D1204329

CAMPUS HOTTIE

JENNIFER SUCEVIC

Campus Hottie

Copyright© 2021 by Jennifer Sucevic

All rights reserved. No part of this book may be reproduced in any form or by any electronic or mechanical means, including information storage and retrieval systems, without written permission from the author, except for the use of brief quotations in a book review.

This is a work of fiction. Names, characters, businesses, palaces, events, locales, and incidents are either the products of the author's imagination or used in a fictitious manner. Any resemblance to actual persons, living or dead, or actual events is purely coincidental.

Cover Design by Mary Ruth Baloy at MR Creations

Editing by Evelyn Summers of Pinpoint Editing

Home | Jennifer Sucevic or www.jennifersucevic.com

ALSO BY JENNIFER SUCEVIC

Campus Flirt (Novella)

Campus Heartthrob

Campus Player

Claiming What's Mine

Confessions of a Heartbreaker

Crazy for You (80s short story)

Don't Leave

Friend Zoned

Hate to Love You

Heartless

If You Were Mine

Just Friends

King of Campus

King of Hawthorne Prep

Love to Hate You

One Night Stand

Protecting What's Mine

Queen of Hawthorne Prep

Stay

The Boy Next Door

The Breakup Plan

The Girl Next Door

Chapter One

ELLE

The TA avoids all eye contact as he sets my paper facedown on the desk before moving on to the next row.

Crap.

The knot in my belly tightens as I realize that's probably not a good sign. What I can't afford is to barely scrape by on yet another test or quiz. I'd rather drop out of college than retake this class. And just to be clear, my mother would kill me if I actually did that.

Someone needs to explain what statistics has to do with being a theater major anyway. How is this supposed to assist me in pursuing my dream career as a stage actress?

The short answer is that it won't, which is exactly why I made a last-ditch effort to persuade my advisor on the third day of class that I should be given an exemption from Western's graduation requirement. His response was to sigh heavily as he removed his horn-rimmed glasses and pinched the bridge of his nose before effectively telling me to suck it up, buttercup.

So I'm stuck for the duration. A puff of air escapes from me as my shoulders slump. Failing this class is not an option.

"Aren't you going to look?" Mike asks from the desk parked next to mine.

I scrunch my nose and give my head a few violent shakes. "If it's bad, it'll ruin my entire day." And that's the last thing I need.

He rolls his hazel eyes before pushing his sandy-colored hair away from his face. "God, you are *so* dramatic."

A reluctant smile tugs at the corners of my lips. "That's what you love about me."

He tilts his head as if seriously considering the statement. "Hmmm...is it?"

I give him my most winsome smile before batting my eyelashes. "Yup, pretty sure it is."

"Maybe," he admits before pointing to the paper. "If you won't do the honors then I will."

The thick ball of tension that has taken up residence in the pit of my belly turns painful. "Stop trying to peer pressure me into doing something I'm not ready to."

His eyes ignite with humor as he elbows me. "Come on," he cajoles, "do it or I won't be your friend."

With a frown, I smack his shoulder and shift on the chair. "You're such a jerk."

He shrugs, looking unaffected by the insult. "Never said I wasn't."

When a few seconds trickle by, he raises his brows expectantly.

Ugh. I can already tell he won't drop the topic until I show him.

"Fine," I grumble. Air gets wedged in my throat as my heartbeat picks up tempo. I do a silent countdown before quickly flipping over the paper and staring at the number circled in red ink in the top right corner.

Sixty-five.

Shit. That's worse than I'd assumed it would be. My lips sink at the edges as my eyes widen. It's official, my Friday has just gone down the tubes.

"Sorry," he mumbles, looking equally surprised by the dismal score. "I really thought it would be better. We spent a ton of hours studying last week."

My hand drifts to my right temple where a headache is beginning to brew. This class will be the death of me, I just know it. All of my other courses are going great. Since day one, statistics has been a gigantic pain in my ass. No matter how much time I spend preparing for the tests or slogging through the daily assignments, I can't seem to wrap my mind around the concepts. I have some kind of mental block when it comes to math. It's always been a struggle, but I've usually been able to pull off a C. I would be thrilled with that at this point. We're talking happy dance and everything.

All of the red check marks decorating the page blur before my eyes until it looks like the paper is bleeding and should be promptly put out of its misery.

"Good morning, everyone," Dr. Holloway greets with a cheerful smile from behind the podium at the front of the room. "It's Friday, so I'll attempt to make this as painless as possible. Sound good?"

Ha! It's much too late for that.

His comment is met with a lone grunt or two that echo off the walls. By the blurry-eyed expressions filling the packed lecture hall, my guess is that most of my fellow students decided to jumpstart their weekend early. If they're expecting this material to do the trick and bring them back to life again, that won't be happening. Even though our professor does his best to breathe life into statistics, it's still dry and tedious.

Not one to be put off by the unenthusiastic response, he claps his hands together. "Excellent. Let's dive right in, shall we?"

Precisely forty-eight minutes later, my brain is on the verge of exploding from information overload. Statistical confidence intervals and the difference between populations swim around in my brain. If I'm not careful, the material will leak right out of my ears and onto the floor in a gooey mess.

As soon as he glances at his silver wristwatch and dismisses class for the day, everyone perks up and comes alive as if a switch has been flipped.

"Oh, I see how it is. Now you've all got something to say, huh?" Professor Holloway shakes his head as if disappointed in the caliber of student who populate his lectures. "Maybe I should assign a few pages to complete over the weekend."

The room erupts into noisy protests.

"Yeah, I didn't think so." He waves a hand in mock irritation. "Get out of here before I change my mind." His gaze travels over the sea of students loading up their bags before homing in on me. "Except you, Ms. Kendricks. Would you mind sticking around for a few minutes?"

Great.

"Sure." It takes effort to lift my lips into a smile.

Mike leans toward me. "Ohhh, the sexy professor wants to speak with you all alone. Lucky girl."

When I glare, he waggles his brows. "Give me a break," I mutter. "We both know he wants to discuss my dumpster fire of a grade."

Mike's gaze shifts to our instructor, who's shuffling around paper-work as undergraduates flee his classroom like rats from a burning building. "I'd be more than happy to have a little private tutoring from the likes of him."

An unwilling smile quirks my lips. This isn't the first time Mike has made just such a remark. "Something tells me the private tutoring you're looking for isn't in math." Especially since the big jerk received a ninety-three on his test.

A ninety-three!

That's the kind of grade I can only fantasize about.

His eyes turn dreamy as he leans his elbows on the laminated desktop before resting his chin on clasped hands. "I'll take whatever that man is willing to give me."

A chuckle bubbles up in my throat as I glance at our professor. I totally understand what Mike is saying about Dr. Holloway. He's good looking with dark hair and blue eyes. If I had to guess, I'd say he was somewhere in his early to mid thirties. The man obviously takes care of himself. Beneath his sport coat and khakis, he's lean and muscular.

Once I've packed up my belongings, we rise to our feet and move to the center aisle of the large space.

"All right, girl. I gotta get moving. I'll see you at three for rehearsal."

"Yup, I'll be there."

I live for play practice. It's what makes everything else in life bear-able. Even statistics. I've been involved in the theater since I was a kid, and it's what I channeled all of my grief into after Dad died four years ago. I'm not sure I would have gotten through the loss of him without it. Instead of being constantly steeped in grief, I was able to escape, at least for short bursts of time, by pretending to be someone else.

With one final wave, Mike takes off and I turn, moving down the staircase to the front of the room where Professor Holloway waits. As the last student heads out, a heavy silence falls over the space. I clear my throat and hitch my backpack higher onto my shoulder.

"You wanted to see me?"

He glances up from the handful of papers he's in the process of organizing. "Yeah, thanks for sticking around. I was hoping we could touch base. I noticed you didn't do so well on the last test."

That's something of an understatement, and we both know it.

My grimace has the corners of his lips bowing up. Straight white teeth flash through the artificial light filling the room.

As he shifts his stance, his blue blazer falls open, revealing a perfectly pressed white button-down. "Oh, come on now. Is it really that bad?"

I huff out a breath as my shoulders loosen. "I know it doesn't look like it, but I'm actually trying. I studied for this test with Mike, and he got a ninety-three."

A thoughtful expression crosses his face as he nods. "Mike is doing well in this class. He seems to have a firm grip on the material."

I shoot him a sour look. "Unfortunately, his knowledge doesn't seem to be transferrable."

"In this particular case, I would agree with that statement," he says easily. "I wanted to mention that I have office hours every Tuesday and Thursday from four to six. You should stop in early next week, and we can spend some time going over your test and rework the problems you had trouble with."

"That would be all of them," I admit.

"Luckily for you, Ms. Kendricks, I just so happen to have a Ph. D in Applied Statistics. With a little one on one attention, I think we can get that grade up before the end of the semester. Right now, you're sitting at a D. And contrary to popular belief, that doesn't stand for 'darn good.' More like 'danger zone.' I don't think either of us wants to see it drop any further."

I suck in a sharp breath before blowing it out and jerking my head into a tight nod. With the upcoming production on campus, my schedule is jampacked, but there's no other way around it. I need help. And Dr. Holloway is offering it.

"Thank you. I'll plan to stop by on Tuesday."

"Excellent. You'll see, a little extra help will go a long way."

He's being really nice about this. Even though I loathe stats with the passion of a thousand burning suns, I'm appreciative of the lifeline he's throwing me. Plus, I can rub the fact that I'll be spending a little time alone with our sexy professor—as he likes to refer to him—in Mike's smug face.

"You obviously don't understand how terrible I am at the subject," I joke.

"Have a little faith, Elle. With enough hard work, nothing is impossible."

It takes effort to rein in my snort.

I certainly hope he's right about that. Or I'll be suffering through this class for a second time.

Chapter Two

CARSON

"**A**ll right, man," Rowan Michaels says as we cut across campus. "I gotta take off. I'll catch you later at practice."

"Yup," I say with a wave. "See you then."

Rowan moves in one direction as I head in another toward the English building for my communications class. Since I hate speeches, I put it off freshman, sophomore, and then—much to my advisor's annoyance—junior year. Now I'm stuck taking it with a bunch of overeager underclassmen. Had I been smart, I would have gotten it out of the way my first year and been done with it.

My gaze coasts over the crowd of people moving across campus. A good number of them look hungover from the previous night's antics. Around here, Thursday night kicks off the weekend. Even though Western is an academically rigorous school, most of the student body enjoys kicking back and having a good time. I'm not adverse to partying, but I don't make a habit of getting shitfaced like a lot of my friends and teammates do. Even when I was a freshman, that was never my MO.

My attention gets snagged by every girl that I pass with long, dark hair.

Sure, I could lie and try to convince myself I'm not searching for

Elle Kendricks, but what would be the point? I've been doing it since she came in last year as a freshman. If I time my trek across campus just right, we'll run into each other. Timing it 'just right' means leaving my house an hour before I actually have to. The couple of minutes I'm in her presence will feed the need for the rest of the day.

Definitely pathetic.

I should stop torturing myself by looking for her around every bend. I'm certainly not doing myself any favors by engaging in this behavior.

From the corner of my eye, a flash of dark hair catches my attention and my head whips in the direction of the mathematics building. Unconsciously, my feet stumble to a halt as my gaze rakes over the length of her body. With her head angled forward, her long locks shield her face like a shiny curtain. That familiar hollowed out sensation takes up residence inside my belly. It's the same kind of feeling one experiences when constantly denied something they desperately need for survival.

From the pink turtleneck sweater that clings to every slender curve to the black, button-down jean skirt, and the tall, knee-length boots wrapped around her calves, she always looks put together.

Hot.

Sexy.

I really shouldn't be thinking along those lines, but I can't help myself. Which is precisely why I go to such great lengths to keep my distance. Being anywhere near Elle is dangerous. Every day, my self-control slips a notch, becoming more of a paper-thin veneer. I'm afraid of what will happen if it continues to fall away. Right now, she has absolutely no idea how I truly feel, and that's exactly the way it needs to stay.

Her face lifts, and even from the yawning expanse that separates us, I notice her forehead is creased as if something in her world isn't right.

Turn away, asshole. Don't you dare say one damn word.

Instead, I shout, "Elle!"

The moment her name leaves my lips, I wince.

Fuck me.

Could I be any more of a glutton for punishment?

Her head snaps up as her gaze scans the thick crowd until it lands on me. I have to steel myself against the electricity attempting to sizzle its way through my nerve endings, making them snap and crackle with life. It's been like this for as long as I can remember.

Craving the one person you can't have sucks ass, but there's nothing to be done about it.

Brayden is my bro. My teammate. And nothing will ever change that.

Not even his little sister.

I spent most of my childhood at the Kendricks' house. From day one, Bray's parents welcomed me with open arms and made me feel like I was part of their family. For as long as I can remember, I've had a soft spot for Elle. I watched out for her when we were in elementary, middle, and then high school. Somewhere along the way, my feelings changed, morphing into something different. Something stronger. I started to notice things about her that I probably shouldn't have.

Have I ever mentioned this infatuation to Brayden?

Ha!

Are you out of your fucking mind?

The dude is ridiculously protective of her. When she started at Western last year as a freshman, he spread the good word that if anyone so much as glanced in her direction, he'd pummel their asses.

And no, it wasn't an idle threat.

We might go way back, but the warning pertains to me as well.

Jake, their father, was struck and killed by a drunk driver when Brayden was a senior in high school. The loss of him blew a gaping hole in all of their lives. Brayden never asked to be man of the house, but those are the shoes he was forced to fill much too early in life. Instead of shirking that responsibility, he embraced it, taking it seriously.

I force those thoughts away as Elle's face transforms into a smile and she lifts a hand to wave before cutting across the sidewalk until she's a few feet away.

"Hi!"

I tamp down the urge to reach out and tug her into my arms. It's the very same impulse that demands I bury my face in her hair and breathe in the sweet scent of her.

"Hey." Instead of giving in, I search her expression for clues as to what's going on. "Everything okay?"

She blinks as confusion flashes across her face.

When she continues to remain silent, I nod toward the mathematics building. "You looked upset when you were leaving stats."

Is it pathetic I know her class schedule by heart?

Don't answer that.

"Oh." Her teeth sink into her plump lower lip before worrying it.

My gaze drops to her mouth, and it takes every ounce of self-control to stop my cock from stirring and making its presence known. We've barely exchanged a handful of words and already I know this conversation was a shit idea. The last thing I want is for Elle to realize the effect she has on me. I won't bother to pretend that getting through the rest of senior year hinges on her remaining oblivious to my feelings.

At this point, it's my dirty little secret that I keep buried in the darkness.

I clear my throat and jerk my gaze from her pink-slicked, cupid's bow of a mouth. I can only imagine what it would be like to nip at it with my teeth.

Or have it wrapped around my cock.

Fuck.

This was definitely a bad idea. I need to get the hell out of here before I totally lose it. Although, I'm not going anywhere until I get to the bottom of what's going on.

"Is there a problem?"

Her shoulders wilt as color invades her cheeks. "I failed my latest stats test."

"Oh." Well, hell. I shift my stance as guilt surges through me. "I'm sorry to hear that." We've met up several times at the library since the beginning of the semester. Spending time alone with Elle is both heaven and hell, which is when I realized that I couldn't do it any longer and stopped offering my assistance.

Now I feel like a complete asshole. She obviously needs the help.

Her dark brows pinch together as she shrugs. "I'm a hopeless case when it comes to math. No amount of studying seems to make a difference. I just came from speaking with Dr. Holloway. He suggested I drop by during office hours next week to go over my test."

"That sounds like a great idea. I'd offer my assistance but..."

"Don't worry about it," she says. "I know how busy you are with football and classes."

Yeah...

"If you still need help," I blurt like the masochistic dumbass I am, "just let me know and I'll rearrange my schedule. I'll figure something out, all right?"

The way she beams is like being hit with a ray of undiluted sunlight. I really need to get out of here before this conversation spirals any further out of control.

"Thanks, Carson. I really appreciate that."

Just as I'm about to retreat, her fingers drift to my forearm and squeeze the bare skin. Tiny electrical pulses surge through every nerve ending. If I don't get away from her, I'll end up doing something I regret.

Her eyes widen when I jerk out of her grasp and her arm floats back to her side.

"No problem," I bite out. Even though I've got a good forty minutes before the start of my next class, I mumble, "I should get moving."

Unaware of the effect she has on me, Elle slips her phone from her bag and glances at it. "Okay. I'm meeting up with Madison, Sierra, and Kari to look for costumes for the Sig Ep party Saturday night."

My lips flatten at the thought of her attending a rowdy frat party. "You're going to that?"

"Yup. The girls are dragging me with them." She glances at me with curiosity. "What about you?"

Up until two seconds ago, I had zero intention of going anywhere near that place. The Sig Ep's are known around campus for throwing the craziest bashes with a ton of free-flowing booze and a wide array of party favors.

"I wasn't planning on it." Although it looks like that's changed. I shift my weight and narrow my eyes. "Does Brayden know?" The question shoots out of my mouth before I can stop it.

Her expression cools as she straightens her shoulders. "No, and I would appreciate it if you didn't mention it. You know how ridiculously overprotective he is." Her face scrunches as she shakes her head. "If I'd realized he was going to be all up in my business every second of the day, I would have attended a different university."

Whether she wants to admit it or not, there was no way Brayden would have allowed that to happen.

"There's a good chance he'll show up on his own. I'm pretty sure I heard Sydney and Demi talking about it earlier this week." If I'm lucky, that will be enough to change her—

"Thanks. I appreciate the warning." She shoots me a conspiratorial smile. "I'll keep my eye out for him."

Great.

Before I have the chance to throw out any other deterrents, she waves before taking off down the path.

Fuck.

Looks like I'm in need of a costume for tomorrow.

Chapter Three

ELLE

"Girl, you look totally hot!" Sierra says as we walk from the dorms to Fraternity and Sorority Row, which is located a few blocks off campus.

I tug the backside of the red and black sequined short shorts I'm wearing. They barely cover my cheeks. Thankfully the weather cooperated this evening or I'd be freezing my assets off. Fishnet stockings and a pair of lace-up boots that match the shorts are the only thing covering my legs. A midriff baring T-shirt that says 'Daddy's Lil Monster' along with a red and blue jacket completes the ensemble.

Madison tugs one of the colorful pigtails from the blonde wig I'm wearing. "If I didn't know it was you beneath all that clothing and make up, I would never have guessed."

I snort. "Thanks...I think."

She grins and knocks her shoulder into mine. "You know what I meant. You always look so damn polished and put together with your matchy-matchy outfits. It's nice to see you slum it with the rest of us for a change."

I roll my eyes before giving her a little shove in return. "They're hardly matchy-matchy," I grumble under my breath. Not that I'll admit it to her, but I like to color coordinate. Is that such a crime?

"What?" she chuckles. "It's true. Don't get your sparkly panties in a twist, I still love you. Matchy outfits and all."

The one-fingered salute I aim in her direction only makes her laugh harder.

"See?" she continues. "Now your personality is more in line with your costume."

My lips lift into a good-natured smile. "You better hope I don't go all Harley Quinn on your ass."

"Save all that sass for the boys," she shoots back. "Of which there will be many. Hopefully they won't be a bunch of drunk assholes."

I've had enough run-ins with the guys from this fraternity to know that it could go either way.

As we turn the corner, the Sig Ep house comes into view. Even if you lived under a rock and were totally clueless about tonight's festivities, it would be impossible to miss. Loud music emanates from the two-story Victorian as people loiter on the front lawn with the requisite red Solo cup in hand. There isn't one single person who isn't in costume. It's the only ticket into the party.

The four of us make our way up the crowded cement walkway to the rickety front porch steps. A pledge who barely looks old enough to be in college mans the door. He gives every girl a once-over before waving us inside the dark interior. Strobe lights flash through the first floor. Here's hoping no one is prone to seizures or we're all in trouble.

"Looking good, Harley!" he calls after me.

I give him a quick wave before getting swept away by a sea of rowdy revelers.

"Let's make sure we all stick together," Sierra yells in order to be heard over the pulsing beat of music that reverberates off the walls and in my bones.

"Good idea," Madison calls back, scanning the thick press of bodies. "It's even more crowded than last year!"

Sierra, who's dressed as a sexy nurse since she's in the registered nursing program, leads the charge, pushing and shoving people out of her way. She might be small and pixie-like, but she has a big personality. And she's not afraid to stand up for herself or her friends when the occasion calls for it.

I take in all the great costumes until my gaze lands on a familiar blond head and my heart stutters unwantedly in my chest. After our conversation yesterday morning, I hadn't expected to see Carson this evening. His costume—if you can even call it that—is a football jersey with his name stamped across the back above his number.

I shake my head. It's not a surprise to find him outfitted like this. The guy has always hated dressing up. Even for Halloween. Which, I'm not going to lie, is just plain weird. Who doesn't like Halloween costumes? This isn't the first time he's thrown on one of his jerseys and passed it off as appropriate attire.

Me, on the other hand?

I love dressing up—we're talking full-on hair and makeup—and getting into character. It's fun. And incredibly freeing. It allows you to step into someone else's shoes even for a couple of hours and lose yourself in make believe.

Madison nudges my shoulder. "I see you've found your man."

I roll my eyes.

Carson Roberts is *not* my man. More like one of my keepers. He enjoys playing the part of protective older brother, which is completely unnecessary. Brayden already enjoys making life difficult for me in the guy department. Anyone who has ever shown the slightest bit of interest gets run off before anything can actually happen.

I wasn't joking when I'd said I should have chosen a different university. One far away from here. Maybe a place like New York. Even thinking about the possibility has my heart flip flopping in my chest. After Dad died, there was no way I could moved so far away from Mom or Brayden. At least, not at eighteen years old.

That's my plan after graduation.

I blink and refocus my attention on Carson as a sexy devil saunters over and runs her fingers along his broad chest. That's all it takes for jealousy to ignite in the pit of my belly. After all these years, you would think I'd be used to girls hanging all over him and seeking out his attention. It's been happening since we were in middle school, and yet, it never gets easier to watch.

If I had any brains whatsoever, I'd turn away and stop inflicting further damage on myself. Instead, I stay fixated on them. Even though I'm too far away to hear what's being said, the conversation must be scintillating by the way she throws her head back and laughs, continuing to paw at him the entire time.

Everything I've eaten today threatens to revolt. Unable to stomach any more, I force my gaze away, only to realize that my friends have disappeared from sight. I push forward, searching for them in the crowd. With about twenty fraternity members living here, the house is massive. It takes time to fight my way into the dining room where people have congregated on a makeshift dance floor. I stand on my tiptoes and crane my neck, looking for Kari, Madison, and Sierra but don't see them anywhere.

My name gets shouted before someone grabs hold of my arm. I swing around, only to find Batman with a huge grin lighting up his partially concealed face.

"Hey!" My gaze slides over him, taking in all the intricate details of his costume. "You look fantastic!"

"Damn, you knew it was me?" Mike asks.

"It's not like I haven't seen you dressed up a bunch of times."

Mike and I go back to first semester of freshman year when we met in theater class, and we've been fast friends ever since. This year, we've both been cast in the university's production of *Heathers: The Musical.* There have been a lot of long nights running lines, but it's been a blast. The show opens in less than two weeks. We both have larger roles than the previous year when we were lowly freshmen.

"True enough." Mike glances around. "Where's the crew? Please tell me you didn't show up by yourself."

"Nope, they're around here somewhere. Probably went to the kitchen for liquid refreshments. They'll be back soon." Thankfully I can always hang out with Mike until they turn up again.

He throws an arm over my shoulder and tugs me close. "Guess it's just you and me, Harley."

I give him a bright smile and attempt to shove Carson from my mind. "Yup."

It's not as simple as I wish it were.

Chapter Four

CARSON

Monica continues to yap my ear off as I comb over the crowd of drunken students busy partying their asses off. With the dim lighting, it's difficult to see. Plus, everyone is wearing a costume, making it even more of a challenge to find her. I have no idea what Elle decided to wear. I probably should have asked. Hell, for all I know, she changed her mind about attending or decided to hit a different house. Although the probability of that happening is low. The Sig Ep bash is an annual event that continues to swell in size each year. It's one the entire university shows up for. There's not another sorority or fraternity that would dare to throw a rival party.

"Carson?"

I blink back to the conversation as her sharp fingernails bite into my flesh. "Yeah?"

"I was just saying that we should really get together sometime." Her gaze stays pinned to mine expectantly. "Soon."

Well, shit.

This isn't the direction I thought this conversation was going to swerve in when I mentally checked out a few minutes ago. In fact, she'd been blathering on about her sorority and...

Oh, who the hell knows. I stopped paying attention about twenty seconds after she stepped in front of me.

My bad.

Put on the spot, I scramble to come up with an answer. "Umm, yeah..."

She perks up, looking thrilled. Like she just won the lottery.

"I'd like that," I lie. "It's just a really bad time with football."

Her hopeful expression nosedives as disappointment sets in.

"You know," I gesture vaguely, "with the playoffs and the bowl game coming up."

Before I can untangle myself from this sticky situation, she presses closer, her tongue darting out to moisten her lips. "I'm more than willing to wait until after your season ends."

Damn.

I clear my throat, wanting only to get away from her. "How about we play it by ear, and I'll let you know."

She beams as if I've just agreed to be her bona fide boyfriend. "That sounds great."

"Um," I point toward the kitchen. "I'm going to grab something to drink." Before she can attach herself to my hip and offer to be my side-kick for the rest of the evening, I add, "I'll catch you later."

"Sure! I'll be here waiting!"

That's exactly what I'm afraid of.

And then I'm off, shoving my way through the mass of bodies. My plan is to make another sweep of the house, and, if I can't find Elle, I'm calling it a night and taking off. I can't deal with this mob. The more alcoholic beverages these girls guzzle down, the clingier they become. Most guys wouldn't have a problem with that, but since I have zero interest in finding a hookup to take home at the end of the night, it's more of a pain in my ass than anything else.

Crosby slaps me on the back as I stumble across the group I came here with. Like me, the only thing he bothered to do is throw on a jersey. Brayden, Rowan, and Easton on the other hand, are all here with girlfriends. They're decked out in full-on costumes whether they want to be or not.

I almost shake my head. They're all so pussy whipped.

Demi and Rowan are wearing matching seventies disco outfits, Sydney and Brayden are dressed as Barbie and Ken, which is hilarious, and Easton and Sasha have come as Jon Snow and Daenerys from *Game of Thrones*. Let's hope their relationship doesn't end as badly as the fictionalized one.

"Looks like you and I are the only ones who didn't have chicks help dress them tonight," he says.

"That would be because we don't have girlfriends."

He raises his beer as if I've offered up a toast before downing it. "Damn straight."

Crosby has never had any interest in getting tangled up in a relationship. The guy has all the pussy he wants and seems perfectly content with the parade of jersey chasers who rotate through his bed. After three years, he's still going strong.

Instead of admitting the truth, I say, "I'm gonna grab a bottle of water. I'll be back."

Just as I take a step toward the dining room, I bump into a girl. Her eyes flare as she teeters on sky-high heels. I spring forward, reaching out to steady her before she topples over.

"Hey, are you all right?" I ask, getting a better look at her face.

When she smiles, I realize it's Sasha's friend Brooke. "I'm fine. Thanks for the impromptu save."

"No problem." I take in her outfit. She's wearing a short, sparkly gray dress that hits mid-thigh and hugs her body like a second skin. Delicate feathers sprout from her back and there's a matching halo suspended above her head. "Cool costume."

"Thank you!" she says with a grin before flicking her gaze over me. "Um...you, too."

My lips quirk. "Yeah, Crosby and I went all out this year."

Her attention reluctantly strays to the guy behind me before growing frosty. The smile disappears as her lips tighten into a brittle slash across her face.

Right. I almost forgot how much these two can't stand each other. For reasons I haven't been able to figure out, Crosby took an instant dislike to her from the very beginning. Even when she was dating his roommate, Andrew, he was a complete dick.

I glance at my friend, hoping he isn't paying attention to our conversation.

No such luck.

Instead, his steely gaze slowly crawls over the length of her body. When his eyes finally meet hers, he flashes a shitty smile. "Wait, wait —let me guess." He taps his chin with the tip of his finger. "You're a blowjob queen."

Her eyes narrow as she gives him a perfectly polished finger. "Fuck off, Rhodes."

He smirks, seeming pleased with the direction their interaction has gone. Which is straight down the shitter. "I'd be happy to."

With that, he turns away, giving us the wide expanse of his back. Even with the flash of the strobe lights, I can see the dull red color flooding into her cheeks. Awkwardness descends as I shuffle from one foot to the other, unsure how to smooth over their skirmish. What I'd like to do is kick Crosby in the ass right about now.

"Sorry," I mumble, offering up an apology even though I didn't do anything wrong. "He can be a dick sometimes."

She raises a sculpted brow. "Only sometimes?"

My lips quirk in relief that she's not letting the comment ruin her mood. "Well, probably more than that. I was attempting to be generous."

Her attention shifts and she glares daggers at his back. "Don't bother when it comes to that guy. He's a raging asshole."

I've known Crosby since freshman year, and we've become good friends. I should defend him, but I find myself unable to summon the words. Especially when he treats Brooke like such crap. So, yeah, I get why she dislikes him.

What doesn't make sense is that her ex is the one who was sleeping with other chicks behind her back. He's one of those guys who enjoys having a pretty girlfriend at his side but also wants to fuck all the jersey chasers he can. Unfortunately, Brooke was the last one to find out about his side dishes. Rumor has it that a clap diagnosis is what ultimately tipped her off. I have no idea if that actually happened or if it's just an ugly bit of gossip that made the rounds. Regardless, she dumped his ass and has refused to give him the time of day. Instead of moving on to any number of the females who vie for his attention, Andrew is on a campaign to win her back. He's taken groveling to a whole new, embarrassing level.

"It was nice running into you, Carson. Her lips hitch. "Literally. But I should get moving, I need to find Sasha." She glances around. "She has to be here somewhere."

"Yeah." I point to the group next to us. "Last time I saw her, she was hanging out over there." I hesitate, unsure if I should ask. Before I can weigh the consequences of my decision, the words are shooting out of my mouth. "Hey, you haven't seen Brayden's sister around, have you?"

"Actually, I just ran into her." When she flashes a grin, it's a relief to see that Crosby's nasty comment has been relegated to the past where it belongs. "She looks totally amazing as Harley Quinn."

Harley Quinn?

Fuck me. I can just imagine.

And it's not good.

"See you later," she says before melting into the crowd.

"Yeah, later," I mutter, taking off, searching through the writhing mass of bodies for Elle. Even though I'm looking for one specific costume, there are a lot of girls dressed as the *Suicide Squad* member. It's like hunting for a needle in a haystack.

After fifteen minutes, I'm about to throw in the towel when I finally catch sight of her across the room. She's grinning at a guy outfitted in a full-on Batman suit. The way she's dressed is like a punch to the gut. Elle usually wears shirts or sweaters with high necklines and skirts that are short to show off her long legs. Her preference for tall boots never fails to make my dick stir.

Tonight, it's the total opposite. She's wearing a blonde wig with pigtails that have red and blue colored strands. A thin, white T-shirt clings to her chest. Thank fuck for the jacket or I'd probably kill someone.

The obvious choice being Batman.

My gaze roves further down her body.

What the fuck is she wearing?

Or maybe I should say—where the hell are her pants?

Are those booty shorts? Or straight up panties? I'll tell you what…it better not be underwear. The guy she's with throws his arm around her shoulders and tugs her close. A thick haze of jealousy clouds my vision as I barrel through the crowd, cutting a path straight to her. As I pull up to the couple, I snake my arm around her waist before hauling her against me. Batman's arm falls away as they both stare in surprise.

"Carson!" she says.

"Hey." I glare at the guy, mentally willing him to leave before bodily injury becomes a necessity. Whatever delusions he thought would come to fruition tonight have been blown to shit by yours truly.

You're welcome.

"I didn't think you were going to show up."

Tension fills every muscle, ratcheting up as I try to play it cool by shrugging. "Changed my mind."

"I can see that." Her gaze bounces to the caped crusader as she waves a hand in his direction. "You remember my friend Mike, right?"

Oh…Mike. He's a theater buddy.

Everything inside me loosens as I give him a chin lift in greeting. "Yeah, sure. I didn't recognize you."

"Thanks!" He flexes his muscles. "I wasn't sure if I could pull off the costume."

"You did. It's great."

He grins at Elle. "What do you think of our little Harley Quinn over here? She looks amazing, right?"

Yeah. A little *too* amazing. I don't like the way she's dressed.

All right, that's not precisely true. I fucking love it. I just don't want other guys staring at her. And they're definitely doing that.

Mike chats my ear off for five minutes before disappearing to the kitchen for a refill. The entire time he talks, I can't take my eyes off Elle. That thin T-shirt and shorts—or sparkly panties—are going to be the death of me. All I want to do is lay my hands on her.

Instead, I clear my throat. "Interesting outfit choice." My gaze slides down the length of her, eating up every inch of bared flesh on display.

"Thanks." She preens before doing a little twirl.

I hiss out a sharp breath as my attention falls to her ass. This is bad. It's a struggle to keep my dick in check. I need to get out of here before all hell breaks loose.

In my jeans.

"So," I glance around, "did you come here with friends?" All I have to say is that she'd better not be here on her own. If so, I'll be carrying her damn ass out of this party. No ifs, ands, or buts.

Her brows pinch together as she cranes her neck. "I did, but we ended up getting separated. I'm sure they'll show up at some point."

In this fucking crush?

Good luck with that.

Her expression changes, becoming serious, as she tilts her head. "You don't have to babysit me, Carson. I'm perfectly capable of taking care of myself."

Maybe.

"There's no way I'm leaving you alone." I add the first thing that pops into my brain. "Your brother would kill me."

Her eyes narrow as her body stiffens. "Brayden needs to chill out and let me enjoy myself every once in a while."

Yeah, that's not going to happen, and we both know it. If her brother could lock her away in a tower for safekeeping, that's exactly what he would do. And I can't blame him for it. Elle is gorgeous. I see the way guys eye her up. Without Brayden beating them away with a stick, she would be inundated with interest, and that, I don't think I could stand.

The conversation is abruptly cut off when a drunk guy stumbles into us. "Hey, Harley—what do you say we go upstairs so I can rock your world?"

Barely am I able to make out his words as he leers at her. And this is exactly why I won't be leaving Elle's side until I find her friends or convince her to get the hell out of here. Preferably the latter.

Instead of responding—because if I do, I'll likely plow my fist into his face—I grab her hand and drag her through the mass of writhing bodies until I'm able to carve out a small space for the two of us before tugging her into my arms. Her eyes go wide as she stares at me.

"I thought you might want to dance," I mumble, feeling like a jackass.

"Um, sure." She slips her arms over my shoulders. "I love busting a move."

I'm aware. Just like I know everything else about this girl.

In the middle of this mob with the lights turned low, I pull her even closer. We've danced a few times in high school, but this feels decidedly different. It doesn't escape me how perfectly our bodies fit together. Almost as if she were made for me. My arms slip around her ribcage, settling on her back as hers entwine around my neck. With our gazes fastened, we're like an island onto ourselves. I lose track of how long we stay pressed together as one song bleeds into the next. My breath stalls when she untangles herself and flips around until her back is aligned against my chest. Even though I should put a stop to this madness before it spirals any further out of control, I find myself unable to push her away. Instead, my hands settle around her bare waist, the tips of my fingers grazing the soft skin of her taut belly.

Fuck me. This is absolute torture.

And yet, I want it to last forever.

I want to hold her in the middle of this crush and never let go. The bodies hemming us in along with the music melt away as my hands drift upward, slipping beneath the cotton of her T-shirt to strum over her ribcage until my thumbs are able to rest beneath the silky fabric of her bra. A few inches higher and I would be cupping her breasts.

How many times have I fantasized about touching her like this?

Too many to count.

With the back of her head resting against my chest, she tilts her face and meets my gaze through heavy-lidded eyes. My cock throbs even harder. I know a fuck-me gaze when I see one. If this were any other girl, I'd drag her up the stairs to a bedroom before screwing her brains out. I wouldn't give a rat's ass about doing it at a random frat house.

That's how turned on I am.

"Carson?" she whispers, breaking into the thick haze clouding my better judgment.

When her tongue peeks out from between red-slicked lips, my gaze falls to her mouth, and I feel myself leaning—

I jerk back as if scalded.

Fuck!

I can't believe that almost happened. What I need to do is step away and get some air. I'm too wrapped up in this girl. Instead, my fingers lock around her wrist before dragging her from the dining room and down a long stretch of dark hallway where the crowd has thinned. With a gasp, she teeters on her boots, trying to keep pace with me.

Even though I know this won't end well, I can't stop myself from hurtling headfirst toward this disastrous decision.

Chapter Five

ELLE

I blink, attempting to regain my bearings as Carson drags me through the thick press of bodies. His fingers are still shackled around my wrist as we wind our way through the crowded rooms. I'm not sure what happened. It's like a switch flipped inside him. One minute we're dancing and the next, we're on the move without any explanation. For a sliver of a moment, it almost felt as if he might want me the same way I've always desired him. I'm sure it's wishful thinking on my end. More like my mind conjuring up what it wants to see and believe.

Nerves scuttle down my spine as I try to get his attention. "Carson?"

His movement never falters. If he heard my voice, he doesn't acknowledge it.

Before I can force myself to repeat his name, louder this time, his fingers grab hold of a handle, and he throws the door open. The couple making out on the bed gasps before jumping apart.

"Get out," Carson says, sounding as if he's barely holding onto his temper, which doesn't make sense.

What's he so angry about?

"Hey," the guy sputters, irritated by our untimely interruption. "We were here first. Get your own room. There are more than enough of them."

A thunderous expression crosses his face as he growls, "Get the hell out of here right now or I'll throw your ass out myself."

My eyes widen as they bounce from the couple, whose clothing is in various stages of disarray, to the guy at my side.

"Fine," the dude grumbles as the girl buttons up her shirt and rises unsteadily to her feet. "We're going. Chill out, man. It's a party."

Carson waits, muscles tensed as if prepared for a fight, until they slink past. As soon as they step over the threshold, he slams the door shut, locking us inside the room. Silvery light pours in through the unadorned windows, giving me just enough illumination to see his face. My mouth turns cottony at the strained tension that hums in the air between us. I don't understand what's happening here. He's always been so easy going and quick to laughter. It's one of the qualities that has drawn me to him over the years.

This Carson...the one who seems so pissed off and quick tempered...is little more than a stranger.

Now that we're alone, he releases the grip on my wrist. Needing distance, I scramble backward until my spine hits the wall. Air clogs my throat as his narrowed gaze stays pinned to mine. The oxygen in the room gets sucked out, making it impossible to breathe.

My tongue darts from between my lips to moisten them. "Carson," I whisper, needing to right whatever is careening out of control between us.

When he gives his head an abrupt shake, my voice stalls.

Every nerve ending inside me goes on high alert as he closes the distance and I'm able to feel his warm breath feather across my parted lips. My heartbeat increases, pounding painfully as it slams against my ribcage. Any moment it'll explode from my chest. I flatten against the wall as his thick forearms settle on either side of my head, caging me in until I'm surrounded by his brute strength and he's all I'm cognizant of.

His lips are flattened into a tight slash across his face as he silently searches my gaze.

Before I can fully consider the ramifications, I stretch onto my tiptoes and press my lips against his. For a moment, he freezes, going impossibly still. When he remains impassive, I pull away to search his gaze. Just as I break contact, a low growl rumbles up from deep in his chest and he wraps his arms around my body, yanking me to him until all of my curves are pressed against his hard lines. My arms slip around his neck. We're so close that I can feel the heat radiating off him. It's exactly like when we were dancing a few minutes ago except so much better. It feels like I've been waiting half my life for him to open his eyes and see me as something more than Brayden's little sister.

And now it's finally happening.

When he licks at the seam of my lips, I open, allowing him entrance until our tongues can tangle. Hot sensation explodes inside me, rocking me to the very core as our mouth fuse, becoming one. In that moment, I realize nothing in my life will ever be the same again.

There is no way to go back in time and not know how amazing it feels to have Carson's mouth coasting over mine, taking me to a place I've only dreamed about.

He presses into me, pinning my body to the wall as he explores. Our teeth scrape as he tilts his head one way and then another, devouring me one bite at a time. Never in my life have I been kissed quite so thoroughly. It's raw and unexpectedly rough. Barely am I able to catch my breath as his lips roam over mine. When he grinds his thick erection between my legs, my knees weaken and I'm unable to keep the desperation buried inside me any longer.

The whimper breaks free, shattering the silence of the room. Carson jolts, cutting off contact before quickly retreating. The loss of him is sharp and swift. I lock my knees so that I don't slide to the floor in a boneless heap of simmering emotions. He stares with wide, hazel eyes that are full of shock as his fingers drift across his lips.

My gaze drops to them. The only thing I want is to feel them roving hungrily over me again, dragging me to the very bottom of the ocean where thought becomes an impossibility.

"What the hell are you doing?" he rasps.

The deep vibration of his voice sets off another explosion of arousal within me. Only now do I realize how hard I'm breathing and that it matches his deep inhalations. It's almost as if we've both run a marathon.

My head continues to spin as I shake it, unsure how to respond to that question.

"I thought..." My voice trails off as I gulp down the rush of nerves that are multiplying within me. Instead of giving in to the fear clawing its way from deep inside, looking for an escape, I straighten my shoulders. I'm tired of keeping all of these pent-up emotions locked up tight where they can't see the light of day. I've been doing it for years and it's exhausting.

The words escape in a torrential burst. "I've wanted you for a while and I'm tired of pretending these feelings don't exist or that you're nothing more to me than my brother's best friend." Even though I'm scared to death of the rejection, I take a tentative step in his direction. No more than a foot separates us, but it feels as if there is a gaping chasm of distance that keeps me from him. "You're the only guy I've ever wanted." I gulp in a breath of courage before forcing out the truth. "It's why I decided to save myself."

His eyes widen to the point of being comical. Until they look like there's a very real possibility of falling out of his head.

When he remains silent, desperation claws at my insides and creeps into my tone. "Did you hear me? I'm a virgin."

Chapter Six

CARSON

H oly shit.

Exactly what am I supposed to say to that?

I can only stare as my mouth opens and closes like a beached fish gasping for its last dying breath. Those three words whip through my head until it becomes the roar of the ocean and I'm deaf to everything else.

I'm a virgin.

I'm a virgin.

I'm a virgin.

Did I have my suspicions that Elle was probably inexperienced when it came to the opposite sex?

You bet my ass I did. Brayden stands guard over her like a sentinel, not allowing any guy to come within sniffing distance. In some ways, his overprotective behavior has been a relief. I've never had to worry about her hooking up with other people.

Dating douchebags.

Or falling for a guy who won't love her the way she deserves.

To hear her not only confirm this information but blurt that she's been saving herself for me—that she wants *me*—blows a hole through all my self-control. It also makes my cock unbearably hard. All I want to do is yank this girl into my arms and claim what is rightfully mine, what I've been dreaming about for years. A growl works its way up from my throat as I fight to maintain a firm grip on my restraint.

I'm so damn close to losing it. To ripping free and breaking loose. To throwing it all to hell.

Fuck.

A silent war erupts in my head. I've wanted Elle for longer than I care to admit. And the one thing that has kept that need in check is my friendship with Brayden. How can I betray him?

The guy is like a brother to me. No matter what has happened in my life, he's always stood steadfast by my side. And the one thing I know with certainty is that he would never be okay with me dating his sister. Not in a million years. In the end, it would destroy our friendship. And I can't risk that.

Not even for Elle.

It takes effort to fight my own body's natural inclination and clear the thick emotion from my throat.

"I'm sorry, Elle. I don't feel the same way." The lie tastes bitter on my tongue. It's difficult to force it out. "You've always been like a sister to me."

It takes effort to steel myself so she doesn't see through the fib, down to the truth buried beneath it. I don't know what I'd do if she figured me out.

Her eyes widen. "But...you kissed me, and I could feel your erection." The husky words are barely more than a forced out croak as her gaze drops to my groin. "Even now you have an erection."

I don't have to glance down to know she's telling the truth.

I feel it.

I'm ridiculously hard.

Impossibly hard.

Painfully hard.

Any moment, I'm going to explode—and it's all because of the dark-haired beauty who is telling me exactly what I've always dreamed of hearing. Before I can manufacture another lie, she reaches out. A hiss escapes from me when her fingers settle over my rigid length. It takes everything I have inside to knock them away instead of pulling her close.

"I'm a twenty-two-year-old dude," I grunt. "I'm always hard. Don't take it personally."

She sucks in a sharp breath as her expression turns slack. "But I thought..."

I shake my head before forcing out a gruff response. "Sorry, you're wrong."

"Oh god..."

As much as I want to reach out and comfort her, I don't. Instead, I ball my hands at my sides to keep from doing exactly that.

"I feel like such an idiot." Misery laces her words and fills her expression.

It's painful to observe.

A gurgle of despair escapes from her before she pushes past me and flies toward the exit, yanking on the knob and escaping from the room. The door slams against the wall and reverberates on its hinges. The urge to rush after her pulses through my veins, prompting me into action. I take a quick step toward the door before grinding to a halt. As much as I want to chase her down and tell her the truth, I can't.

Dragging her away from the party was a mistake that shouldn't have happened. I lost control and because of that, she's hurt. I need to get it through my thick head that Elle Kendricks will never belong to me. No matter how much I want her.

I plow a hand through my hair in frustration and force myself to stay in the room. It takes a couple of minutes to wrestle all of my ferocious emotions back under control. One sweep of my tongue across my lower lip and the taste of her sweetness comes flooding back. I push out of the room and stalk down the darkened hallway, scanning the costumed crowd as I go. In the fifteen minutes or so that I was gone, the number of students crammed into this house has exploded. Everywhere I look, there are people making out, laughing, drinking, and dancing as if this is their farewell bash.

I should get the hell out of here before I can fuck up this night any more than I already have. But I can't do that. I need to make sure Elle is safe. That she found her way back to her friends or—at the very least—Brayden. I force my way through the mob, searching each face as I go. There are a ton of girls dressed as Harley Quinn, but none are Elle. I scour the first floor of the house.

Twice.

And still manage to come up empty handed.

By the time I run into my teammates, there's a pit the size of Texas sitting at the bottom of my gut, and I have the feeling I've just made the biggest mistake of my life.

Chapter Seven

ELLE

Embarrassment scorches my cheeks as I shove my way through the mass of writhing bodies crammed together on the first floor. Even though my costume is flimsy, I'm burning up inside. Any moment I'm going to spontaneously combust. Then again, maybe that would be for the best.

I have no idea how I'll ever look Carson in the eyes again. It's not like he's some random guy at a party I can pretend doesn't exist. This is Brayden's best friend we're talking about. The very same one my mother considers more like a second son. He turns up for holiday dinners and birthdays. I can't stop by my brother's rented house off campus without running into him. In the past, that's usually been a good thing. I'm always secretly hoping to catch sight of him.

That's no longer the case.

A groan escapes from me.

I can't even fool myself into believing this isn't anything other than a disaster. Not only did I blurt out that I've been saving myself for him, but then I groped the guy. My fingers tingle as I recall how his thick length felt beneath my hand. This isn't an incident you live down. It's the kind that forces you to change your name and address and relocate in hopes of starting your life over.

If only it were possible to chalk up this momentary lapse in judgment to being wasted. The problem with that excuse is that everyone knows I don't drink. Not after my father was ripped away from us four years ago by a drunk driver. In my brain, the two will forever be tied together.

The longer it takes to fight my way to the front door, the more pressure builds in my chest, making it impossible to breathe. Any moment, I'll gasp for my last dying breath. Not once does it occur to me to search for my friends in the frenzied mob of revelers. All I know is that I need to leave before I pass out from lack of oxygen.

By the time I burst through the front door, the edges of my vision are fuzzy and I'm lightheaded. I stagger across the dilapidated porch as the cool night air stings my overheated cheeks. With my hands braced on my knees, I squeeze my eyes shut and suck in a deep, cleansing breath before gradually releasing it back into the atmosphere.

"Hey, Harley," a deep voice booms, "if you're gonna be sick, do it over the railing. I don't want to be hosing off your puke in the morning."

My eyes spring open as I swing my head and meet the gaze of a six-foot-tall condom.

When I say nothing, his voice sharpens. "Did you hear me?"

It takes effort to straighten to my full height. "I'm not sick."

He eyes me dubiously as if I'm full of shit.

Since I have zero desire to be judged by this oversized piece of protection, I force my feet into movement, walking down the rickety front porch steps. My fingers wrap around the banister, clinging to it for dear life. The cherry on top of the sundae that is tonight would be to fall down the stairs and hurt myself. It would be yet another humiliation to add to the growing heap. And that, I don't think I could survive.

Once I reach the concrete path that cuts through the front lawn, I hurry to the sidewalk before swinging left in the direction we came earlier this evening. All I want is to return to the dorms, get out of this stupid costume, and lick my wounds in private.

There are a ton of students milling around with drinks in hand, laughing and talking. A few are singing at the top of their lungs. One girl is hunkered over, throwing up on the grass near the street while her friend holds back her hair. I glance at the pile of puke. Seems rather symbolic for how this night has turned out.

The girl groans, and more of tonight's festivities make a reappearance on the lawn. I give her friend a pitying look before picking up my pace. After about a block, the crowd begins to thin.

Now that I've cooled off and some of my shame has dissipated, my scalp begins to itch. I yank off the wig before picking out the pins and rubber band holding everything in place. Once all of the fasteners have been removed, I shake out my hair and the thick mass tumbles around my shoulders. A sigh escapes from my lips. Oh my god, that feels so much better. The breeze wafts through the strands, drying the perspiration.

By the time I'm two blocks from the party, there are far fewer people wandering around. Even though the streetlights are on, illuminating the area, unease scampers down my spine as I realize that leaving the party alone wasn't the smartest idea. I should have tried to find my friends or requested an Uber. I could have even looked for my brother. Although, after what happened, I don't want to see him. The most I can hope is that Carson keeps what happened between us to himself and never speaks of it. My brother would probably become unhinged if he discovered that I'd thrown myself at his friend.

It's the low vibration of a passing car that knocks me from those thoughts. I glance at the vehicle as it passes, slowing in the process as the driver turns his head and stares. There's too much distance between us to clearly make out his face. When he's about twenty feet in front of me, red brake lights flash in the darkness.

Oh fuck.

My heart spasms, thumping into overdrive, as I grind to a halt. I scrutinize the sleek sedan. From this distance, I can't identify the make, model, or color. My pulse flutters as I wait to see what will happen next. If I have to make a run for it, I won't get far in these boots. They were made for standing around and looking pretty, not actually walking.

Why the hell did I leave the party?

Humiliated or not, I should have stayed put. In hindsight, it seems like an impulsive decision that could come back to bite me in the ass.

So what if I'd been embarrassed?

It's better than ending up raped and left for dead on the side of a desolate road, right?

Oh god...I'm too young to die.

I steel myself as the driver's side window disappears between us. If there's one thing I've learned from years of drama classes, it's how to project my voice so that it'll carry over a distance. I'll yell my damn head off if I have to. There's no way I'm going down without a fight.

A scream bubbles up in my throat.

"Elle, is that you?"

All of my limbs shake as I blink.

Wait a minute...that voice sounds familiar, but I'm not sure where I recognize it from. It's deep. Older sounding. More like an adult than a student on campus. I remain silent as my mind flips through memories, trying to place it. I don't answer or make a move in the car's direction.

Are you kidding me?

Of course I don't!

I've watched enough episodes of *Dateline* to know better than that. Well, maybe not. I left that stupid party, didn't I?

"Elle, it's Dr. Holloway. From your statistics class."

"Dr. Holloway?" And just like that, my muscles turn lax, and my knees weaken with relief. It's all I can do to stay upright.

"Yeah." There's a beat of silence. "What are you doing walking around by yourself at this time of night? Don't you know how dangerous it is?"

Heat blooms in my cheeks. I certainly do now. I'll more than likely remember this moment for the rest of my life.

"Oh, um..." I stammer, feeling like an idiot. "I was at a party and decided to leave early."

"Where are your friends?" Before I'm able to respond, he hurtles another question at me. His voice sharpens. "You weren't at a party alone, were you?"

I shift from one foot to another before reluctantly admitting, "No, I was there with my roommates."

Even from where I stand, I can see his expression darken as the edges of his lips sink. "I really thought you were smarter than that."

I wince at his chastising tone. What I've learned tonight is that I'm not only terrible at statistics, but my survival instincts are shit.

"Get in the car and I'll drive you home."

What?

I couldn't possibly do that.

I shake my head. "No, that's all right. It's not much further."

His tone turns steely. "Get in the car, Elle. This isn't up for discussion. I'm not going to let you walk home alone at this time of night. I wouldn't be able to forgive myself if something happened to you."

I draw my lower lip between my teeth as indecision spirals through me. When I remain motionless, he growls, "Now, Elle."

Ugh.

This night has become an endless string of humiliations. Ones that I won't be able to live down. First Carson and now one of my professors.

Left without any alternative, I mumble, "Fine."

I force myself to walk toward the vehicle idling in the middle of the street. His attention stays fastened to me in the driver side mirror as I sidle around the trunk before pulling open the door and slipping into the passenger seat beside him.

"Thanks." My gaze flickers in his direction before hastily bouncing to the road beyond the windshield.

"I assume you were at the Sigma Epsilon party tonight."

It's not a question.

I glance down at my clothing as a fresh wave of mortification crashes over me.

Why did I allow Madison to talk me into this costume? It barely covers my ass, and the T-shirt is so thin that you can probably see my nipples poking through the cotton.

"Yeah." I shift awkwardly on the butter-soft leather seat, unable to meet his eyes.

"At the very least, I hope you had fun." He switches the gear into drive and the car shoots forward, surging down the tree-lined street.

I almost snort but rein it in at the last moment. "Not really."

More like not at all, but I keep that little tidbit to myself.

He turns slightly until I feel the brief touch of his gaze. His voice softens, losing the sharp edge it had held moments ago. "I'm sorry to hear that." There's a pause. "Is there anything you want to talk about?"

My eyes widen as they swing toward him.

As much as I like Dr. Holloway—he might teach one of the subjects I hate, but he seems like a nice enough guy—the man is still one of my instructors. I can't imagine opening up and sharing what happened with Carson.

I press my lips together and shake my head. I want to forget about tonight, not rehash it in gory detail.

"All right, that's fine." We fall into silence before he asks, "Where do you live?"

Grateful for the change in topic, I blurt, "Sutton Hall."

He nods, not bothering to ask for further directions. His attention stays locked on the ribbon of road stretched out in front of us. Without his inquisitive stare resting upon me, I'm able to study him more closely. He's younger than I originally assumed. During class, he usually wears khakis and a button-down shirt. Sometimes he adds a blazer to the ensemble along with black, horn-rimmed glasses. His hair is longish with a slight wave to it in the back, near the collar of his shirt.

Tonight, his attire is more casual. A simple black T-shirt that hugs his chest and biceps along with dark wash jeans. The glasses are conspicuously absent, and his hair is more disheveled than I'm used to seeing. Before, I'd thought he was somewhere in his late thirties. Maybe even early forties. Dressed like this, he looks to be more in his late twenties or early thirties.

My phone dings, knocking me out of my silent perusal. I blink back to the present, a little embarrassed that I've spent so much time examining him and dig through my small cross body purse. Once I find the slim device, I pull it out and stare at the screen.

The message is from Carson.

Where are u? U ok?

My heart skips a painful beat as my brows slam together.

You know what?

Screw him.

Not bothering to reply, I return the phone to my purse and glance at Dr. Holloway, only to find him watching me with a curious gaze.

"Was that your boyfriend?"

I shake my head before breaking eye contact. It's much easier to have this conversation while staring out the windshield. "No, just a friend. Actually, he's my brother's friend." I have no idea why I blurt out the last part, but it's the truth, right?

At the end of the day, that's all Carson is to me.

Brayden's friend and teammate.

"Are you sure there's nothing you want to talk about? You might not realize this, but I'm a really good listener if you're in need of one."

My shoulders droop as I force a thin smile to my lips. "Thanks, but I really don't."

Honestly, it's a little surreal to be sitting in his car. We've never had any conversations that went beyond statistics or spoken two words to each other outside of the lecture hall. In a way, it almost feels like when you were a kid and you'd run into your teacher at the grocery store or a restaurant. It always blew my mind that they existed outside of the school building, let alone had an actual life with kids and a family.

"Just know I'm always available if you want to talk or vent, okay?"

"Yeah, thanks." Even though I appreciate the offer, there's no way in hell I'm taking him up on it.

The breath rushes from my lungs in relief when the sixteen-story dorm comes into view. A minute later, he's pulling up to the curb in front of the building and shifting into park. My fingers snake around the handle, ready to leap out of the vehicle and put the entire night behind me. I don't want to think about it ever again. And I certainly don't want to run into Carson on campus anytime soon.

Is it possible to avoid him until he graduates in the spring?

That's what I'm shooting for.

"Thanks again for the ride."

His lips quirk. "It wasn't a problem, Elle. I'll see you in class on Monday."

I nod and jerk the handle before slipping from what I now realize is a high-end BMW.

As I stand on the sidewalk alongside his car, our gazes stay locked. A strange energy passes between us, and I have to resist the urge to tug at my shorts before turning away and quickening my step to the building. It's only when I've slipped through the glass door that he pulls away. The red taillights fade into the night before finally disappearing into the darkness.

Chapter Eight

CARSON

It's been more than forty-five minutes since Elle disappeared from the bedroom, and I've scoured this party at least a dozen times trying to locate her. It's like the moment she stepped out of the room, she disappeared into thin air. Every minute that ticks by has the lump sitting at the bottom of my gut expanding in size until I feel nauseous.

I know who her friends are, but there's no way I'll recognize them in costumes. I keep glancing at my phone, hoping she'll respond to my text. Even if it's one telling me to go to hell. At least I'd know she was safe. Instead, there's been nothing but stereo silence from her end.

It's driving me crazy.

Even though I don't want to do it, I finally bite the bullet and ask Brayden.

"Hey, have you seen your sister around?"

He scowls, which is his usual response when discussing his sibling in a party situation. After more than a year of attending the same school, that hasn't changed. "No, I didn't realize she was here." His brows slam together as he cranes his neck and searches the sea of bodies. Although, it's still a madhouse. "I really fucking hate when we end up at the same place."

Shifting his stance, he pulls out his phone from his back pocket and taps the screen a couple of times. A few seconds tick by before he shoots me a confused expression. "What are you talking about? She's at the dorm."

Now that I know she's safe, my muscles loosen as a wave of relief crashes over me. There were too many scenarios playing out in my head, and the longer I went without knowing where she was, the uglier the endings became.

It's only when Brayden claps me on the back that I'm knocked out of those thoughts. "I really appreciate you looking out for Elle. You're a good friend."

Guilt floods every cell in my body. It's doubtful Brayden would be saying that if he knew how I really felt about her. Or if he'd caught sight of us dancing together. And I'd already be dead—no questions asked—if he found out that I'd yanked her to one of the back bedrooms and kissed her.

I've done the worst thing I could do and broken bro code.

I drag a hand across my face and consider the merits of 'fessing up. Brayden has a right to know what happened between us. I should have the balls to be honest with him. The guy is like a brother to me. Always has been. When my parents were too busy getting their business up and off the ground, I spent an endless amount of time at the Kendricks house. There came a point when Katherine, Brayden's mom, would set a place for me at the dinner table without even asking if I was planning to stay. It was just assumed I would. As if I were a de facto part of the family. Her easy acceptance meant the world to me. My childhood would have been far lonelier without the Kendricks filling it. Who knows if I'd even be playing football in college or have a chance of making it to the pros without Jake Kendricks encouraging me to get involved in the sport? He stood on the sidelines for every game, rooting me on, more times than my own father did.

Taking advantage of his daughter isn't how you pay back your friend's dead father for stepping in and guiding you through all of the pitfalls of being a teenager when your own parent couldn't be bothered to take the time.

Self-loathing bubbles up inside me. Even thinking about it leaves me feeling like an ungrateful asshole. It's those thoughts that solidify my decision to stay away from Elle. Maybe she doesn't realize it, but I'm doing what's best for both of us.

"Carson!"

I blink and stare at the girl I'd been talking to earlier this evening before all hell broke loose.

"Oh, hey..."

"Monica," she supplies helpfully.

I nod and lie through my teeth. "Yeah, sure...I remember."

When her grin intensifies in wattage, I realize that was probably the wrong thing to say.

"We were about to head over to my friend's house for a more," she pauses as her tongue darts out to moisten her shiny red lips, "*intimate* gathering." Her palm drifts to my chest. "Why don't you come with us? It'll be fun."

Fun?

That's debatable.

Will it get my mind off a certain someone I have no business thinking about?

Also unlikely.

The best thing I could probably do at this point is spend a little time with this girl in an attempt to forget about the one I forced away. If I squint, there's a slight resemblance. They both have slender figures and long, dark hair. Although, I made it a point to stop screwing girls who look like Elle when I realized that all I was trying to do was fuck her out of my system.

Because guess what?

It never worked. They ended up being nothing more than a poor imitation for the one I really wanted. Instead of feeling loose and satisfied after rolling out of bed and hauling up my jeans, I felt empty and a little dirty.

Who the fuck needs that?

"Thanks for the invite, but I'm good." The words pop out of my mouth before I can stop them.

The brightness of her smile fades. "Are you sure?"

"Yeah, I'm going to stick around here for a bit longer."

It's a relief when she shrugs off the disappointment. "Okay. If you change your mind, come find me. I'll be here for about ten more minutes."

I nod. "I'll keep it in mind."

As luck would have it, a friend waves her over and she takes off.

When I glance at Brayden, he shakes his head. "That was a mistake. You need to get laid, dude. You're way too tense. And that girl was totally interested."

Little does he know that I haven't gotten laid in six long months. I've unfortunately become intimately acquainted with my hand. Screwing a random girl at a party won't alleviate my problems. It'll only exasperate them.

It's a shit situation that doesn't have a solution.

The only hope I have at this point is that once I graduate from Western and get away from Elle, I'll be able to get my mojo back. I won't be looking for her around every damn corner. I won't be seeking her out, trying to keep her close. I can move on with my life and maybe even meet someone else. I just need to get through the next six months before that can happen.

"I need a bottle of water." Although it's doubtful anything will wash away the bitter taste that lingers in my mouth.

"Whatever," Brayden calls after me with a shake of his head.

I should have realized this night would turn out to be a total bust. If I'd been smart, I would have sat my ass home. Instead, I kissed the one girl I shouldn't have and nearly fucked over my friend.

Chapter Nine

ELLE

I rattle off my drink order at the Roasted Bean and step to the side to wait.

It's been more than a week since the Sig Ep party, and I'm relieved to report that I've been able to avoid Carson on campus. There were a handful of times during the week when we'd bump into each other—like when I'd leave stats.

In order to prevent this from happening, I began exiting from the opposite end of the building and taking a different route. On Tuesdays and Thursdays, I'd usually run into him while grabbing something to eat for lunch at the union. Instead of taking a chance on that happening, I now pack something portable I can eat on the run or at the library. A protein bar, piece of fruit, or trail mix.

Normally, I'd drop by Brayden's house on the weekend to visit him and Sydney or stop by one of their parties. I skipped the get-together they had, just like I plan on avoiding any other future events. The further I can stay from Carson, the better off I'll be. I can almost fool myself into believing that the whole ugly situation never transpired.

Almost.

The only time I've caught sight of him was when I attended the football game Saturday afternoon. And that was unavoidable. I've never missed one of Brayden's games and I'll be damned if I start now. Especially since this is his final season playing for the Wildcats. As much as I tried to keep my attention off the blond tight end, that's exactly where it ended up. All I can say is that Rome wasn't built in a day, and it'll take time to forget about him.

Until now, I never realized how much I looked forward to seeing him around campus or talking with him. Distancing myself has been a challenge. I'm like an addict attempting to detox cold turkey without assistance.

If it were possible to rewind time and make different choices, I'd do it in a heartbeat. I have no idea what got into me Saturday night. When we'd been dancing, it had almost felt like he might want me.

Clearly, nothing could be further from the truth.

A dull flush creeps into my cheeks as his clipped words ring unwantedly throughout my head.

I'm a twenty-two-year-old dude. I'm always hard. Don't take it personally.

Every couple of days, he sends a text. Even though it's difficult, I ignore them. I wish he would get the hint and leave me alone.

When the barista calls out my vanilla latte, I grab the to-go cup and wind my way through the cafe-style tables before arriving at a ratty couch that has seen better days near the front window where bright sunlight pours in. I set the drink down on the scarred coffee table and pull out my statistics book, notebook, and AirPods before getting to work. I met with Professor Holloway on Tuesday during office hours, and we went over the last test one problem at a time. It was painful. The only positive to come out of that situation is that I now have a firmer grasp on the material.

I think.

Three problems in and it's all too tempting to bang my head against the table. All right, so maybe I'm being a bit dramatic. What I do know is that I really hate this class. It just doesn't seem to get any easier. It's like trying to comprehend a foreign language I've never heard before. For the record, I suck at that too. No matter how much I try to understand the information, it just doesn't seem to penetrate.

Tumbling down the rabbit hole of statistics, I lose all track of time. I only glance up when a shadow falls over me, cutting off the beam of sunlight pouring in through the picture window. I blink as Dr. Holloway's lips lift into a smile. His gaze settles on the book spread wide on the stretch of table in front of me.

I quickly pull out my AirPods.

"Working on my favorite subject, I see. How's it going?" There's a beat of silence. "Or shouldn't I ask?"

I hesitate, embarrassed to admit that it's not going well. Having so much trouble with a subject makes me feel like an idiot. Brayden has always aced his math classes with minimal effort. I, on the other hand, have always struggled to pull off passing grades. Over the years, I've worked with a handful of tutors, and I still didn't do as well as my brother. It's frustrating to work so hard and not see the payoff. One reason I love the theater is because it has absolutely nothing to do with numbers.

"It's going," I mumble.

His brows furrow as he quietly studies my notebook. It's tempting to lay a palm over my chicken scratches so he can't attempt to decipher them. Instead, I keep my hands locked tightly together in my lap. My eyes widen as he settles on the couch next to me. The cushion dips, tipping me toward him until his khaki-covered thigh rests against the bare skin that peeks out from beneath the hem of my skirt. He's so close that I'm inundated by the spicy scent of his cologne.

Our shoulders brush as he leans forward and picks up my pencil, erasing the last couple steps of the problem I'd spent ten minutes working on. "This is where you went wrong." He writes out the sequence before arriving easily at the answer.

My brows snap together as I stare at the paper. How does he make it look so effortless when it's anything but? Without his assistance, I probably would've wasted another fifteen minutes before I figured out where I went wrong.

If I ever figured out where I went wrong.

It's tempting to pick up the book and hurl it through the window.

"Do you see what I did there?" he asks as I silently stew.

"Yeah. It was a stupid mistake," I admit.

His head turns until our gazes can lock and hold. With him sitting this close, I'm able to see the vibrant color of his eyes more clearly behind the black-rimmed glasses. They're a deep and rich blue, like cobalt. All the tiny flecks that dance around within his irises are mesmerizing.

I clear my throat as a jolt of unease shoots through me. It's tempting to shift away so that there's more space between us, but I resist the urge. It's not like we're alone together in some dark room. Or he's making moves on me. For goodness' sake, it's mid morning and we're in the middle of the coffee shop on campus where dozens of students are milling around. No one seems to be paying us the least bit of attention. I'm overreacting. I need to chill out and be thankful the guy took pity on me and decided to offer his assistance. He's saved me from a lot of headaches.

"Tell you what," he glances at the chunky silver watch adorning his wrist, "I've got about thirty minutes before my next class. Why don't we work through a few more problems?"

His generous offer takes me by surprise. "Really?"

"Yeah." The sun-kissed skin around his eyes and mouth crinkles as he smiles. "I'm happy to help."

"Thank you." I nod, grateful I don't have to figure out the rest of the assignment on my own. Especially when I wasted so much time on answers that weren't even correct. There are a few people I usually go to for help. Sierra is a whiz when it comes to science and math. Since she's in the nursing program, she's already taken statistics, but she's overloaded with coursework and always busy. Sometimes I work with my brother, but with football, Sydney, and classes, he doesn't have a lot of free time. As much as I enjoy studying with Mike, after about thirty minutes, we end up goofing around and running lines for the play.

And then there's Carson...

After the Sig Ep party, I'd sooner fail then ask him for anything.

"All right," my professor says, "let's get to work."

Chapter Ten

CARSON

I haul my backpack onto my shoulder as I cut through the heart of campus before glancing at my sports watch. There's about twenty minutes before class begins. That's more than enough time to grab a coffee. I need a dose of caffeine, and I hate sucking down too many energy drinks. All they do is make me feel jittery. At the moment, I'm running on fumes. I haven't gotten a decent night's sleep in a week.

And it's all because of the dark-haired beauty who has gone into avoidance mode. The girl won't even respond to my texts. Not only has she disappeared from campus, but she's vanished from my life without a trace. It's tempting to show up unannounced at her dorm room just to make sure everything is all right, but I know it is. The fact that she has no problem answering Brayden's text messages is all the proof I need.

Deep down, I realize this separation was inevitable. Over the years, we've become too close, and I enjoy spending time with her a little too much. And what occurred at the party can't be allowed to happen again.

So yeah...

This is for the best.

What I didn't anticipate is how hard it would be to have her ripped from my life. This is the longest we've gone without talking since she stepped foot on campus freshman year. Somehow, when I wasn't looking, Elle Kendricks managed to burrow her way into my heart. If I'm being brutally honest with myself, I'm desperate to catch sight of her. I'm like a man dying of thirst.

All I want is one damn drop.

Just one.

I drag a hand through my hair before pushing through the glass door of the Roasted Bean and taking my place in line. To kill time, I slip my phone from my back pocket and contemplate firing off another text to Elle. My fingers hover over the keyboard before I blow out a steady breath and stop myself. I need a clean break from her, and this is it. I can't afford to back peddle.

When someone calls out my name from across the small shop, I glance up before automatically lifting my hand to return the greeting. As the guy shifts to talk with someone else, I catch a glimpse of long dark hair. Everything inside me goes on high alert as I crane my neck to get a better look at a girl who bears a striking resemblance to Elle as she disappears behind a bunch of people standing around, enjoying their drinks.

I almost wince.

What the hell am I doing?

This seriously needs to stop. I'm more out of control than I realized.

Even as I tell myself not to do it, I step out of line and maneuver my way through the crowd until I have an unobstructed view of the worn couch. My feet grind to a halt. It wasn't my imagination at all. Elle is actually here. It takes a moment to realize she isn't alone. I blink before narrowing my eyes.

Who the hell is the old dude sitting next to her?

All right, so maybe he's not exactly a relic. From what I can see, he's probably in his mid-thirties. But still...that's too damn old for Elle. Jealousy bubbles up inside me like a geyser, overtaking all rational thought. Without considering the ramifications of my actions, I stalk closer, swallowing up the distance between us before pushing some random guy out of the way.

"Watch it!" he grumbles as his coffee sloshes over the rim of his cup.

I mutter an apology before arriving at the couch and clearing my throat. When neither bothers to glance up, I snap, "Hey."

It's like the bubble they've been encapsulated in pops as both of their heads jerk up and two sets of eyes land on me. My gaze bounces from Elle to the guy sitting entirely too close to her for comfort. It takes every ounce of self-control not to grab him by the shirtfront and yank him to his feet. My guess is that we're roughly the same height, although my shoulders are broader and I'm more muscular. I probably outweigh him by a solid forty pounds. The odds are stacked in my favor if it comes to blows. And with the way I'm feeling, that's exactly the direction this confrontation is headed in.

"Carson." An uncomfortable silence ensues. "What are you doing here?"

"Grabbing a coffee before my next class," I say tersely, firing back with my own question. "What about you?"

Before she can respond, the interloper glances at his expensive watch and rises to his feet. It's just as I suspected—we're roughly the same height. I shift my stance, squaring up.

"I'd better get going. I'll see you in class, Elle."

He gives me a polite smile before picking up his briefcase and walking away. I glare, torn between following the guy and having a private word with him or staying at Elle's side. The need to stick close to her wins out. Once the door slams closed behind him, my gaze slices back to Elle.

I jerk a thumb toward the entrance. "Who was that?" Better question—why were they together?

I'm almost taken aback by the frostiness that enters both her eyes and tone. I don't think she's ever looked at me like that.

"Dr. Holloway, my stats professor."

My attention deviates to him again as he walks past the picture window that stretches across the front of the shop. He glances at her and then me. We hold each other's gazes for a second or two. What I see in his eyes is enough to have the possessiveness I've always felt where Elle is concerned roaring back to life.

Professor or not, do I think he wants her?

You bet your damn ass I do.

What guy in his right mind wouldn't?

She's absolutely gorgeous in that untouched, pristine kind of way. She has all of this barely contained energy radiating off her where life is concerned. Especially for the things she's passionate about. It's enough to make a man want to be the first one to dirty her up. To channel all that untapped passion into—

Fuck.

"You need to stay away from him," I growl, hands tightening at my sides.

Her brows pinch together as she stares at me for a long moment before shoving her books into her bag and rising gracefully to her feet. She tips her head back to hold my gaze. "That would be difficult to do, given the fact that he's my professor. I'm not sure what you think was going on, but he was helping me with homework. That's it."

Before I have a chance to respond, fury leaps into her espresso-colored eyes as she takes a step toward me, invading my personal space. With her this close, the scent of her floral shampoo swirls slyly around me, teasing my senses. It's a battle not to lay my hands on her and drag her to me. To kiss her the way I did a week ago. It's all I can think about as my attention drops to the angry slash of her mouth.

She rams a finger into my chest. "And even if something were going on, it's none of your business."

The fuck it is!

A potent concoction of rage-infused jealousy rushes through my veins as she swings away and stalks toward the door before shoving against the glass and stepping over the threshold without another glance in my direction.

I gape at her retreating form, unsure what to do. As soon as the door slams shut behind her, I wake from the strange paralysis that has taken hold.

Did that really happen?

Has Elle ever gotten in my face? Or talked to me with so much pent-up fury?

Nope. She's always stared at me with adoration. If that girl thinks this conversation is over, she couldn't be more wrong. Spurred into action, I beeline for the exit. People scurry out of my way with their drinks in hand as I barrel through like a locomotive. A few call out greetings, but I don't bother returning them. All I can think about is Elle.

She's wrong about this not being any of my concern. Whether she realizes it or not, anything that happens with her is my business.

Once outside, I scour the walkway until my gaze fastens on her retreating form. Her spine is ramrod straight as she blows through the crowd. And then I'm off, closing the distance between us. Just like in the coffee shop, people see me coming and scramble out of my way. No one wants to get run over this early in the morning. The moment I'm within striking distance, my fingers wrap around her arm. Shock transforms her expression, and she gasps at my sudden arrival on the scene as I maneuver her off the crowded pathway and out of student traffic.

Elle stares at me like she has no idea who the hell I am, and I'll admit—at this particular moment—I'm not quite sure either. All I know is that I don't want her around that guy. Maybe she doesn't see the desire in his eyes, but I do.

"The hell it isn't my business!" I growl, responding belatedly to the last comment she threw at me in the Roasted Bean before stomping away, leaving me to hold my dick in my hand.

The flare of surprise that had leapt to life in her eyes swiftly dissipates as irritation and resentment overtake her expression. "And why is that?" she challenges, attempting to wrench her arm free with a soft grunt.

But there is no way I'm allowing that to happen. If anything, I haul her closer. We're going to hash this out here and now. When my grip tightens, she bares her teeth and growls. For a second time, I'm bowled over that all of this rage is directed at me. We've always had an easygoing relationship.

Until now.

At the moment, there's nothing effortless about it. Instead, it feels explosive. Like a powder keg that could detonate with one wrong move or misplaced breath.

I stare silently, unsure how to respond. What I can't do is reveal the truth. It takes a few heartbeats to wrangle myself under control and moderate my voice. "Because I care about you and don't want to see you get hurt." That's as close to the truth as I can get without crossing the line and giving myself away.

Her brows rise across her forehead. "You...care about me?" There's a pause as the energy crackling in the air ratchets up. She drops her chin but continues to hold my gaze. "Like a sister?"

I force down the thick lump of sawdust that has wedged itself in the middle of my throat, making it impossible to breathe. I should force out the lie and be done with it.

But I can't. That's not how I feel about Elle, and the words refuse to budge from my lips.

When I fail to respond, the high color in her cheeks drains away and she growls, "I already have one overprotective brother. I don't need another. Got it?"

God dammit.

This conversation isn't going the way I expected it to. Instead of smoothing over our strained relationship, all I've done is blow it further out of the water.

"Elle..." Desperation creeps into my tone as my mind cartwheels. Normally, I can assess a situation in a matter of seconds and think swiftly on my feet. It's what makes me invaluable at my position on the field. In this instance however, it's like my brain has taken a temporary hiatus and I have no idea how to reel this interaction in again.

"No! You need to leave me alone, Carson!"

When she attempts to yank her arm free, I do the only thing I can and release her. As much as I want to hold on tight, I can't. When she stumbles back a step, I spring forward to steady her. Instead of allowing me to help, she lifts her hands as if to ward me off. Almost as if she can't bear the thought of me touching her. Wounded by her behavior, my arms drop back to my sides.

I seriously can't believe this is what it's come to.

She straightens her skirt, giving me one final glare that could freeze the balls off a yeti before spinning on her heels and stalking away for a second time as she disappears down the pathway.

A feeling of helplessness settles over me as I realize there's nothing more I can do. If I continue to chase her, the situation will only escalate, and I don't want that to happen. Allowing her to walk away when we have so much unfinished business to work out feels wrong.

It sucks to realize that all I can do is give Elle the space she's so intent on forcing between us.

Chapter Eleven

ELLE

A message pops up on my phone from Brayden, letting me know that he's here and waiting downstairs. Tonight we're headed to Mom's for dinner. Honestly, it'll be a relief to escape from campus, even if it's only for a few hours. Between play practice, my classes, and this growing issue with Carson, I'm both mentally and emotionally exhausted.

I need a homecooked meal and to spend a little quality time with the fam. As a result of avoiding the football house, I haven't seen very much of my brother. He might be overprotective and annoying, but I miss seeing his ugly mug. I'm struck with the realization that this is a little glimpse into the future and what it'll be like when he graduates in the spring.

We're closer to that happening than I've allowed myself to dwell on. Sadness bubbles up inside me at the thought of Brayden moving on to the next phase of his life when I'll still be stuck here. We won't know where my brother will end up playing football until the draft in the spring. It could be halfway across the country.

The same goes for Car—

As soon as an image of him pops into my brain, I shove it aside. It doesn't matter where Carson gets drafted. In fact, I'll be glad once he's gone. Maybe if I repeat the mantra enough times, I'll actually start to believe it.

With a quick goodbye to my suitemates, I close the door behind me and take the elevator to the first floor before exiting the dorm. I wave to a few girls from class and jog to where Brayden's black truck is idling alongside the curb. When I'm close enough, I catch a glimpse of Sydney in the front seat. My brother introduced his new girlfriend to Mom last month and she's been joining us for dinner when she can carve out time. Since she plays soccer, she isn't always able to make it. Luckily for me, play practice was scheduled for earlier this afternoon and I was able to plow through most of my homework, which freed up a few precious hours.

I yank open the backdoor, ready to slip inside. "Hi..." The rest of my greeting dies a quick death on my tongue as I lock gazes with Carson.

He's the last person I expected to see this evening.

When I remain frozen in place, Brayden glances at me from the front seat. "Hey, you gonna get in or what?"

It's tempting to select the *or what* option, but then I'd have to explain why I have zero interest in being in a certain someone's presence, and I'm not really in the mood to watch my brother lose his shit.

Instead, I huff out a breath before reluctantly sliding onto the seat next to the one person I've been trying so hard to avoid. I slam the door shut with a grunt and stare straight ahead, refusing to acknowledge his presence. Tension fills every muscle in my body as Brayden peels away from the curb before pulling into traffic. Even though I try to pretend I'm alone in the backseat, that's impossible. I couldn't be more aware of the muscular guy next to me. I feel every shift of his body, every intake of air, every glance in my direction like the ripple of a pebble in a calm pool. I'm bombarded by his very existence.

Just when I feel like I'll come unhinged, Sydney asks, "How's the play going? We're excited to see it."

I release a steady inhalation and tell her about the fall production of *Heathers* the university is putting on. Since I'm only a sophomore and competition is fierce in the theater department, I was given a minor role. The part has more lines than last year, which is a plus. I'm trying to look at it through the lens of there being no small parts, only small actors.

We're about halfway to Mom's when the conversation ebbs and music from the radio fills the cabin of the truck. Now that I'm no longer distracted by the back and forth of our banter, I become acutely aware of Carson. I turn toward the window and focus on the passing scenery. I have no idea how I'll make it through the next few hours in his presence. For an evening that was supposed to be relaxing, it's turned out to be the complete opposite.

Thick tension blankets the atmosphere until it becomes suffocating. Unable to sit still, I shift restlessly on my seat and wonder if my brother and his girlfriend feel it as well. Normally, when the four of us are together, there's a lot of joking, laughing, and lighthearted discussions.

That's not the case tonight.

If I had realized Carson would be joining us, I would have come up with an excuse and bailed on the evening.

I don't have to glance in his direction to know his gaze is burning holes into me. I can practically feel the intensity of his scrutiny. I grit my teeth, refusing to give him the time of day. The humiliation of what happened at the Sigma Epsilon party is still fresh enough in my memory to make me wish the leather seat would open up and swallow me whole. I can't imagine looking him in the eyes without being forced to remember the incident in full Technicolor clarity. And our run-in the other day at the Roasted Bean certainly didn't help matters. It only made everything worse, which I didn't believe was possible. It's painful to admit that our relationship has careened so far out of its orbit it will never be the same again.

"What's going on with your professor?"

Even though his voice is nothing more than a gruff whisper, it sounds like a gunshot in the echoing silence of the truck.

I jerk my head until my wide gaze can slam into his.

Oh my god...did he really just ask that?

Brayden frowns from the front seat as his attention fastens onto mine in the rearview mirror. "Are you having a problem with one of your teachers?"

My heartbeat pounds into overdrive as my gaze narrows before slicing back to the guy next to me. If only there were a way to smite him on the spot. When Brayden continues to stare, waiting for an answer, I ground out, "Nope. Everything's fine."

Unconvinced, my brother's attention slides to his friend for the truth. "Is there something going on that I need to know about?"

A groan gurgles up from my chest as I slump on my seat.

Carson's gaze stays pinned to mine.

Just when I think he might brush off the question, he says instead, "Elle was at the Roasted Bean the other day with one of her instructors. The guy couldn't have sat any closer to her if he tried."

Heat floods into my cheeks as I shoot daggers at him. "He was helping me with homework," I ground out. "That's it. Dr. Holloway is my stats professor—it's his job to help me. He actually gets paid for it. And we were in the middle of a crowded coffee shop on campus. If you're trying to insinuate that something was going on, you couldn't be more wrong."

Brayden's lips flatten as he stares straight ahead. I can almost see the wheels in his head turning. "Is that the only time you've met with him outside of class?"

I press my lips together as my head falls back against the cushion and I stare at the ceiling.

"Elle?" Brayden's voice sharpens.

"This entire conversation is ridiculous," I grumble, not wanting to lie. Although, there's no way I can tell him the truth. "I can't believe you think—"

"That's not an answer," my brother fires back.

Carson shifts toward me on his seat. "When?"

"What?" It's tempting to snap my teeth at him. I'm so aggravated by this line of questioning. Why couldn't he have kept his big mouth shut? Why does he have to cause more problems for me?

"When else did you spend time together?"

"We never," I raise both hands in order to make air quotes around the first three words, "*spent time together*. You're blowing the entire situation out of proportion." I am so over this conversation.

And Carson.

The guy can take a flying leap for all I care.

He twists toward me, looming closer. "When was it?"

"Answer the question, Elle," my brother cuts in.

"After the Sig Ep party," I growl. "I was walking home, and he stopped and gave me a ride. That's it. All right?"

"Why would you walk home alone?" my brother asks. "You know how dangerous that is. I was at that party. You could have texted, and I would have given you a lift to the dorms." There's a pause before he adds, "Carson was there, too. He would have made sure you got home safely."

From the corner of my eye, I watch as guilt flashes across his expression. He knows *exactly* why I chose to leave the house party by myself.

Wanting to put a swift end to this conversation, I say, "You're right. I should have texted. It won't happen again."

Thankfully, we roll to a stop in front of Mom's house before any more questions can be fired off. As soon as Brayden shifts the gear into park, I throw open the door, needing to escape from the thick tension permeating the atmosphere. I'm so pissed that he brought up Dr. Holloway. He knew damn well Brayden would get all fired up.

Had I really thought tonight would give me a chance to relax and recharge with my family?

Ha!

Looks like the joke is on me. It's turned out to be the complete opposite. I would have been better off staying home and making a bowl of ramen. Maybe hitting the books and trying to get ahead in a few of my classes. Instead, I'm sweating bullets and dodging questions.

As I slam the truck door and stalk up the walkway, heavy footsteps pound behind me, closing the distance between us. I hasten my pace, wanting to avoid any further interactions with Carson. Just as I reach the front porch, a deep voice whispers at my ear, "You and I need to talk."

"Actually," I snap, "we don't."

I throw open the heavy glass door of my childhood home and attempt to slam it shut before he's able to make it over the threshold. His large hand whips out, wrapping around the edge before that can happen.

As much as I've always loved our house and have found comfort in spending time here, that's not the case at the moment. Given the choice, I'd rather be anywhere else. If there's any silver lining to be found, it's that the evening can't get any worse. Anger swirls through every cell of my body as I stalk into the foyer and the long stretch of hallway before arriving at the kitchen.

"Hi, Mom," I call out.

She swings around from the stove with an oven mitt in hand. "Hey, sweetie. How are you?"

I open my mouth to answer when movement from the corner of my eye catches my attention and I twist toward it. The lie poised on the tip of my tongue gets forced down as I lock gazes with a stranger standing near the kitchen table with a glass of wine in one hand. My feet stutter to a stop as I stare in surprise.

Not even a second later, Carson plows into me from behind. When I pitch forward, his hands wrap around my upper arms to lock me in place. Electricity sizzles through my veins and it takes every ounce of self control not to bare my teeth.

Why am I still reacting like this to him?

Especially now that I know how he feels about me.

Once I regain my bearings, I growl, "I'm fine. You can let go."

Our gazes stay fastened as regret twists his expression. I get the feeling he wants to say more but ultimately decides to remain quiet at the last moment. Instead, he releases his grip before retreating a step and giving us both some much needed space. It takes effort to tamp down all of the rioting emotions attempting to break loose inside me. More voices fill the room as Sydney and Brayden burst onto the scene.

"No way," my brother says with a laugh before his feet grind to a halt as he stares at the guy.

The room becomes so quiet that you could hear a pin drop. Mom sets down the oven mitt before silently making her way across the room to where the man loiters.

She shoots him a reassuring smile before slipping her arm through his. "Brayden and Elle, I'd like you to meet Theo." There's a pause as the energy in the room ratchets up to unprecedented heights. "My boyfriend."

Chapter Twelve

CARSON

U nder normal circumstances, I've always enjoyed spending time at the Kendricks' house. Especially when dinner is involved. Katherine is a phenomenal cook. If I hadn't practically grown up here, scarfing down meals five nights a week, I would have been left to my own devices, which more than likely meant nuking something from the freezer in the microwave or ordering take-out. Tonight, however, there's an air of tension that fills the atmosphere.

Amusingly enough, you wouldn't have guessed it from Katherine's easy demeanor as she keeps up a steady stream of conversation, asking everyone questions and regaling comical stories from her children's past.

I glance at Brayden, who sits across from me in the formal dining room, expecting him to have the toughest time with his mother deciding to move on, but he seems strangely at ease with the situation.

I suspect his chilled attitude has something to do with his new girl-friend. I've known Brayden for a long time and didn't think he would ever settle down. He's always been one to play the field where girls are concerned, enjoying all the perks that went along with being a Division

I athlete at Western University. It was a surprise when Sydney changed all that.

My gaze shifts to his sister.

Elle, on the other hand, has been uncharacteristically quiet throughout the meal. She's usually outgoing and talkative. Always smiling and quick to laughter. No matter what's going on in my life, the sound of her happiness has always had the power to lighten my mood. Katherine has made several attempts to draw her daughter into the conversation, but Elle is having none of it. She politely responds to whatever question is posed, but there's a subdued quality to her demeanor.

I don't like it.

It makes me want to comfort her and somehow alter the trajectory of this evening. Although that's difficult to do when she refuses to meet my gaze or even acknowledge my presence. As far as Elle is concerned, I have ceased to exist. If it were possible to go back and erase everything that transpired since the Sig Ep party, I'd do it in a heartbeat. Anything would be better than the iciness radiating from her.

Once dinner is finished, Elle quietly slips away from the table. I assume she's going to use the bathroom, but when she doesn't return within five minutes, I decide to look for her. When Theo asks Brayden about the upcoming bowl game, I excuse myself and beeline for the kitchen.

The Kendricks' home is over five thousand sprawling square feet. After Jake died, I'd wondered if Katherine would downsize to something smaller, something more manageable, but that didn't happen. I doubt Elle or Brayden could have handled any more change.

The first place I check is the small powder room located off the back hallway near the laundry. When I'm halfway across the kitchen, movement from outside catches my attention and I turn my head, expecting to see a squirrel or maybe a deer near the tree line at the back of the property. Instead, my gaze fastens on the slim figure a couple of yards away from the rectangular-shaped pool.

When we were kids, we'd spend hours splashing around in the water. Once we were in high school, I couldn't keep my eyes off Elle.

She lived in colorful bikinis. Some smaller than others. And I enjoyed every damn minute of it. Even when I had to stay in the deep end of the pool to hide my arousal. With the winter months fast approaching, all of the outdoor furniture has been packed up and put away for the season, giving the patio a desolate feel and appearance.

Her arms are wrapped tightly around her middle as she stares toward the woods with a distant look in her eyes. It's as if the weight of the world is resting on her slender shoulders. There's a distinct chill to the air, especially now that the sun has dipped beneath the horizon. With only a thin shirt covering her, she must be freezing. After the silence of the last hour, I'm fully aware that she has little interest in speaking to me, but I don't give it a second thought before detouring toward the set of French doors that lead outside.

The one thing I've never been able to bear is Elle's pain.

Even when I'm the architect of it.

When I'm no more than a few feet away, her head snaps in my direction. Her dark gaze flickers toward mine before dismissing me and returning to the trees.

"What are you doing here?"

Her voice is hollow as if she can't even be bothered to muster up her previous irritation.

Since she hasn't told me to get lost—which is exactly what I was expecting—I edge closer. "I was concerned after you disappeared from the table."

She jerks her shoulders. "Don't be. I'm fine."

My attention sharpens, taking in the tightness of her jaw and the sadness lurking in her eyes. "Are you sure about that?"

A puff of air escapes from her lips as she trails her hands over her bare arms. Goose flesh rises in the wake of her fingers. I grab hold of the back of my sweatshirt and whip it off before closing the distance between us and pulling it over her head.

"What are you doing?" she gasps. "I'm fine. I don't need your hoodie."

What Elle is really saying is that she doesn't need *me*.

But she does.

Whether she wants to admit it or not.

"Yes, you do," I say, tone hardening in an attempt to stymie any further arguments. "You're freezing. For fuck's sake, your teeth are chattering."

Her annoyed gaze returns to mine as I maneuver her limbs through the sleeves as if she's a small child. Once the black Western Wildcats sweatshirt settles around her, I run my hands down her covered arms.

"Better?"

A silent war breaks out across her features before she reluctantly gives in with a terse nod. "Yes, but aren't you cold?"

"Nah. You know the weather has never bothered me."

One side of her mouth hitches. "Yes, I remember. In high school, you'd wear shorts until January."

It's the first semi-smile I've been treated to in weeks. Even though it's in no way full-blown, I still want to bask in its warmth.

An answering expression tugs at my lips as the memories roll through my head. "Yup." My mom would nag the hell out of me, insisting I would catch a cold and end up getting sick. It never happened.

As my gaze roves over the length of her, a wave of possessiveness slams into me. There's something about the sight of her wearing my clothing that claws at my insides. It's like a small claim of ownership that I have no right to make. Silently I admit that the need to put my stamp on her is nothing new. The desire has always been there, pounding like a steady drumbeat beneath my skin, even when I did my damnedest to deny its existence.

It takes effort to blink back to the present as she grabs hold of the thick curtain of dark strands before lifting them from the back of the hoodie until they spread around her shoulders like a silky waterfall. It's so damn tempting to reach out and sift my fingers through the heavy mass. Instead, I tighten my hands and keep them locked at my sides.

Needing a distraction, I clear my throat along with those thoughts before glancing toward the back of the house. "I'm guessing you didn't know about Theo."

Further clarification isn't necessary. The fresh wave of sadness that seeps into her eyes leaves me wincing, making me wish I'd left well enough alone.

Her forehead furrows as she stares at the stone façade of the expansive structure before slowly shaking her head. "Until I walked through the door, I had no idea he existed."

Ouch. That's tough.

I'm not sure why Katherine chose to spring her new boyfriend on them at a random dinner. Seems like it might have been easier to talk to her kids about the situation and give them a little time to adjust before introductions were made.

Then again, what the hell do I know?

I've royally fucked up my relationship with Elle and we're not even going out.

I shift my stance, fighting the impulse that demands I tug her into my arms in order to offer comfort. "If it's any consolation, he seems like a nice guy."

Her teeth sink into her lower lip before she worries it. Instead of answering, she pops a shoulder and breaks eye contact before staring off into the distance.

Even though I should do us both a favor and keep my big mouth shut, I say, "It's been four years since your dad died. That's a long time to be alone." I wince as the words leave my lips. It's not like I understand what it's like to see one of your parents with another person. Mine are still together, happily bickering with one another.

Her entire body wilts, deflating before my eyes. It only leaves me feeling like a bigger jackass for inflicting more heartache.

"I know exactly how long it's been."

My gaze flickers to the massive residence. "It's a big house for just one person. It must be lonely with both you and Brayden at school." I know exactly what it's like to rattle around all alone in an empty house. It's the reason I spent so much time with the Kendricks while growing up.

Air escapes from her lungs like a tire that has sprung a leak. "I'm sure you're right." Her voice dips, flooding with pent-up emotion. "It's just hard to see her with someone else. Before, it wasn't something I could even conjure up. Now, I can't get the image out of my head. It feels burned into my retinas."

No matter how much self-control I pretend to have where this girl is concerned, those words are my undoing. Powerless to resist the urge, I reach out, nabbing her fingers with my own before towing her to me. It's almost a surprise when she comes willingly. Once there, I wrap her up in my arms, cocooning her in my embrace.

If it were possible to leech away her pain and take it onto myself, I would do it without question. Even though her body is stiff as a board, I hold on tightly, securing her to me. With the side of her face pressed against my chest, I close my eyes and simply enjoy the feel of her.

With my face buried in her hair, the floral scent of her shampoo inundates my senses. Gradually her muscles loosen until she sinks fully into my arms. Time stops and I lose track of how long we stand wrapped up in one another. I don't understand why everything always feels so much better when I'm holding her, pretending that she belongs to me.

It's a problem I don't know how to solve.

Because at the end of the day, Elle isn't mine.

And she never will be.

Chapter Thirteen

CARSON

Stretched out flat on the bench, I focus on the bar, gradually lifting it above my chest before bringing it down again with measured movements. Once I finish the rep, I repeat it fourteen more times. The second I stop focusing all of my energies on the precision of the exercise, Elle relentlessly forces her way back inside my brain. Permanent eviction doesn't seem to be a possibility. The more I try to untangle myself from these thoughts and feelings that have slyly taken hold, the more I find myself ensnared in them. It's like I'm caught in a trap of my own making.

For as long as I can remember, I've wanted Elle. In the past, I've been able to keep those emotions locked up tight where they couldn't see the light of day. Where life couldn't be breathed into them. I could be around her and pretend the need to tug her into my arms and bury my face against the delicate hollow of her throat didn't exist. I was able to deny the ache inside me that demanded I claim and mark her as my own.

That option no longer exists.

The battle to keep all of this emotion contained is exhausting.

Especially now that I know she's a virgin and has been saving herself for me.

For me.

How the hell am I supposed to walk away from that?

From her?

The simple answer is that I can't. Each day that passes, it becomes increasingly more difficult to do the right thing.

I snap back to the present when the metal door to the team weight room opens and Brayden walks in. He gives me a chin lift in greeting before stopping near the end of the bench.

"You just get here?"

"About twenty minutes ago." I refocus my attention before raising the bar. "I've already done a few sets."

When we're in season, we aren't supposed to lift. The time to build muscle and get stronger is in the off-season. My problem is that it's the only thing that takes my mind off her. I'm tired of going round and round in my head and trying to figure out a solution where none exists.

Even though nothing has happened with Elle since the party, it still feels like I've betrayed Brayden. Guilt swamps me, making it difficult to concentrate on anything else.

The heavy metal music pumping in the background fills the silence that stretches between us as he begins his own reps. The words are on the tip of my tongue, fighting to break free, just waiting to assuage the remorse that hangs around my neck like a debilitating weight. I've imagined broaching the subject of his sister with him a hundred different ways and the conversation always ends the same.

With him punching me in the face.

"Hey," he says, interrupting the chaotic whirl of my thoughts. "You mentioned something the other day about one of Elle's professors." When his gaze flickers in my direction, I jerk my head in acknowledgment. "Do you really think there's something going on between them?" Concern weaves its way through his voice.

I wince, realizing that specific conversation should have taken place with Elle in private. At the time, I'd been pissed off, unable to stop thinking about seeing them together at the coffee shop. The question had escaped before I could rein it in.

"I don't know," I mutter. "Probably not."

I've spent a lot of time going over the interaction in my head, and the answer I've arrived at is that it's more than likely just as she's claimed—harmless. The guy understands she's a student who struggles in his class and simply stopped to offer his help. Not that I'll be mentioning it to Brayden, but I'm pretty sure my jealousy got the better of me.

"You don't think it's weird he drove her home?"

"No."

Maybe.

On one hand, I'm glad she didn't walk all the way back to the dorms alone. It was a stupid decision on her part to leave the party without her friends. What I can't tell Brayden is that I'm the reason she left in the first place. I'm the one she was trying to escape from.

But...I know how guys think. Even older ones who have no business checking out their students. Deep down, we're all the same. No matter how much we've evolved as a species, we all think with our dicks.

And Elle is a gorgeous girl. She's tall and slender with the right amount of curves. Her breasts are high and tight, and she has legs that go on for miles. They're long and lean. Have I fantasized on more than one occasion about having them locked around my waist while I drove deep inside her heat?

Guilty.

I've dreamed about winding the thick length of her hair around my hand and pulling her head back until my lips could fasten onto hers. Those images are all it takes for my cock to stiffen up. I have to shake myself out of the dangerous thoughts that are slyly attempting to wrap their way around me.

Willing down the growing erection is another thing altogether.

So, yeah...I know *exactly* how men think and what they want.

"I could always drop by during office hours and have a little chat with the guy," he says with a grunt, lifting the weight above his head.

I snort as the edges of my lips quirk. "I'm sure that would go over well with your sister." And by that, I mean not at all.

He flashes a tight smile. "She's used to my overprotective nature by now. In fact, I think she probably enjoys it."

We both know that's a lie.

"You know damn well she hates you interfering in her life. You keep it up and you'll push her right off the edge one of these days."

I glance in his direction, wondering if he'll heed my warning.

"That's tough shit. I don't care how old she is, it'll always be my job to look out for her."

I shake my head and mutter, as I lift the bar, "I almost feel bad for any future daughters you might have. They're gonna hate your ass."

"Correction," he shoots back with a grin. "They'll love me because I'll always keep them safe."

Before I can say anything else, he brings us back to the original topic at hand. "So, about this professor...you think I should get involved? Cause you know damn well I will."

Oh, I have zero doubts in that regard. Even before their father died, Brayden always watched out for his sister. That behavior only intensified after Jake's death.

I think if he did that, Elle would totally lose it. She's already out of sorts with what happened between us and her mother springing her new relationship on them out of nowhere. I don't think she can take much more.

"Nah, I wouldn't. It's probably just like she said." My mind tumbles back to the coffee shop. "It's not like they were grabbing a drink together. He was helping her with homework. Pretty innocent."

He grunts in response before we both finish up our sets and switch places. I guzzle down a quarter of my water before moving on to the next rotation.

As I take my place on the bench, I say, "One of these days, you're gonna have to loosen your hold on her."

He frowns. "Who says?"

"Come on, Bray. Your sister is almost twenty years old, and to my knowledge, she's never even had a boyfriend. Don't you think you're—I don't know—stunting her growth or something?"

"That's not true. There have been a few boyfriends over the years," he mumbles, focusing on the weight he's lifting.

"Maybe one or two, whom you promptly chased away."

"Tell you what, when she brings home someone who's actually worthy of her, I'll consider it."

"You realize it's not your decision to make, right?"

He keeps his gaze trained on the ceiling as he straightens his arms, steadily pushing the bar above his chest. "Sure, it is."

Frustration churns inside me. It's tempting to blurt out the truth. I'm tired of pretending I don't have feelings for Elle. This secret has become more of a heavy weight, and every day it grows more burdensome. At some point, it'll be too much to bear.

If I were smart, I'd shut my mouth and focus on my own workout. "What if she got involved with someone you knew who was a good guy?" There's a pause before I add through stiff lips, "Would that make a difference?"

His forehead furrows as he scowls. "What do you mean? Like one of my friends? Or someone from the team?" His voice rises with each question.

Sweat breaks out across my forehead. "Yeah, I guess."

There's a moment of silence before he sets the bar on the holder and sits up to face me. His expression morphs into a scowl. "Have you lost your damn mind?"

It's entirely possible.

When I remain silent, he continues to foam at the mouth. "Over my dead body is Elle going out with some jackass from the team. You know what most of them are like. They're out to screw as many jersey chasers as they can. Look at Andrew." He shakes his head. "I've already warned her to stay as far as she can get from the athletes on campus. Elle knows better than to even look twice in their direction. And more importantly, they know to stay the hell away from her. At least, the ones who enjoy having their balls intact do."

Even though I realize that what he's saying—for the most part—is true, it still rankles me. Is Bray forgetting that he spent the better part of his college career screwing all the groupies he could get his hands on? Most of the students on campus were shocked when he called it quits and decided to settle down with one female.

And now look at him...

The guy is totally domesticated.

He'd never look twice at another girl besides Sydney.

Or how about Rowan Michaels? He's the QB for the Wildcats.

Until Demi, rumors used to run rampant around Western about all of his sexcapades. Now he's a one-woman guy.

This entire conversation is pissing me off. When I can't hold the words back any longer, I point out, "I hate to break it to you, bro, but you're an athlete. And you were certainly never a slouch in the hookup department."

An uncomfortable stillness falls over us. It was a mistake to bring any of this up. A discussion that has to do with his sister dating was never going to end well.

Just when I think he might drop the conversation, he says, "We both know I fucked around a lot before Sydney. What's your point?"

Good question, because I'm no longer sure.

I huff out a breath and do my best to backtrack before this convo blows up in my face. "I'm just saying that not all athletes are bad guys."

"Never said they were. They're just not good enough for my sister. End of story."

And that's exactly how it feels.

Like the end of the story.

Chapter Fourteen

ELLE

As soon as the elevator doors open, I rush into the corridor before making a sharp left and continuing down the narrow hallway. Once I locate Dr. Holloway's office, I rap my knuckles against the door and wait. My chest heaves, rising and falling with harsh breaths as if I just ran a marathon.

When he calls out a greeting, I nudge it farther open before poking my head inside. We were scheduled to meet twenty minutes ago, but play practice ran over. With opening night being less than a week away, most of the cast stuck around to run through lines and make last minute adjustments.

He glances up from his computer with an easy smile and waves me in. "Elle, glad you were able to make it."

Now that I'm here, I slump onto the chair parked in front of his desk. The auditorium is all the way across campus, and I've never been much of a runner, but I jogged the entire way. In thanks for my effort, I now have a stitch in my side. If this has taught me anything, it's that I need to work on my endurance. "I'm really sorry about being late. Practice ran over. I finally had to tell the director that I needed to get to an appointment."

To say that Marcel Littlehouse was irritated with my impromptu departure is a vast understatement. He'd glared for a full thirty seconds —just enough time to make sure I squirmed beneath his heavy disapproval—before informing me in a nasally voice that life was all about priorities and then dismissing me with a flick of his wrist. I have little doubt that my part in next semester's production will be reduced to barely a line or two.

He sits back in his chair. "It's not a problem. I didn't realize you were involved in the theater department. That's great."

Now that I realize he isn't upset, the thick tension vibrating through my body leaks from my muscles and my heartrate gradually slows to a steady thump. "I'm a theater major. This year's production is *Heathers: The Musical*, and it opens next week."

"That sounds like a lot of fun. I'll have you know that I once tried out for a play in high school." He grimaces before shaking his head. "It didn't go well. I got on stage, took one look at the audience, and promptly forgot my lines." When my mouth trembles at the corners, he says, "It was a fairly traumatic experience that continues to haunt me to this very day."

Now my lips do more than just quiver—I'm full on laughing at the image of a young Professor Holloway being struck with stage fright. "I doubt it was that bad."

"Trust me, it was actually much worse. Even my poor parents were embarrassed. They'd invited all of our family from out of town to watch my theatrical debut. After that dismal failure, mathematics seemed like the best route." He leans forward and lowers his voice to a conspiratorial whisper. "Here's a little-known secret. Numbers are safe. There aren't any surprises with them. And every problem has a solution."

Ha!

How can the man even say that?

I shake my head in disagreement. "Numbers are terrifying. And statistics is like trying to decipher hieroglyphics. There are times when I think I'm actually starting to understand the material and then you set a test before me. Everything swims on the paper, and it's like I've never seen it before in my life."

Dr. Holloway straightens before glancing at the chunky silver watch adorning his left wrist. "Which is exactly why you're here. Hopefully, we can clear up some of your confusion and stats will start to make a little more sense. We have roughly forty minutes to work through some of these problems."

I nod before shrugging off my backpack and pulling out my book and notebook. Even though this is my least favorite subject, it has nothing to do with the instructor. What I've discovered these past couple of weeks is that Dr. Holloway is a really nice guy and easy to work with. There are a few other statistics professors in the department who have the reputation of being hard asses. Since this class is a graduation requirement for most majors on campus, it doesn't make a difference to them if you pass or fail.

"That sounds good."

Eyes dancing with humor, he rubs his palms together. "Then let's get to work, shall we?"

For the next forty minutes, we go over the latest assignment in painstaking detail, making sure I understand each concept before moving on to the next problem. I actually did pretty well on this one, earning a whopping seventy-six percent. Unfortunately, that's not going to do much to nudge my grade in the direction it needs to go.

"Does that make sense?" He glances up, searching my face for understanding.

I've scooted my chair around the side of his desk so we can both look at the problems together.

"I guess," I mumble, knowing that as soon as another quiz is placed in front of me, all of the numbers and terms will blend, and the second guessing will begin.

After ten more minutes, Dr. Holloway removes his glasses and sets them on the desk. "I think we've tackled enough for today. I haven't announced it yet, but we'll be having a quiz on the material later next week. So, let's plan on getting together at least one more time before that happens, all right?"

I nod, realizing I could hire a private tutor and study for ten hours straight and it still wouldn't be enough.

"I have faith in you, Elle," he says, interrupting the whirl of my thoughts.

The snort slips out before I can stop it. "That makes one of us."

He releases a deep chuckle and the laugh lines around his eyes become more prominent. Now that I'm taking a closer look, I understand what Mike sees in him. The man is attractive in that nerdy, sexy professor type of way.

"You'll see. All the effort you're putting in will pay off in the end."

I really hope so. At the moment, I'm not so sure. I've been spending so much extra time studying statistics, I'm starting to slack in my other classes.

It's not a good situation.

Certainly not one I can maintain for the long term.

Dr. Holloway rises to his feet before swinging around and grabbing his leather jacket from the coat rack in the corner of the cramped office as I pack up my things, shoving them into my backpack. Once his briefcase is in hand, he moves around the metal desk before extending an arm toward the door.

"After you."

With a quick nod, I hustle over the threshold. He follows me out, stopping to lock up. I'm tempted to take the stairwell, but he keeps up a light chatter as we head to the elevator and ride to the first floor. When I'd arrived almost an hour ago, the sun had been in the process of sinking below the horizon. A mixture of red and orange had been splashed across the skyline, creating a stunning picture. With the sun no longer shining, it's turned dark, and the temperature has dropped.

After descending the wide stairs in front of the mathematics building, we both pause on the walkway as a slight wind whips through campus.

"Thanks again for meeting with me," I say, ready to head back to the dorms. If I weren't so tired, I'd return to the theater. My guess is that everyone is still hanging out there. They've probably ordered a couple of pizzas so they could continue practicing late into the evening.

"It wasn't a problem," he says, shoving one hand into the pocket of his khakis. "That's what I'm here for."

I shift from one foot to the other before pointing in the general vicinity of the residence halls. "I should probably get moving. I have a couple more assignments to finish up."

As I take a step in retreat, prepared to swing around, he says, "I was just about to get something to eat. Between play practice and here, did you manage to wolf down dinner?"

My footsteps falter as I blink, parroting the word back to him. "Dinner?"

His lips quirk as I continue to stare. "I know the cafeteria on campus closes by six o'clock and it's a little after that. I was going to grab something before heading home. Do you have any interest in joining me?"

Join him?

For a meal?

"Oh." I nibble at my lower lip, uncertain what to do. I've never spent time alone with any of my professors. Off campus, that is. The exception being when he drove me home from the party. But we were only together for a few minutes. "Um..."

"There's this great little Italian place about ten minutes away. It's a real hidden gem in the community. We could eat and then I'll drop you off at Sutton Hall. Plenty of time for you to finish up your other work."

I don't know...

I mean...that's weird, right?

Having dinner with your professor?

"I'm not sure if you've ever had linguini in clam sauce before, but trust me, it's exceptional. One of the specialties this place is known for."

My mouth waters at the mention of the pasta dish. That sounds so much better than heating up chicken-flavored Ramen in the microwave. Even though I had dinner at Mom's last week, all I really did was push it around on my plate. And caf food gets old after a while. There might be a rotation of entrees, but it's pretty much the same thing over and over again.

"Okay," I blurt before I can give it too much thought.

His smile broadens as his teeth flash in the darkness. "Great. Let's go." He nods toward the nearby parking lot. "My car is over there."

He peppers me with a series of questions about the play as we fall into line and traverse the walking path that leads toward the well-lit lot next to the athletic center.

Just as we reach his black BMW, my name is shouted from a distance. The deep voice that resonates through the night air sends a shiver dancing down my spine. Even before I turn, I know who I'll find. I can't deny that part of me wants to hasten my pace and slip into the front seat before he's able to reach me.

As tempting as the idea is, I can't do that. After what happened on the ride to Mom's house, I wouldn't put it past Carson to run straight to my brother with this information.

Embarrassment stings my cheeks as I bite down on my lower lip. My guess is that Dr. Holloway probably won't remember that Carson is the one who interrupted us at the coffee shop. At least, I hope he doesn't.

I clear my throat when my name is called for a second time. "I'm sorry. Can you give me a minute?"

"Of course." He nods toward the sleek vehicle. "I'll warm up the car."

I swing around, only to find Carson jogging through the empty parking lot. I quicken my pace, wanting to keep him as far away from my instructor as possible. When it comes down to it, his presence is as irritating and over-protective as my brother's. He doesn't need to be all up in my business.

A frown tugs at the corners of his lips as his feet stutter to a stop. His steely gaze darts to the BMW before slicing to mine.

He tips his chin toward the vehicle. "Who is that?"

I hitch my backpack higher onto my shoulder and shift under his penetrating stare. "Hello to you, too," I shoot back, not wanting to answer the question.

His eyes narrow as he takes another step closer. "Don't play games with me, Elle. I'm not in the mood for it. Were you about to leave with that guy?" There's a moment of silence as he eats up more of my personal space. When I fail to respond, his voice dips, turning incredulous. "Wait a minute. Is that your professor? The one I saw you with last week?"

I'm not proud of the fact that I consider lying before quickly disregarding it. There's no reason for me to hide the truth. At the end of the day, Carson is nothing more than my brother's friend. Another jailkeeper, as far as I'm concerned. I don't owe him any explanations as to who I spend time with.

With those thoughts buzzing through my brain, I straighten my shoulders and force myself to admit the truth. "Yes, it is."

Shock flickers across his face as his brows crash into his hairline. "Where are you going with him?"

"I stopped by earlier for office hours and now, because it's dark out, he's driving me back to the dorms." All right, so maybe that's not the unvarnished truth, but it's close enough.

He folds his arms across his T-shirt clad chest. I hate the way the quick movement makes the brawny muscles in his arms and chest pop. He must have come directly from working out.

"That's not necessary. I'll make sure you get home safely." His voice sharpens as he bites out the words.

Maybe if I'd never thrown myself at him in such a humiliating way, I'd do as he says and tell Dr. Holloway that it's easier to catch a ride back to the dorms with my friend. But I'm still smarting over that conversation. Along with the ones that have followed it.

I've told Carson more than a dozen of times that I don't need another brother, and I meant it. I'm more than capable of taking care of myself.

"No."

He blinks before scowling as if he didn't hear me correctly. "What?"

"I said no," I reiterate, louder this time. "We're actually on our way to get something to eat. I didn't have a chance to grab dinner and the caf is now closed." I give a tiny shrug as if it can't be helped.

"The hell you are," he grounds from between clenched teeth.

When he advances another step so that we're practically toe to toe, I straighten to my full height, refusing to be intimidated. Even if I'd been waffling over joining him for dinner, I'll be damned if I allow Carson to force me into canceling my plans.

"I'm going, and there's nothing you can do to stop me," I blurt, hardening my stance.

"Elle," he growls.

I stab a finger at his rock-hard chest. "I'm not your sister, and I sure as hell aren't your girlfriend." When a tiny pang of sadness attempts to bloom in my chest, I snuff it out.

Just as he opens his mouth to argue, I swing around and stalk toward the BMW. Tension seeps into every line of my body as my ears prick for the slightest noise. As I close the distance to the car, I pray that Carson doesn't scoop me up and carry me to his truck, which I now realize is parked a few rows over in the deserted lot. That would be the ultimate embarrassment. And I've already suffered more than enough at his hands.

My fingers tremble as they wrap around the handle and yank it open. I release a pent-up breath as our gazes collide across the distance that separates us. His stony glare stays fastened on mine as I slide onto the leather seat and slam the door shut, locking myself inside with the older man.

Only then does the air escape from my lungs in a torrent as I slump onto the seat.

What I hate most is that this feels like a mistake. One I'll probably end up regretting in the not-so-distant future.

"Is everything all right?"

The quietly asked question startles me from my thoughts. I blink before pasting a thin smile across my face.

"Yup, it's fine," I lie.

"Are you sure?" His brow furrows as concern threads its way through his voice.

"Positive." I just want to get out of here before all hell breaks loose. I have the feeling that Carson is in a weird state of shock because I didn't immediately comply with his barked-out command. It's only a matter of time before that changes.

When he glances out the window, I do the same. The blond football player is still standing in the parking lot, gaze glued to the vehicle. The wind rustles through his hair, mussing it.

"Is that your boyfriend?"

"Nope." I shake my head. "Definitely not."

"All right." He tries again. "Maybe an ex-boyfriend?"

"No." I flick my gaze toward Dr. Holloway, only to find him carefully watching me. I shift on my seat, reluctant to explain the situation. "He's just someone I grew up with. He's always been more like family." The words taste bitter on my tongue. More than anything, I wish they were the truth. Life would be so much easier if that were the case.

"Would it be better if I dropped you off at the dorms and we skipped dinner? We could always do it another night."

Probably. But I'll be damned if I allow Carson to interfere in my life any more than he already has.

Screw him.

"No, it's fine."

He lifts a brow. "Are you sure?"

I force a smile to my lips. "Yes."

With a nod, he shifts the BMW into drive, and we exit the parking lot. The more distance there is between Carson and me, the easier it is to breathe.

Chapter Fifteen

CARSON

A nother wave of shock crashes over me as I watch the red taillights disappear from the parking lot before fading into the distance.

What the hell just happened?

Did she seriously take off with that guy?

I thread both hands through my damp hair, tempted to rip the strands from my scalp.

It's only when she vanishes from sight and it's too late to do anything about it that I come alive.

Fuck.

I could fire off a dozen texts, but I already know she won't respond. I'd hoped after the evening spent at her mom's house that maybe our relationship had fallen back into place, but clearly that's not the case.

Instead of continuing to stand like a slack-jawed idiot, I stalk to the Tahoe, wrench open the driver's side door and slide behind the wheel before peeling out of the parking lot. Even if I wanted to follow them, the car is long gone. Left without any alternatives, I return to the house we rent off-campus. Everything that just happened churns in my head as I slam out of the truck and jog up the front porch stairs before shoving through the door. As soon as I do, voices assault my ears. A handful of guys are in the living room, chilling out, drinking beer, and playing video games. There are a couple boxes of pizza on the dining room table.

Even though Crosby's name isn't on the rental agreement, his ass is parked on the velour recliner shoved in the corner of the living room. He spends more time here than he does at the place he and Andrew share a couple of blocks away. His roommate is one of those guys who is constantly in the gym, pumping iron. Rumors have always circulated that he takes SARMS, which is just a healthier version of steroids. As far as the NCAA is concerned, it's still an illegal substance and therefore a big no-no. Obviously, he doesn't take cycles during the season. One positive drug test and Coach Richards would boot his ass from the team.

Crosby glances at me before his gaze darts back to the television screen and the game he's playing. "You just work out?"

"Yeah." Normally, after lifting, I feel energized. All those endorphins are flowing, which puts me in a good headspace. That, however, is not the case tonight. In fact, it's more like the opposite. I'm worked up and out of sorts. Barely am I holding it together.

"Bray returned about thirty minutes ago."

"Yeah, I stayed behind and ran the track," I mutter, not really paying attention to the conversation. I can't stop thinking about Elle and that fucking guy.

Know what I should have done?

Jumped in my truck and followed them.

Another thought crashes through my head. What if he's not taking her to dinner at a restaurant?

What if they're headed to his house and—

"Dude, what's the deal? Why are you pacing?"

Huh?

I grind to a halt and realize that Crosby is right. I'm walking the entryway outside the living room.

Before I can come up with a plausible excuse, Brayden jogs down the staircase. His dark hair is damp from his shower and he's wearing fresh clothes.

He points to the dining room before hitting the last tread. "Asher

ordered a few pizzas. After that lift, I'm starving. I need some carbs."
He smacks my belly.

Wordlessly, I stare after him as he disappears into the kitchen.

I don't know what to do.

Should I tell him that Elle took off with her professor?

The dude from the coffee shop. The very same one who gave her a
lift home after that disastrous party?

About an hour ago, he'd asked if I thought something was going on
between them. At the time, I hadn't been sure. Now, however, I'd say
the likelihood was high. If Brayden finds out, he'll tear this town apart
with his bare hands until he finds her. And if that happens, Elle will
know I tipped him off. That girl is already pissed and won't give me the
time of day. Her brother going off half-cocked and beating her
professor to a bloody pulp will only make matters worse.

But I can't allow one of her instructors to take advantage of her.
Especially since I know she doesn't have much experience in that
department. The thought of that asshole laying his hands on her—*on
what's mine*—drives me fucking nuts.

God dammit! I really should have followed them. Better yet, I
should have thrown her kicking and screaming over my shoulder
before tossing her into my truck. Then I wouldn't be in this mess. My
mind wouldn't be spinning with every possible outcome tonight could
have.

I swear a blue streak under my breath.

You know what?

I can't sit around here with my thumb shoved up my ass. I need to
do something. That realization has me spinning around and stalking
toward the front door.

"Hey," Brayden shouts from the dining room where he's busy
loading down his plate with pepperoni pizza. "Where are you going?
Thought you just got back?"

I glance over my shoulder and meet his confused gaze. There is no
way I can reveal the truth. "Umm, yeah. I did, but there's something I
need to take care of."

A knowing smirk spreads across his face. "Maybe you should
shower first."

I plow a hand through my hair. He's right. After that run, I'm a sweaty mess. Five minutes won't make much of a difference. I swing around and beeline for the staircase, taking them two at a time.

"Trust me, whomever you're in such a hurry to take care of will thank me for it."

A humorless laugh bubbles up in my throat.

That's doubtful.

Chapter Sixteen

ELLE

I shift on the padded chair and glance around the tiny Italian restaurant. This is my second year at Western and I'm familiar with a lot of eateries in the area, but this is one I've never been to before. In fact, until ten minutes ago, I had no idea the place even existed. That's probably because it has more of a romantic vibe to it with the dim lighting and red votives decorating each white, linen-covered table. The wait staff is outfitted in crisp, white button-downs with black pants. Thick, black aprons cover their lower halves. It feels upscale and yet intimate.

It's not what I'm used to.

As soon as we pushed through the glass door, we were immediately shown to a table and given menus describing the appetizers and entrees written in Italian, along with a separate wine list. Dr. Holloway glanced at the alcohol selection before ordering a bottle of something I'd never heard of and probably couldn't pronounce if my life depended on it.

Instead of our original waiter returning to the table with the wine, an older gentleman with a bushy mustache and a shiny head stops by. His skin is deeply sun-kissed with a weathered quality as if he's spent his entire life tromping around outdoors. When he smiles, wrinkles break out across his face, making it look more like a busy road map.

"*Buona sera*, Gabriel," he says with a small bow.

My professor smiles, greeting him warmly in the same language, which I assume is Italian. My attention bounces back and forth between them as they speak for a few minutes.

It's only when the older man's gaze darts to me that he clears his throat. "*Mi scusi, signorina*. Sometimes I forget and lapse into Italian."

I smile. There's something both charming and endearing about him. "It's not a problem."

"Elle, I'd like to introduce you to Dante." My professor waves to encompass the beautiful space. "And this is his restaurant. He and his wife have owned it for over thirty years."

The man beams, standing a little bit straighter. "Yes, and Gabriel has been coming here for nearly as long."

Interesting. That can only mean that Dr. Holloway grew up around here.

Instead of giving me more of their backstory, Dante opens the bottle and pours us each half a glass. "I promise you will love it," he says, voice overflowing with enthusiasm.

Even though I don't drink, I find myself unable to refuse. "Thank you."

"Let me know if you need anything else." He places the wine on the table before disappearing from sight.

With a nod, my instructor swirls the golden-colored liquid inside the delicate stemmed glass, making sure not to slosh it over the rim before raising it to his nose. My fascination grows as he closes his eyes and inhales deeply. There's a sweep of dark lashes against the fragile skin before they flutter open again. His gaze locks on mine as he brings the glass to his lips and takes a drink.

"Exquisite." He waves a hand toward my untouched beverage. "Take a sip and tell me what you think."

When I hesitate, he cocks his head. "You don't like white wine?"

For a few seconds, I contemplate whether or not to reveal the truth. If I do, it'll lead to questions I don't particularly want to answer. "I'm not sure, I've never had it before."

His brows rise before a chuckle slips free. "I almost forgot you were still in college. Let me guess, your palette leans more toward beer and shots."

I glance away before clearing my throat. "Actually, I don't drink."

Surprise laces his voice. "At all?"

"Nope."

He sits back before lifting the glass to his lips as he silently contemplates me from across the table. "I would imagine there's a reason for that?"

I nibble at my lower lip, trying to decide if I want to delve into something so personal. The extent of our previous conversations has mostly revolved around statistics. It's strange to take our relationship beyond the realm of school.

"Elle?"

The sound of my name has me blinking back to the present. I hadn't realized I'd become lost in the tangle of my own thoughts. Instead of responding, my fingers wrap around the fragile stem before lifting the glass until it's eye level. Mimicking his movements, I cautiously swirl the liquor. The motion becomes almost mesmerizing as the liquid rises before washing down the side.

"What you're doing aerates the wine, which helps release more aroma into the air. If you bring the glass to your nose, you should be able to notice the differing notes."

I do as he instructs, burying my nose in the stemware and sniffing delicately.

He leans closer to the table as enthusiasm leaps into his eyes. "Now, tell me what you smell."

Hmmm. Something...zesty yet fruity. It's so different than the overpowering scent of hops and barley I'm used to catching a whiff of at the parties I normally attend.

"Definitely fruit. Pears?" I inhale a little more deeply. "Maybe lemons?" I don't know. It's just a guess.

A satisfied smile lifts the corners of his lips as he nods. "Very good. You're absolutely right. This particular grape is grown in Sardinia. You can actually smell and taste the flavors of the earth where the grapes were raised."

Curiosity gets the better of me and I find myself bringing the glass to my lips before taking a tiny sip.

"Allow it to sit on your tongue for a moment," he directs. "Can you taste the rich tapestry of scents you were able to identify earlier?"

Actually...I do.

Surprised, I nod.

He looks pleased by my willingness to learn. "What do you think?"

Hmmm. Good question. I'm not sure.

"I don't hate it," I admit sheepishly.

He laughs just enough for his broad shoulders to shake. The sound is deep and rich.

I take another small taste to see if there are other flavors that stand out.

This experience is so different than being at a crowded house party and watching college kids pound cans of beer or play drinking games. Their end goal is always the same—to get hammered. Sampling this wine feels more like a challenge to discover the ingredients that went into making it.

When I take a third sip, still trying to figure out the flavor combination, he says, "Please don't feel as if you need to finish it." He lifts his hand to catch our waiter's attention. "I can order you a water or coke instead. Whatever you want."

My gaze fastens on him before sinking to the glass still clutched in my fingers. It's almost a surprise when I find myself admitting, "No, I kind of like it."

There's a moment of silence before he says, "You never mentioned the reason for your abstinence. From what I've heard about this particular campus, it seems more like a rarity."

I take another swallow before setting the drink down and running my fingers over the thick fabric of the tablecloth. I hate talking about what happened with my father and how it irrevocably changed all of our lives. No matter how much time passes, I have to steel myself for the wave of grief that will crash over me. It doesn't feel like a heartache that will ever dissipate.

"About four years ago, my father was hit in an accident." I jerk my shoulders, forcing myself to finish. "It was a college kid who had drunk too much at a party. He got behind the wheel of his car and struck him in a head-on collision. They both died instantly. That one stupid decision caused so much destruction in all of our lives. I was only fifteen when it happened, but I've avoided alcohol ever since."

Dr. Holloway's dark blue eyes cloud with sympathy before he reaches across the table and lays his palm over the top of my hand. "I'm sorry, Elle. That's a tragic loss for any child to suffer, especially one so young."

I will away the wetness that stings the backs of my eyes. My father has been gone for a long time. Normally, I can get through the story without getting overly emotional. I think seeing my mother with another man has forced all of these unresolved feelings to the surface. She's moving on, and I'm not sure I'm ready for that.

"Thank you."

My gaze falters, dropping to our clasped hands as a heavy silence falls over the table. Just as it turns awkward, a waiter arrives with two steaming plates. A rush of breath escapes from my lips as I carefully slip my hand free from his.

The server sets the plates down in front of us before asking if we need anything else in heavily accented English.

My gaze flickers from the delicious looking pasta to the man across from me. "I didn't realize we'd ordered our meals."

His lips quirk. "Dante knows I always request the linguine. I hope you don't mind that I took the liberty of ordering for both of us."

I shake my head, relieved to have my dinner to focus on instead of our previous conversation. "Not at all. It smells delicious."

He gives me a wink to go along with the easy smile. "Trust me, it tastes even better."

Taking his word for it, I wind my fork around a few strands of pasta before bringing the utensil to my lips. A symphony of favors explodes on my tongue as I make a little hum of pleasure deep in my throat.

"It's good, right?" He asks with a grin.

My eyes widen as my appetite rushes back and I realize that not only did I skip dinner but lunch as well. "Oh my god, it's amazing!"

Even though my thoughts and feelings surrounding alcohol have always been non-negotiable, I find myself sipping from my glass of golden-colored liquor as I finish my meal. The flavors of the wine and the pasta seem almost complimentary. Drinking isn't something I can see myself doing often, but tonight, with Dr. Holloway, it feels strangely right.

Chapter Seventeen

ELLE

B y the time my professor pulls up to the curb outside Sutton Hall and cuts the engine, it's after nine o'clock.

Before I can say a quick goodbye, he swivels toward me, breaking the companionable silence that has fallen over us on the ride from the restaurant. I'm in no way drunk, but I feel pleasantly buzzed.

"I'm glad we could do this. I always enjoy getting to know my students and discovering who they are on a more personal level." There's a pause as his gaze searches mine. "And this evening, I feel like we were able to scratch beneath the surface and do just that."

"Me, too." Surprisingly, I mean it. What I've discovered is that he has a good sense of humor and is knowledgeable about more than statistics. At the end of our meal, I offered to pay for my portion of the bill, but he quickly waved off my concern, which made this feel more like a date. "Thanks again for dinner, Dr. Holloway."

His lips lift into an easy smile. "When we're outside of the class-room, feel free to call me Gabriel. I think we've moved past such stuffy formalities, don't you?"

Ahh...I don't know. I've never referred to any of my professors by their first names. Certainly not to their faces.

It feels a little...weird.

When I continue to stare, a chuckle erupts from him, and he moves closer.

"Honestly Elle, it's fine. All of my grad students call me by my given name. It's not a big deal. You don't have to make it one."

Is that what I'm doing?

Making a non-issue into something more?

I don't know. I can't tell. And I'm unsure if it's the wine clouding my better judgement or not. Instead of arguing, I nod. "Okay," there's a pause as I force out his name, "Gabriel."

Definitely strange.

He shifts toward me before stretching his arm along the back of my seat. "Was that so difficult?"

"No." Yes.

"Good. My hope is that you won't hesitate to stop in after class or during office hours for extra help now that we've gotten to know each other better. Even though statistics isn't a subject you enjoy, I want you to be successful in my class. I think with more of a tailored approach, it's possible to raise your grade to a B."

I almost snort out my disbelief. There's little more than a month remaining in the semester. That's not a lot of time. And with ramped-up rehearsals, I'm busier than ever.

When he holds out his palm, I glance at it in confusion before raising my gaze.

"Hand over your phone."

Uncertain, I remain perfectly still.

"Come on. Give it to me. I want to add my number to your contact list. That way if you're ever studying, and need help, you can reach out to me directly. We can even FaceTime and work on problems."

I release a steady breath as the tension gathering in my shoulders dissolves before slipping my hand inside my bag to grab my phone. There's another moment of hesitation as I tap in the passcode and carefully set it on his outstretched hand.

As soon as I do, he opens the texting app and inputs his name and number before hitting send. There's a corresponding ding from his pocket before he returns the device to me. Our fingers brush and there's an odd moment where I'm not quite sure what's happening between us.

Are the lines of our relationship becoming blurred?

Or, like he claimed earlier, am I reading too much into what's happening?

It's not like Dr. Holloway is coming on to me, right?

I shove those ridiculous thoughts from my head as the need to escape the confines of the vehicle explodes inside me. Nerves scamper down my spine, making the fine hair on my arms rise to attention.

I clear my throat, only wanting to banish the odd thoughts trying to take root in my brain. "Thanks again for dinner. It's one of the best meals I've had in a long time. When my mother comes for a visit, I'll have to take her there. She would love it."

"You're welcome. We'll have to do it again sometime. Dante enjoyed meeting you. I know he would love to see you again."

"Yeah, okay." I force out the response. I can't deny that the evening was pleasant, but it was also a bit bizarre as well. My fingers wrap around the door handle before yanking it open. The cool night air swirls around me, and I immediately feel more settled as I slip from the vehicle.

Once my feet hit the pavement, I lift a hand to wave. After he returns the gesture, I head to the front entrance of the dorm before pulling open the door. I sneak a peek over my shoulder only to find his sleek BMW idling at the curb. As I take the elevator up to my floor, my mind replays everything that happened over the last couple of hours. I never expected the evening to end at an Italian restaurant with my professor. Once the doors slide open on the sixth floor, my nerves vanish. It makes me wonder what I had been concerned about in the first place. As I walk toward my suite at the end of the hall, a few friends wave and say hello.

I shove the key in the lock and turn the handle, glad today is finally over. As I step inside the darkness, I'm surprised by the silence that greets me. Usually, the girls will sit around in the shared living space and do homework or gossip. Instead, all three are conspicuously absent. It's probably better that way. I'm not sure if I want to tell them about Dr. Holloway inviting me to dinner. I can just imagine it now—

they'd all jump to the wrong conclusion, and I would never hear the end of it. Even though he alluded to dinners in the future, I don't plan on it becoming a habit.

As far as I'm concerned, it was a one-time deal.

As for him inputting his number into my cell at the end of the evening, I can't actually imagine calling him. Even if I did need help.

I grab my phone and fire off a text to the group chat, wondering where all of my roomies have disappeared to. Madison responds almost immediately that she's with her boyfriend and I shouldn't wait up for her (she adds a winky face and a few food emojis I won't bother to mention), Sienna is with her study group, and Kari went to see a movie with a couple girls from the floor.

Looks like I've got the place all to myself. When you share a suite with three other people, alone time is a rarity.

As I peel off my jacket and push open the door to my room, I take two steps inside the dark space when a voice snaps, "It's about damn time you got back. I was just about to come looking for you."

Chapter Eighteen

CARSON

A high-pitched scream fills the air as I rise to my feet from the pink fuzzy chair near the window I've been lounging on, waiting for her to finally make an appearance.

"Relax," I grunt, still pissed off, "it's me."

A shaky inhalation leaves her lips as she almost collapses near the door. A sliver of light from the common area falls over her startled features. "Carson?"

"Who the hell else would it be?" Cause if there's another guy making himself at home in her room, I want to know about it.

And then I'll kill him with my bare hands.

Her shoulders jerk back as she straightens to her full height, which is still a good six inches shorter than me. Elle is tall for a female, which gives her slim body a willowy look.

"What are you doing here?" The fear that had been filling her voice moments ago dissolves as her tone turns sharp. I'd bet money our last interaction in the parking lot is rolling through her head. "And how exactly did you get in here?"

The need to be closer thrums through me as I stalk toward her. "Your roommates let me in before they took off."

She plants her fists on her hips. "I'll be sure to have a word with them. They shouldn't have done that."

When I advance another step, her eyes widen, and she scrambles back in retreat as if only now realizing that she should keep a healthy distance between us.

"Actually, you should be glad they did."

Her tongue darts out to moisten her lips. "And why is that?"

"If they hadn't, I would have driven all over this damn town until I found you." There's a pause as the tension filling the air ratchets up, turning the atmosphere oppressive. "Want to know what I would have done after that?"

She gulps before giving her head a violent little shake.

"Why not? Aren't you interested to know what would have happened?" Fury bleeds into every bitten off word. Even remembering how worried I'd been only fans the flames of my anger.

"No." When I'm close enough, her palms slap against my chest as if her will is enough to keep me at bay.

Guess what?

It's not.

Elle has no idea how far she's pushed me tonight. I spent most of my time here pacing the small area, all the while tearing my hair out and thinking about all the terrible things that might be happening to her.

"That's too damn bad, because I'm going to tell you anyway. Consider it fair warning for the next time you decide to do something stupid."

"Stupid?" she gasps, shoving at me for a second time with all her might.

"Yeah, that's right, *stupid*. If I'd gone out and searched for you, you better damn well believe I would have found you. Once that happened, I would have thrown you over my shoulder and carried you out kicking and screaming." My face looms closer. "Then I would have spanked your ass for taking off with a guy who is practically old enough to be your father."

She gulps, eyes flaring wide before whispering, "You wouldn't have dared."

I arch a brow, challenging her to tempt me into proving it. "Do you really want to test that theory?"

Her bravado wavers as she bites down on her lower lip. "No."

"Smart girl. Before this conversation goes any further, I want to know where the hell he took you. And so help me if you say it was back to his place." A growl rumbles up from deep within my chest even thinking about the possibility. Elle is too damn naïve for her own good. As much as I love it, it'll ultimately be my undoing. It'll be what pushes me into taking her for myself.

The delicate column of her throat works as she gulps. With the shaft of light streaming in, I can almost see the pulse fluttering beneath the fragile flesh. "We went to a restaurant."

I cock a brow as my fingers tighten against my palms. It's taking all of my self-control not to reach out and grab hold of her. "You were there the entire time?"

"Yes."

"Did you mention that you're still a virgin?"

A choked-out gurgle of distress bubbles up from her throat. "Of course not! Why would I tell one of my professors that? It's none of his business, and it's certainly none of yours!"

"Actually, if you'll remember correctly," I remind her, "*you* made it my business."

"That was a mistake." Anger and resentment swirl through her dark eyes.

"Trust me, it's just one of many."

Confusion flickers across her features as her brows slant together. "What does that even mean?"

How can I begin to answer that question when it can't be with the truth?

How do I tell her that as close as we are physically at the moment, it's not nearly enough? That I want to feel the heat of her naked body pressed against mine. That my cock is so damn hard, it's painful.

The one girl who has always been off-limits is the very same one who drives me fucking crazy. She's the one I secretly fantasize about when I'm alone in bed at night. I'm not proud to admit that she's the one I conjured up in the past while screwing other girls. Just being in her dorm is dangerous and I damn well know it. It won't take much to shove me over the edge. And if that happens, there'll be no way to come back from it.

The feel of her warm breath drifting across my lips is too much of a temptation. It's all I can do to stand rooted in place and inhale her sweet scent. One that smells suspiciously like—

My eyes widen. "Have you been drinking?"

Guilt flickers across her face as she sucks in a shuddering breath.

"Since when do you drink?" My temper skyrockets. "I've never known you to take even a sip of alcohol." It's one of the reasons I don't get wasted like most the guys on the team. I know how Elle feels about it. Just like I know the reason behind that choice.

"It was one glass of wine," she whispers.

Even though her hands are still splayed against me, I force my way into her space until I can feel the sharp rise and fall of her chest pressed against my own. As close as we are, it's still not enough.

Deep down, I know it will never be enough.

My eyes narrow. "Was that asshole trying to get you drunk?" I'll fucking rip his head off and shit down his throat if that turns out to be the case.

She shakes her head almost frantically. "Of course not. It was one glass. That's it."

"You're not even of legal age. The restaurant had no business serving you alcohol. You realize they can lose their liquor license because of that, right?"

"You're overreacting, it wasn't like that at all."

"Then explain to me what it was like, because I want to know." I can just imagine him sitting next to her, pouring her a glass, encouraging to drink it down so he could ply her with more. A red haze clouds my vision.

The guilt flickering in her expression vanishes as her lips thin and she shoves her palms against my chest. A soft grunt escapes from her as she tries to force me back a step. "I don't owe you any explanations!"

I don't budge. Her strength is no match for mine.

"The hell you do." I shackle my fingers around both wrists, pulling them from between us before forcing her hands behind her back. The movement makes her spine arch, and her breasts thrust forward until they're pressed into my chest. "I'm not going anywhere until we hash this out."

"I've already told you that there's absolutely nothing to talk about." A frustrated growl leaves her lips as she twists against me, trying to break free from my hold. Little does she know that all her squirming does is excite me more. If I'm not careful, she'll realize how turned on I am. "You're making a big deal out of nothing. It was dinner. That's it."

"Christ, Elle. Please tell me you're not that naïve."

Her chin lifts as I force her closer. "Maybe you should trust me to know what I'm doing and to take care of myself."

"How can I do that when you don't even see that this fucker is trying to seduce you?"

"Seduce me?" An abrupt laugh tumbles from her lips as she shakes her head. "You're crazy."

Like hell I am.

Her gaze searches mine. Whatever she sees there is enough to have the mirth in her expression dying a quick death.

I've spent so many years longing for this girl. Wanting to touch her. To stroke her soft skin. To simply breathe her in. I've done everything in my power to keep my attraction tightly under wraps so she wouldn't realize that it exists.

When her tongue darts out to moisten her lips, my attention drops to the movement and the last of my resistance crumbles as my mouth crashes into hers.

Chapter Nineteen

ELLE

O h.
My.
God.

Is this really happening?

It feels more like a delicious dream than reality playing out. Any moment, the alarm on my phone will go off and I'll wake up all hot and bothered. I don't think I could stand for that to happen.

Not now.

Not when it's been weeks since I felt the firm pressure of his mouth roving over mine.

All it takes is one sweep of his tongue for me to open and he's swallowing me whole. At least, that's the way it feels. One hungry gulp and I'm completely consumed. His mouth moves furiously over mine as our tongues tangle. It doesn't take long for his breathing to turn labored. As if he's not only fighting me, but himself as well.

I've known Carson for a decade, and other than Saturday night at the Sig Ep party, I've never witnessed him lose control or his temper. This is now the second time it's happened. The abrupt change in his behavior should scare me. Strangely enough, it doesn't. At the core of it, I know exactly who he is.

No matter what happens between us, that will never change.

There's a scrape of teeth as he licks and nips at me until I'm dizzy with the sensation. Our bodies are pressed so tightly together that I don't know where he ends and I begin. With every shift of his hips, he drives his thick erection into my belly. Excitement spirals through me as a deep ache grows in my core.

The kind of desire unfolding inside me is new. Before this very moment, I had no idea that it even existed. Now that I do, I can't imagine never feeling my blood boil or my heart race the way it is now. The need to explore him explodes through me and I break the hold he has on my wrists, slipping my hands between our bodies until they're flattened against his chest. My fingers curl, digging into the solid slab of muscle that lies beneath the soft cotton of his T-shirt.

I've been kissed a handful of times over the years, but none have been to this level. They've been more tentative. There has never been this kind of intoxicating concoction of anticipation and excitement pumping wildly through my being, making every nerve ending crackle with electricity.

Before I can fully sink into the embrace, his arms band around my ribcage and he swings me around, walking me backward until my calves hit the bedframe and I'm falling onto the thin twin bed. Barely do I catch my breath before he's following me down. He maneuvers our bodies until we're stretched out fully on the mattress before his full weight settles on top of me. The thickness of his erection presses against the juncture between my thighs and it's so tempting to spread my legs wide so he can nestle more intimately against my core. His warm breath feathers against my lips as his gaze searches mine. I still, afraid that he'll pull away and put a halt to what's unfolding between us the same way he did at the party. If that happened, I'd probably break down and cry. There is too much pent-up arousal ricocheting through my body.

Instead, he lowers his face, slanting his mouth one way before angling it the other, peppering me with a thousand tiny kisses.

"You taste so fucking sweet," he mutters, drifting lower. He nips at the curve of my jaw before sliding down the column of my neck. "Even better than last time."

I whimper in response, unable to string together a few passable syllables. I'm so dizzy with the sensation that grasping on to a single coherent thought has become an impossibility. When I bear my throat, he sucks the fragile flesh into his mouth before biting down on it. A tidal wave of pleasure crashes over me, threatening to drag me to the very bottom of the ocean.

Just when I'm about to spin completely out of control, he pumps the breaks and slows things down. His movements turn almost lazy as he continues his descent before arriving at my collarbone. The velvety softness of his tongue sweeps over the skin left uncovered by the fabric of my shirt. There's a pause as he arrives at the first button. Air gets wedged in my lungs as the sound of his harsh breathing breaks the silence of the room and fills my ears until it's all I'm aware of and the world shrinks to encompass just the two of us.

"This is so damn wrong," he groans.

I don't understand how he can say that when nothing in my life has ever felt so right.

Half-afraid that I'll burst this strange bubble we find ourselves in, I remain silent.

"We shouldn't be doing this," he continues.

If he stops, I'll likely self-combust. He's barely touched me and already it feels as if I'm on the verge of coming undone. It's as if my body has been set ablaze and I'm in imminent danger of burning up from the inside out. I'm not ready for this to be over with.

Or for him to tell me it was another mistake.

He shifts until his weight is balanced on one arm as the fingers of his other hand settle on the first pearly button before freeing it from its loop.

Relief rushes from my lungs.

Silently, each subsequent button meets the same fate until all of them have been released and there's a pale strip of flesh bisecting the right and left sides of my body from my collarbone to my belly button. My heartbeat flutters against my ribcage as his breathing turns labored. Carefully he parts the thin material, baring the lacy cups of my bra. Even in the darkness that swirls around us, I feel the hot burn of his gaze licking over every exposed inch.

And still, it's not enough.

I need so much more.

"Tell me to stop," he growls, breaking into the chaotic whirl of my thoughts.

Unable to follow the directive, my teeth sink into my lower lip as I give my head a little shake.

A defeated sound rumbles up from within his chest as one finger trails from the middle of my clavicle, skimming over the front clasp of my bra before halting inches away from my belly button. I can't help but tremble beneath his touch as his finger gradually slides in the opposite direction. Once he returns to the plastic fastener, his fingers hesitate.

"Tell me to stop," he repeats, harsher this time.

I shake my head. There's no way I can do that.

A furious growl erupts from him as his fingers curl around the plastic before releasing it. Even though the cups spring apart, they continue to cling to the tips of my breasts. His gaze burns into me as he impatiently shifts his weight.

Air gets clogged in my throat as one hand knocks the material aside so that I'm finally exposed. It's the heady concoction of cool air hitting my naked flesh and his attention trained on me that has my nipple pebbling.

A guttural groan rumbles up from him before he lowers his head and fastens his lips around the tightened peak, drawing it deeply into his mouth. My eyelids feather shut as pleasure explodes inside me, rushing to fill every single cell. My fingers tunnel through his thick hair, curling around his skull in order to keep him in place.

Never have I experienced anything this amazing. Every pull of his lips sends another spike of desire shooting straight to my core. It's as if there's an invisible string connecting the two parts of my body. Unable to stay still, I shift impatiently beneath him, trying to find some relief from the avalanche of need that has settled in my core.

Just when it seems like I'll die from the sensation, he releases my nipple with a soft pop. Chilled air wafts over my damp skin as he sweeps aside the material covering my other breast before giving it the same ardent attention.

As his teeth rake over me, gently biting down on the delicate flesh, a strange mixture of pain-infused pleasure swirls through me, becoming a tempest. A moan works its way from deep inside me before breaking free as I wriggle beneath his muscular body that pins me in place. The feel of his hard length pressing into the V between my thighs has my panties dampening. It leaves me craving something I've never experienced before but have always yearned for when it comes to Carson.

Whether he realizes it or not, it's always been him.

He draws the bud between his lips, giving it one final tug before releasing me. The over-sensitized little peak aches from all of his delicious attention. His mouth drifts across a sea of newly revealed flesh, sinking lower with every caress before sweeping around the indentation of my belly button. Once he reaches the band of my denim skirt, there's a pause. The air thickens between us as his rapid breaths feather across my shuddering skin.

Everything in me stills as my teeth sink into my lower lip. I'm so afraid this fragile moment will shatter into a thousand jagged pieces. One beat passes, and then another. Slowly he lowers his forehead until it can rest against the quivering muscles of my belly.

"Has another man ever given you an orgasm?"

The rough scrape of his voice is so low and chock-full of need that it strums something deep inside me. Or maybe it's the intimate question that has a million butterflies exploding inside the confines of my abdomen before winging their way to life.

"No." Even though I'm embarrassed, I find myself unable to lie. If there's anyone who should know the truth, it's him. How could I possibly let another guy touch me when he's the only one I've ever thought or dreamed about?

Possessiveness flares to life in his eyes as he pulls the elastic band down an inch or two before lowering his face to my bared flesh and brushing his lips against me. He's so close to the part of me that pulses with a life of its own, it's almost painful.

The way his hot breath drifts over me is sheer torture, and I can't help but twist in order to get closer. He tugs at the fabric until it slips further down my hips, revealing the very top of my slit. The air gets sucked from my lungs as his tongue darts out. A whimper escapes as sensation explodes inside my body, ricocheting through every cell.

His heated gaze stays locked on mine as he repeats the maneuver, only slower this time. He draws out the pleasure until it becomes almost too much to bear. Until I want to tear at my hair and scream with the need that spirals through my entire being.

With his thumbs, he spreads my lips until my clit is fully exposed. His elbows sink into my thighs, trapping them as he focuses his attention, lapping at the tiny bundle of nerves. The way his tongue scrapes over me sends a million shockwaves cascading through my system. My back arches off the mattress as my muscles tighten.

It's almost as if he can sense just how close I am from leaping off the precipice and into oblivion. His movements turn demanding as his thumbs hold me captive, exposing the most delicate part of me as he keeps up the torment. The intensity vibrating throughout my body is almost painful. There's too much sensation rampaging through my veins, lighting me up from the inside out. Any moment, I'm going to come undone at the seams.

"You taste so damn sweet," he growls.

That little nudge is all it takes to send me tumbling through the stratosphere. The sensation blows apart everything I thought I knew. All the times I've touched myself while thinking about Carson. And while that was satisfying and did the job nicely, it never felt anything like this.

Not even close.

When I subconsciously lift my hips, he presses them back into the mattress, keeping me tethered to the Earth. My clit throbs an insistent beat as I continue to convulse. He laps at my softness until every last shudder has been expertly wrung from my body and I melt bonelessly into the mattress. I have no idea how much time passes as my heartbeat echoes in my ears. It takes effort to crack open my eyelids as I stare sightlessly at the ceiling. Carson's heated breath ghosts over me before disappearing. With deft fingers, he tugs my panties into place before yanking up my zipper and refastening the skirt.

The abrupt movement shatters the bliss filling me.

A soft string of obscenities falls from his lips as he wrenches himself away from the bed and rises to his feet. The loss of his body heat leaves me feeling exposed and vulnerable. My gaze shifts, only to find him staring down at me. Even in the darkness, I'm able to see the wild tangle of emotions that floods his features.

My tongue slips out, moistening my swollen lips. I open my mouth, wanting to say something that will banish the guilt and anger that have transformed his expression, but nothing escapes.

Without another word, he swings away, stalking to the door. When his feet stutter to a stop and he pauses, everything inside me lifts. All I want to do is smooth over the heavy emotion that claws at him. Instead, he grabs hold of the handle and rips it open before disappearing into the common area. The tension gripping me slowly ebbs from my body as the suite door closes with a resounding thud.

I suck in a lungful of air, wondering if the last thirty minutes really happened or if it was just a figment of my overactive imagination.

But I know it did. There's too much adrenaline pumping wildly through my system, filling me with a strange restlessness.

What I don't know is if it will change anything between us.

Chapter Twenty

ELLE

A gust of chilly wind follows me as I push through the heavy glass doors and step inside the toasty warmth of the union. I pause, gaze coasting over the sea of students and faculty that have gathered to grab a quick meal in search of my mother's dark head. Twice a month, she drives to Western, and we make plans to catch up. Sometimes we meet at a local restaurant that isn't far from campus. With the play opening in a few short days, I don't have enough time in my schedule for that.

Cafeteria fare will have to do.

My head is on a constant swivel as I move through the wide, open space. Laughter and chatter bombard my ears. Just as I'm about to reach inside my bag and pull out my phone, I catch sight of her as she stands and waves from the other side of the room. I return the greeting before beelining in her direction. Once I'm close enough, she envelops me in her arms for a quick hug before we settle on opposite sides of the table. I glance at the smooth surface, surprised to find matching salads and sandwiches along with a drink already waiting for me.

I flick open the buttons of my jacket and pull it off, throwing it over the back of my chair. "You picked up lunch already?"

"I arrived fifteen minutes ago and thought I'd grab our food, so you didn't have to waste any time."

A huge smile breaks out across my face. "Thanks, Mom."

Her lips quirk at the edges. "It wasn't a problem. I thought the Caesar salads and club sandwiches looked good. And then there are chocolate chip cookies for dessert."

"Mmm. My favorite." Now that I'm sitting with all of this food spread out in front of me, my belly grumbles and I realize I haven't had anything more than the banana I grabbed while running out the door this morning before my first class.

"I figured you needed a solid lunch since who knows what time you'll be able to grab dinner tonight."

"If rehearsal runs over, then we usually order a few pizzas."

"From everything you've said, it sounds like the play is going well. Will everything be ready by opening night?"

"Yup, it's great." I nod as excitement bursts inside me like an over-inflated balloon. There's nothing I love more than the anticipation of the curtain rising for the first time. "I can't wait for you guys to see it. The script is hilarious."

She opens the clear plastic container of her salad before digging in. "I remember going to the theater to see the movie when it first came out. It was amusing in a dark, satirical kind of way."

"As soon as I found out what this year's production would be, I found it online and watched it. So funny. I loved Christian Slater and Wynonna Ryder together."

She grins. "He was quite the 80s heartthrob."

I dig into my salad and continue chattering about the play as Mom takes a bite of her sandwich. You'd think all the drama would be saved for the stage, but that's not the case. There are people cheating behind their partners' backs and one of the lead actresses is talking shit about her understudy. And that's only the tip of the iceberg.

Just like always, the conversation flows easily. Even before Dad died, Mom and I had a close relationship. Now we're even tighter. I suppose that's why my feelings are bruised that she didn't immediately tell me about Theo. Instead, she chose to spring it on me when I was least expecting it.

When we're halfway through our meal, she sets her sandwich down and clears her throat. "We didn't get a chance to talk when you stopped by for dinner. What did you think of Theo?"

With my fork paused midair, I carefully lower the plastic utensil to my bowl. Not that I would admit it to Mom, but I've been doing my best to avoid a conversation about her new dating situation. I've been so busy with the play and—

We'll just leave it at that.

Maybe I was hoping that if I didn't bring it up, their relationship would fizzle out and there wouldn't be a reason to discuss the fact that she's finally moving on after Dad. By the cautiously optimistic expression on her face, that hasn't happened. Although, I know Mom well enough to realize that she wouldn't have introduced us to him if she didn't have some degree of certainty he'd be part of her future moving forward.

Even though I'd been famished a few minutes ago, my appetite vanishes, and I push the bowl away from me.

"He seemed nice," I finally admit, shifting uncomfortably on my chair. Hopefully that response will be enough, and we can talk about something else. Anything else. From her expression, that isn't going to happen.

She nods, a relieved smile blooming across her face. When was the last time she looked this content or happy? It doesn't take long to figure out the answer.

"He's a real sweetheart," she gushes.

"How long have you two been seeing each other?"

"Oh, let's see." Her brow furrows. "About four months."

I blink.

What? No way...that can't be right.

"Four months," I parrot. While I don't live at home during the school year, I'm still surprised she managed to keep this a secret from us. I straighten on my plastic chair as that thought resonates through my brain. "Does Brayden know about this?"

Come to think about it, he didn't seem all that bent out of shape when we'd found Theo in the kitchen. The idea that she might have confided in my brother but withheld information from me cuts deep.

Her expression falters, her smile dimming as she reaches across the table and lays her hand over mine before giving it a squeeze. "Of course not. I would never tell one of you something and not the other. Especially something as important as this."

I nod, slightly mollified by her response. But still...four months. That seems like a long time to keep a lid on their relationship. My brain tumbles back in time, counting out the months.

"So that means you began dating in July?"

This time when she nods, it's more cautiously. "Yes, that's right."

"Why didn't you say something then?"

Her shoulders slump under the heavy weight of my question before she releases a steady breath. "When Theo first asked me out in June, I turned him down. Even though it's been years since your father passed away, I wasn't sure if I was ready to date or get involved with another man. He seemed to understand that and said he was happy to be friends. We grabbed coffee a few times and it was nice. Easy. He made me laugh, and I hadn't done that in a long time."

The way her dark eyes turn wistful has a lump of wet sawdust settling in the middle of my throat.

"After that, we began spending more time together, discovering all the things we had in common and," she shrugs, "I guess it grew from there. I didn't want to mention anything to either you or your brother until I knew it was serious."

It's frightening to realize that Mom is already in a committed relationship with this guy. I understand her not wanting to introduce random men to her children, but the flip side is that we now need to get used to someone who she's already developed strong feelings for. And vice versa.

"I want both of you to get better acquainted with Theo. It's important to me that you like him. I can't imagine bringing someone into our family who you or Brayden didn't get along with."

I release a steady breath as she runs out of steam. There are so many conflicting emotions churning inside me that it's difficult to pinpoint exactly what I'm thinking or feeling.

Am I happy for Mom?

Sure. Of course.

Does that necessarily mean I want someone taking Dad's place in her life or ours?

Not really.

When I remain silent, her fingers wrap more tightly around my hand. "I think I'm ready to move on, and I need you to be all right with me taking that next step. It's been the three of us for so long. I'm hoping there's enough room for Theo in all of our lives. Do you think that's possible?"

Even though I'm conflicted about the situation, I'm loath to tell her that I'm not interested in getting to know her new boyfriend.

The word has a pit forming at the bottom of my gut.

Mom has a boyfriend.

Boyfriend.

This was something I'd worried about immediately after Dad died. But when the months turned into years and she failed to express any real interest in dating or men, it seemed like we'd dodged a major bullet. And, rather selfishly, I enjoyed it just being the three of us and having Mom all to myself.

Now that she's ready to move on, I'm not sure if I am. It seems like a lot to wrap my head around.

It doesn't escape me that Mom is still young, beautiful, and full of energy. She deserves to have a partner who makes her happy to share the rest of her life with. She's always been supportive of everything I've wanted to do. Even acting. She understands that the end goal after college is to move to New York and make it on Broadway.

There have been a handful of students in my acting classes whose parents refuse to pay for their education unless they majored in something more realistic that will lead to a good job that pays well and offers benefits. The reality of the situation is that most people who end up with a theater degree will do something totally different with their lives. Even though the odds are stacked against me, I can't imagine pursuing another career. Maybe at some point in the future, I'll change my mind and redirect my energies. But for the time being, I'm pouring everything I have into turning my dreams into a reality.

Which is exactly what prompts me to say, "Yeah, Mom. I'd like the chance to get to know him better. If he's free, you can bring him to the play."

A sheen of tears brightens her eyes as she beams at me. "Thank you, I think he'd enjoy that very much."

Even though it's difficult, I force my lips into a smile. "Then it's a date."

Chapter Twenty-One

CARSON

"Hey, you ready to go or what?" Brayden asks, pausing outside the living room where I'm sitting on the couch, playing a video game. "We're leaving in ten."

I keep my gaze focused on the big screen TV and shake my head. "No, sorry. Can't make it."

A surprised silence follows that response. I know my friend well enough to realize he's studying me with a quizzical expression. I can practically feel the burn of his gaze, and it takes every ounce of self-control not to squirm beneath it.

"How come?"

I clear my throat and do my best to avoid eye contact. "I've got a shit ton of homework to finish up tonight. I'm just taking a ten-minute break before hitting the books again."

"That sucks," he says, drawing out the two words. "I can't remember the last time you missed one of Elle's opening night performances."

This will be the first.

I shrug. "I'll try to catch a different show next week." In all honesty, I have zero plans to show up for a performance. I'm doing my best to avoid her right now. Sitting in a dark theater for a couple hours while staring at her won't help matters.

He stuffs his hands into the pockets of his khakis. "I'll let her know."

It's only after his footsteps fade from the entryway that I release the pent-up breath I'd been holding hostage in my lungs and toss the controller onto the wooden coffee table after I crash and burn on the screen.

If that's not a fitting metaphor for my life, I don't know what is.

Stroking my hands over Elle was a big fucking mistake. One I regret and yet can't stop thinking or fantasizing about. I won't even tell you how many times I've locked myself in the bathroom and jerked off to thoughts of her. Reliving the precise moment she fell apart beneath the stroke of my lips and tongue. The way she'd clutched my head, holding me to her as I lapped at her clit.

The memory alone is enough to have my cock stirring in my athletic shorts.

Which is exactly why I've gone into avoidance mode. At this point, I'm hanging on to the last shreds of my self-control by my fingertips. It won't take much for it to come crumbling down around my head and I'll finally take what was never meant to be mine.

The worst part of all this is that I'm lying to my best friend, a guy who has always been there for me no matter what. I'm avoiding him as much as I am his sister because I'm afraid that if he looks hard enough, he'll figure out my dirty little secret.

The Kendricks are like family. Brayden, Elle, and Katherine. I can't risk losing them.

When the front door slams shut, my shoulders collapse and I bury my head in my hands, wishing there were a way to evict her from my brain once and for all. How the hell am I going to get through the remainder of the year without laying my hands on her again?

Without taking what she saved for me alone?

That knowledge leaves me groaning. It's sweet torture to realize that no other guy has touched her. Has thrusted inside her tight heat. Has given her an orgasm with the stroke of his cock.

I want to be the one to give her all of that.

And more.

I glance up to find Asher staring at me. His brows are drawn together, and there's a quizzical expression on his face.

"Huh?" If he asked a question, I have no idea what it is.

He points to the controller before enunciating his words carefully. "Are you playing the game?"

I shake my head. "Nah. Go ahead." My brain is too full of Elle to focus on anything else. Even a stupid video game. And I feel guilty as shit for blowing off her play. It's already eating me up inside.

He drops onto the couch and grabs the controller before waiting for the game to load. A few beats of silence creep by before he gives me a bit of side-eye. "What's your deal?"

I shrug before crossing my arms against my chest and staring sight-lessly at the screen. "Don't know what you're talking about. Everything is fan-fucking-tastic."

"I don't know about that. It kind of seems like something's crawled up your ass. I'm just wondering what it is and how we dislodge it."

This isn't a conversation I want to have.

Especially with Asher.

Which is exactly the reason I pull something out of my ass. "There's a lot going on with playoffs and the conference championship. Not to mention the bowl game, draft, and school." When I rattle off all the bullshit that could be giving me issues, even I'm astounded that I'm holding everything together as well as I am. Except none of those things are weighing on me. Classes are going well. I've always been a straight A student without much effort on my part.

Hey, don't hate the player. Hate the game.

As far as the playoffs go, I think our chances are good for winning them and making it to the conference championship. That's the only way I see this season ending for me.

With one last ring added to my collection.

At this very moment, my agent is fielding calls from several prospective NFL teams who are interested in what I can bring to the table.

So, no...I'm not concerned about any of that.

"It's little Kendricks, right?"

His words have me straightening in my seat like someone just rammed a two-by-four up my ass. "What did you say?"

Cause there is no damn way I heard him correctly.

His bored gaze flickers in my direction before refocusing on the football game unfolding on the screen. "You heard me. Do I really have to repeat myself?"

I shake my head and attempt to force down the thick lump lodged in the middle of my throat, making it impossible to breathe. "I'm not—"

He scrunches his face. It would be comical if I didn't feel so gut sick.

"Dude, come on. The fact that you're even trying to deny it is embarrassing."

My eyes widen as I moisten my lips and make a second attempt. "I don't—"

With a snort, he shakes his head. "Just own up to it, Roberts. You've got major wood for that girl."

"It's not like that." It's difficult to push the words through stiff lips. I don't want anyone talking about Elle in that way. In fact, I'm tempted to beat the piss out of him for even—

"Ahh, so you admit she's not just messing with your dick, but your head. Now we're getting somewhere." One corner of his mouth hitches as he gives me a sly smile. "Was that so difficult?"

Heat floods my cheeks. "I haven't admitted to anything." I wish there were a way to backtrack from this uncomfortable conversation.

"All right, so do us both a favor and deny it." Interest lights up his face as he watches me with a raised brow. "Tell me I'm wrong."

I can only stare.

What the hell is going on around here?

Since when does Asher pay enough attention to anything that doesn't involve football or pussy?

Strictly in that order.

And I can already tell by the way he's digging in that he won't be dropping the topic anytime soon. I glance desperately into the dining room, hoping to find someone I can pull in here and distract Asher with but there's no one. The house is surprisingly empty for this time of the evening. Where the hell did everyone go?

Before I can steer this one-sided conversation in a different direction, he says, "You realize that Bray is gonna kick your ass if he finds out you've got the hots for Elle."

That's all it takes for my head to fall back against the cushion as if it weighs a thousand pounds. The words escape before I can stuff them back inside my mouth where they belong. "Tell me something I don't know."

When he chuckles, I wince and squeeze the bridge of my nose between my fingers.

Well, fuck me.

"Now that you've finally fessed up and admitted the truth, what are you going to do about the delicate situation you find yourself embroiled in?"

"Absolutely nothing." The way I see it, I've gone this long without giving in—the other night notwithstanding. Surely I can get through the next six months. And then we can go our separate ways. Out of sight, out of mind, right?

"I think you're making a mistake."

My head jerks up so fast that I nearly give myself whiplash. "Why would you say that?"

His attention stays locked on the screen. "Because you've obviously had these feelings for a while. It sure as shit doesn't sound like a passing thing to me."

I blink. "How the hell would you know?"

His tongue peeks out at the corner of his mouth as he stays laser focused on the game. "Dude, you've been hovering over that girl since she stepped foot on campus freshman year. Anytime she's at the house, you're hanging all over her, making sure that every guy in the vicinity is keeping their distance. Frankly, it's shocking as hell that Kendricks hasn't figured you out."

He's right about that.

I drag a hand over my face. "We both know he would lose his proverbial shit if he discovered the truth."

Asher snorts. "Damn right he would."

"And it would seriously fuck up our friendship." I add the last part more to myself than him.

He nods as if I've offered up an excellent point. "Probably. It's a total breach of bro code."

This conversation isn't making me feel better. Scratch that, I feel worse than when it started.

Why the hell are we discussing this again?

"Look, I've known you since freshman year and have never seen you into a girl. Even before little Kendricks got here." He sends me a speculative look. One that punches me right in the gut. "Now I'm thinking there's a reason for that."

I press my lips together and glare.

Like I need him figuring shit out.

Figuring me out.

No thanks.

"Seems like she's more than just a piece of groupie ass at a party." When my expression turns thunderous, he shrugs. "I'm just giving you my thoughts on the matter."

"Yeah, well, maybe you should keep your thoughts to yourself from now on."

He bobs his head a few times before shrugging. "Maybe."

A sigh of relief escapes from me when he remains silent. Asher is the last person I'd take advice from when it comes to the ladies. He doesn't know his ass from a hole in the ground. Hell, just a couple of weeks ago, he pissed off the hostess at Taco Loco and we almost didn't get a table. We were dangerously close to missing out on all you can eat tacos because of this bonehead.

So, no...I won't be listening to him anytime soon.

"You think she's worth it?" When I lift a brow, he rolls his eyes. "Can you please keep up with the conversation?" Before I can tell him that I want no part of this one-sided discussion he's ramming down my throat, he continues. "Is she worth upending your friendship with Bray?"

All of the air deflates from my body.

That's the million-dollar question, isn't it?

"You treat her well and I would imagine that Kendricks might come around at some point in the distant future. Like when you're sitting around in an old folks home wearing your Depends."

Nice image.

"I think we can all agree," he says, "that she could do a hell of a lot worse than you."

He chuckles when I flip him the double birds.

"You really gonna miss the opening night of her play because you're trying to prove a point to yourself?"

I shift on the couch and glare. "Am I paying you for therapy and didn't realize it? Is that what's happening here?"

"Sure, I'll take payment in beer and weed." He points a finger in my direction. "And don't buy the skunky shit the Sig Eps sell."

I roll my eyes, already swamped with guilt for ditching something so important to her. It's nearly eating me up inside. I just thought...

Aww, hell. I don't know what I'd been thinking.

Before I can second guess myself, I rise to my feet and head to the staircase.

"That's my boy. Now go get your girl and make me proud."

"I'm not going to get my girl." Elle will *never* be my girl. "But that doesn't mean I shouldn't support her." There's a pause before I tack on, "As a friend."

"Sure, man." He shakes his head. "Whatever you gotta tell yourself to sleep at night."

I scowl before stomping up the staircase.

Fucking Asher Stevens. The guy needs to mind his own damn business and stop trying to stick his nose in mine where it doesn't belong.

Thirty minutes later, I'm freshly showered and dressed in a light blue button-down and khakis. The show is already underway as I slip into the auditorium and find a seat in the backrow. As soon as Elle steps onto the stage, my heart skips a beat and I lean forward to get a better view. The way she lights up the theater blows me away. It always has. She doesn't have one of the lead roles and every time she disappears from sight, I grow impatient, waiting for her to reappear.

If I had any willpower where she was concerned, I would have done us both a favor and stayed away. Already I know that nothing good will come from this. In fact, all I'm doing is tempting fate. If Asher, who's not the most astute guy on the face of the planet has figured me out, then anyone can. I need to do a better job of hiding my feelings.

Starting now.

The final act is just about to end when movement catches the corner of my eye, drawing my attention to the side. I glance over and see a guy standing near the exit with his arms crossed against his chest. Even though the theater is shadowy, I've been here long enough for my vision to have adjusted to the darkness.

What the hell?

I squint, trying to get a better look at the man, and hope I'm wrong. Although, deep in my gut, I know I'm not. It's that fucking professor who took Elle out to dinner.

My hands tighten into fists as every muscle tenses.

Even though there are a ton of rational explanations as to why he could be here taking in the show, my gut tells me it's because of the dark-haired girl, and that knowledge sinks to the bottom of my gut like a massive bolder.

What the hell is this dude doing? Is he really trying to get something going with one of his students?

I glance at the stage as Elle makes another appearance. Instead of focusing on her the way I want, I keep my attention locked on him.

The way his gaze sharpens, never deviating from her tells me that my intuition is spot on.

Motherfucker!

If there weren't people hemming me in, I'd stomp over and rip him a new one. I'm so intent on keeping my eyes on him that I don't realize the play has ended until the heavy curtain drops and the theater is once again illuminated. A few moments later, the red drapery rises, revealing the gathered cast as they hold hands and take a bow. The audience climbs to their feet en masse as applause echoes throughout the auditorium.

Elle beams from ear to ear. I've never seen her look happier than when she's performing on stage. She's a natural born actress and this has always been her happy place. I'm glad I didn't miss it. I would have been kicking myself for months if I'd stayed away. It's galling to realize I have Asher to thank for it.

Let's just hope the guy can keep his big trap shut when it comes to our previous discussion.

When the curtain drops for a second time, I glance back to where professor *I'm-gonna-take-advantage-of-the-young-girls-in-my-class* is loitering, only to find he's disappeared.

Dammit!

I crane my neck, combing through the crowd but don't see him anywhere. Part of me wonders if my eyes weren't playing tricks on me and he was never really here.

Just as I'm about to slip from the theater, my name is called out.

About a dozen rows in front of me, I spot Katherine, the guy she's seeing, Brayden, and Sydney. They're steadily moving up the center aisle, making their way toward me. Once they're close enough, Katherine pulls me into her arms for a quick hug. After we break apart, I shake her boyfriend's hand.

"Thought you couldn't make it?" Brayden raises a brow.

I shrug and try to play it cool. After my convo with Asher, I don't want to do anything that will tip him off. "I shifted a few things around. No big deal."

Katherine smiles. "That was so sweet of you. I know Elle will appreciate you showing up to support her."

"Of course." I point toward the double doors, only wanting to make a hasty escape. I've done my due diligence, now it's time to scram. "I should really get back and get cracking on my work. It's gonna be a long night."

Before I can slip away, Elle joins our small group. She's still grinning. Her face is radiant and she's vibrating with pent-up energy. She must feel the same way I do after a big game when we've crushed our opponents into the ground. I can only imagine the adrenalin pumping wildly through her veins. She looks as if she's on top of the world.

It's tempting to stare and simply drink her in.

Katherine's boyfriend steps forward and hands Elle a carefully wrapped bouquet of fresh flowers. Surprise lights up her eyes as she buries her nose in the blooms.

"Thank you! They're beautiful."

"You were really wonderful up there," Theo says. "The play was fantastic. I told your mother that we should see it one more time."

Dammit. I should have picked up flowers. Why didn't I think about that?

Katherine nods, agreeing with the idea. "We'll have to figure out a day next week."

Brayden and Sydney congratulate her, each pulling her in for a hug.

"Hey, Elle!" A guy in costume saunters over. "Great job!"

"You, too!"

"Everyone's heading to Anthony's for an afterparty. Are you coming with?" His gaze flickers to encompass the rest of us. "Your friends are welcome, if they want."

She nods before glancing at the group. "Are you guys interested?"

"Sure," Sydney answers before Brayden can beat her to the punch. Although it's doubtful his response would have been the same.

I smirk at him.

"Awesome! I'm going to change and then we can head over."

Elle gives her mother and even Theo a hug before bounding away. It's so easy to see that the theater is her element. I can't imagine her doing anything else that would make her this happy.

Now that I've come here and done what I needed to, it's time to take off. I jerk a thumb over my shoulder before retreating a step. "I should probably—"

Brayden shakes his head before throwing an arm across my shoulders. "No way, dude. If I have to attend this artsy party, so do you."

I groan. "But I have—"

"Tough shit. We won't stay long."

He gives me the same smirk I'd flashed at him about thirty seconds ago.

Asshole.

Chapter Twenty-Two

ELLE

There's an air of excitement as I stop and chat with the different groups of people who have gathered to celebrate the success of our opening night. Everyone from the production has shown up for the party—cast members, crew, costume and set designers, lighting and sound engineers, along with the director.

This was our first performance and we slayed it. Hopefully the rest of the shows will run just as smoothly and be as well received by the audience.

Large hands grab hold of me before swinging me around. I squeal when my feet are lifted off the floor and hang on for dear life.

"Best. Show. Ever," Mike singsongs mid-swing.

I fasten my arms around his shoulders. The last thing I need is to fall and break my leg. That would be a major bummer. "It went off without a hitch."

"Sure did. Let's hope it just continues to get better and better."

He's all smiles as he sets me back on my feet.

I keep my arms loosely wrapped around his neck as he drops his voice. "What's up with tall, blond and brooding in the corner?" He pauses before adding, "I'm so intrigued."

I don't have to glance over my shoulder to realize who he's asking about.

Carson.

Unable to help myself, I turn until my gaze can settle on him. Electricity zips through my veins, lighting up every nerve ending. We haven't seen or spoken since the night I found him in my room. After he stalked out, I wasn't sure where we stood with one another.

Even now, I'm still not certain. The stereo silence that followed after the incident seemed to be a pretty good indication of the answer.

"There's nothing up with him. We've known each other since we were kids." I pause before forcing myself to add, "He's like a brother to me."

Mike's narrowed eyes bounce between the two of us as if he's trying to silently puzzle out a problem. "Methinks you might be lying."

Wanting to avoid the conversation, I shift my gaze. "No, I'm not."

"Ha!" he crows. "You've got the hots for him!"

I swat at his arm. "Shhh! He'll hear you."

Mike rolls his eyes and huffs out a breath. "From across the room? Unless he can lip read, that's doubtful. Don't worry, your secret is safe with me."

Heat rushes to my cheeks. "I don't know how much of a secret it is."

He perks up and moves his fingers in a give-me-more gesture. "Do tell. I'm all ears."

Of course he is. Mike lives for all the juicy gossip. All right, we both do. It's what we originally bonded over in theater class.

"I might have forgotten to mention that I've been holding out for him."

His eyes widen as his mouth falls open. "No way! I love it. Have you told him yet? Did he jump your bones?" His gaze cuts to the football player. "Ohhh, I just bet he did, and I can only imagine that it was fantastic."

I glance away, embarrassed to share the details of that night with someone. "Hardly." More like the opposite.

"Let me guess, you took matters into your own hands and jumped him instead?"

I shake my head. "There was absolutely no jumping of any kind going on."

His expression falls. "Well, that's a rather disappointing end to this story."

I don't bother to mention the last time we were together. How he made me orgasm before promptly walking out of my dorm.

Pursing his lips, Mike shifts his stance and stares across the room. "Think it's possible he bats for the other team?" Excitement lights up his eyes. "Or...could he be persuaded to? You know me. I'm always up for a challenge."

Laughter gurgles up from my throat. "Definitely not."

He sighs. "That's too bad. The guy has hot sex written all over him."

I tilt my head as my gaze locks on Carson. A sizzle of electricity zips down my spine. Ever since we arrived, I've been acutely aware of his presence. No matter where I was or who I was conversing with, I could feel the burn of his gaze singeing me alive. The longer we stare, the more impossible it becomes to look away. He can deny it all he wants, but there's a combustible attraction that pulses between us, drawing us to one another. Or am I the only one who feels the intense lure of it?

After the other night, I'm not sure.

"The guy certainly can't take his eyes off you. He looks ready to stomp over here, throw you over his shoulder, and carry you away. I, for one, would pay good money to see that happen."

The thought of Carson doing exactly that has a burst of arousal exploding in my belly. "It's not like that." More like wishful thinking on my part.

"I think it could be. Why else would he be here?"

I shrug. "He came with my brother and his girlfriend. He's just as protective of me as Brayden."

"Hmm." Mike glances around the thick crowd. "Where did they disappear off to?"

I pull my gaze from Carson and search the vicinity for the newly minted couple but don't find them anywhere. "Good question. Maybe they went to the kitchen to get something to drink."

Mike unwraps his arm from around my waist before giving me a little shove in Carson's direction. "You should keep him company until they return. He looks lonely. Plus, I've noticed that bitch, Sara, circling like a hungry shark. Once she sinks her teeth into him, she'll gobble him up in one tasty gulp. I've seen it happen before and trust me, it's not a pretty sight."

With a frown, I search the throng. "What?"

"I'm surprised you haven't noticed." He points out the lead actress who was cast as Veronica. She's gorgeous with long, golden-blonde hair. Rumor around the theater is that she was sleeping with our director. I can't say whether it's true or not. She flirts with everyone.

I watch as Sara meanders from one group of people to the next, soaking up adoration and accolades as she goes. As pained as I am to admit it, she was fantastic. She hit every mark, had the audience laughing, and belted her way through the show.

It only takes a second to realize that Mike is right in his assessment of the situation. It's like her sights are locked on a target. And that target just so happens to be Carson. A hot bolt of jealousy slices through me before I can stomp it out. It certainly isn't new. I've spent years watching girls hang all over him.

"Uh-oh, looks like Sara the shark is going in for the kill."

Before I realize it, I'm on the move, pushing my way through the crowd as Mike's chuckle echoes in my ears.

Chapter Twenty-Three

CARSON

S omeone needs to tell me what the hell I'm doing here.

I lift the bottle of water to my lips as my gaze locks on Elle as she talks with Mike.

I really need to stop hovering over her, acting like Elle belongs to me.

Like she'll *ever* belong to me.

She doesn't.

And never will.

That's just the way it is.

End of story.

The only thing Asher was spot on about is how pissed off Brayden would be if he caught wind of the situation.

"Hi."

I blink and realize that someone has snuck up on me while I wasn't paying attention. I've spent the last thirty minutes by myself, hanging out in the corner, watching Elle like a creepy stalker. Am I aware that I've jackhammered to an all new low and should probably seek out immediate treatment?

Yup.

I shift and take a discrete step away from her. "Hey."

"I'm Sara." She flips her long, blonde hair over her shoulder in a practiced move.

"Carson." I clear my throat and force myself to add, "Nice to meet you."

"I know who you are." She sidles closer, invading my personal space for a second time. "I'm a huge Wildcats fan."

"Oh. Well, thanks."

She grins, revealing bright white teeth. "This party seems to be winding down. Any interest in getting—"

"Hello. Am I interrupting anything here?"

My gaze cuts to Elle as she slips her arm through mine before giving the other girl a pointed stare.

"Oh...hi." Her lips sink at the corners as her attention drops to the hold Elle has on me. "I take it you two know each other?" The blonde doesn't seem pleased by the notion.

She presses closer. "Yup, Carson is an old family friend."

Sara's blue eyes light up at that bit of information. "So...you're not together?"

My brows rise. There's not a hint of coyness in this female.

"Sorry, Sara." Her voice turns frigid. "He's not available."

The other girl glances at me with a raised brow as if looking for confirmation. I shake my head once.

"Hmm. That's too bad." She gives me a full-on pout before running one long fingernail up my chest. "After that performance, I could have gone for a fuck with a hot guy. Maybe next time."

With a little wave of her fingers, she saunters away without a backward glance.

I can only stare as she disappears into the crowd before looking at Elle with raised brows. Her arm is still looped through mine. "That was kind of frightening."

She snorts, and the tension filling her muscles dissipates. "Sara is like a barracuda. She'll chew you up and spit you out before you even realize it happened."

Damn. "I don't doubt it."

Now that I've been saved, we fall into an awkward silence as she releases her hold and steps away.

Avoiding eye contact, Elle glances around. "Where are Brayden and Sydney?"

"They took off about thirty minutes ago."

Her brow furrows as her gaze resettles on mine. "How come you didn't leave with them?"

I shrug, realizing the innocuous question is a veritable minefield that needs to be carefully navigated. "I wasn't sure how you were getting home and didn't want you walking by yourself."

"Oh." The air between us intensifies as she glances at her fingers. Color slowly seeps into her cheeks. "Should we talk about what happened the other night?"

Hell no.

That topic is more dangerous than the previous one.

"No reason to." My voice comes out sounding gruffer than I intend. "It was a mistake that won't be repeated."

The flush staining her face drains away as her wide gaze jerks to mine. "Do you really think that?"

Even though the music is loud, and the incessant sound of chatter presses in on us from all sides, her whispered words are perfectly clear.

"Yeah, I do." It takes effort to force the lie from my lips.

She looks like a puppy that has been repeatedly kicked as her teeth sink into her bottom lip. It takes every ounce of self-control not to pull her into my arms and kiss the expression away. To tell her that I don't mean one goddamn word of the bullshit coming out of my mouth. But it's my lack of self-control that got me into this mess in the first place. I need to hold it together and right our relationship. If that's even possible.

She straightens to her full height and says through stiff lips, "You don't need to worry about staying at the party. I'll catch a ride home with Mike."

Even though I should say goodbye and get the hell out of here, my feet refuse to obey the commands of my brain.

Reluctant to leave, I shift my weight. "Are you sure?"

"Positive."

Before I can say anything else, she swings away and disappears through the crowd. I would be lying through my teeth if I didn't admit there's a voice inside my head demanding I take off after her.

But how can I do that?

How can I give in to this deep need I have for her when it'll only end up ruining a different relationship in the process?

Maybe she doesn't understand it, but what I'm doing is for the best.

Chapter Twenty-Four

ELLE

Can you stick around after class?

I stare at my cell for a moment before lifting my gaze to the front of the lecture hall where Dr. Holloway loiters behind the podium. His attention is already locked on me. The question on the screen is evident in his blue eyes.

I give my head a slight nod in silent response before refocusing on my paper and the problems he assigned a couple of minutes ago. A weird sensation takes up residence in the pit of my belly. It seems kind of odd that he would send a text instead of asking me to stay once class is released. As soon as that thought tries to sneak its way into my consciousness, I shake it away.

I've been alone with him several times and there's never been anything inappropriate about his behavior. Nothing that would lead me to believe this is anything more than a professor who is concerned about one of his students.

Just as I glance at the clock on the wall, his voice cuts through the quiet chatter of the room. "All right everyone, we'll meet back here on Friday. If you have any questions about the assignment, I have office hours tomorrow afternoon. Don't be afraid to pop in."

I slam my book shut and shove it into my backpack.

"Hey, any interest in grabbing a coffee before your next class? You know I'm addicted to pumpkin spice."

It's one of Mike's favorite coffee drinks. This might be an unpopular opinion, but I can't stand it. It's probably the only thing Mike and I disagree about.

Vehemently.

I shake my head. "No, I need to stay after and talk to Dr. H."

"If it's quick, I don't mind waiting around. I've got a bit of time to waste."

"Honestly, I don't know how long it'll take. You should go without me so you can grab your drink." My lips quirk at the corners. "I'd hate to be the reason you fall asleep in your next class."

"Please, girl. Even with a PICC line pumping caffeine straight to the vein, I'd still fall asleep in poli sci."

We both rise to our feet before moving to the center aisle. With a quick wave, he joins the herd of slow-moving students making their way to the doors of the lecture hall. I swing in the opposite direction toward the front of the room where Dr. Holloway waits.

"Hi, you wanted to see me?"

His lips curve as his eyes crinkle at the corners. "Yeah, thanks for sticking around. Do you have a couple of minutes to talk?"

I nod. "I don't have another class until twelve."

"Okay, good. First off, I wanted to mention that I caught the play last night and it was fabulous. The whole cast was incredible."

"Thank you!" Any unease swirling around inside me evaporates with the compliment. I'm still riding high from the performance. This weekend is the official opening, and I'm so excited. It's an amazing feeling to see a production come together after pouring blood, sweat, and tears into it. There were so many late nights spent running lines and wolfing down cold pizza, all the while trying to squeeze homework in.

He pulls out a sheet of paper and holds it up. "This is your homework from the other day. Well done! It's obvious that all of the hard work you're putting into this class is paying off."

My gaze falls to the sheet. This is the first time one of my assignments hasn't been marked up with so much red ink that it resembles some poor animal slowly hemorrhaging to death.

Even though this is good news, I have a long way to go toward lifting my grade and not a lot of time to accomplish it. "Maybe if I'm lucky, I'll be able to eke out a C minus." Trust me, I'm not complaining.

He chuckles before shifting his stance and angling his body toward mine. "I know the prospect seems daunting, but it's completely doable. If you're interested, I have some extra credit that will help."

"Sure." I'm always interested in earning a few bonus points. You never know when they'll come in handy. Although, with this class, I need every single one I can grade grub.

"Great." His smile widens. "I have some paperwork that needs to be organized and it shouldn't take more than a few hours of your time. It's nothing pressing that has to be completed in one sitting. I know you're spread thin with your other classes and the play. So whatever schedule works for you is fine with me."

I shift the backpack on my shoulder as his words run through my brain. "You want me to file paperwork in your office?"

"That's exactly what I want." Humor leaps into his eyes. "Were you hoping for a couple pages of stats problems?"

A gurgle of laughter bubbles up in my throat as I nod. "Maybe I was."

He shrugs as if warming to the idea. "Well, I can certainly pile on more work if that would make you feel better."

More statistics?

I quickly shake my head. "No, thanks. I have enough trouble with the assignments as it is."

"Then it sounds like this could be a situation that'll be beneficial for both of us."

He's right. It does seem that way.

When he's finished packing up his briefcase, he grabs the handle and steps around the podium. "Are you ready to leave?"

"Yup."

Side by side, we move up the carpeted staircase to the exit.

"You must have a lot of students taking advantage of this offer."

I'm certainly not the only one doing lousy in this class. Every time tests and quizzes get passed back, there are always plenty of people bitching and moaning about their grades.

Dr. Holloway stares straight ahead. "You're the first person I've offered it to, so if you wouldn't mind, let's keep it between the two of us for the time being."

Oh.

Before I can dissect the comment, he tacks on, "I'm sure as the semester winds down, more students will stop in, begging for an opportunity to lift their grade." His gaze flickers to mine. "Not everyone is as conscientious as you are."

Hmm. I suppose that makes sense.

He reaches out and grabs hold of the door handle before flashing me a smile. "After you."

"Thanks."

The moment I cross over the threshold and step into the hallway, my attention locks on the blond football player and my feet stutter to a halt. His muscular arms are crossed against his chest as he leans against the brick wall. With narrowed eyes, his mouth tightens into a thin slash across his face. One look is all it takes for me to realize he's pissed off.

"Carson." Anxiety leaps into my voice, making it high pitched and reedy. "What are you doing here?"

"I wanted to talk after last night."

I shift under the heaviness of his stare as my heartbeat kicks up. Any moment, my knees will buckle, and I'll slide to the floor in a boneless heap. Thick tendrils of tension swirl through the air as Dr. Holloway follows me into the hall, stopping alongside me. Fury sparks from the younger man's eyes as he straightens to his full height and takes a step forward.

Just when it seems like I might choke on the suffocating silence that has fallen over the three of us, Dr. Holloway clears his throat.

"I'll see you on Friday, Elle. Take care and congrats again on a successful first performance."

"Thanks," I say faintly, relieved the older man is taking off before Carson can totally lose his shit.

He scowls at my professor's retreating form for a few seconds before his steely gaze slams into mine. By now, the corridor has emptied of all students, and the only sound is Dr. Holloway's fading footsteps as he disappears from sight.

"What the hell were you doing alone with that guy?" His voice is so low and tightly strung that it strums something deep inside the pit of my belly. Nerves skitter down my spine.

"Nothing. We were just walking out of the classroom."

Wait a minute...

I don't owe Carson Roberts any explanations for my behavior. I'm free to do what I want, when I want, no matter what he thinks.

I straighten my shoulders and lift my chin. "Not that it's any of your business."

That last comment has his nostrils flaring as he closes the space that separates us with two quick strides before shackling his fingers around my wrist.

"That's where you're wrong."

A squeak of protest escapes from my lips as he drags me down the hallway. My feet trip over each other to keep pace with him. By the time I consider fighting the tight hold, he's yanking me inside an empty classroom and slamming the door shut behind us. The click of the lock is like a gunshot ringing out in the stillness of the room. My heart leaps into my throat as I watch him with wide eyes.

We're so close that I'm able to see the various shades of brown and green flecks that dance within his irises.

Only now does it occur to me that I've pushed him too far.

Chapter Twenty-Five

CARSON

O nce we're locked inside the empty space and she can't escape, I release my grip on her before retreating a few steps. If I'm going to keep my cool, I need to put some distance between us. Having her this close—smelling the floral scent of her shampoo, staring into her dark eyes, feeling her pulse thunder beneath my fingers—screws with my head, and that's the last thing I need. Even though my hold wasn't punishing, she rubs her wrist with delicate circles, all the while watching me warily.

"I told you before I didn't want you hanging around with that guy." The idea of them alone together has me seeing red. It makes me want to rip him apart limb by limb.

"You're being ridiculous. He's my professor. We were walking out of the room together."

Unmoved by the explanation, I lift a brow. "Ten minutes after the end of class? What were you doing?" Actually, I can just imagine what he was trying to do.

Finagle more time alone with her.

Asshole.

"He wanted to discuss an assignment."

Right.

I cock my head. "So you're telling me that you two didn't talk about anything other than a stats assignment?"

Her teeth sink into her lower lip as her gaze flickers toward the window.

Yeah, I didn't think so.

When she gulps, the muscles in her throat convulse. "He mentioned some extra credit that's available to lift my grade."

"And what exactly would that entail?" When she lapses into another silence, I prompt, "Elle?"

She shifts. "There are some files in his office that need to be organized."

Is this girl being serious?

For a long moment, I can only stare. It takes effort to keep from raising my voice. "Did you tell him no?"

When she glances away and gives her head a slight shake, I drag a hand through my hair. How doesn't she see through this caring professor bullshit act he's putting on? It's so obvious.

"Don't you understand what he's doing here?"

Her wide gaze slices to mine as she takes a quick step in retreat. "Yeah, he's trying to make sure I pass his course. And you know what? I'm appreciative of that. There are a lot of professors on campus who wouldn't give a damn how many times I have to retake their class. Dr. Holloway actually cares about his students. I don't see what the issue is."

I'm not buying his altruistic bullshit act. It's beyond frustrating that Elle doesn't see through it. She's smarter than this.

Tight-lipped, I spell it out for her. "The guy is trying to get into your pants. *That's* the problem."

She rolls her eyes. "Oh my god, when did you become so delusional? You know what? You're becoming more like Brayden every day, and it needs to stop. He's never done anything remotely inappropriate. So chill out."

I fold my arms against my chest. If I don't, I'll reach out, grab her by the shoulders and shake her senseless. Or maybe try to shake some sense into her. "Really? Because I can think of a few things he's done that have been suspect. Like picking you up from a party and driving

you home or taking you out to dinner and plying you with wine."
There's a beat of silence before I add, "And now he's trying to entice
you into being alone with him by offering some bullshit extra credit?
Yeah, it's *all* inappropriate."

"For one, I didn't ask you. And two, we've been over this. He never
plied me with anything." She grits her teeth as a dull red color stains
her cheeks. "He's my teacher. That's it. You keep trying to find bad
intentions where there are none and I'm tired of it. I'm not even sure
why you care. We're nothing to one another."

Her words are like a punch to the gut, and if I'm being honest, they
knock the wind from my lungs. I'm not a dumbass. I'm aware that I've
been the one forcing her away, but, in this moment, that doesn't matter
one damn bit.

Barely can I push out the word. "What?"

Her glare turns icy. "You heard me. How many times have you said
that I'm nothing more than a little sister to you? Too many to count,"
she answers for me. "You know what? I don't need you watching out
for me. I'm more than capable of taking care of myself." She purses her
lips before spitting out the rest like a spray of gunfire. "So why don't
you just fuck right off."

My eyes widen. Holy shit. Did she really say that to me?

My arms fall to my sides as I eat up the distance between us. "Fuck
right off, huh?"

Her gaze stays pinned to mine. Instead of cowering, she draws
herself up to her full height as if preparing for battle.

"Yup."

Even though there's a slight waver to her voice, she shows no sign
of backing down.

"I don't need you."

The fuck she does. "You're so naïve. You have absolutely no idea
when a man wants you."

Every muscle goes still. When her tongue peeks out to moisten her
lips, my cock stirs in my boxer briefs. A groan fights to break free, and
it takes every ounce of self-control to force it down and regain the
upper hand on my lust.

"That's not true."

Her answer is laughable. She doesn't have a clue.

Not a single one.

I shake my head. "Yeah, it is."

She blinks as her brows pinch together. A suffocating silence falls over us as she searches my eyes. That's all it takes for understanding to dawn in hers.

I clamp my lips shut, wishing I could stuff the words back inside.

What the hell am I doing?

Dragging her in here and then locking us inside this room was a huge mistake. But I couldn't help myself. Seeing the two of them together—especially the expression on his face when he thought no one was looking—sent my temper skyrocketing and my vision turning hazy. You'd think after all these years, I would be used to controlling my baser instincts where this girl was concerned.

Turns out that's not the case.

Elle's gaze sharpens as she tilts her head and studies me carefully, almost as if she's trying to sift through all the secrets buried in my eyes. "What are you trying to say?"

"Nothing," I mutter, hoping she'll believe me as I attempt to backtrack from this dangerous conversation. "The last thing I want to see is some asshole professor take advantage of you. It's nothing more than that."

She takes a tentative step in my direction. "Are you sure?"

I remain silent in hopes the glare will speak for itself.

Her expression turns contemplative. "Maybe you're right and I don't know when a guy wants me."

Fuck.

What I need to do is put an end to this disastrous conversation and get the hell out of here before she figures out the truth. When I remain still, she slowly inches toward me. Every bit of space she swallows up has my heart hammering harder. Faster. Until it feels as if it might explode from my ribcage. Already I know there's only so much more I can take. She needs to keep her distance.

Hasn't she figured out that I have very little self-control when it comes to her?

"Carson?"

I blink and realize she's no more than a handful of inches away. She's so close that the delicate scent of her perfume is able to tease my senses. Her palms rise before settling on my chest. I steel myself as their warmth burns holes through the material of my shirt straight down to my flesh. There's never been a girl who has affected me this way. And it's doubtful anyone will ever make me feel these kinds of out-of-control emotions again. I wish it were possible to douse everything brewing dangerously inside me.

"Have I misinterpreted the situation?"

Almost desperately, I shake my head. "No."

She presses into me, tilting her chin to hold my gaze. "I think that's exactly what I've done."

I clear my throat and force out the lie. "You're wrong."

With deliberate strokes, her hands drift from my chest to my shoulders before reversing direction and sinking lower. Her fingers leave a trail of nerve endings sparking to life in their wake. With every stroke, it becomes more of a challenge to keep all of the desire and need from breaking loose inside me.

Her gaze drops, tracking the lazy movements. "Do you know that I've always wanted to touch you like this?"

The muscle in my jaw tics as my molars grind together until it feels as if they'll shatter.

What she's doing is both heaven and hell. All I want to do is squeeze my eyes closed and immerse myself in her tentative touch. And yet, at the same time, I need her to back off before I say fuck it and take what I've been salivating over for years. It's a dangerous line she's forcing us to walk.

When she sucks in a sharp breath, I realize that my body has betrayed me once again. My attention stays locked on the crown of her head as she stares at my groin.

For a heartbeat, neither of us moves a muscle. The air in the room turns thick and oppressive as her hand descends, drifting over my taut abdominals before hesitating at my fly. Before I can find the willpower to knock her away, her fingers wrap around my throbbing length through the material and squeeze.

A hiss of pain escapes from my lips as my cock turns to steel beneath her touch. If I could dig deep and muster even a kernel of strength, I'd take a step back and get the hell out of there before any more damage can be inflicted. But that's not possible. I'm frozen in place as a tidal wave of pleasure crashes over me.

"Don't you realize how wrong this is?" My teeth clench as I wage war against every instinct to reach out and drag her into my arms.

She flicks her gaze upward, assessing me from beneath the thick fringe of her lashes. "Actually, I don't."

The fight inside me recedes. "We shouldn't be doing this. And you certainly shouldn't be touching me."

Instead of letting go, her fingers tighten around my throbbing erection. The sensation is enough to leave me feeling lightheaded. If I don't put the kibosh on this now, I won't be able to. In two minutes, it'll be much too late. I'll force her against the wall and take her the way I've dreamed of doing for so long. I can't begin to imagine what it would feel like to sink inside her warmth.

I shove that image from my head. If I focus on it, I'll explode in my jeans. And just to be clear, that's never happened before. It's yet another telltale sign as to how different my feelings are for this girl.

My fingers shake as I reach down and grab hold of her wrist before wrenching it away. It's only when I'm no longer able to feel the burn of her touch that the thick haze clouding my brain clears enough for rational thought to once again prevail.

Holy fuck.

That was close.

Too damn close.

With her wrist held captive between us, her gaze locks on mine. There's an unexpected steeliness in her dark eyes that takes me by surprise. This is not the same stunned girl I'd dragged in here a handful of minutes ago.

"Why?" Her voice turns sultry. The deep cadence of it goes straight to my dick. It's the last thing I need.

"What?"

"Why shouldn't I touch you?" There's a pause. "Don't you like it?"

Refusing to touch the second question, I focus on the first. "You know the reason."

When she attempts to break free, my grip tightens. There is no way I'll be able to survive if she lays her hands on me for a second time. My self-control is already in tatters. Anything more will shove me right over the edge.

"Because of Bray?"

Barely am I able to force the words through clenched teeth. "He would fucking kill me. That's exactly why nothing will ever happen between us." I search her eyes for understanding. "Period."

Instead of arguing the point, she examines me with more care than is comfortable. "But you want me."

Fuck.

Fuck.

Fuck.

She needs to do us both a favor and let this go.

I smash my lips together, refusing to engage in this conversation.

Hasn't she figured out that it doesn't matter what I want? It never has. My grip tightens on her delicate wrist before I force myself to release her and take a giant step in retreat, giving us both some much needed room to breathe.

When she doesn't spring forward, I put even more distance between us until I'm halfway across the room. Only then does my head clear. Warily, my gaze stays pinned to hers as I make my way to the door before turning the lock and pushing it open.

As I cross over the threshold, I hesitate. "Stay the hell away from that guy. Whether you realize it or not, he wants to do more than tutor you."

"That's going to be difficult given the fact that he's my professor and I need his help with stats." Her attention stays fastened on me as she lifts her chin a notch. "Are you offering your assistance in his place?"

After this fiasco? "No."

A challenging light fills her eyes. "Then I'll take the help where I can get it."

My hands tighten as a growl rumbles up from deep within my chest. It's so tempting to march back inside the room and kiss her into submission. I have to ball my hands until the short nails bite into my palms so I don't do exactly that.

"Don't push me, Elle."

Before she can come up with a way to detain me, I swing around and stalk down the empty corridor. For reasons I can't explain, the power balance has shifted between us. There's a clock ticking in my head, and when the alarm goes off, time will be up.

What I can't allow is for that to happen.

Chapter Twenty-Six

ELLE

"There's an empty table over there," Madison says, leading the charge with her tray in hand.

The three of us follow suit as she winds her way through the thick crowd of students who are busy grabbing something to eat before settling at a booth in the back of the union.

Once we're seated, everyone digs into their lunches. Madison is an if-I-feel-like-a-bacon-cheeseburger-loaded-with-the-works, I'm-gonna-eat-it kind of girl. She doesn't give a damn. She's got curves for miles and the boys go crazy for them. Being a nursing student, Sierra is more health conscious. She's partial to smoothies, wraps, and bowls. Quinoa and grilled chicken breasts are her best friends.

Besides us, that is.

And Kari is a vegan with a bazillion food allergies. So, she's careful about steering clear of gluten, dairy, nuts, and eggs. Thank god she enjoys a good chopped salad or I have no idea what she would eat. I'm somewhere in the middle. I like to eat healthy, but I also want to splurge when the urge strikes me. I'm luckier than most with a fast metabolism. I can pretty much eat what I want within reason and not gain weight.

"Hey, isn't that your brother over there?" Madison asks, straightening on her chair as she stares past me. "Have I mentioned how damn hot he is?" A dreamy look enters her eyes.

I scrunch my nose, disgusted by the comment. Especially when I'm trying to eat. "Yes, and I've told you not to." There have been times when she's gone into graphic detail on the subject.

Doesn't she realize I can never unhear those words?

Her gaze tracks his movements through the open space. "What are the chances of him breaking up with that girl?"

"*That girl* has a name. It's Sydney." I shake my head before taking a sip of Diet Coke. It's one of my guilty pleasures. "And to answer your question, I don't see that happening any time soon." If ever. I've never seen my brother so crazy over a girl before. But that's exactly the way he is with her.

If there's a spark of sadness that I'll never have the same kind of relationship with Carson, I sweep those feelings aside and pretend they don't exist. It's something I've had a ton of practice doing over the years.

Neglecting her half-eaten burger, Madison sets both elbows on the table and rests her chin on clasped hands. "That's too bad."

"No, it's not. I love Sydney. She's the absolute best."

Brow furrowing, she shoots me a dirty look. "But if we were dating, I could be your sister from another mister."

My lips tremble at the corners. "You'll always be that. Whether you're dating my brother or not."

That comment does exactly what it's meant to, and she grins before shrugging. "Fine. I suppose I'll allow that dream to fall by the wayside."

"It's probably for the best."

"It really is," Kari adds. "You've been going on about him since freshman year."

Not embarrassed in the least, Madison waves the comment away.

"Speaking of crushes, there's your hottie," Sierra says.

It's so tempting to swivel around and take a look. I'm hungry for the sight of him. It's been a few days since the incident in the class-room and we haven't run into each other again. It's almost like he's deliberately going out of his way to avoid me.

Now that I think about it, that's exactly what he's doing.

My brother is the first one to cross my line of sight. His arm is wrapped around his girlfriend as if he can't bear to be separated from her for even a moment. Just like always, my heart constricts at the sight of them. They're so good together. Sydney is the perfect match for him. She doesn't take any of his crap and she's fiercely loyal. She's everything he didn't know he needed or wanted.

A few seconds later, the guy who has held a piece of my beating heart since middle school trails behind them as he talks with his friend. I'm much too far away to hear what's being said. An easy smile flashes across Carson's face as he shakes his blond head. The other football player scowls in return. I would be hard pressed not to admit that there's something appealing about Crosby's brooding presence. Or maybe it's the silver lip ring. I've never been attracted to guys with piercings, but he pulls it off spectacularly. Even though he's never been anything but kind to me, I still find his presence intimidating.

He's the bad boy athlete of the Western Wildcats.

Kari sighs. "Can I just add that Crosby Rhodes is dreamy?"

"I think the word you meant to use is scary," Sierra says before shoving a spoonful of quinoa into her mouth.

"Scary. Dreamy." She shrugs. "Same thing."

"Hardly."

It's not difficult to tune out the conversation as I track the group's movements through the union. I'm certainly not the only one watching. Heads turn as they saunter past. Everyone on campus knows who these guys are.

From where I'm seated, buried at one of the crowded booths in the back, none of them have spotted me. Which is kind of nice. I can stare at Carson to my heart's content without him being aware of it. Once they find an open table, Brayden drops down on a chair and Sydney settles beside him. Carson and Crosby find places on the other side, giving me the perfect view.

"Girl, you're drooling on your sandwich." Sierra elbows me in the side, knocking me out of my Carson-filled thoughts.

When I swipe at my chin, all three of my so-called friends laugh.

"It was more of a figurative statement than a literal one," she says with a smile.

I stick out my tongue as heat floods into my cheeks. It doesn't take long before my gaze resettles on Carson. Only this time, there's a girl seated next to him. If the blonde were any closer, she'd be perched on his lap. Jealousy rears its ugly head, bubbling up inside me like a geyser. I have no right to feel this way. Carson doesn't belong to me. And, after our last conversation, he never will.

My heart constricts painfully. It's not like I thought there was a snowball's chance in hell we would get together, but to hear him say it so bluntly was like a punch to the gut. After he stalked out of the room, I'd wanted to curl up into a ball and cry. Refusing to dwell on the ugly memory, I shake myself out of it. Even though I should ignore them, that's impossible. It's like a car accident unfolding before my eyes and I'm powerless to look away.

The girl smiles coyly before leaning toward him and trailing her fingertips along his bicep. It's not a conscious decision to dig through my bag until my fingers wrap around my cell and pull it free. I open the home screen and scroll through my messages until I find the texts from him. Then I tap out a sentence before hitting send.

Any chance you can help me with stats tonight?

My gaze remains fixated on him. There's a part of me that wonders if he'll even—

The girl continues to paw at him, inching closer, as he reaches into his pocket and pulls out his phone. A satisfied smile tips the corners of my lips when his brows snap together, and he frowns. Maybe he won't bother to respond, but at least he's no longer paying attention to my competition.

I wince.

According to Carson, I'm not even a contender.

My shoulders collapse.

Why am I putting myself through this?

I've never been that girl who throws herself at someone who isn't interested. Over the years, I've stood on the sidelines and watched scores of females do that with both my brother and Carson. Actually, most of the guys on the team.

Just as I'm about to shove my phone back into my bag, a message pops up.

Can't. Busy

Yeah, I can just imagine what he'll be occupied with.

Or maybe I should say *whom.*

Ugh.

The only positive in this situation is that the girl parked next to him looks irritated by his lack of attentiveness. Her brows are slanted together as she flips her long hair over her shoulder.

Even though I know I shouldn't...

My fingers swiftly tap out another message.

No worries. I'll just work with Dr. H

I hesitate, recognizing that I shouldn't be playing these games with him. Although, that realization isn't enough to stop me from pressing the send arrow.

I don't have to wait long for a reaction.

Even from this distance, I see the way his jaw clenches. When the girl next to him attempts to recapture his distracted attention by running her hand across his chest, he grabs hold of her wrist and removes it without so much as a glance in her direction. She scowls before rising to her feet and flouncing off in a huff.

Well...at least I don't have to watch them flirt for the rest of lunch.

That's something, right?

I'm busy gloating when a second text pops up on the screen.

Like hell you will

I glance at him from across the space. Everyone is talking and laughing, but he isn't paying attention to their conversation. When Crosby waves a hand in front of his face, he glances up long enough to glower before staring down at his lap.

Guess there's no other choice

I tack on the shrugging emoji.

He plows a hand through his hair before his head falls back and he stares at the ceiling.

His reaction is just so...interesting.

Fine. Library. 6pm

Too loud. Dorm. 7pm

He shakes his head as his lips flatten until they're barely discernible. It's the funniest thing. Am I a terrible person for enjoying this?

Probably.

Anticipation thrums through me as I stare at my phone and wait for a response. I'm not sure why this feels so important—like we've reached a turning point in our relationship—but it does. The longer he goes without responding, the antsier I become, wondering if I've pushed him too far.

Fine

Relief rushes from my lungs as I carefully set the phone next to my plate and smile.

And just like that, everything is looking up again.

Chapter Twenty-Seven

CARSON

I stab the button for the elevator and impatiently wait for the doors to close. This decision already feels like a mistake, but that knowledge isn't enough to stop it from coming to fruition. My foot taps as the two girls in the elevator whisper to each other, all the while sending coy looks at me from beneath their eyelashes. Instead of making eye contact, I keep my attention focused straight ahead. The last thing I want is to get embroiled in a conversation. I know exactly where it'll lead, and I have zero interest in going there.

It's a relief when the elevator stops on the fifth floor and the doors spring open. An explosion of giggles erupts from them as I stride down the hallway, glancing at the name plates hanging next to each office until I find the one I'm looking for. I hesitate and reconsider my actions. If I were thinking clearly, I'd forget about this and get the hell out of here while I still can. Once I rap my knuckles against the heavy wood, there won't be any turning back. No sooner does that thought flit through my head than I raise my hand, knocking on the slightly ajar door.

"Come in," says a deep male voice from the other side. "It's open."

The easy-going cadence of it pisses me off. Once I'm finished with him, he won't sound quite so jovial. This asshole is using his stature at the university to get close to Elle, and I don't like it one damn bit. I've been looking out for her since we were kids. I don't care how old she gets, that's something that will never change.

I push the door wide before stepping over the threshold and into the small space. His gaze locks on mine from where he's parked behind his desk as his head jerks up. Surprise flashes across his face before it's carefully masked.

"Hello." He removes the black-framed glasses perched on the bridge of his nose before leaning back in his chair. "Is there something I can help you with?"

"I'm a friend of—"

"I know who you are," he says, cutting me off.

Good. It'll make everything easier if we don't have to pretend.

He points to the chair opposite of him. "Want to take a seat while we talk?"

I shake my head, unwilling to give up my position of power. Even for a few minutes. "What I have to say won't take long."

His brows rise as he remains silent.

"I'm not sure what you're trying to do, but it needs to stop."

He holds my gaze with steady eye contact. There's not a flicker of guilt within his blue eyes. "I think you have the situation confused. Elle Kendricks is one of my statistics students and nothing more."

I shift my stance. If he thinks he can fool me, he's wrong about that. "So...going out to dinner with your students is a normal occurrence for you?"

There's a moment of silence as we size each other up.

"Upon occasion—yes. I enjoy getting to know the kids in my class on a deeper, more meaningful level."

I almost snort.

Yeah, I'll bet.

"From now on, you need to stay away from her."

"And how am I going to do that? She's one of my students. Us interacting is inevitable."

I tilt my head and narrow my eyes. His calm, I-have-an-answer-for-everything demeanor pisses me off. Maybe Elle can't see through his schtick, but I do.

"You know exactly what I mean. Offering her extra credit to work in your office, grabbing coffee and dinner...you're trying to get her alone, and it needs to stop."

"All I'm trying to do is give her an opportunity to earn more points and lift her grade before the end of the semester. I have absolutely no interest in her other than seeing that she succeeds."

It's tempting to believe him and put a swift end to this uncomfortable conversation, but I've seen the way he stares at her when he thinks no one is looking. Like she's a juicy Big Mac he can't wait to sink his teeth into. Maybe he thinks he can blow smoke up my ass, but it won't work. "From where I stand, it seems like there's more to it than you're willing to admit."

He shrugs. "You would be mistaken."

"I really hope that's the case. The last thing I want to see is her being taken advantage of by someone she trusts to have her best interests at heart."

He folds his arms across the perfectly pressed button-down that stretches across his chest. "Here's the thing you need to remember. Elle is a nineteen-year-old young woman. More than old enough to make her own decisions, don't you think?"

"I do," I say in agreement. "Even though she's a smart girl, she still might not see what a guy like you is up to until it's too late, and I'm not going to allow that to happen." My eyes sharpen. "Correct me if I'm wrong, but aren't there rules against professors fraternizing with their students? I mean, something like that would probably be easy enough to check with the head of your department, or even the chancellor of the university." I throw down that comment like a gauntlet.

He stiffens, the smug expression disappearing from his face. "Are you implying that my relationship with Elle has been in any way inappropriate?" He doesn't give me a chance to respond. "Those are awfully strong accusations."

"You're right, they are." I wrap my fingers around the back of the chair before leaning forward until we're practically eye level. "I'll do whatever it takes to protect that girl from anyone who tries to hurt her. And that includes you, Dr. Holloway. If I catch so much as a whiff of impropriety going on, I have no problem reporting you for misconduct."

His jaw tightens as his nostrils flare. "If you're finished, I think it's time for you to leave."

With a nod, I straighten to my full height. "Just as long as we understand one another."

One side of his mouth curls with disdain. "Oh, I think we understand each other perfectly."

I swing around and call over my shoulder. "You be sure to have a good day, professor."

He remains silent as I close the door behind me.

Chapter Twenty-Eight

ELLE

I carefully assess myself in the full-length mirror to make sure everything is on point.

A sweater that hugs my curves paired with a short skirt—check.

Light application of makeup that doesn't make me look like the kid sister he grew up with—double check.

Hair straightened to an inch of its life, so it falls down my back in a shiny curtain—triple check.

I blow out a steady breath as my hand flutters against my lower abdomen to settle the butterflies currently winging their way to life. The light rap of knuckles against the suite door has them exploding into furious movement.

Instead of allowing the nerves to get the best of me, I swing away from the mirror and stride into the common area. With my fingers wrapped around the handle, I pause for a second and jerk my shoulders as if headed into battle. If I have my way, tonight will change everything between us.

So, you know...no pressure.

I pull open the door and find Carson waiting on the other side of the threshold. As soon as our gazes lock, a sizzle of electricity zips down my spine. It's impossible to imagine experiencing this kind of reaction with anyone else. Maybe it's wrong to push him the way I am, but I need to know how Carson truly feels. I understand what he keeps trying to tell me, but after the other morning in the classroom, I'm almost positive he's lying.

Maybe even to himself.

Tonight is all about unearthing those answers. No matter what they are. If there's not a chance for us, then I want to move on with my life. I can't pine over this guy forever. At least, I hope I don't.

How depressing would that be?

"Hey."

There's a cautious look filling his eyes as his mouth remains a tight slash across his face. The thick tension wafting off him in heavy waves couldn't make it any more obvious that this is the last place he wants to be. I'm not under any illusion that I didn't strong arm him into showing up at my door. I would be lying if I didn't admit there's a tiny part inside me that wants to end this.

Instead, I step aside and allow him in. "Thanks for coming over."

He grunts. "You didn't really give me much choice in the matter, now did you?"

Ouch.

But accurate nonetheless.

I shrug. "There's always a choice."

If it's possible, his lips flatten even more. The guy is definitely pissed off. It only sends my nerves skyrocketing.

He stalks into the suite, making sure to keep as much physical distance between us as possible before beelining toward the square table at the far end of the room. The common area is laid out in the shape of a T with the entryway making up the bottom part of the letter. Kari's bedroom is on the right with a communal bathroom situated across from it. Sierra's room is next to Kari's, and then there's a small living area with a futon, coffee table, chair, and television. My private space, along with Madison's, is at the back of the suite. On the opposite side is a table and small kitchenette with a fridge and microwave. As much as I'm looking forward to moving off campus next year, I've enjoyed living here with my friends.

Just as he drops his bag on the table, I say, "Would you mind if we study in my room?"

His brows snap together as he shakes his head. "Actually, I would. There's no reason—"

The door to the suite crashes open and a bunch of girls pour in, arms filled with takeout bags. Not only is it my roommates but three other friends from the floor. Chatter and laughter fill the space.

Madison is the first to spot us. Her gaze slides from mine to Carson's before she points to the bag in her other hand. "Hey, we just picked up a ton of Chinese. Are you guys hungry?"

We both shake our heads. With the anxiety roiling dangerously inside me, I don't think I could eat a single bite without it making an encore appearance. And that's not really the vibe I'm going for tonight.

"No, we were just about to study, but thanks."

She shrugs as the other girls stare in curiosity. Or maybe I should say they're gawking at Carson. And who can blame them? Even in a navy-colored hoodie and jeans, he looks damn near edible.

"Your loss. I'll save you an eggroll."

I need to get out of here before these girls grow bold and attempt to distract him with conversation. Not wanting that to happen, I grab hold of his hand and tow him to my bedroom before closing the door behind us. Even from the other side of the thick wood, a burst of chatter follows in our wake.

A frown settles on his face as he glances around the small space. "We should have met at the library. There's nowhere to work in here."

I point to the most obvious place—the twin bed shoved up against the wall—and try not to think about the last time he was here. "Right there is fine."

He stares at the mattress for a long moment before shifting his gaze to mine and shaking his head. "Forget it."

I raise a brow and plant a fist on my hip. "What's the problem? Are you afraid you won't be able to control yourself around me?"

His expression darkens as the muscle in his jaw tics. My heartbeat picks up tempo, crashing against my ribcage. I'm afraid he'll swing around and storm out of the room.

And then I'll have my answer, won't I?

One tense second passes and then another.

"Let's just get this over with," he grumbles, stalking to the bed and gingerly taking a seat at one end.

The room is roughly ten by eight feet in size, with just enough space for my bed, a chair, and desk. There's a dresser shoved in the closet. With Carson here, it shrinks around him, making it feel even smaller. Standing over six feet tall, he's all rippling muscle. A shiver works its way through my body. One of my favorite things while growing up was watching him play basketball with Brayden in the driveway. After a couple of games, he'd strip off his T-shirt. It was all too easy to sit on my window seat and watch him for hours.

As far back as I can mentally trip, it's been Carson.

Clearing away those memories, I grab my stats book, notebook, and a pencil from my desk before settling next to him. I'm careful not to sit too close. We get straight to work without any of our normal chitchat to smooth the way. With the thick tension permeating the atmosphere, I don't even try to make conversation. I know it'll be met with reluctant one-worded answers. After about fifteen minutes, his broad shoulders gradually loosen as he explains the answer to a problem.

"What's the heat set at? It's really warm in here," he mumbles, rising to his feet before grabbing the edges of his sweatshirt and yanking it over his head. As he does, the gray T-shirt beneath rides up his stomach, revealing a rock-hard six-pack. My mouth turns cottony, and it takes every ounce of self-control to resist reaching out and stroking my fingers over every sculpted ridge. Instead, I squeeze my hand into a tight ball and focus on the questions we've been painstakingly working our way through.

When he drops down on the mattress for a second time, I scoot closer. Nothing crazy. Just an inch or two until our thighs touch. With our heads bent together over the notebook, he uses his finger to point out where I went wrong. For a moment, I forget about my plans of seduction as my brow furrows, and I squeeze my eyes shut in frustration.

I really, *really* hate statistics.

"Come on, it's not that bad," he chuckles, voice softening. He sounds more like the Carson from weeks ago before I threw myself at him. "You're doing great."

My eyes snap open, only now realizing that I must have muttered my hatred for the subject under my breath. How embarrassing. But then again, that seems to be how everything involving Carson turns out lately.

It's one humiliation after another.

With our faces scant inches apart, his minty breath feathers across my lips and his gaze searches mine as if he's just become aware of our proximity and isn't sure what to do about it. We remain paralyzed, rendered incapable of movement as the moment stretches. Anticipation dances down my spine as sexual tension explodes in the air.

I'm not sure who eats up the distance first. All I know is that I blink, and the warmth of his mouth is ghosting over mine. Barely touching. It feels more like a delicious dream that I don't ever want to wake from. As I sink into the caress, the pressure becomes firmer. A deep, guttural groan escapes from him as he angles his head until we fit together perfectly. The moment his tongue sweeps across the seam of my lips, I open. Sensation explodes within me as he plunges inside, brushing against my own. He tilts his head a bit, realigning his mouth with mine before deepening the caress. Our lips are the only place where we are completely fused together. There's the barest scrape of teeth as the kiss continues to unfold. It doesn't take long to spiral out of control, taking on a life of its own.

Needing to touch him, my hands slip over his shoulders before sliding up his neck and tunneling through his hair. When my nails rake against his scalp, his eyes pop wide as he breaks away and jumps to his feet. He stares in horror before dragging a hand over his face and turning away to pace the cramped room.

"Fuck. Brayden would kill me if he found out about this."

His darkly muttered words have me pointing out, "We've done worse."

Even as the response tumbles from my mouth, I know it's the wrong thing to say.

He swings around to stare as if he can't believe I brought that up. "Yeah, and he would *definitely* kill me for that."

Unable to sit still any longer, I rise to my feet. His expression turns wary as I close the distance between us until we're standing toe to toe. Hesitantly, I place both palms on his chest. The moment I touch him, his muscles stiffen beneath my fingertips.

My gaze stays pinned to his. "What my brother doesn't know won't hurt him."

He snorts, brows lifting. "Are you sure about that?"

"I'm almost twenty years old. He can't control my life forever. One of these days, he'll have to let me grow up." When he doesn't pull away, I rise onto the tips of my toes until my lips can brush across his. "I can have sex with whomever I want."

Thunderclouds erupt across his expression. "It'll be over my dead fucking body that you give yourself to anyone else."

A mixture of joy and relief explodes in my heart.

"I guess that works out perfectly, since you're the only one I want to give myself to."

"Elle..." His voice turns tortured. "You need to stop saying those kinds of things to me."

I blink. "Why?"

"You know why." A groan works its way free from deep within his chest.

"All I know is that I want you." I suck in a steady breath before forcing out the rest. "And I'm pretty sure you want me, to—"

Before the last word can fully escape, his lips capture mine. This time, there is nothing soft or hesitant about the caress. It's forceful and dominant. His tongue delves inside my mouth as his hands wrap around me, dragging me close enough to feel the thickness of his erection digging into my belly. As our tongues tangle, every thought evaporates until all I can focus on is Carson and how good it feels to have him touching me again.

When he finally pulls away, we're both breathing hard. He lowers his face until his forehead can rest against mine. Our gazes stay fastened as if we're both afraid to look away for even a heartbeat.

"Is there anything I can say or do to talk you out of this?" Conflict rages in his voice. In his eyes. In his head.

One side of my mouth quirks. Deep down, he already knows the answer to that question.

"No."

His shoulders sink as he huffs out a breath. "I didn't think so." There's a pause as his voice drops. "I need to think this over, Elle. Brayden is like a brother to me, and the last thing I want to do is hurt him."

It's tempting to push him into giving me an answer. Instead, I remain silent, knowing he has to arrive at this decision on his own. I'd secretly hoped tonight would end like this, but I didn't actually expect it to happen.

"All right."

His mouth swoops in, pressing another quick kiss against my lips. Before I'm able to sink into the caress, he steps away. The loss of his presence and warmth rushes in to fill me.

"Give me a few days."

My fingers drift across my lips as he grabs his sweatshirt from the bed and strides toward the door. When his hand is wrapped around the knob, he glances back one last time before slipping into the common area.

As soon as the suite door clicks into place, I do a little happy dance.

Chapter Twenty-Nine

CARSON

Exhausted from a two-hour practice, I drop my helmet onto the bench as I strip off my jersey and pads. Sweat drips from my forehead as I wipe it away with my forearm. It's been a couple of days since I kissed Elle at her dorm. I've been doing everything possible to keep my distance and get a little perspective before I make a decision that will change everything between us.

Nothing helps.

The more I force myself to stay away, the more she pops into my brain. Not that she's ever far from my thoughts. But I'm no longer able to fool myself into believing that everything is under control.

It's the knowledge that she wants me in the same way I desire her that kills me. It took every ounce of self-control not to take her on the narrow mattress in her room. I've had girls throw themselves at me before and sure, it's always flattering, but with Elle, it meant so much more.

Actually, it meant everything.

Know what another turn-on was?

The way she blurted out her feelings without there being any coy games. She just put it all out there.

All it takes is the memory of her saying she wants me to be her first for my cock to rise to attention.

For the record, that happening in the locker room after practice is no bueno.

I squeeze my eyes tight and try to think about anything but the dark-haired girl. The very same one who's had a starring role in my dreams for too many years to count. This was so much easier when she had no clue that I wanted her. Now she understands the depth of my needs, she's using that knowledge to steadily chip away at all of my defenses.

My eyes pop wide when a heavy hand lands on my shoulder.

Crosby's brows pinch together. "What the fuck is going on with you lately, dude? You're just standing here in the middle of the locker room, spacing out."

"Nothing," I mumble as heat rushes in to fill my cheeks. This is exactly what that girl does to me, and it's becoming a problem. Asher has already figured out my dirty little secret. I don't need anyone else seeing through my lies.

"You sure about that?" He tilts his head as if to study me more closely. "You've been acting weird lately."

I roll my shoulders and scoff, hoping to brush off this whole line of questioning. "What are you talking about? I've totally been myself."

His eyes narrow. "Uh-huh."

Nerves jangle in the pit of my gut as I strip off my sweat-soaked pants and toss them into the laundry bin, only wanting to hit the shower and get the hell out of here.

"I've been working on a theory," Crosby says conversationally, knocking me out of my thoughts just as they circle back to Elle. "Wanna hear it?"

"Sure, I'm all ears." Actually, I don't have the slightest interest in what he has to say. But I've known the guy long enough to realize that the best way to get him off my ass is to let him get it out of his system. If I protest too much or try to shut him down, he'll dig in deeper.

I hook my fingers into my boxers, ready to yank them down my thighs when he says, "I think you've got a thing for little Kendricks."

My fingers curl, biting into the elastic band as my mouth turns bone dry. "What?" It takes effort to keep my voice level as I glance around to make sure no one is paying attention to our conversation.

Especially Brayden.

Luckily, he's busy yapping with Rowan about one of the plays they were running on the field during practice.

When I finally shift my narrowed gaze to Crosby, his lips are curved into a satisfied smirk that scares the hell out of me. "Oh, you heard me the first time, Roberts."

This is un-fucking-believable.

First Asher and now Crosby. And here I'd assumed I was doing a decent job of hiding my feelings. Apparently not. It would seem like everyone and their damn mother knows.

His smile widens as I take a menacing step toward him. "So, I'm right, huh?"

"That's not a topic I'm going to discuss with you." I can't help but look around for a second time. The last thing I need is any of these assholes sticking their nose into my business. Crosby will be a fucking handful as it is.

"Why not?" His brows rise as he cocks his head. "Maybe we should ask Bray what he thinks of his friend having the hots for his little sis. I'm sure that would go over like a lead balloon. Can I watch him beat your ass to a bloody pulp?"

When I bare my teeth and knock into his chest, he straightens to his full height. Crosby and I have become pretty tight over the years, but that won't stop him from giving me shit if he unearths a juicy secret.

"Shut the fuck up," I growl.

Brayden steps between us, shoving me back a step as his surprised gaze bounces back and forth. "What the hell is going on over here?"

The smirk never falters from Crosby's lips. It's tempting to punch the expression right off his face. He has that effect on people. Most of the ladies on campus being the exception to that rule.

When I remain silent, Crosby says, "Nothing. I'm just giving Roberts a little shit."

Brayden rolls his eyes. "Oh yeah, what about?"

"Nothing," I mutter.

Certainly nothing I'm going to tell you about.

When Crosby clears his throat in an attempt to cover his laugh, I gnash my teeth together as my hands tighten at my sides.

"Dude," Brayden says, "you need to chill. You get laid lately? It might take the edge off."

"Yeah," Crosby snickers, wrapping a thin, white towel around his waist. "That's exactly what our man needs." A wicked gleam enters his eyes. "Isn't that right?"

I press my lips together, refusing to answer the question.

"Don't worry about it." Brayden claps me on the shoulder. "We'll get you fixed up this weekend and then you'll be a new man."

Crosby laughs his ass off as he saunters into the shower room.

I can only glare after him.

That guy is really going to get it.

I wind the fuzzy scarf around my neck as Mike and I head out of the theater. The nights have grown colder as the temperature dips lower. As much as I like wearing shorts and T-shirts, sweater weather is my favorite. I enjoy knee-length boots and short skirts paired with cozy sweaters and maybe a knit cap. Let's face it, the fashion choices are endless.

"Look who showed up," Mike says, "it's Mr. tall, hot, and incredibly muscular."

My gaze snaps up before landing on Carson like a heat-seeking missile. Even in the darkness, it's not difficult to find him parked on a bench outside the auditorium. My heartbeat picks up its tempo at the mere sight of him.

I've been a mass of nerves since we last saw each other. He said he needed a few days to mull over the situation, and it felt important to give him that. I had to fight myself not to reach out. Every time I pulled out my phone to call or text, I had to stop myself before slipping it back into my pocket for safekeeping.

When I fail to respond, Mike whispers, "Please tell me he has a brother. Or a cousin. I'm not picky."

Those comments have me blinking out of my thoughts. "No, sorry. He's an only child. And all of his cousins live out of state."

A heavy sigh escapes from him as his shoulders slump. "That's a shame."

The corners of my lips lift, and for that I'm grateful. Already I can tell from the serious expression on Carson's face that I won't like what he has to say. As I force myself to move down the short flight of stairs, he rises to his feet and shoves his hands into the pockets of his jeans.

"Has something happened between you two that I should know about?" Mike's voice drops. "I get the distinct impression that it did. More shocking than that, you didn't tell me about it." He knocks into my shoulder with his own. "Bitch."

I glance at him and shake my head. "No." All right, so maybe that's a teeny tiny lie.

"Hmmm." His eyes narrow as he contemplates me. "Why don't I believe you? You're both wearing similarly strained expressions. And just in case you're wondering—you two look miserable."

His observation only confirms my previous suspicions as to how this conversation will go.

Normally, whenever I catch sight of Carson, I gravitate toward him like a flower seeking out sunlight. This is the first time I have to physi-cally prod myself to close the gaping distance between us.

"Hi." It takes effort to keep all of the rioting emotion that's attempting to claw its way to the surface tamped down where it belongs. Upon closer inspection, his eyes are hooded and there's a tightness to his expression that only reinforces the knowledge that this won't be a pleasant conversation. This is not the easy-going Carson I grew up with. Now that I think about it, he hasn't been that person for a while.

"Hey." His gaze flickers to Mike, who remains steadfast at my side. Recognition sets in and he gives him a chin lift in greeting.

Mike beams. "Congrats on the season so far. There's no way you guys won't make it to the championship."

Carson's lips tug into a tight smile. "That's the plan."

His attention returns to me, where it settles. "Do you have a moment to talk?"

As much as I want to shake my head, I don't. There's no point in prolonging the inevitable. "Sure."

We glance at Mike, who straightens as if only now realizing he's the odd man out. "I guess that would be my cue to leave."

I pull him in for a quick hug before he can retreat into the darkness. "I'll see you tomorrow, okay?"

His arms tighten around me, and he presses his lips against the side of my face. "Call me later if you need anything."

My heart sinks with the realization that I'll probably need a shoulder to cry on. After we break apart, Mike gives us one last wave before taking off.

It's only when he rounds the corner of the building and disappears from sight that Carson says, "How about I drive you home and then we can talk?"

A knot forms in the pit of my gut as I nod.

A suffocating silence falls over us as we walk side by side through the parking lot to his shiny black Tahoe. The truck is decked out with all of the bells and whistles. It was a high school graduation present from his parents.

With every step that brings us closer to the vehicle, my anxiety ratchets up even higher. Did I think there was a distinct possibility that he would turn me down?

Of course.

But after the way he kissed me the other night, I'd thought the odds were tipped in my favor. I'd thought that maybe—just maybe—I might be worth taking a risk on.

Foolish, I know. He and my brother have been friends for a long time.

Once we reach the SUV, Carson clicks the locks before silently opening the passenger side door. The longer this unease stretches between us, the more my nerves lengthen until it becomes excruciating. I grip my bag as if it's a lifeline and slide onto the leather seat.

For a second, our gazes lock and hold. He pauses and my breath catches as a sizzle of awareness shoots through me, lighting up every nerve ending in its path. My heart beats into overdrive as I wonder if he'll close the distance and kiss me. Just as my body strains toward him, he closes the door, trapping me inside the vehicle. Air rushes from my lungs as all of the hope swirling inside me evaporates. I can't help but wonder if anyone else will ever make me feel as alive as Carson does.

There is nothing more depressing than longing for someone who doesn't return the sentiment. Or isn't willing to overcome the obstacles standing in your way. My shoulders collapse under the heavy weight of that knowledge.

I'm so lost in the tangle of my own thoughts that I don't realize he's settled on the seat next to me and has turned on the engine until we're pulling out of the lot and swinging onto the tree-lined street that wraps around campus and ultimately leads to Sutton Hall.

He keeps his attention focused on the road beyond the windshield. There are a thousand words perched on the tip of my tongue, but none of them fall from my lips. It takes a handful of minutes until he's pulling to the curb in front of the dorm. Only then does he put the truck into park and swivel toward me.

A rush of air gets clogged at the back of my throat as nerves explode inside the confines of my belly. Even though I'm fairly certain how this conversation will end, I can't help but hold out a sliver of hope that I'm wrong. I've never wanted anyone the way I want Carson.

I just wish he felt the same way.

"I don't know what else to say other than I'm sorry. I never meant for this situation to spiral so far out of control. If I could take it all back—everything that happened between us —so that our relationship could return to normal, I would."

His words slice into my heart, cleaving it in half. The pain is enough to leave me doubling over.

How can he say that?

Doesn't he realize these feelings have been brewing beneath the surface for years?

"No." I shake my head, refusing to accept this outcome. Or, at the very least, I need to fight for what I want.

I need to fight for *him*.

"No?" His brows draw together as if he's uncertain what to make of my response.

"Whatever this is, it's been festering between us for years. It was only a matter of time before it came to a head." Hot emotion stings the backs of my eyes. "You have to feel it, too."

He glances away. "It doesn't matter what I feel. Nothing more can happen between us."

"Carson." It's only when his gaze slices to mine that I say, "Why are you so insistent on stomping this out?"

A potent concoction of regret and anger flashes across his face and fills his voice. "We've already been over this. I don't understand why we have to rehash it again. It won't change anything."

"Brayden." The corners of my lips twist in irritation.

"We both know he'd go off the deep end if he found out I laid a finger on you."

When I fail to respond, he continues. "As much as I want you," there's a pause as his jaw locks and he reluctantly admits, "I can't break his trust more than I already have."

I release the burst of air wedged in my lungs. Even though I'd hoped my brother wouldn't stand in the way of this relationship flourishing into something more—something I've always longed for—deep down, I knew it would end this way. They've been friends for more than a decade. But still, I can't help but feel hurt that Carson is choosing my brother over me.

I twist on my seat, wanting him to see reason. The more I try to pull him closer, the further I end up pushing him away. "Exactly how does us being together impact my brother? How does it hurt him?"

He blinks before plowing a hand through his blond hair. It's so tempting to smooth down the thick strands. Instead, I keep my hands locked in my lap.

"Brayden has always been a good friend. Probably the best one I've ever had. No matter what, he's been there for me. The only thing he's ever asked is that I don't mess with you. Even though I knew better, I did it anyway."

My throat closes up, making it impossible to suck in full breaths.

"He'd fucking kill me if he ever found out, and you know what? I wouldn't blame him for it. So, no...this can't happen. I won't hurt him any more than I already have."

The conviction of his words turns his features to granite, making him appear even more resolute than when I stepped into his truck. Unconsciously, I lift my hand to rub at the delicate flesh over my heart. His words feel like a dagger piercing the center of it.

I shouldn't push out the next question when he's already given me a definitive answer, but I find myself unable to contain it. "Is there anything I can say that will change your mind?"

An uncomfortable silence ensues, turning the air oppressive.

"No, there isn't."

My teeth sink into my lower lip until it becomes painful. I'll admit part of me is tempted to argue but ultimately, what good will it do?

I can't force him to be with me if he doesn't want to.

My fingers wrap around the door handle. "You know what sucks most? That I waited all these years to be with you because I thought, in the end, you'd be worth it. Turns out I was wrong."

His eyes widen, but he remains stoically silent.

I grab my bag before pulling open the door and slipping from the truck. Once my feet are on the sidewalk, I straighten my clothing and lift my chin before walking to the entrance of Sutton Hall. Not once do I turn to look at him. The tears pricking my eyes slide down my cheeks as I leave Carson where he belongs.

In the past.

Chapter Thirty-One

CARSON

God fucking dammit!

I stare after her as she slips inside the brick building and disappears from sight before slamming my palms against the leather steering wheel. A hiss of breath escapes as pain ricochets throughout my hands.

Was I worried that Elle would put up more of a fight and make the situation even more difficult to deal with?

Yup.

It's a relief that she accepted the outcome and didn't try to change my mind. I'm not sure how much prodding it would have taken to push me right over the edge. It already feels like I'm walking a tightrope. One wrong move and I'll plummet to my death. Or straight into her waiting arms, as the case might be.

I keep trying to convince myself that this is what's best for everyone involved. But, if that's the case, why is every cell in my body screaming for me to take off after her and beg forgiveness? Already I know the hurt that had filled her dark eyes will haunt me for the rest of my life. Elle is the last person I'd want to inflict pain and yet, that's exactly what I did.

I drag a hand down my face, wishing there were a way this could end differently.

Now that I know she's safely inside the building, there's no reason for me to sit here idling in my truck. I need to leave before I do something stupid. Something I'll end up regretting in the not-so-distant future. Something that will end up getting my ass kicked by the guy I've always considered to be my closest friend. And yet, I can't shift the gear into drive and pull away from the curb. I can't do anything other than stare at the last place I saw her before she disappeared from sight.

Start the truck, asshole.

Leave right now.

She's not even here to wear me down, and I'm crumbling like a cheap house of cards.

A decision has already been made, and I'm wavering. Rethinking everything that was said. Before I can talk myself out of this shit idea, I'm slamming out of the Tahoe and stalking up the walkway that leads to the front entrance. Just as I arrive at the set of glass doors, a couple exits the building. As soon as they walk past, too lost in their conversation to notice me loitering in the vicinity, I spring forward and grab the metal edge with the tips of my fingers before slipping inside and beelining to the stairwell. Maybe by the time I reach her floor, I'll have miraculously come to my senses. I can turn around before blowing up my friendship with Brayden.

That, unfortunately, doesn't occur. Not once do I reconsider my actions. By the time I reach her floor, I'm more resolved than ever. The idea of walking away from Elle is unbearable. I can't do it.

Once at her suite, I rap my knuckles on the thick wood and shift my weight impatiently from one foot to another. Just as I lift my hand to knock again, the door swings open and one of Elle's roommates fills the space. She stares at me curiously from the other side of the threshold.

"Oh, hi." She tilts her head, sizing me up. "You're here for Elle?"

Even though the words are arranged in the format of a question, we both know it's more of a statement. I jerk my head in response. "Is she here?"

For a moment, her forehead furrows and I wonder if she'll allow me inside or tell me to get fucked before slamming the door in my face.

My muscles tighten, ready to spring forward and plead my case if that's what it takes to gain entrance.

A moment of silent debate plays out across her face before she huffs out a resigned sigh and moves aside. "Come in."

My shoulders loosen as I step into the cramped entryway. "Thanks."

The girl with the pixie cut points toward the back of the suite. "She's in her room."

"Thanks." I don't get more than two steps when her hesitant voice halts me in my tracks.

"Carson?"

I swing around and meet her gaze in silent question.

"Don't hurt her. Elle doesn't deserve that."

Her words hit me like a punch to the gut, knocking the air from my lungs, making it impossible to suck in a full breath. Even if I could respond, I have no idea what to say. The last thing I want is to cause her pain, but part of me wonders if it can end any other way.

With my lips pressed together, I jerk my head into a nod and turn back around. Not wanting to get ambushed by any of her other room-mates, I keep my gaze focused straight ahead. Once I reach the door to her bedroom, I don't bother knocking. After the way our conversation ended, I'm not going to give her an opportunity to turn me away. I twist the handle and slip inside before closing it softly and leaning against the wood.

A gasp escapes from Elle as she swings around and meets my gaze. "What are you doing here?"

Surprise flashes across her face as she stands motionless in nothing more than a pale pink bra and matching panties. The clothing she'd been wearing earlier has been shed, piled loosely on the chair near the window.

"This."

I shove away from the door before eating up the distance between us. It only takes two long-legged strides until I'm within striking distance and able to nab her wrist before tugging her into my arms.

Her eyes flare as the soft curves of her breasts are crushed against my chest and my mouth crashes onto hers. Unlike the previous times we've kissed, she doesn't immediately grant me access. Instead, she keeps her lips pressed firmly together.

Does she really think that will keep me from taking what I want?

What I know she wants to give?

What's mine?

Or has she already changed her mind in the time it took for her to leave my truck and arrive at her room?

The knowledge that I might have actually let her slip through my fingers sends my heart into freefall. That's not something I'm willing to contemplate.

A growl rumbles up from deep within my throat as I pull away just a fraction. "Open for me." A stubborn light enters her eyes as she presses them together. Unwilling to let this end here, I nip at her lower lip. It's not enough to inflict damage, only to get her attention. I've already spent way too much time denying myself the feel and taste of her.

I'm over that.

She pushed and prodded, tempting me to lose control. Now Elle has what she's been asking for all along. She'd better figure out fast what she's going to do with my undivided attention.

When she sucks in a sharp breath, my tongue slips inside her mouth to mingle with her velvety soft one. For a heartbeat, her muscles tense. Just when I think she'll protest, her body turns pliant. Only then am I able to relax and slow things down. To tease her until she's as needy for me as I am for her. For the first time in my life, all of the pretenses have fallen away. I'm no longer strong enough to hold them in place.

I want to devour her one breath at a time until I've consumed every single part of her, and even then, it could never satiate the deep well of need I have for this girl.

By the time I pull away, we're both breathing hard.

"You're mine now. I've spent years fighting against the attraction I felt for you, but I refuse to do it any longer. For better or worse, this is happening. Do you understand?"

"I do."

With that, I take her mouth in a searing kiss.

In this moment, Brayden is the furthest thing from my mind, and that's exactly the way it needs to stay.

Chapter Thirty-Two

ELLE

Bright sunlight slants across my face as my eyelids flutter open. It takes more than one attempt to fully awaken. As I shift against the cottony sheets and stretch, my leg bumps into something hard.

What the—

My head swivels and my gaze lands on Carson, who sleeps soundly beside me.

I...

Oh.

How could I have forgotten—even in slumber—the way he barged into my room yesterday evening and yanked me into his arms, kissing me until I wanted to melt into a puddle of wax at his feet? My fingers drift to my lips in silent confirmation before feathering over them. They're still swollen from the ardent attention he showered on me. It's as if now that the flood gates have been opened, there's no way to slow the spigot. Not that I'd want to. We spent most of the night making out before eventually falling asleep in each other's arms during the wee hours of the morning.

Have I ever been kissed quite so thoroughly?

What am I saying?

Of course I haven't.

I fill my lungs with air and squeeze my eyelids tightly closed, reliving every delicious moment we spent together. We didn't do anything more than kiss and cuddle, but it had been amazing. Better than anything my fantasies could have conjured up.

"Morning," a deep voice growls, breaking into the whirl of my thoughts.

My eyelids fly open, only to find Carson's head turned, gaze locked on mine. That's all it takes for need to spark to life deep inside my core. He looks sleepy and delightfully disheveled. It's tempting to run my fingers through his hair.

I've become so used to resisting the urge that it takes a moment to realize I no longer have to hold myself in check. Almost hesitantly, I reach out and brush the thick strands away from his eyes. Instead of drawing away, my fingers glide over his sculpted cheekbone before drifting across a strong jaw and shadowed chin. The entire time I touch him, learning his features, his gaze stays pinned to mine.

My attention drops to his lips as I stroke my forefinger over the pillowy softness. His lower one is full and generous. A groan rumbles up from him as his teeth close around my finger before gently biting down. My surprised gaze snaps to his, and my breath catches at the dark look swirling through his eyes.

Before I can decide on my next move, he pounces, and I find myself flat on my back with a heated-up looking Carson looming over me. His hard body is stretched out on top of mine. His forearms press into the mattress next to my shoulders, effectively caging me in. Not that escape is even a thought in my head. His thick erection is nestled against the juncture between my thighs. All that separates us is a thin scrap of panties and the cotton of his boxers. My heartbeat thumps against my ribcage, echoing hollowly in my ears.

He watches me closely as he thrusts against my core. The gentle rocking motion sends a thousand shivers cascading through my body, lighting me up from the inside out.

"Are there any regrets swimming around behind those dark eyes?"

Regrets?

I shake my head. "Not a single one."

He flexes his hips and pleasure continues to build inside me. "Good."

I gasp as need dampens my panties.

"You have no idea how much I want you. How much I've always wanted you. Now that you've unleashed the beast, there's no way to rein him back in again. He's out there, Elle."

My hands drift to the sides of his face, cupping each scruffy cheek in my palms. "I wouldn't have it any other way. You're the only one I've ever wanted. Don't you realize it's always been you?"

A softness enters his eyes, overtaking the heat of the moment.

Not in a million years did I ever think that Carson Roberts would look at me like I'm the only girl on the face of the planet. It almost feels too good to be true. I'm afraid the alarm on my phone will go off and I'll wake with a start before realizing this was nothing more than a sexy dream.

The need to prove this is really happening thrums through me as I pull his face to mine. He braces himself on his elbows as his tongue dances across my lips. A whimper escapes as he continues to tease. Round and round his tongue licks, edging my mouth until I want to scream as need builds inside me.

"Do you like that?"

Barely am I able to groan out a response.

"Give me your tongue," he demands.

Almost hesitantly, it peeks out from between my lips. Instead of drawing it into his mouth, he licks at me. His head slants one way before angling the other, driving me to distraction, stroking and caressing my flesh until I'm on the verge of exploding. Just when I don't think I can stand another moment, he draws my tongue into his mouth until our lips are fused together. It takes a moment to realize that his cock is thrusting against me, mimicking the steady rhythm of his tongue.

By now, my panties are completely soaked as his boner presses insistently against the cotton, sinking no more than an inch inside my body. I can't help but squirm as he pins me to the mattress.

"Mmmm," he groans. "You feel so damn good."

Tiny fireworks explode deep within my womb. There's too much pleasure rushing through my veins, suffusing every cell to wrap my mind around one coherent thought.

I can't imagine anything feeling better than the press of his hard body against mine, taking me to places I've only—

A startled gasp escapes from me as his heavy weight disappears and he rolls onto the sliver of mattress next to me before throwing one brawny arm over his eyes. His breath is short and choppy, as if it's a struggle to maintain control over himself.

He groans when I shift against his nearly naked body. Every nerve ending feels like it's on fire from the way he was touching me moments ago. Even though he hadn't been buried deep inside me, I'd been so close to coming. A few more strokes and I would have shattered around him.

Sexual tension crackles in the air, turning the atmosphere explosive. I'm so turned on that it's painful.

"Carson," I whisper. "Why did you stop?"

With a huff of breath, he lifts his arm from his face before rolling toward me and smacking a kiss against my lips. "As much as I need you, I don't want your first time to be like this. Nothing more than a rush when we're barely awake. I want to take my time and enjoy this. Enjoy you. Okay?"

I squirm, my clit throbbing as if it has a life of its own. The only thing I'm able to focus on is getting a little bit of relief any way I can. I don't want to be left hanging. Not like this. "I don't care about that. I need you. *Now*." I emphasize the last word, hoping he understands that he's the one who stoked the fire raging inside me to a veritable inferno. Now he needs to do something about it.

One side of his mouth quirks as his hazel eyes flare with humor. "Aww, is my poor baby frustrated?"

I pout. "It's not funny. You ramped me up. Now you're just going to leave me high and dry?"

The warmth of his large palm skates over the curve of my hip before cupping my panty-covered pussy and squeezing. "That's funny. You don't feel so dry to me."

A moan escapes before I can stop it as my hips lift, attempting to get closer.

He rubs gentle circles over my center as his voice sharpens, becoming so low that it claws at my insides. "Fuck, you're so wet."

Closing the distance between us, he brushes a kiss against my mouth before drawing my lower lip between his teeth and biting down on it. The pulse between my legs becomes more insistent until it echoes in my ears.

Once he releases the plump flesh, he murmurs, "I love that you saved yourself for me and that my cock will be the only one you've ever had."

Oh god...

"Please..." Even though the firm pressure of his fingers is a constant presence, it's not enough to send me careening over the edge. It's like he's deliberately holding back. Only giving me enough to stoke the flames of my desire but nothing more.

"Do you want to come?" His warm breath ghosts over the outer shell of my ear.

My breathing kicks up a notch as my eyes roll back in my head. "You know I do."

"Then take your panties off."

He doesn't have to tell me twice. My fingers tremble as they slip beneath the elastic band, shoving the material over my hips and down my thighs before kicking it off. His hand is no longer stroking over me, and I want it back.

Desperately.

I'm almost to the point of begging.

"Take off the bra, too. I want you spread out before me like a goddamn feast."

I blink, bowing my back so my hands can slip around my ribcage before fumbling with the clasp. Just as I grow impatient, the pale pink fabric springs apart and I'm able to pull the straps from my arms and toss it to the floor.

Bright sunlight pours through the unadorned window, spilling over me as I lie perfectly still against the mattress. A potent concoction of nerves, adrenaline, and desire rushes through my veins, flooding every cell in my body with painful awareness. Carson remains stretched out beside me. His head is propped up on one arm as his heated gaze takes a leisurely tour of my body, licking over every inch on display. I can almost feel his laser focus as it singes me alive.

"You're so fucking beautiful." His gaze flicks to mine. "And now you belong to me."

The possessive sentiment has warmth blooming in my chest before spreading outward until it reaches my fingertips and toes. I've been waiting my entire life for him to say that.

With his other hand, he strokes over one breast before wrapping his fingers around the taut peak and giving it a gentle tweak. There's a strange mixture of pain-infused pleasure that arrows through me before exploding in my core. I gasp as he gives the same attention to the other side. His fingers glide down my body to the part of me that throbs with painful awareness.

"Do you like touching yourself?"

My gaze slices to his before widening. "What?"

He smirks. "I want to know if you enjoy masturbating."

A rush of heat floods into my cheeks, making them feel like they're on fire. "I..."

Have no idea how to answer that.

Are we really having this conversation?

Now?

His fingers stroke over the lips of my pussy, rimming the edges until I'm twisting beneath him. The more pleasure that unfurls inside me, the more difficult it becomes to focus on what he's saying.

"It's a yes or no question. You either do...or you don't."

Just when I think I can't stand another moment of this sweet torture, one finger dips inside my heat. He doesn't thrust all the way in. Just an inch or two. Just enough for my muscles to contract around him.

"Mmmm," he growls. "I felt that. You're so damn tight."

I clench again, attempting to lock him inside me. This feeling is much too delicious to end.

"Tell me, Elle. I want to know exactly what you do when you're alone in bed at night."

His thick digit continues to tease my pussy, forcing me to the precipice before yanking me back so I don't crash over the edge. Frustration spirals through me until I want to scream.

"Yes," I choke out as my hips gyrate, matching the excruciating rhythm he's set. "Okay? Yes."

"How often?" he asks, voice dropping.

Arrgghhh!

"I don't know...a few times a week?" I continue to shift, silently begging him to send me over the edge and into oblivion. I just want—

"Look at me," he growls.

I turn my head until my dazed vision can lock on him.

"Do you think about me when you stroke this pretty little pussy?"

"Carson," I groan, embarrassment swamping me.

He presses closer until his lips are able to hover over one nipple. His warm breath sends a cascade of shivers rampaging across my flesh before he sucks the taut bud into his mouth. My back arches off the bed as my fingers tunnel through his thick hair to keep him in place.

It doesn't work.

Instead, he releases me. His attention once again locks on mine before he repeats the question. "Do you fantasize about me when you touch yourself?"

When I remain silent, his fingers still over my heat, the heel of his palm pressing into my soft flesh. A gentle reminder that he's there, holding me but nothing more. And no amount of grinding against him is enough to give me the satisfaction I so desperately crave.

"All you have to do is answer the question."

"Yes," I blurt. "Every. Single. Time."

His lips curve into a slow smile as heat floods into his eyes. "Better only be me, baby, or we're gonna have a problem."

Before I can say anything more, he's sliding between my thighs and spreading them wide. With his thumbs, he stretches me until every delicate inch is on display. Embarrassment surges through me as I try to close my legs, but he won't allow it.

"I want to look at you."

A groan slides from me as my face heats. I've never had anyone stare at me so openly. It's as if he's committing every part to memory. Even when he made me orgasm a few weeks ago, my panties and skirt had been in place. He'd only pulled them down enough to bear my clit. This is totally different. I couldn't be stretched any further. And with his hands holding my thighs wide, there's nothing I can do about it.

"You're so fucking gorgeous," he whispers, reaching out to stroke his fingers across my lips. "Just remember that you gave yourself to me and now this pussy is mine." His gaze flicks upward, daring me to argue. The possessiveness shining from his hazel depths is enough to turn my mouth bone dry. "Do you understand?"

"Yes."

All I've ever wanted was to belong to him.

"Good."

He leans forward until his warm breath can skate over my shuddering flesh. With his tongue, he takes a leisurely lap, licking me from the bottom of my slit to where my clit is buried. Pleasure cascades through me as he slows things down and repeats the maneuver. His fingers dig into the soft skin of my thighs as he holds them open. Only now, I have no desire to close them. My back arches, offering him everything. He wanted me laid out like a feast before him and I am. With lazy strokes, he circles my clit before stabbing the velvety softness of his tongue deep inside my heat.

As amazing as the first time he touched me was, it's nothing compared to the pleasure he's now evoking. It feels as if I've died and gone to heaven.

I don't realize my eyes have feathered closed until they're flying open as the warmth of his breath disappears. I stare at Carson in question as he rises above me, closing the distance between us. A second later, his lips are aligned with my own and he's thrusting his tongue inside my mouth.

"Do you taste your sweetness on me?" he whispers. "So fucking delicious. How will I ever get enough of you?"

A whimper breaks free. It's the only response I'm capable of giving.

He pushes away to kneel between my spread thighs. His fingers wrap around my hand before drawing it between my legs and placing it over my core. The haze filling my vision clears as I stare at him in confusion.

"I want to watch you touch yourself."

My mouth falls open.

No. He can't possibly—

"Show me how you stroke that sweet little pussy of yours when you're all alone and thinking about me."

Oh god.

Just as I'm about to shake my head and deny the request, he yanks his boxers down until his thick length springs free. My gaze stays riveted to the sight as he fists his erection.

Holy crap.

He's so big and hard.

Need explodes inside me like a firework as I eat him up with my eyes. I don't realize that my fingers are moving, circling my own damp flesh until he groans and begins to pump his cock in tandem with my movements. Moisture beads the tip. I'm so enamored by the sight that looking away feels impossible. For years, I've fantasized about what it would feel like to be with Carson, but nothing compares to the reality.

"That's it, baby. Stroke all that softness for me."

His low voice strums something deep within that I had no idea was lurking beneath the surface, just waiting to break free. Wanting to please him, my fingers dip inside my heat before circling my clit. The little bundle of nerves throbs a steady beat until I'm to the point of shattering into a million jagged pieces. As tempting as it is to close my eyes, I don't. I've never seen anything hotter than Carson fisting his hard dick. As he pumps it slowly, his erection becomes even thicker. He cants his hips, thrusting himself forward as the swollen head turns a deeper shade of purple. Moisture continues to bead the tip, leaking from him.

The longer I stare, the more arousal spikes through me, propelling me higher and higher into the stratosphere. It barely takes a few flicks of my fingers and I'm splintering apart, falling to pieces beneath his steady gaze. My spine arches as I widen my legs, spreading them until my knees are pressed against the sheets. His name falls from my lips as wave after wave of pleasure crashes over me, pummeling my senses, threatening to drag me to the very bottom of the ocean. My heart pounds a painful staccato against my ribcage before echoing in my ears.

As soon as the first moan slides from me, a hot spurt of cum splashes across my lower abdomen, decorating the pale skin. His head is tipped back, the column of his throat on display as his body shudders with release. The way his grip tightens around his cock, pumping it forcefully, sends another little spasm of pleasure spiraling through me.

Only when every last drop has been wrung from my body do I sink bonelessly into the mattress. With a huff, his muscles loosen, and he releases his softening erection.

A satisfied smirk curves his lips. "And that is exactly how you start the day."

Barely can I muster a chuckle as he takes me in his arms, and we float back off to sleep.

Chapter Thirty-Three

CARSON

I t's Saturday night, and the first floor of the house is jampacked with people. I lift the bottle of water to my lips and take a swig as my gaze coasts over the sea of partiers, looking for one girl in particular, but she continues to remain elusive. Elle had a performance earlier tonight and promised to make an appearance as soon as it ended. Impatience bubbles up inside me as I check my phone for the umpteenth time.

It's almost eleven o'clock.

She should be here by now.

Even though I spent last night in her bed with my arms wrapped around her body, it's not enough. She's like an addiction pumping wildly through my veins. I've spent years trying to beat back my lust and pretend it didn't exist. Now that I've finally given in and had a taste, there's no going back.

We've been stealing time together whenever we can, but it's not easy. I live with a houseful of dudes, including her brother, and she lives with three girls in a suite with very little privacy. She sneaks me in after everyone has gone to bed and then I'm out the door before they wake. Even though I hate secrets, we've decided to keep this on the downlow for the time being until we figure out exactly what it is.

I startle to awareness when someone claps me on the shoulder.

"What are you doing, standing around all by your lonesome? It's a party, man. We won this afternoon. Victory is ours! That means it's time to celebrate!" Brayden's voice booms over the music.

My gaze shifts to his girlfriend, who's tucked beneath his arm. They haven't been a couple for long, but already it's impossible to imagine Brayden without her. They complete each other in a fundamental way.

I hate the hot rush of jealousy that careens through my veins. That's exactly the kind of relationship I want. One where I can walk around out in the open with my arm draped over Elle's shoulders. Right now, I can't do that. Hell, I have no idea when that will be possible.

I shrug. It's not like I can tell him the truth—that I'm waiting for his sister to show up. Instead of heaping yet another lie onto the growing pile, I remain silent. It's just easier this way.

Brayden shakes his head as if he doesn't understand what the hell is going on with me. Thank fuck for that. We'd have real problems if he did.

"When the hell did you become such a moody bitch?"

Sydney elbows him sharply in the ribs. He flinches before chuckling. "What? That's exactly the way he's acting. I'm just calling it like I see it."

She rolls her eyes before her gaze settles on mine. A knowing look fills her green depths. It's one that leaves me shifting uneasily beneath her penetrating stare. I get the feeling she sees way more than I'm comfortable acknowledging. I loosen my shoulders and attempt to shake off the odd sensation. Crosby and Asher have already figured me out. I don't need anyone else—especially Brayden's girlfriend—getting clued in to what's going on.

Hopefully, this is nothing more than a bout of paranoia on my part. This is exactly what secrets will do to you.

I clear my throat. "It was a tight game this afternoon. We're too close to the playoffs to have that happen again."

Any curiosity filling his expression drains away. "You're right about that. There were too many little mistakes that could have ended up costing us big time. We got lucky."

"Luck doesn't win championships." Thank fuck I've managed to steer the conversation in a different direction. Even if it is to what happened earlier today on the field.

You better believe Coach ripped us a new one in the locker room after the game. Most of us won't be sitting for a few days because of it. And just so we know he's serious, he scheduled a mandatory practice for the butt crack of dawn tomorrow, when we would normally have Sunday off. So yeah...

Sucks to be us.

I glance around and notice a few of my younger teammates knocking back bottles of beer. I almost shake my head. They'll pay for their stupidity when we're running suicides before the sun has fully risen in the sky.

Tonight, I'm like Cinderella. I'll be out of here by midnight so my head can hit the pillow and I can get a good night's sleep.

My attention gets snagged by Brayden as he raises his hand in a wave. Even before I swing around and glance in that direction, I know who I'll find. A gut level sensation has taken up residence deep inside me, indicating that Elle has finally walked through the door.

Wanting to play it cool, I tamp down my growing excitement and take another pull from my bottle. I've spent years pretending this girl is nothing more than my best friend's sister. Now that she's discovered the truth and forced me to acknowledge my own feelings in the process, it's become increasingly more difficult to act indifferent where she's concerned.

Although there's something to be said for having a secret. It's fun to tease her, all the while driving her crazy. Not to mention making myself just as nuts in the process. I love grazing the soft flesh of her inner thigh beneath the table when we're studying at the library. Or rubbing delicate circles against her palm when no one is paying attention. Heat will flood her eyes, and it's all I can do to set her free when I'd rather sink inside her warmth.

By the time I meet her dark gaze, she's pushed her way through the crowd and has sidled up beside her brother. With a smile, she reaches out and pulls Sydney in for a quick hug. That's one of the things I like about Elle. She's affectionate. There was a time when I didn't think there was a snowball's chance in hell for us to have a future and lived for those fleeting touches. Now, I'm greedy for them all.

"How was the play, squirt?"

I wince.

That's always been Brayden's pet name for his sister.

Her gaze flickers in my direction before returning to the couple. "Fantastic. It went off without a hitch."

"Good," he says with a nod. "Did you just finish up?"

"Yup. Someone was having another cast party, but I wanted to come here and celebrate with you guys. Congrats again on the win. It was a great game."

"Thanks. It might have been by the skin of our teeth, but we'll take it."

"You were great, Bray." Warmth gathers in my chest when her gaze settles on me. "You, too."

"Thanks."

Knowing she was in the stands this afternoon was all the incentive I needed to make sure I was playing to the best of my ability. I was everywhere on that field. Creating holes in the defense and protecting my QB during passing plays.

Do you really think I was going to allow the other team to show me up in front of my girl?

No fucking way.

The four of us spend a few minutes shooting the shit before Elle takes off to use the bathroom. With one last look thrown over her shoulder, she disappears through the crowd. It takes every ounce of self-restraint to keep my ass firmly in place and not shadow her every movement. I hate the idea of her being off on her own at a party. Most of the guys here are football players and know to stay away from her unless they want to feel the wrath of Brayden come down on them.

And trust me, no one wants that. Especially if he decides to take it out on your ass on the field.

When my attention returns to the couple, I find Sydney watching me with a speculative look in her eyes.

Fuck.

I clear my throat and bring up the bowl game we'll be playing in.

Once enough time has ticked by, I drain my bottle of water and make up an excuse about the need to stay hydrated.

Before either of them can respond, I take off, searching the thick sea of people for Elle's dark head. Need spikes through my veins, spurring me on. The more time that passes, the antsier I get to find her. This need rampaging through my system feels more like a living, breathing entity. Every day that passes has it growing stronger as it continues to multiply.

As soon as I catch sight of her, relief washes over me and I change direction, beelining for her. There's a smile on her face as she chats with Easton, Sasha, Rowan, Demi, and Asher. The guys in this house have always looked out for Elle as if she were their own sister. I'd trust her with any of them.

As I pass by, I tug on her fingers to get her attention. There's a moment of eye contact as I make my way to Asher's bedroom. More often than not, the guy leaves it unlocked. A simple twist of the handle has the door springing open. I step inside and wait for her to show up. When the door creaks, I tug her inside before slamming it shut and jerking her to me. Her eyes widen as she lands against my chest with a gasp.

"Missed you," I growl seconds before my lips crash into hers.

That's all it takes for her to open and my tongue to delve inside her mouth. Her arms twine around my neck to hold me close. It's the sweet taste of her that calms the beast rampaging dangerously beneath my skin. I adjust my stance and angle my head a different way in order to claim more. The whimper that escapes from her only ratchets up my own desire. It feels like I'm on fire and nothing will ever douse the flames.

It's as frightening as it is exhilarating.

All of the emotion swirling inside me has been lying dormant beneath the surface, just waiting for the opportunity to flare to life. And now that it has, there's no tamping it down or pretending it doesn't exist.

It's only after we surface for air that we break apart.

"I missed you, too," she whispers.

"The play went well? You had a good night?"

Even in the shadowy darkness of the room, it would be impossible not to notice how her face lights up or the excitement that threads its way through her voice. "It was one of the best performances we've given. Everyone hit their marks and it went off without a hitch."

Just listening to her talk brings a smile to my face. "I'm glad."

"Me, too. I'll be sad when it's over. We've had such a great time. All the rehearsals, running lines late into the night, and the shows..." Her voice trails off.

Wanting to take her mind off the production and its inevitable end, I angle my head and press my lips against hers. Elle's parents got her into a community acting class when she was in third grade, and she fell instantly in love with it. There's never been another sport or activity that she's felt this passionate about. When we were younger, I secretly enjoyed helping her run lines and watching her slip effortlessly into character.

As we break apart for a second time, I rest my forehead against hers. We're so close that her soft inhalations become my own and vice versa. It's intoxicating.

"Are you going to sleep at my place tonight?"

As much as I want to...

I shake my head. "Not with the early morning practice Coach mandated."

"Okay. Then maybe I should sleep here." Her brows rise as hope dances in her eyes.

"Hell, no. Can you imagine your brother barging in on us by accident? I'm already worried about his reaction when I tell him what's been going on, and that's without a visual. If he catches us in the act, he'll probably kill me on sight."

She thrusts out her lower lip as her brows slant together. "I'd really hoped he would loosen up now that he's with Sydney."

"Oh, he's loosened up all right. Just not where you're concerned." Before she can fire back with a response, I add, "You should probably get back to the party before he realizes you're MIA. I'll follow you out in a couple of minutes."

Emotion churns on her face and I can tell she wants to argue.

Instead, she rises onto the tips of her toes and gives me one last kiss before slipping out the door and into the hallway.

I pull out my phone and scroll through ESPN before deciding enough time has passed for me to exit the room unnoticed. As soon as I pull the door closed behind me and swing around, my feet grind to an awkward halt as I come face to face with Crosby. He's leaning casually against the wall with his arms crossed over his chest. As soon as our gazes collide, one brow wings its way upward. The ever-present smirk is firmly in place and aimed right at me.

"Looks like someone's trying to get his ass beat."

"Yeah," I growl, not in the mood for his shit, "and that someone is gonna be you."

He snorts before straightening to his full height. "You know what they say about playing with fire, right?" There's a pause. When I refuse to respond, he finishes, "Eventually, you're gonna get burned."

My shoulders collapse, because we both know it's the truth. Sooner or later, I'm going to go up in flames.

"Yup."

Chapter Thirty-Four

ELLE

E ven though I've grabbed food here dozens of times over the last year and a half while at Western, I study the menu, trying to choose between a barbeque chicken wrap or lime cilantro chicken bowl with black beans and quinoa. I think Sierra's uber healthy eating habits have rubbed off on me. How else would you explain the choices I'm contemplating? She's been trying to get us to branch out and try new entrees. Baking is something she enjoys and helps her to destress. She likes to make nutritious snacks in the oven on the dorm floor. Sometimes, they're shockingly delicious. Like roasted nuts with everything bagel seasoning. Other times, not so much—I'm talking about you, baked kale chips.

Deciding on a bowl, I step closer to the counter. The line is about six customers deep and I'm a little crunched for time. I'm hoping to order and wolf it down before making it to my next class.

"Do you have any idea how much I want to kiss you right now?" a deep voice says from behind me.

A shiver scampers down my spine as Carson's warm breath feathers across the outer shell of my ear. It takes every ounce of self-control not to spin around and throw myself into his arms. But how can I do that when we're in the middle of the union and there are a ton of students buzzing around?

The answer is that I can't.

"Probably as much as I want to kiss you back," I whisper, turning my head slightly to meet his gaze.

One side of his mouth quirks as he steps closer, until I'm able to feel the heat of his muscular body pressed against my backside. It sucks that we're still hiding our relationship and forced to steal moments in the shadows. I don't know how much longer I can keep this up.

I'm knocked from those thoughts when he says, "I was thinking after the game this weekend, we could get out of town for the night and away from everyone. Would you like that?"

Yes!

"That sounds amazing." The idea of having Carson all to myself for even twenty-four short hours fills my heart with so much happiness that it feels like it'll explode like an overinflated balloon. We could actually go out to dinner and hold hands, or even kiss.

In public.

All the little things normal couples do when they aren't keeping their relationship on the downlow.

He grins. "We could drive like an hour or so away. Maybe a place like Cold—"

"What about the cabin?" Excitement threads its way through my voice. "I could ask Mom if we could go there. I'll just tell her that the girls want to get away for the night. I'm sure she wouldn't mind."

His eyes darken before he glances away. "I don't like the idea of lying to your mother."

What difference does it make? At the moment, we're hiding the truth from everyone. Both friends and family.

"If you want, I'll tell her what's going on." Under normal circumstances, I tell my mother everything. We've always been close. "I don't have a problem doing that." Honestly, it would be a relief to finally share the news with someone. Keeping all of this to myself makes me feel like I'm going to explode.

He sucks his lower lip between his teeth and chews it thoughtfully.

Before he has a chance to respond, Brayden and Sydney appear out of nowhere. At least, that's the way it feels. Maybe we were just too involved in our conversation to notice their approach. Carson takes a quick step in retreat to put an appropriate amount of distance between us.

"Hey. Everyone's over there." My brother nods toward a table full of rowdy football players on the other side of the union.

Carson shakes his head as he continues backing away. "Sorry, I have to take off."

"What?" Brayden frowns. "I thought we were grabbing lunch today." There's a pause. "For fuck's sake, wasn't it your idea?"

"Yeah, I know, but something just came up. I'll catch you later at practice," he says with a wave.

And then he's gone, disappearing through the crowd.

My brother stares after him with a frown before turning back to me. "Anyone else notice that he's been acting weird lately? I seriously don't know what's going on with him."

That's one question I won't be touching with a ten-foot pole.

Instead of lying, I shrug. My gaze flickers from Brayden to Sydney, who raises a brow. The knowing look in her eyes has heat creeping into my cheeks as I glance away.

If Sydney has figured out our secret, it's only a matter of time before my brother catches on as well.

Chapter Thirty-Five

CARSON

I crest the second floor of the library and glance around for Elle. I know she was planning on being here for a while, and I told her I'd stop by after practice. It only takes a few seconds to catch sight of her and Mike studying at a table off to the side. Her long, dark hair covers her face like a shiny curtain as she bends over a book. Mike has his laptop open and is typing away across from her.

After not seeing her all day, I'm starving for the sight of her. "Hey."

Both of their heads whip up as a smile breaks out across her face. For just a second, everything swirling through my brain leaks out of my ears, and I'm dazzled by the sheer brilliance of her. It's like having the warmth of the sun beating down on me.

Which is—trust me, I know—corny as fuck.

But that doesn't make it any less true. I've spent so many years denying what I felt that, for a while, I almost started to believe it. This is all it takes to make me realize how futile the struggle was.

I clear my throat along with those thoughts. "Getting any work done?"

"Yup. We've been camped out here for a couple of hours and I've already plowed my way through my stats homework along with a few other subjects."

I nod and glance at Mike as I shift my weight. I'm dying to yank her into my arms and kiss the hell right out of her. It takes every ounce of self-restraint to resist the urge to do exactly that.

A knowing glint enters her eyes as she tips her head toward her friend. "The secret is out. He knows."

I raise my brows. "Is that so?" We're supposed to be keeping this on the downlow for the time being. The last thing I want is for Brayden to catch wind of our relationship. When the time comes, he needs to hear it from me.

"You two are adorable together. I couldn't be happier." There's a pause as Mike corrects himself. "Well, if you had a brother…then I'd be happier."

Huh?

Elle snorts out a laugh. "We've already discussed this. Carson is an only child."

When Mike opens his mouth, she cuts him off. "And his cousins live out of state."

He cocks his head. "What about distant ones?"

She rolls her eyes as her shoulders shake. "You need to give up the dream."

I have no idea what they're talking about, but if the cat is already out of the bag, then there isn't a reason for me to resist a quick kiss. I glance around before closing the distance between us and brushing my lips across hers. Even though it's not nearly enough to feed the intense need I have for her, a feeling of calm settles over me. I've waited all damn day for this.

"Yup." Mike sighs. "Totally adorable."

Elle's lips curve into a smile as she chuckles.

"Do you have time for a quick break?" Now that I've laid my hands on her, I need more. One peck isn't going to be enough.

"Yup."

With that, I pull her from the chair and tow her to the stacks where there's a bit more privacy from prying eyes.

"I'll just be over here," Mike calls after us, "all by my lonesome."

"We'll only be a few minutes," she shoots back.

I glance at Elle. "What was all that about?"

"Mike thinks you're pretty hot and muscly. For the record," she winks, "I agree one hundred percent. He wanted to know if there were any brothers or cousins who might be his type."

A chuckle slips free as I shake my head. "Nope. It's just me."

"That's what I told him."

Once we wind our way through a couple of bookshelves, I stop and tug her into my arms. Her slender body presses against mine, fitting perfectly.

"The only thing that matters to me is that I'm your type."

"You don't have anything to worry about. You are *definitely* my type."

I slant my lips over hers until our tongues can dance and mingle. As soon as she opens more fully, I deepen the kiss and crush her against the bookshelves. She twines her arms around my neck, clinging to me as if she'll never let go. At the moment, I don't want her to.

Once we come up for air, she whispers, "I'm so tired of sneaking around and pretending we're not together."

"I know. That's exactly why I'm looking forward to having you all to myself this weekend."

Her eyes soften. "Me, too."

I press another kiss against her mouth. "We can talk and get everything figured out, okay?"

She nods. "We'll have the place all to ourselves..."

"Oh?" I waggle my brows. "It sounds like you might have some plans in mind."

Her expression turns coy. "Maybe a few."

The corners of my lips tilt as they hover over hers. "Care to share? Give me a little preview?"

"Nope. You'll just have to wait and see what happens."

My cock stirs with interest in my sweatpants. "Tease."

Her fingers settle over my hard length before gently stroking it. A groan escapes from me as she continues to play with my growing erection.

In the middle of the library.

Just as I'm about to suggest we take this somewhere more private, a familiar voice says from the other side of the bookshelf, "Dude, I'm so wrecked after that practice. This is the last place I want to be."

"Agreed. But I need to finish up this paper for econ. Then we can get the hell out of here."

Fuck.

Brayden and Easton.

Elle's eyes widen as she recognizes the voices. Either of them could turn at any moment and catch sight of us.

We need to get out of here.

Quietly.

If her brother finds us, he'll string me up by the balls. No questions asked.

It only makes me realize that Elle is right. All the sneaking around might be kind of fun, but it gets old after a while. At some point, we're going to have to tell him.

The question is when.

I navigate the Tahoe through the woods that push in at the edges of the narrow strip of road. By now, the trees have completely lost their leaves. A thick carpet of browns, reds, and golden colors decorate the forest floor. Since we played an early game today, Elle and I were able to take off by three o'clock. Even though I tried to slip out of the house unnoticed, I ran into the one guy I was hoping to avoid. Instead of coming clean, I pussied out and said I was heading home to see my parents. Not thinking much about it, he'd clapped me on the back and told me to have a good time.

Omitting the truth is one thing. Flat out lying is another.

After this weekend, I need to talk with him and explain the situation. I'm not under any illusions that it'll go well. I've been friends with him for long enough to realize that he'll be pissed. I'm just hoping I can convince him my feelings for his sister are genuine, and that I'd never do anything to hurt her.

I've spent most of my life protecting Elle.

He has to see that...right?

When Elle squeezes my hand, I blink back to the present and glance over at her. She flashes a smile and all thoughts of her brother vanish. As much as I hate sneaking around, I'm glad we're taking this time to get away. It's exactly what we need.

As we turn onto the rutted road that leads to the cabin, the trees close in even more, the branches almost scraping against the side of the truck. I've been coming to the lake with the Kendricks since Brayden and I became friends in elementary school. I have so many good memories of this place. Of fishing, camping, swimming, tromping around in the woods, having bonfires in the backyard, and riding ATV's. For a kid whose parents weren't outdoorsy at all, it was paradise, and I looked forward to our trips every year.

When Jake died our senior year of high school, all that came to an abrupt halt and Brayden stopped coming here. Their father was the embodiment of this property, and there were too many painful memories lurking around every corner. It's been four years since I've stepped foot on this land. Even though my feelings are tinged with sadness around the edges, it feels very much like coming home.

Once we drive over a small hill, the lake and log cabin come into view. The sun shines brightly from the sky, and the water is calm and glassy, reflecting the pine and poplar trees that flank the other side of the bank like a scenic photograph. Everything is so much more overgrown than I remember. It's yet another marker as to how much time has passed.

Cutting the engine, I glance at Elle and smile. She returns the expression before giving my hand a gentle squeeze. While Brayden has avoided the place, Elle and her mother spend the weekend here every couple of months. She's made her peace with the past, no longer wanting it to overshadow her future.

"Are you ready?" I ask.

She nods and we both exit the vehicle. As soon as I step out of the truck, I suck in a deep breath. There's something invigorating about the air. It's fresh, crisp, and full of pine. If I squeezed my eyes shut, I would be propelled back to my childhood.

It's a comforting feeling.

Popping the hatch, I grab our duffels from the back. Since we only plan to stay for one night, we didn't pack much in the way of clothing. On the way out of town, we stopped at the store and picked up a few bags of supplies to get us through. Elle grabs the grocery bags as we haul everything to the front porch. She slips the key from her purse before sliding it into the lock and pushing open the front door.

As we step inside, my gaze travels around the spacious interior. It looks exactly like I remember. At the far end of the room is a massive fireplace made up of gray and blue fieldstones that take up the entire wall. A chandelier created from antlers hangs suspended from the two-story ceiling while a white, oversized sectional curves around the far wall, creating an inviting space to sit and take in the long stretch of windows that overlook the lake. It would be a challenge to not find a gorgeous view from anywhere in this house.

Elle takes the duffels upstairs to her bedroom on the second floor as I put the groceries away in the kitchen. This place is more like a home than a cabin. The Kendricks spared no expense when they built it decades ago. Everything is stainless steel, granite, and an ocean of shiny hardwoods that stretches throughout the open spaces. Across from the kitchen is a dining room with views of the forest and a massive table that can seat twelve people.

By the time I'm done putting away all the food, Elle is back. She's changed into yoga pants and an oversized Wildcats sweatshirt. When I open my arms, she immediately steps into them before being engulfed by my embrace. A soft sigh falls from her lips as she lays her cheek against my chest.

A deep sense of rightness washes over me.

I suck in a lungful of air, holding it inside before releasing it back into the atmosphere. Only now do I realize that I'm finally able to breathe again. For the past few weeks, I've been holding my breath, unable to relax or lower my guard. Now that she's in my arms, my airways no longer feel constricted the way they do on campus. If I had any doubts about pulling Brayden aside and divulging our relationship, they're laid to rest. I can't do this anymore. I can't continue to sneak around behind his back. I need everything to be out in the open.

No matter what happens.

Unaware of the thoughts rampaging through my brain, she tilts her head back to meet my gaze. The softness filling her eyes is like a punch to the gut. Maybe we haven't been together long, but these feelings have been in the making for years.

"I'm glad we decided to do this," she says.

"Me, too."

Unable to hold back any longer, my lips descend, slanting over hers. Unlike most of the frenzied kisses we've been forced to steal when no one is around, this caress is more of a lazy exploration. It unfolds gently as our tongues dance and mingle. I move my head one way before tilting it the other, trying to find the perfect angle. Her arms wrap around my neck before pulling me closer until every slender curve is aligned against my harder ones. My hands skim along her sides before dropping to her ass until they're able to palm her cheeks. A groan rumbles up from my chest as my erection digs into the softness of her belly.

Over the years, I've done everything in my power to eradicate the emotions that have always bubbled beneath the surface where Elle is concerned. None of the other girls I've been with have ever come close to touching what I feel for her. In hindsight, I realize that I've been biding my time, waiting for the chance to make her mine. Elle belongs to me, and, if I have anything to do with it, nothing will ever change that.

Including her brother.

It's taken me a long time to arrive at this conclusion. Now that I have, there's no turning back or talking myself out of it.

Hot spikes of need rush through my veins, suffusing every cell in my body until it feels like I'll explode. When I finally break away, we're both breathing hard, and there's a dazed look filling her eyes. It's sexy as hell. The urge to scoop her up and carry her to the bedroom thrums through me.

Instead of doing that, I say, "Should we head outside for a while?"

I need to cool off before we get carried away.

From beneath the dark fringe of her lashes, she gives me a coy look. "Is that really what you want to do?"

Hell, no.

But I also don't want the time we spend here to be all about sex.

What I feel for her is so much more than that. And I want to make sure she knows it.

I press a quick kiss against her lips. "I think it would be for the best. Let's take the ATV out and explore some of the trails. We can see everything that's changed since we were kids." It's an activity we both used to enjoy.

Her eyes clear as she nods. "Sure, that sounds fun."

"After that, we can make dinner."

Her brows rise as she drops her chin. "And then what?"

My lips tremble around the edges with a smile. "I don't know. Probably watch a little TV before hitting the sack."

She blinks as her brows slam together. "Are you being serious?"

"I'm exhausted after that game. I was hoping to get a little extra shuteye." There's a pause. "Isn't that what you had in mind?"

With narrowed eyes, she tilts her head. "I can't tell if you're screwing with me or not."

I tug her to me as my lips hover over hers. "When I'm fucking you, baby, you'll know it."

Her body melts against mine. "I want you so much, Carson."

Her soft admittance has everything crumbling inside me. How the hell did I go so long without making her mine?

It seems crazy.

As I get lost in her fathomless depths, it occurs to me that when I take this woman to bed, it'll be different from any other past experience. This won't be fucking or screwing. I'll be making love to her, and that's not something I've ever done before. The fact that this is Elle's first time makes it all the more special. It's important I slow things down and make it the best it can possibly be.

Tonight will change everything between us.

It's a lot of pressure, but I wouldn't have it any other way.

Chapter Thirty-Seven

ELLE

I'd be lying through my teeth if I didn't admit I'm nervous. Sure, I've scrolled through Tumblr and listened to my friends gossip about what it's like to have sex, but I think we can all agree it's one of those things you can't fully understand until you experience it firsthand.

And tonight, that's what will happen.

That being said, there's no one else I'd want to do this with other than Carson. When I've laid awake at night in my bed and imagined the man who would be my first, it was always him.

From where I'm sitting at the long stretch of granite counter, I watch him move around the spacious kitchen, preparing dinner for us. He's been here so many times that he knows where all of the pots and utensils are located.

Earlier this afternoon, we picked up lettuce, tomato, bread, and bacon to make BLT's. When we were kids, it's a meal my mom would make for us when we came in for lunch after being out swimming or fishing all morning. There's something familiar about it that settles the butterflies that are attempting to wing their way to life in the pit of my belly.

I shift on my chair, wondering if it would help to busy myself with a meaningless task in order to take my mind off what will be occurring in a few short hours. As much as I want it to happen, that doesn't mean I'm not anxious.

What if I'm not good at it and he's disappointed?

Or it really hurts?

Or I hate it?

Those butterflies now feel more like pterodactyls trying to fight their way free. It takes effort to gulp down the burst of nerves and clear my throat. "Are you sure I can't help with anything?"

He glances at me from the stove where the bacon is sizzling in a pan. There's a dish towel thrown over one shoulder, making him look adorably domesticated. "Nope. Everything is under control; you don't need to do a thing."

My fingers twist in my lap beneath the counter as I suck in a breath before steadily forcing it out again.

Once the bacon has crisped, he sets the pieces on a paper towel covered plate so the grease can drain and places four slices of bread in the toaster. Humming beneath his breath, he pulls out the mayo and lettuce from the fridge before expertly cutting up the tomatoes. When the toast pops up, he assembles the sandwiches, splitting them in half and delivering them to the breakfast bar with a small bag of potato chips for each of us.

"Dinner is served," he says with an easy smile.

"Thank you."

We dig in, talking about everything that has changed on the property since he was here five years ago. The loss of my father was difficult for all three of us, but it was especially rough on Brayden. The two of them had a close relationship. My father was a professional football player, and from the time Brayden could walk, they were always tossing around a ball. When they were at the cabin, they spent a lot of time outdoors fishing in the lake, tromping through the woods, riding ATV's, and camping in the backyard.

Even though I enjoy nature, I'm more like my mother in that regard. Neither of us has any interest in sleeping outside when there was a perfectly good bed under a roof where the bugs —or anything larger—couldn't get at us.

Once we've finished off our sandwiches, I grab both plates before taking them into the kitchen and dropping them in the sink to wash later. A fresh burst of nerves skitters across my flesh as I swing around and find Carson watching me intently.

There's a moment of silence before he asks, "Any interest in watching a movie?"

The air wedged in my lungs rushes out in a burst. It doesn't make sense how I can want something and yet be filled with so much anxiety at the same time.

It takes a concerted effort to loosen my shoulders from around my ears. "Sure."

His penetrating gaze never relinquishes mine as he rises from the stool and holds out his hand for me to take. It's not a conscious decision on my part. Before I can even think about it, my feet shuffle forward until his hand can close around mine. It only takes one small tug for me to tumble into his arms. Some of the anxiety rioting inside me settles at the innocuous contact.

"You know that we don't have to do anything, Elle. We can chill out and enjoy the cabin if that's what you want. There's no pressure."

I nod.

Of course he would say that.

Carson would never force me into anything I wasn't ready for. I think the fear gripping me has more to do with the great unknown. I have a faint idea of what to expect, but the details of it are still murky. Without a doubt, he'll make this the best experience it can be and won't do anything to purposefully cause me pain. That knowledge has the remaining tension in my shoulders dissolving as I tilt my chin upward until my gaze can lock on his. I rise onto the tips of my toes before brushing my lips across his. Everything about Carson is solid and hard.

Except his lips.

Those are soft and cushiony.

A shiver works its way through me when I think about what it felt like to have them coasting over certain parts of my body and how much pleasure he's capable of giving.

"On second thought," I say, surprising even myself, "I'm not interested in watching a movie."

"Oh?" His brows furrow. "What do you want to do then? Check out the hot tub? Maybe start a fire in the pit and roast a few marshmallows?" Before I can respond he tacks on, "There were always tons of board games upstairs. We could grab one of them. You used to love Monopoly."

I still do. I always end up owning Boardwalk and Park Place like a boss bitch. Then I load up the properties with hotels and bankrupt the other players. As fun as that always is, it's not what I have in mind right now.

I suck in a shaky breath and force out the words. "I want you to make love to me."

His body grows impossibly still. "Right now?"

Pressing my lips together, I jerk my head into a tight nod. I've never been more certain of anything in my life. I want Carson, and I want him now. There's something empowering about being the one to voice the decision. As if I'm the one in control of the situation.

He studies me for a long moment as if he's able to see all of the conflicting emotions warring inside me. His voice drops as his expression softens. "Are you sure? You seem nervous."

"I am," I admit. "But that doesn't mean I don't want this to happen." Especially since I've been waiting so long for him to make me his.

"All right." Flames ignite in his eyes. "Lead the way."

Huh?

I gulp. "You want me to..." My voice trails off as I wave toward the staircase.

When I continue to stare, hoping I've gotten it all wrong, he presses a kiss against my mouth before whispering, "I want you to grab hold of my hand and take me upstairs to your room, Elle. Show me how much you want this."

The pterodactyls are back in full force. My heart flutters madly beneath my breast as my fingers tighten around his. "Okay."

I can do this.

It's no big deal.

With every step that brings me closer to the staircase, I try not to overthink the situation. Once we reach the second floor, I lead the way, walking through the spacious loft area with its cozy couch and big screen television. Just like Carson mentioned, there's a cabinet stuffed full of board games.

Instead of stopping, we bypass the space and continue moving down the long stretch of hallway where four of the five spacious bedrooms are located. Each one was designed with its own en suite. Mine is the last one on the left. The entire house has a north woods vibe to it, including my room. The walls are painted a light blue gray with white trim. There's a dark wood mission style dresser with a matching nightstand next to the bed. A large mirror is positioned over the rectangular piece of furniture, and a white ceramic deer head hangs opposite. The bedspread is a light blue plaid that matches the over-stuffed chair parked in the corner.

A potent concoction of excitement and anxiety rushes through my veins as I pull him over the threshold and into my private space. Now that I have him here, I'm not quite sure what to do with him. My fingers open and I release his hand as my arm flutters back to my side.

Another burst of nerves explodes in my belly.

"Come here, Elle." His voice dips, becoming so low that it strums something deep inside me.

One step is all it takes to close the distance between us until we're standing chest to breast. Mine rises and falls in rapid succession with each quick inhale and exhale. His hand lifts, feathering across my cheek before slipping around the side of my head until he can hold the back of my skull in his wide palm. Carefully, he pulls me to him until his lips can slant across mine. Each caress is soft, barely there before disappearing.

In between kisses, he murmurs, "I want you to be sure about this. If you're not ready, we don't have to do anything. This isn't about me, Elle. It's all about you. I couldn't stand it if you had regrets afterward. This experience is too important for that to happen."

His words do the unthinkable and settle everything rioting danger-ously inside me. "I'm ready. You're the one I've always wanted. Even before I fully understood what that meant."

He pulls away just enough to examine my face. "If you want to slow down or stop at any time, all you have to do is say the word. You're the one in control here. Understand?"

I jerk my head in response as he rains down kisses that are as light as a butterfly wing against the corners of my mouth before descending to my jawline, where he nips at me with sharp teeth. Not a heartbeat later, his tongue darts out to soothe the tender flesh. A whimper escapes from me as I bare the column of my throat for him to feast upon.

His hand drifts from the back of my skull to my shoulder, sweeping down my ribcage before snaking around my body and tugging me against him until we're perfectly aligned, and I can feel the thickness of his arousal.

My fingers dip beneath the fabric of his T-shirt, gliding over the grooved ridges that lie beneath. Slowly I gather up the soft cotton in my hands. He bites down on the delicate skin just hard enough to leave me gasping before breaking contact and retreating a step until my arms have no other choice but to fall away. In one swift movement, he grabs hold of the material and whips it over his head before discarding it on the floor.

As soon as the shirt disappears, I pause, drinking in the sight of him. Everything about Carson is hard and chiseled perfection. From the broad set of his shoulders to the bulging muscles of his biceps, it's evident that he spends hours lifting in the gym. His chest is sculpted—looking as if it's been carved from marble—before tapering to a trim waist. There's a smattering of hair that arrows down his six pack before disappearing beneath the waistband of his denim.

I don't realize he's standing perfectly still, allowing me to look my fill, until my attention flicks up to his face and I see the tightly leashed control being exerted. A flurry of arousal explodes in my core like a firework before dampening my panties.

He is ridiculously beautiful.

Most guys couldn't be described using such a word, but it's the only one that springs to mind when I think about him. Every time we're together, it's a struggle not to reach out and brush the thick blond strands away from his eyes. I completely understand why girls have been throwing themselves at him since he was fourteen years old. I remember the way a few of the younger female teachers would eye him up in the hallway when we were in high school. Even though I couldn't lay claim to him, it never failed to ignite a firestorm of jealousy inside me. I hated it.

What now seems surreal is that he's wanted me for just as long as I've secretly yearned for him. How has this become my reality? Half a year ago, I couldn't have imagined it. Even two months ago, the possibility of us getting together seemed farfetched.

And yet, here we are.

As I shake off those thoughts, I realize his fingers have settled at the hem of my shirt.

"Can I remove this?"

I nod as my heart thunders beneath my breast. It's not like he hasn't seen me naked before, but still...

I know exactly where this is leading.

He must sense my sudden spurt of apprehension because he pulls me close and kisses me again, drawing my lower lip into his mouth and sucking on it. Just when it seems like I'll melt into a puddle at his feet, he releases the plump flesh with a soft pop. His gaze stays pinned to mine as he gathers up the thick fabric of my sweatshirt before gently pulling it over my head and dropping it to the floor on top of his discarded shirt.

His attention sinks to my chest. I can almost feel the heat of his stare licking over my bared flesh.

"And the bra?"

I gulp and force myself to say, "You can take it off."

Without further ado, he reaches around my ribcage and unfastens the clasp. The delicate straps slip down my shoulders and arms as the silky cups fall away, revealing my breasts. With gentle fingers he tugs the garment free, tossing the pale pink material onto the growing pile of discarded clothing.

A shaky exhalation escapes from my lungs as I stand before him in nothing more than leggings. It takes everything I have inside not to raise my arms and shield myself from his piercing gaze. Slowly his hands rise to palm the soft flesh. The moment he makes contact, my teeth sink into my bottom lip as sensation explodes inside me.

"Do you have any idea how beautiful you are?" he murmurs, continuing to toy with my body. "I've spent years dreaming about your breasts, wishing I could play with them just like this."

His quietly spoken words send an arrow of lust straight down to my core.

After a tortuous amount of time that leaves me squirming beneath his touch, his gaze once again settles on mine. The blazing inferno within their golden depths nearly singes me alive. He bends, head lowering, until his warm breath is able to drift across my chest. His tongue darts out to lap at one stiffened peak before sucking it into his mouth. A million shockwaves erupt across my flesh before burying me alive in an avalanche of intensity.

Just when I don't think I can stand another moment of this torment, he releases me before giving the same ardent attention to the other nipple. My fingers tunnel through his thick blond hair, trailing over his scalp, in order to hold him in place. Once he breaks contact, the cool air of the cabin wafts over me and goose flesh ripples across my skin.

I watch from beneath eyelids that are at half-mast, unsure what will happen next. Instead of doing the expected and straightening to his full height, he drops to his knees in front of me. His gaze locks on mine as he presses a kiss against my belly button. Air gets trapped in my lungs as his fingers settle at the elastic band at my waist before shoving the fabric over my hips and down my thighs until it can puddle around my ankles. My hands go to his shoulders as he carefully lifts one leg and removes the material before repeating the maneuver on the opposite side. Once the stiff fabric has been discarded, I'm left in nothing more than pale pink panties.

As he stares up at me, my hands gravitate to the sides of his face, stroking across the light scruff that shadows his chiseled jawline. There's so much tenderness brimming in his eyes. More than I ever thought possible. It only reinforces that what we're about to do is the right decision and the wait was well worth it.

Breaking eye contact, he leans forward and presses a delicate kiss against the front of my panties before rising to his feet. My arms slide around his neck to draw him closer as his hands slip down my sides, strumming along my ribcage before cupping an ass cheek in each palm. When he lifts me into his arms, my legs tangle around his waist. He turns, walking us to the queen-sized bed that takes up residence in the middle of the spacious room. When his mouth captures mine, our tongues mingle as he lowers us to the mattress, and the hard stretch of his body follows me down before I'm pinned in place. He readjusts himself until his thick erection can nudge my center. Each slow stroke is like throwing a large stone into a calm pool of water. Desire ripples outward until every vibration can be felt in the tips of my toes and fingers.

Every time he makes the subtle movement, pleasure ratchets up inside me. When the sensation becomes almost too much to bear, he breaks contact and trails hot kisses over my jaw, along my throat, down my collarbone before ending up at my belly button and sinking lower still. His fingers slip beneath the slim band before slowly pulling the scrap of material down my hips and over my thighs until I'm totally bare.

His heated gaze locks on mine.

Before he can ask, I whisper, "I'm sure."

Humor ignites in his eyes as his mouth quirks at the corners. "All right."

He rises to his knees and widens my thighs until I'm completely exposed. I can almost feel the burn of his gaze as it licks over me. With his hands on my inner thighs, his thumbs gently sweep over my delicate flesh.

"So damn pretty," he growls before lowering his face.

A heartbeat later, his warm breath ghosts over me. I shift beneath the firm hold, desperate for his touch. Anticipation spirals through me until I can barely stand it. The velvety softness of his tongue sets off a firestorm of sensation within me. It's like a raging inferno sweeping over dry kindling. I can't help but wonder how I'll survive as he laps at me again before zeroing in on my clit. The tiny bundle of nerves throbs a painful beat as he dips his tongue deep inside. It doesn't take long until I'm dancing precariously close to the edge. My fingers tangle through his thick strands as my back bows off the mattress.

"Mmm, you taste so damn good. I want to eat you up all night long."

Oh god.

I don't think I could stand that.

Already it feels as if I'll come undone at the seams.

A whimper falls from my lips. It's the only response I'm capable of giving at the moment.

"Are you ready to come for me, baby?"

That question is all it takes to shove me over the edge and into oblivion. Every muscle becomes whipcord tight as I groan out my orgasm. Stars explode behind my eyelids as Carson nibbles at me, making sure to wring every last drop of pleasure from my body. It's only when I turn boneless, sinking into the mattress, that he drops one last kiss against my over-sensitized flesh before lifting his head and carefully crawling up my body until he can press his mouth against mine.

"Did you enjoy that?"

"Yes." Even to my own ears, the word comes out sounding slurred.

A smug smile lifts the edges of his lips. "You ready for more?"

"Mmm hmm." It seems surreal that there could be more. I feel utterly blissful. As if I'm floating on a cloud. This isn't the first orgasm he's given me, but it is the most intense.

"Are you sure?" His gaze turns serious before searching mine. "It's not to late to pump the breaks."

Even though it feels like each of my arms weigh at least a thousand pounds, I force them up until my hand can feather across the scruff of his cheeks. "I'm positive. No regrets."

"Okay." The heavy weight of his body disappears as he rises to his feet.

It takes a herculean effort to prop myself up on my elbows and watch as he unbuttons his jeans and shoves the material down his muscular thighs before kicking it away. Some of my lethargy recedes as the boxers meet a similar fate. His thick erection springs free, jutting out as if it has a life of its own. For a moment, Carson stands at the end of the bed, legs spread apart as if bracing for a storm and simply allows me to study him at my leisure.

He has the most gorgeous body.

Hard and muscular.

Totally masculine with thick slabs of muscle and a smattering of dark blond hair that begins at his chest before arrowing down his belly to his cock and covering his thighs.

Even though I've just orgasmed, a fresh wave of need crashes over me. Unconsciously, my thighs fall open. His gaze drops to my core, and, if it's possible, his dick swells.

Becoming harder.

Thicker.

Desire surges within me until it's all I can focus on.

He hunkers down, snatching the denim before slipping something from the pocket. Once he straightens, I notice the slim foil packet clenched in his fingers. Only now do I realize that we never discussed protection.

My tongue darts out to moisten parched lips. "We don't have to use that. I'm on the pill."

His brow furrows. "Are you sure?" There's a pause before he tacks on, "I haven't had sex in six months. I'm clean. But I don't want to do anything that puts you at risk. If you want me to wear a condom, I have no problem doing it."

If this were any other guy, I wouldn't have even mentioned being on the pill. But this is Carson. Not only do I trust him to tell me the truth, but to protect me as well.

"It's okay."

He sucks his bottom lip into his mouth and chews it as if silently debating the right course of action.

When a few tortuous seconds tick by, I spread my legs wider, wanting to put an end to this conversation. "No condom."

His pupils dilate, the black overtaking the golden brown color, as his attention stays fixated on me. The square package falls to the floor as he returns to the bed and crawls up my body. When he reaches the vee between my legs, he presses his mouth to mine before stretching out until the blunt tip of his cock can nudge the lips of my pussy.

His gaze latches onto mine as he pauses, keeping himself immobile. "Still good?"

I nod as my arms slip over his shoulders to twine around his neck and pull him closer. I draw in a steady breath as he carefully maneuvers himself inside me. The muscles around him stretch to accommodate his girth. Even though I'm slick with need, there's still a bite of pain that leaves me wincing.

His teeth clench as the muscle in his jaw tics. "Fuck, baby. I've never had sex without a condom before. I can't believe how damn good it feels. Your pussy is so tight. It's like you have me in a vise." Beads of sweat pop out across his brow as he continues to gently inch his way inside. "This feels too good. There's no way I'll last long," he groans.

My brows pinch together at the fullness now radiating from my center as he continues to push forward. He can't be more than halfway inside me, and already it feels as if there's nowhere else for him to go.

"Are you all right?" Tension vibrates throughout his voice, making it sound tightly strung.

I press my lips together and nod.

"Do you want me to stop? All you have to do is say the word and we won't go any further."

It's tempting.

All those good vibes buzzing beneath my skin, electrifying every nerve ending, have vanished. Even though there's a smattering of pain and discomfort, I can't imagine putting a stop to what's unfolding between us. More than anything, I want to experience this with Carson. I knew my first time would be painful, but I also realize it'll get better.

"No. I want to keep going."

A tortured expression settles across his face as he takes shallow thrusts before butting up against a barrier. "This is going to hurt, and the last thing I want to do is cause you pain."

The gentleness of his voice soothes everything abraded within me, making it easier to continue. No one else would ever take the time or care that Carson has with me. And that's what makes all the difference in the world.

"It's okay. I'll be all right."

"Give me your mouth so I can swallow down all of your cries."

I tilt my chin, offering up my lips. As soon as his settle over mine, I open until his tongue can slip inside and mingle with my own. As I sink into the kiss, his hips fall into a steady rhythm. The shallow movements steadily become faster and more forceful. They batter the thin membrane until finally, one hard drive breaks through it and he's buried to the hilt inside my body. Pain rips through me as a choked sob escapes. Just like he claimed, he drinks down all of my cries. Hot tears leak from the corners of my eyes as his movements cease, allowing me time to adjust to the foreign intrusion.

It's only when I quiet that he pulls away enough to search my face. "I'm sorry, Elle. I wish it didn't have to be that way."

I can't help but feel like a baby for making such a big deal out of something that's more of a rite of passage than anything else. Every woman who engages in this activity goes through a similar experience. "It's okay. It doesn't hurt quite so much now."

The sharp stab has settled into more of a dull ache.

"Good. Hopefully it'll continue to get better. Just give it a bit of time." He kisses away the wetness from the corners of my eyes until there's nothing left. "I'm going to move just a little bit, okay?"

"Yeah." I mentally prepare myself for the discomfort to rush back full force.

Braced on his elbows, he withdraws his hard cock from my body. Just when I think he'll pull all the way out, he cautiously pushes back inside until he's once again buried in me. My inner muscles stretch around him to accommodate his size. This time, the sting isn't to the same degree. It's still a long way from feeling good, but it no longer seems like I'm being stabbed from the inside out.

"You need to tell me if it hurts, and I'll stop."

Even though his strokes are tempered, they're sure. With each one, the ache continues to fade, becoming more of an uncomfortable twinge. After a while, even that diminishes, and I find myself cautiously lifting my hips to match the rhythm he's set. It doesn't take long before we're moving together and pleasure swirls tentatively through my body.

"You're so fucking tight. I've never felt anything like it before." Carson's breathing grows more labored as his pace picks up.

The slide of his cock propels me higher and higher.

"Fuck, I'm going to come," he growls, teeth clenched together.

His muscles tense as his erection grows harder and a rough groan falls from his lips. I lock my arms around him, holding him close as he loses control. His orgasm seems to go on forever until finally, his muscles slacken, and he collapses. Burying his face against the crook of my neck, his warm breath drifts over me before he presses a kiss against my throat and pulls away.

"I'm sorry. I'd wanted to last longer."

"Don't apologize, it was perfect."

He searches my eyes. "I know it hurt in the beginning, but did it get better?"

I nod as a small smile lifts my lips. "It did."

"It'll feel so much better next time, I promise. If I'd been thinking clearly, I would have jacked off earlier. Maybe then I wouldn't have come so soon."

Laughter bubbles up inside my throat as I raise my brows. "You would have masturbated in an attempt to last longer?"

The bright whiteness of his teeth cuts through the darkness as he grins. "Yeah. Like I said before, it's been a while since I had sex. I should have realized that would happen."

"Six months, huh?"

"If I couldn't have you, there didn't seem much point in sleeping with anyone else."

My heart swells with thick emotion.

Carson leans down and captures my mouth with his own. Just as I'm about to sink into the caress, he breaks contact before carefully pulling out of my body, rolling from the bed, and rising in one swift movement to his feet. There's another twinge of pain as he does. Before I can ask what he's up to, he scoops me from the bed and cradles me against his chest.

"Where are we going?" I squeak as he rearranges my naked body in his arms.

"I think we could both use a hot shower, don't you?"

Oh.

"It'll help with the soreness," he whispers against my ear.

My cheeks burn as I bury my face against the hollow of his throat. "If you say so," I mumble, kind of liking the idea of us showering together.

"I do."

With that, he carries me inside the bathroom before setting me down on the counter and swinging away to step into the glass enclosure.

I can't help but admire his firm backside. Like the rest of him, it looks like it's been carved from granite. His body is so hard and unyielding.

Even the part that is now soft and flaccid.

A rush of warmth washes over me.

Once steam begins to rise from the hot water, he swings around and takes one step before stumbling to a halt. One brow slinks up before he slowly shakes his head.

Eyes widening, I sit up a little straighter. "What?"

"I see the look on your face, and you can forget about it."

"Forget what?" I have no idea what he's talking about.

He quickly closes the distance between us before wrapping me up in his arms. "As much as I want back inside that sweet little pussy tonight, it's not going to happen." His hand slips between our bodies before pressing against my core. I wince as his fingers slide inside me.

"Exactly."

I'm about to protest when he whispers, "But that doesn't mean I won't lick and kiss you."

Arousal flares to life as I realize that's *exactly* what I want.

His arms fasten around me before I'm hoisted against his chest, and he carries me into the steamy enclosure. As I burrow against his comforting strength, I realize there's no place I'd rather be than here with him.

Chapter Thirty-Eight

ELLE

My eyelids flutter open, and I wake with a stretch. As soon as I shift, I'm instantly reminded that I'm no longer a virgin. There's a soreness between my thighs that wasn't there before.

Last night was...

In a word...

Amazing.

Maybe I hadn't orgasmed when he'd been inside me, but I had liked the feel of his weight pressing me into the mattress and how he'd buried himself deep in my body. The fullness of it. The natural rhythm we'd found. It's a closeness I've never experienced with another human being, and I can't imagine feeling this way about anyone else.

For me, there's only Carson.

Rolling onto my side, my gaze settles on his sleeping form. His blond hair is mussed and it's entirely too tempting to reach out and rake my fingers through it, pushing the blond strands from his eyes. My hungry gaze roves over his handsome features, from eyebrows that are thick and prominent before sliding to high, chiseled cheekbones and then sinking lower to a strong jawline that's covered with a light scruff. His nose would be straight but there's a slight crick to it from being broken a few years ago. Maybe others would see it as a flaw, but I think it gives his face character. He was way too pretty before.

That thought has the edges of my lips curling. God, he would hate if I told him he was pretty.

A soft sigh falls from my lips.

I'm so in...

Something.

I'm so in *something* with this guy.

Having sex has only intensified all of the emotions fighting their way to the surface, making them even more undeniable.

My gaze falls to his chest. During the night, the sheet has bunched around his waist, covering the part of him I'm most curious about. Last night, his cock had been rock hard. Afterward, in the bathroom, it had softened. Although, that state hadn't lasted very long. In the steamy enclosure, he'd soaped up his hands and stroked them over my body. Within minutes, he's stiffened right up.

There hadn't been much time to inspect him. Not the way I'd craved. I'm dying to see what he looks like now in the early morning light. My teeth chew my lower lip as I consider taking a tiny peek. Roughly thirty seconds tick by before curiosity wins out and I carefully slide the sheet down his prone form. The last thing I want is for him to wake up and catch me ogling him like a creeper. My gaze flicks to his face before dropping again. I want to study Carson at my leisure without him being aware of it. The truth of the matter is that I've stared at him for hours at a time, but never this part of him. Never when he's been wearing so little clothing. Or, like he is now, none.

As the sheet slips past his waist and then hips, his cock is slowly revealed. My breath catches at the back of my throat as I stare in fascination. The root juts out from a patch of dark blond curls, curving along his lower abdomen. I've seen pictures of penises before—Madison has been known to show off a dick pic or two—but I've never found them particularly attractive.

I feel differently staring at Carson. Even in repose, he's long and thick. I take another quick look at his face to make sure he's still sleeping soundly. His chest continues to rise and fall rhythmically.

Wanting to study it more thoroughly, I scoot closer. Almost all the times I've felt him or caught a glimpse of his dick, he's been hard. This is different. He looks almost soft, not nearly as intimidating. When the urge to reach out and stroke him strikes, I curl my fingers into my palms until the nails bite into the flesh.

It's a foreign feeling to realize how fascinated I am with this part of him. The longer I stare, the more curiosity is piqued. Memories of what it felt like when he touched me and went down on me pop into my brain.

Does he enjoy that kind of caressing as well?

Would taking him in my mouth feel just as good for him as it did for me?

I've overheard enough stories from my friends to know that guys enjoy blowjobs. I would never admit it to Carson, but him licking and kissing me had felt so much better than sex. Will that change over time?

I have no idea.

Unable to resist the lure any longer, I reach out and gently stroke the tip of my finger over the long curve of him.

Velvety smooth.

That's the only descriptor that comes to mind.

This time, I trace him from the tip of his bulbous head to the root before running my fingers over his balls. They're equally soft. Using my entire hand, I palm the sac, wanting to learn the weight and feel of it. I squeeze his flesh carefully before caressing him. I'm so enthralled by the sight that I gasp when he shifts beneath me. Within seconds, his cock stiffens, no longer curved against his lower belly. Instead, it rises, becoming harder.

Longer.

Thicker.

When I glance up, electricity sizzles through my veins as our gazes collide.

I clear my throat along with any embarrassment trying to take hold within me. "Morning."

The corners of his lips lift into a slow smile. "Morning. Sleep good?"

The deep scrape of his voice sends a thousand shivers skittering across my flesh. It takes effort to focus on his words and not what they do to me.

"Yeah. You?"

Heat flares to life in his eyes. "Never better."

When he stretches, his muscles flex and his erection swells.

My gaze drops to the movement as I edge closer until my tongue can flick across the blunt tip. As soon as I make contact, a guttural groan escapes from him. My fingers curl around his shaft as I bring the head to my lips and swirl my tongue around it. His cock is like silk-encased steel, and I can't get enough. All I want to do is take this time to explore every inch of him.

"Elle," he growls, shifting restlessly beside me.

My gaze stays pinned to his face as I suck his length into my mouth.

That's all it takes for his eyelids to lower to half-mast. "You're playing with fire."

After a few moments, I allow him to slide free. "Really? Cause it kind of seems like I'm playing with your dick."

A snarl rumbles up from deep within his chest before vibrating in his throat. It makes him sound like something wild. The Carson I've known since we were kids has always been firmly in control. It's sexy as hell to see the façade slip. Even just a little bit. Especially since I'm the one causing it to happen.

"Fuck," he hisses as the cool air in the room rushes over his damp flesh. "Do you have any idea how long I've fantasized about you doing that?"

I shake my head.

"Years." There's a pause as his voice drops. "Longer, if I'm being completely honest."

Does he realize how much that admission turns me on? "And now here I am, doing exactly that."

Before he can respond, I draw him back inside my mouth. I've never done this before, so there's a little bit of a learning curve. Carson's palm settles on the top of my head before he brushes the hair away from my eyes. Maybe I'm not doing this precisely right, but he doesn't seem to mind. If the look on his face is anything to go by, he's enjoying it. I've always been a quick study.

Except in math.

Thankfully, this has nothing to do with algebraic equations or statistics.

"Mmmm, that feels so good, baby." He arches his back, lifting his hips off the mattress.

My movements become voracious. More than anything, I want him to come. I want to give him as much pleasure as he's given me.

Just as his muscles tighten, the front door of the cabin crashes open before slamming shut. Not a second later, an irate voice bellows from the first floor, *"Elle?"*

My eyes widen as my mouth tightens around his hard length. When Carson hisses out a breath, I quickly release him before scrambling up and yanking the covers over my naked body.

"Carson!" my brother shouts again, his voice growing closer as he moves through the first floor before pounding up the staircase.

"Fuck." With that, Carson rolls from the bed and jumps to his feet. "Get dressed."

My mind cartwheels as I sit motionless.

Dressed.

Right.

Brayden.

That's all it takes for me to scurry from the bed. I scan the area, searching for my shirt and jeans before grabbing them from the floor and racing to the bathroom. Thankfully, Carson is already a few steps ahead of me. His boxers are on and he's jerking his jeans up his thighs. I slam the door closed and yank the sweatshirt over my head. My fingers shake as I fumble, lurching to the side before hauling the black stretchy material up my legs and over my hips.

From the other side of the door, my brother yells, "What the actual fuck?"

I wince, squeezing my eyes tight before forcing them open again. As tempting as it is to stay locked behind the thick wood, I can't leave Carson to deal with Brayden alone. From the tone of his voice, I can already tell he's on the verge of losing his shit. I've witnessed my brother get angry, but it's never been directed at me.

Or his friend.

Inhaling a deep breath, I wrap my fingers around the brushed nickel handle and pull open the door before stepping over the threshold. I have to prod myself into movement with each forced step. The heavy tension permeating the air is almost suffocating in its intensity, and I stumble to a halt. Brayden's head whips toward me before his eyes widen. He hovers over the threshold like a vampire who needs to be invited inside.

Have I ever seen him look at me with such shock and disbelief?

It's almost difficult to hold his gaze.

A flash of long, blonde hair catches my attention from the hallway, and I realize Sydney is with him. For a couple of painful heartbeats, there's nothing but silence. The harsh thumping of my heart slams against my ribcage and fills my ears until it's like the dull roar of the ocean. Any moment, it's going to explode from my chest.

Brayden's hands curl into balls that hang limply at his sides as he continues to stare as if he doesn't know who I am. "What the hell are you doing here, Elle?"

My tongue darts out to moisten my lips.

Just tell him the truth!

I open my mouth, but nothing comes out. Another few painful seconds tick by as I wrap my arms around my middle. When I fail to respond, his attention slides to Carson, who has silently moved to stand beside me. Once he's close enough, his arm slips around my shoulders and he pulls me against his body. He's bare chested with only jeans covering his lower half.

My brother's eyes widen before a potent concoction of anger and betrayal leap into his dark depths. "What the fuck is going on here?" His voice escalates until it sounds as if it's reverberating off the walls and inside my head. "What are you doing with my sister?"

With his arm wrapped protectively around me, Carson straightens to his full height. "We've been seeing each other."

"The fuck you have!" Brayden roars, taking a menacing step in our direction.

Sydney lurches forward, grabbing hold of his arm. Her fingers curl, sinking into his bicep. He doesn't spare her a single glance.

His gaze stays fastened to his friend. "Are you really telling me that you've been screwing around with my sister?"

Carson's lips thin as his muscles tighten. "Come on, man. You know it's not like that."

My brother's eyes widen as a humorless laugh falls from his lips. "You know what?" Brayden doesn't pause long enough to give him a chance to answer. "I don't know what it's like because I had no idea you were sneaking around behind my back with Elle, for fuck's sake. You knew damn well I wouldn't have been cool with this, and you did it anyway."

Carson's arm tightens around my shoulders before he hauls me impossibly close. "I was going to talk to you about it after this weekend."

"Guess we don't need to have that conversation, now do we?"

His shoulders droop under the heavy weight of Brayden's disapproval. "For what it's worth, I'm sorry for not telling you sooner. The moment I realized something was going to happen, I should have come to you."

"No, it just shouldn't have happened. You had no business getting involved with her." Brayden stabs a finger at him. "End of story."

"I've always had feelings for Elle. It was never going to end any other way. It just wasn't."

My brother plows a hand through his hair. I can practically see the smoke pouring out of his ears.

"That's seriously fucked up, and you know it! I trusted you to watch over her. Instead, you took advantage of her."

I shake my head. He has it all wrong. That's not what happened. "Bray—"

His icy glare cuts to me. "Get your shit, I'm taking you home."

Every muscle tightens as my brows jerk together. "What? No! I'm a grown adult. You can't tell me what to do."

"Wanna bet?"

When Brayden takes a second step toward us, Carson mutters

under his breath, "Why don't you wait downstairs and let me talk to your brother privately."

Leaving them alone together when there's so much explosive tension in the atmosphere is a disastrous idea. They've always been such good friends. I don't think they've ever had one argument and I don't want to see that change. Nor do I want to be the one that comes between them.

I shake my head. "I'm staying here."

"Please, Elle. Just go. Let me get this figured out. Everything will be fine, I promise."

My shoulders slump as his arm disappears and he gives me a little push toward the door. When I stumble a few steps forward, Sydney sneaks past Brayden and slips a comforting arm around my waist before tugging me close. She gives me a look chock-full of sympathy before propelling me silently toward the hallway. What I don't find in her expression is surprise. I have the sneaking suspicion that she was aware of the situation.

As I maneuver past my brother, his furious gaze locks on me as my footsteps falter.

My tongue darts out to moisten my lips. "Please, Bray. He's your best friend and," I force myself to admit the rest, "I love him."

Another flash of anger cracks across his features as his lower jaw locks, the muscle throbbing in his cheek.

When he remains silent, Sydney breaks away from me to grab my duffle bag before steering me out of the room and into the hallway.

I don't understand how the most perfect night of my entire life has morphed into the worst morning, but that's exactly what happened. And at the moment, there doesn't seem to be a way to fix it.

Just as Elle crosses the threshold, she pauses, glancing over her shoulder until our gazes can collide. Fear and concern swirl through her dark eyes. Her skin is so pale from the confrontation that it looks ghostly. The urge to offer comfort thrums through me like that of a steady drumbeat. All I want to do is eat up the distance that separates us and drag her into my arms. I want to pull her head to my chest and reassure her that everything will be all right. Instead, I remain locked in place. Before I can lift my lips into a small semblance of a smile, she disappears from sight, leaving me alone with the guy I've always considered my best friend.

My gaze reluctantly returns to him. His knuckles are bone white as his hands clench at his sides. Fury churns through his dark eyes. We met in elementary school and have been tight ever since. I've witnessed him lose his shit and get into fistfights. Most of the time, I stood at his side, ready to get involved if it was necessary. I never expected that rage to be directed at me.

All right, maybe that's a lie.

There was a reason I tried so damn hard to not only keep my distance from Elle but keep my feelings for the slim brunette under wraps. Deep down, I knew Brayden would have an issue with it.

And I wasn't wrong.

As I meet his steely gaze, I'm not sure there's anything I can say to wipe away the betrayal filling his expression.

He takes another step toward me before growling, "You've got some fucking nerve bringing her here to our family cabin."

His tone rubs me the wrong way, and I jerk to my full height. "We've been seeing each other for a few weeks and wanted time to talk things out. This seemed like a good place to do it."

He glances around the room before his gaze zeros in on the rumpled covers and his eyes grow frigid. "Talking seems like the last thing you were doing."

Anger crashes through me and I press my lips into a tight line. I don't want to say anything that will make the situation worse, or that I'll regret once we've both settled down. What I'm not going to do is discuss my physical relationship with Elle. I don't give a rat's ass if he's her brother. What we do in private is none of his damn business.

His brows rise when I remain silent. "What? Nothing else to add to the conversation?"

I fold my arms across my chest. "I've already told you that I have feelings for her. That I've had them for a while. If this wasn't serious, I would have never allowed it to happen." I search his gaze for any hint of softening. There's none. "Is there anything I can say at this point that will make a difference to you?"

The corners of his lips curl into an angry slash. "Nope."

I drag a hand through my hair. "Look—"

"Ever since my father died, I've done my best to protect Elle." He forces out a hollow laugh. "And here I thought you were someone I could trust to do the same. I was certainly wrong about that, now wasn't I? All you've done is take advantage of her. And you lied to my face with some BS story about going home to visit your folks for the weekend."

I wince. He's not wrong about that.

"I'm sorry," I mumble, feeling like the world's biggest asshole. "I never meant for it to get this far without talking to you."

He snorts. "You know what? If you were any kind of friend, you would have been upfront with me from the start. Instead, you hid your so-called," he uses air quotes around the word, *"relationship* like a little bitch."

His words are like a kick to the balls. We've been friends for more than a decade and I've always stood by his side. Is that what Brayden really thinks of me?

Some of my guilt recedes as anger sparks to life inside me.

Do I owe him an apology for sneaking around and not being upfront about the situation?

Hell, yeah.

But if there's anyone who should know the kind of man I am, it's him. I would never do anything to hurt his family.

I shift my stance as tension rushes to fill every muscle, making me feel like a tightly harnessed ball of fury. "You realize Elle isn't a kid anymore, right? She's more than old enough to date and make decisions for herself. You need to back off and stop trying to control her life."

A dull red color seeps into his cheeks, turning them ruddy before he stabs a finger at me. "Don't you fucking dare tell me what I need to do when it comes to my family. All I've done is protect her from all the assholes out there who would hurt her. That girl deserves the fucking best."

All of the venom spewing from him feels like an assult.

"What are you trying to say? That I'm one of those assholes?" Even though it's difficult, I force out the rest. "Or that I'll treat her like shit?" I don't give him a chance to respond. "You know me better than almost anyone. At least I thought you did. I've always considered your family like my own." This time, I'm the one pointing at him. "You're like a brother to me. I would never do anything to disrespect your father's memory and that includes hurting you, your mother, or Elle. I fucking love that girl." My shoulders collapse under the heavy weight of that admittance. "I have for a while. As much as I've tried to deny the feelings to myself and her, I just couldn't do it anymore."

"Bullshit." He stalks toward me. "You knew she had a crush on you, and you fucking took advantage of it. You were thinking with your dick, that's all. And you were hoping I wouldn't find out."

Is he crazy?

I shake my head as another wave of anger crashes over me, making my body shake and my voice vibrate with pent-up emotion. "You know that's not what happened."

"What I've learned today is that I don't know a damn thing. Least of all, you."

He pushes into my personal space until we're practically standing toe to toe.

His words knock the air from my lungs, making it impossible to breathe. I blink, attempting to fight my way through the thick haze. I'm knocked from my stupor when he plows his hands into my bare chest and forces me back a step.

"I'm only going to say this once—stay the fuck away from Elle. And while you're at it, do me a favor and stay the fuck out of my way, too. If I catch you anywhere near her, I'll—"

I brace myself, preparing for another attack. Brayden might be tall and muscular, but so am I. We've always been evenly matched.

I lift my chin and surge forward, getting in his face. "What? What will you do?"

His eyes narrow. "Go against me and you'll find out real quick."

Before I can answer, he swings away, stalking from the room.

It's almost hard to believe that our conversation has gone this sideways. While I knew he would be pissed off, I never expected him to end our friendship.

Not like this.

"Brayden."

He pauses, turning his head just enough to glare at me from the corner of his eye. "I meant what I said. Stay the fuck away from both of us."

And then he swings away, disappearing into the hallway and stomping down the staircase in his Timberlands. A few seconds later, the front door slams before rattling on its hinges.

I release a slow breath as my mind spins.

From outside, his truck roars to life. With one rev of the engine, the tires spin on the gravel as he squeals out of the driveway and down the tree-lined road.

I plow a hand through my hair in frustration, unsure where the three of us go from here.

Chapter Forty

ELLE

y heart thumps a painful staccato against my chest as I grab hold of the oh-shit bar to keep from tumbling across the backseat. Brayden careens down the narrow road, whizzing past bare branches as if we're flying through space in hyper speed. My teeth sink into my bottom lip to stifle the scream building in my chest. Any moment, he's going to wrap the front end of this truck around a tree and we're all going to die.

Sydney must feel the same tension because she lays her hand on his forearm before digging her fingernails into his sweatshirt. "Bray, slow down." Even though her voice is steady, anxiety weaves its way through each word.

When his angry gaze slices to mine in the rearview mirror, I hold it for a second before glancing away. Not only am I angry with him about the situation, I'm humiliated beyond belief. How could he barge in and decimate my relationship with Carson?

What gives him the right to do that?

He's not my parent!

My mind is still careening, trying to figure out how I went from being on top of the world to sitting in the backseat of Brayden's truck, being forced away from the one guy I've always had feelings for.

Once the narrow road comes to a T, Brayden swings the vehicle onto a two-lane county highway. The only bright spot is that the forest has opened up and we're no longer surrounded by dense trees. Both Sydney and I breathe a sigh of relieve that we made it out of there alive and in one piece. My brother jams his foot on the accelerator and the truck shoots forward, picking up speed. One peek around his shoulder shows that we're going twenty miles per hour over the limit.

Unsure what to say, I stare out the window at the passing scenery. The countryside is dotted with pockets of trees and fields that will lay dormant for the winter months before a rebirth takes place in the spring. Under normal circumstances, the landscape is enough to quiet my mind and give me a sense of peace. Today there is no joy or relief to be found in the setting. The silence blanketing the three of us is thick and full of unresolved tension. I'm not sure how much more of it I can take without choking to death.

"What the hell were you thinking?" There's a pause before he snaps, "You had no damn business getting tangled up with one of my teammates."

My gaze jerks from a faded red barn and pasture with horses to the rearview mirror, where it latches onto my brother's reflection. "And why is that?"

His eyes widen. "Why?" He parrots the question as if he doesn't understand it. There's a beat of silence before his voice escalates. "Because Carson is my friend. One of the few I trusted." A grim chuckle escapes from him. "Although, that's shot to shit, isn't it? That motherfucker never should have taken advantage of you."

I squeeze my eyes tightly shut in an attempt to block out his words. "He didn't take advantage of me."

Why can't he realize that I'm old enough to make my own decisions? He doesn't need to involve himself in my love life.

"The hell he did. Everyone knows that you've been crushing on him since you were a kid."

I blanch as nausea swirls through my belly before rising up in my throat until I could choke on it.

His brows rise when I remain unresponsive. "What? Did you really think it was some big secret? For fuck's sake, he knew all about it. I told him in high school that if he valued his life, he'd stay the hell away from you."

I slump on the backseat as we hurtle down the country road. My head falls back against the plush cushion until I'm able to stare blindly at the ceiling. It's embarrassing to realize that I've been wearing my heart on my sleeve this entire time. There are so many thoughts crashing around inside my brain that it's almost impossible to keep them straight.

When I'm finally able to find my voice, I lift my head and stare at his reflection in the rearview mirror. Anger still wafts from him in heavy waves.

"Why would you do that?"

His gaze flicks to the mirror and locks on mine. "Do what? What *exactly* have I done that's so terrible?"

"You knew how I felt about Carson, and you did your damnedest to get in the way of that." My voice shakes with the resentment working its way through my body. "He's a wonderful guy who has never been anything but a good friend, not only to you but to me as well. And for some reason, that wasn't enough for you? Or me? Who the hell are you to be the judge of what's in my best interests? Why are you making decisions that involve me without asking what *I* want?"

His eyes widen as his jaw locks. "Don't you see that he took advantage of the feelings you've always had for him?"

I roll my eyes and throw my hands in the air. "For god's sake, you need to stop this overprotective bullshit and let me live my own life. Stop trying to keep me locked away in an ivory tower." My heart is thumping so harshly that it pounds in my ears, drowning out almost everything else. "Do you realize that I'm nineteen years old and up until last night, I was still a virgin. *Nineteen years old!*"

A rush of color fills his cheeks, turning them beet red. "Elle—"

"No!" I lean forward, pressing against the seatbelt. "You've been out carousing, having sex since you were sixteen, and for some reason, no one questioned that. No one tried stopping you from doing what you wanted. No one attempted to control you. We grew up in the same family and our experiences couldn't have been more different. Why is that?"

He focuses on the ribbon of pavement stretched out beyond the windshield and presses his lips into a barely perceptible line.

"Is it because you were a boy, and I'm a girl? Is that the reason?"

"Of course not," he grumbles. But his voice doesn't ring with the same indignation it did at the beginning of this conversation.

"Am I somehow more fragile or not equipped to make the same rational decisions as you are?" When he remains silent, I push onward. "Am I not as smart? Or able to take care of myself?"

"You know none of that is true."

"Then what's the reason?" I strain against the fabric belt as my voice elevates in volume. I'm not sure if I've ever been this furious in my life. But you know what?

It feels good to finally get it all out in the open. This behavior has been going on for far too long, and it needs to stop.

"Come on, Bray," I push. "I want some answers." The already oppressive atmosphere in the truck turns suffocating. "What was the plan? Were you going to protect my virtue until I was forty? Or maybe you had a nice, arranged marriage in mind?"

His expression turns sour before he scoffs, "Now you're just being ridiculous."

"I'm not the one being absurd," I shout. "You are." Even though I'm not looking to drag his girlfriend into our argument, I swing in my seat until she comes into view. "I bet Sydney's slept with whomever she wanted to, and no one attempted to stop her." I might not know her well, but I could tell from the first time we met that she wasn't a girl who put up with anyone telling her what to do.

Including my brother.

It's one of the reasons I admire her so much. Sydney Daniels is her own person who knows her mind. And no one is going to change that.

Instead of answering, Sydney glances at my brother with an arched brow. Their gazes catch before he scowls. When she remains silent, most likely not wanting to take sides, I huff out an exhausted breath and go back to contemplating the landscape that flies by the window. It's a relief when we reach the city limits and Brayden has to slow his speed. I need to get out of this truck and away from my brother before I wrap my fingers around his throat and throttle the life out of him.

An uncomfortable silence falls over us. When it becomes almost too much to bear, he shifts on his seat and mumbles, "You know I'm just trying to protect you, right?"

I huff out a breath. "I don't need your protection. I need you to treat me like an adult and stay out of my personal business the same way I stay out of yours. If I end up making a mistake in a relationship, then it's mine to make and learn from. You might find this hard to believe, but I'm not incompetent. I can take care of myself."

"I never said you were."

My brows rise. "Then why do you treat me like I am?"

"That's not what I'm doing."

My lips flatten as I cross my arms across my chest and go back to staring at the storefronts we're rolling past. There's no point in engaging in this conversation if he won't own up to his behavior.

A few more miles pass by before he clears his throat. "After Dad died, you needed someone to look out for you. To make sure you were safe and taken care of. Don't you think he would have wanted me to protect you the same way he always did?"

My shoulders slump under the heaviness of his words. Dad died when Brayden was just seventeen years old. It forced my brother to step in and fill his humongous shoes. I know that couldn't have been easy for him.

"Yes, but he also wouldn't have wanted you to stunt my growth and keep me from experiencing everything life has to offer." Even though it's harsh, I give him the unvarnished truth. "Whether you realize it or not, that's what you've been doing."

He blinks as his gaze stays pinned to the road. A mixture of grief and confusion fills his expression.

"You're wrong," he whispers thickly.

"No, I'm not."

I've never been so happy to see Sutton Hall than when he swerves into the parking lot before rolling to a stop in front of the building. Without a word, I grab my bag, open the door, and jump out before slamming it shut. For just a moment, I pause and inhale a lungful of fresh air. It's sad. Brayden and I have always been close. Especially after Dad's death. But it's a relief to escape his presence. I think we both need time to think about everything that's happened and been said. Maybe then we can get together and talk.

As I stalk up the front walkway, the door to the driver's side of the truck pops open and Brayden raises his voice. "That's it? You're going to walk away without hashing this out?"

Yup. That's the plan. The ride back from the cabin was excruciating, and I'm mentally and emotionally drained. I don't have anything else inside me to give.

"Elle!"

A prick of guilt wells up inside me and I spin around. "I'm done talking. I'm just...done." Without waiting for a response, I swing toward the dorm.

"Come on, Elle. Don't walk away like this. Just give me a few minutes—"

Once I reach the door, I pull out my key and jam it into the lock before slipping inside the building.

After what happened at the cabin, I have no idea if our relationship will ever be the same again.

Chapter Forty-One

CARSON

I lift the bottle of water to my lips and take a swig. Asher and Crosby are perched on the edge of their seats as they duke it out in an intense game of NHL.

"Ha!" Asher crows as he dekes out Crosby's goalie. "Suck it!"

"Fuck off," the dark-haired guy grumbles. "It was a lucky shot. Everyone knows you have zero skills."

"Ouch, that stings coming from the guy I just creamed." He glances at the two girls who flank him on the couch. "I've got more skills than you'll ever have. Right, ladies?"

Both of the blondes pipe up, attesting to Asher's aptitude in the bedroom. Which, I'll be honest, I have no interest in hearing about. Here's a fun fact I discovered after moving in with the guy—he isn't picky about where he has sex. I have a sneaking suspicion he's christened all of the rooms. And I sure as shit wouldn't shine a black light in the living room. I probably wouldn't be able to sit on any of the furniture again. Hell, it would be tempting to burn the joint down to the ground in a blaze of glory.

Crosby scrunches his face. "Pretty sure I just puked in my mouth."

"Aww, don't be jealous." Asher grins, throwing his arms around both females and hauling them close.

"Jealous of what exactly, I'd like to know," Crosby shoots back.

"That the chicks flock to me in droves while running from you in terror."

Crosby arches a brow as a slow smile tips the corners of his lips. "Yeah, that's exactly what they do."

This is probably my cue to leave. I don't need to get in the middle of a pissing match about who gets the most pussy. Just as I rise to my feet, the front door opens and in walks Brayden with a backpack hoisted over his shoulder. When he catches sight of me, his footsteps falter as a scowl overtakes his features. Without a word to any of us, he stalks toward the kitchen.

Both Crosby and Asher turn and stare at me with curiosity.

"Brrr, that was a chilly reception, brah," Asher says.

"Yeah, my nuts just froze off," Crosby adds.

"Well, it's not like you use them that often," our teammate fires back with an overly cheerful smile. "They're more ornamental in nature."

Crosby glares before giving him a one-fingered salute.

My blond roommate chuckles before dismissing him and turning to the girls. "You two lovely ladies ready to get out of here?"

They scramble up like good little lap dogs. "Yeah, where are we going?"

"I'm hungry," the other whines. "Can we get something to eat?"

"I was thinking we could work up an appetite first and then Uber something afterward. How does that sound?"

They both giggle before pawing at him. He gives Crosby a wink before wrapping an arm around each one and disappearing up the staircase.

My other teammate frowns before rolling his eyes. "It's unbeliev-able how much pussy that guy gets."

I shake my head, not understanding it myself. He drinks, smokes weed, and fucks like it's his sole mission in life. And none of that stops the chicks from clamoring after him like he's the last male specimen on the face of the Earth. It defies logic.

A brief silence falls over us before Crosby shifts on the couch and clears his throat. "So..." He nods toward the kitchen. "What's up with you and Bray?"

I jerk my shoulders, not wanting to field any questions regarding that particular topic. Even though you can cut the tension with a knife in the house and on the field, we've managed to keep our issue between the two of us. Although, that doesn't mean we're not getting a lot of sideways glances and questioning looks.

"Nothing," I mumble, hoping he'll drop the subject.

"My guess is that he found out you're screwing around with his sister."

I straighten on my chair and growl, "We haven't been screwing around."

His expression turns to one of interest. "Oh? What would you call it then?"

I clamp my lips together and glare, refusing to get drawn into another conversation about Elle. Especially with Crosby. To my knowledge, the guy has never even had a girlfriend or gone out with anyone. He's more like Asher than he's comfortable admitting.

The guy fucks.

Pure and simple.

When I refuse to respond, he raises his brows. "Whatever it is, you'd better get it solved fast. Shit like that always bleeds over onto the field, and we can't afford for that to happen. Not now."

My shoulders slump. Crosby might not be someone I'd seek out for life advice, but he just so happens to be right in this instance.

Unconsciously, I glance toward the kitchen where Brayden disappeared a few minutes ago. It's been days since the explosion at the cabin. I'd hoped that if I gave him enough time to cool off, we'd be able to sit down and talk this out like grown-ass adults. So far, that hasn't happened. The guy won't even look in my direction. He's plowed into me a few times on the practice field when I haven't been paying attention and knocked me on my ass.

And Elle...

We've decided to back off until everything with Brayden blows over. My feelings are as strong as they've always been, but how can we have a relationship when the one person I've always considered my best friend doesn't want anything to do with me?

After everything that's happened in their lives, they've always had each other, and I'm loathe to destroy that relationship.

The situation sucks all the way around.

When I reluctantly rise to my feet, he grunts, "Good choice."

I shoot him a sour look and exit the room without another word. As I walk into the kitchen, I find Brayden leaning against the counter with a bottle of orange Gatorade in his hand. His gaze flickers to mine before he straightens, attempting to stalk past as if he doesn't want to even breathe the same air as me.

Before he can disappear into the dining room, I reach out and grab hold of his arm.

He stops, scowling before dropping his gaze to the place where my fingers are locked around his bicep. "You're gonna want to remove your hand before you lose it. I can guarantee you won't get far in the NFL without it."

It's not the snapped-out threat that has me setting him free. I release him because this conversation has already become contentious, and I haven't even opened my mouth. We've been friends for way too long for our relationship to end like this.

"Come on, Bray. Can't we talk this out?"

He jerks his shoulders. "What's there to discuss? I think we said everything that needed to be said at the cabin."

At a loss, I drag a hand through my hair. Any hope that had been flickering inside me dies a quick death. I'd really thought we could work past this issue. Maybe I was wrong. Maybe this is how it ends between us. If that's the case, it's fucking sad. "So that's it? We're just...done? At the end of next semester, we go our separate ways?"

Regret flashes in his eyes before being stomped out. "I don't know."

Desperation bubbles up inside me until it's thick enough to choke on. "You gotta realize that I never meant to hurt you."

He shifts his stance as if the conversation makes him uncomfortable. "Yeah, that's the thing...there are a shit ton of chicks at this school who would have been more than happy to spread their legs for you. There was no damn reason to go sniffing around my sister."

He's right. And for years, that's exactly what I did. I steered clear and stayed away. I banged groupies I didn't want in an attempt to fuck her out of my system.

It's only when I finally gave in to the need coursing through me that I realized it was never going to work. As much as I tried to convince myself that they were all interchangeable and one pussy was just as good as the next, it's not true. Not when feelings are involved. Not when it's more than just sex hanging in the balance.

Brayden of all people should realize that.

"None of them were Elle. I've wanted her for years, bro. There was no way I could stand the thought of her with anyone else."

Anger flashes across his face and I tense when he takes a step toward me, pushing into my space. "Then you should have fucking come to me like a man before anything happened."

"You're right. In hindsight, that's exactly what I should have done. I can't go back and change the past." I pause, thinking carefully about the next words that come out of my mouth. "But you also need to realize my relationship with Elle is between the two of us and doesn't involve you."

His nostrils flare as his eyes darken. "The fuck it does. That's my little sister you're talking about." He rams his finger into my chest. "Doing shit with. You don't think her wellbeing is my concern?"

I stiffen beneath the contact. Even though it's tempting to knock him back a step, I blow out a steady breath and keep a tight rein on my temper. Getting into a physical altercation with Brayden isn't going to solve matters. If anything, it'll only make them worse. And none of us need that.

"No, I don't. She's old enough to make her own decisions, and you need to accept that."

There doesn't seem to be anything I can say to change his mind or make a difference, and that fucking sucks.

"If you know what's good for you, you'll stay the hell away from her," he growls.

Does he have any idea how painful that would be?

Especially now.

I shift my weight, attempting to reason with him one last time. "What if someone told you to stay away from Sydney? Would you be able to do it? Or would you do anything to be with her?"

Fury erupts across his face as he straightens like someone just shoved a two-by-four up his ass. When his hands bunch at his sides, I realize I've probably pushed him too far.

Before he has a chance to jump down my throat, I admit, "Because that's exactly the way I feel about Elle. I love her. Do you get that? I *love* her." It's as if my insides are being ripped apart as I force out the rest. "You and I have been friends for a long time, and we've been through a lot of shit together. If there's one person who knows me— really knows me—it's you. If you don't believe I'm the best thing for your sister, I'll stay away. But don't think for one damn minute it'll change the way I feel about her. And don't fucking fool yourself into believing that she'll ever find someone who loves her the way I do."

Thick tension crackles in the air between us. If there's a tiny kernel of hope inside me that what I've admitted will ultimately sway him, it's snuffed out when he remains stoically silent.

With nothing more to say, I knock into his shoulder and stalk out of the kitchen. Not only have I lost Elle, but our friendship, too. No matter what happens in the future, nothing will ever be the same between any of us again.

Chapter Forty-Two

ELLE

With a quick rap of my knuckles, I push open the door to the office and poke my head inside the tiny room. "Hi, Dr. Holloway."

He glances up from his computer monitor and waves me in. "Hey, Elle." His tone turns chastising. "I've already told you that when we're not in class or with other students, you should feel free to call me Gabe."

"Sorry, guess I forgot." That's a lie. It feels weird to call him by his first name. I know there are other professors who drop the formality with their students, but I've never been comfortable with it.

When he stares patiently with raised brows, I force myself to tack on, "Gabe."

He beams before rising to his feet and moving around the metal desk that takes up most of the space. "The filing cabinet is right here." He pats the tall metal container. "And all of the paperwork is in these two boxes."

I nod, silently assessing the situation.

"My guess is that it'll take a couple of hours, and like I said, it doesn't have to be completed in one sitting. Feel free to spread it out. In all honesty, I'll probably have more work that needs to be filed. Our secretary is great, but she doesn't always get copies and handouts back in time. So, if this is a situation that works for both of us, we could consider making it permanent." There's a pause. "Is that something you might be interested in?"

My schedule is jampacked, but I need all the extra credit I can scrounge. So, I'll have to shift things around and make it work. I should be thrilled that Dr. Holloway is being so generous.

"It'll depend on how often you need help."

"Sure. That's totally understandable. Let's see how it goes and then you can decide." He points to my jacket. "You might want to take that off. The heat is constantly running, and it gets awfully warm in here."

I unwind the bright turquoise scarf from around my neck before unbuttoning my denim jacket and shrugging out of it. When he holds out his palm, I hand over both. He hangs them alongside his on the metal coat rack shoved in the corner. "All right, why don't you come over here. I'll show you the system I've been using, and you can get straight to work."

With a nod, I shimmy past him. The space is tight and with both of us standing near the cabinet, there's not much room to maneuver. He pulls out the top drawer and I step closer, taking a peek inside to get a better look. The last thing I want to do is mess up whatever system he's using.

I don't realize that he's standing directly behind me until he reaches around my body to pick up a folder. I freeze like a deer caught in the bright glare of headlights. My muscles stiffen as his warm breath drifts over the outer shell of my ear.

"All of the papers in the box should be appropriately marked, making it easy to discern which folder they belong in."

As he continues to rattle off information, I try to shift my body so we're not standing in such close proximity. Dr. Holloway has never done anything to make me feel uncomfortable or uneasy, but at this particular moment, there's that strange prickling sensation coursing through me.

And it's stupid.

I'm being stupid.

Why am I being such a baby about this? He's not doing anything wrong. He's simply explaining what he wants me to do. The office is small and there's not a lot of space to maneuver. As soon as he's done talking, he'll go back to his desk, and I'll feel like an idiot for jumping to the wrong conclusion.

"Elle?"

Heat stings my cheeks as I turn my head and meet his blue gaze. "Yeah?"

An amused smile curls around the corners of his lips. "I asked if you had any questions."

I shake my head and realize again how close he is. We're talking a matter of inches. I can see the various flecks of blue and green that make up his irises. It's disconcerting.

"Nope," I say lightly, "none."

His smile widens. "Great. Then you can get started. If you have any questions, don't hesitate to ask."

When he takes a step in retreat, the pent-up breath I'd been holding captive in my lungs escapes in a burst of relief.

"I will."

As he settles behind his desk, returning his focus to the computer monitor, I get to work on the files. The process isn't complicated. It's just like he explained. All of the paperwork is clearly marked, making it easy to find the corresponding file in the cabinet. I glance at the neat pile of stacked boxes. I only have an hour before my next class starts. After lunch, I need to head to the theater for a quick meeting. *Heathers* wrapped up last week, and it's sad to see the production come to an end.

As I make my way through the box, my thoughts turn to Carson. It's been difficult *not* to think about him. It seems like everything finally came together only to fall apart. Even though I didn't want to take a step back from our relationship, that's what we both decided was best for the time being. And my brother is the one I have to thank for that.

There's a part of me that understands his dilemma. He doesn't want to have a problem with Brayden. Not only are they close friends, they're roommates and teammates. And our relationship has created a tense situation for him to contend with.

Carson thinks if we give Brayden time to cool down, he'll gradually come around to the idea of us being together. Honestly, I'm not sure if that will happen. And I'm not willing to wait forever. What I do know is that Brayden only wants the best for me.

Whether he wants to admit it or not, that's Carson.

I jolt out of my thoughts and nearly yelp when strong hands land on my shoulders.

"How are you doing over here? Any questions?"

I clear my throat, only wanting to shrug off his touch. "Um, nope. It's all good."

"Great." He squeezes me, kneading the tensed muscles. "I was just about to grab a coffee from the conference room. Can I get you something to drink? Coffee? Tea? Water? There's also a few snacks if you're hungry."

"No, I'm good, but thanks for asking." Air gets wedged in the middle of my throat, making it impossible to breathe.

Silence falls over us as he steps closer. When his warm breath ghosts over the back of my neck, goose bumps scatter across my flesh. His hands drift down the length of my arms to my elbows before traveling back up again.

A chuckle falls from his lips as his voice drops. "You're so tense. You really need to relax, Elle."

It's on the tip of my tongue to blurt out that he's the reason for my anxiety. Instead, I keep the words locked inside because I'm afraid I've misconstrued what's happening here. He's never been anything but kind and courteous.

His hands resettle along the nape of my neck as both thumbs press firmly into my shoulder blades before fanning outward. My body goes into a strange paralysis as my heart thumps painfully in my chest. I have no idea how to escape from this uncomfortable situation.

My tongue darts out to moisten parched lips. "Dr. Holloway—"

"Gabe," he reminds in a husky whisper that twists my insides into knots.

I clear my throat and force out the words. "You're making me uncomfortable."

Even though his fingers still, he doesn't remove them. "Am I?"

"Yes." I would nod, but I'm terrified to move a single muscle. I don't want the situation to escalate.

"I'm sorry. I hope you realize that was never my intention."

Relief rushes through me, suffusing every cell of my body as I wait for him to step away and give me some much-needed space.

One heartbeat passes.

Then another.

And still, he doesn't move.

I take that back—he steps closer until the hard lines of his body are pressed against my stiffened spine.

"I was under the impression you enjoyed spending time with me. Am I wrong about that?" With his deep voice at my ear, he tugs me even closer until I feel the thickness of his erection digging into my backside.

I squeak out a response "I—"

"Are you uncomfortable because I'm still your professor? In another month or so, that won't be the case. I like being with you, and it seems like the attraction between us is mutual."

Oh god.

How did I not see this coming?

Carson's words roar back to me. Maybe he's right and I've been naïve this entire time. I had assumed Dr. Holloway was being nice because he genuinely cared about my progress in his class. It never occurred to me that it could be anything more.

Still frozen in place, I whisper, "I'm sorry. I—I don't feel that way about you."

I wince when his fingers bite into the flesh beneath my shirt.

He pins me to the front of his body as his lips hover at my ear. "If that's the case, then my guess is that you've been playing a dangerous game, Elle. Leading me on. Pretending to want something more."

What?

No!

I shake my head frantically, uncertain how he could arrive at such an absurd conclusion. "No, I haven't. I didn't realize..."

He snorts as his fingers turn harsh. "How's that possible? We went out to dinner and exchanged numbers. You had to realize that my interest went deeper than you just being my student."

"I'm sorry, I didn't." Emotion wells in my throat, thickening my voice.

"You know what I think?" He doesn't give me a chance to respond. "That you're a cock tease who enjoys showing up to my class in your short skirts and flirting so I'd give you a higher grade."

"What?" The floor drops out from beneath me as his cruel words reverberate inside my head. "No, that's not what—"

"Of course it is. And now I've caught you at it. What do you think the university will do when I make them aware of your disgusting behavior, hmmm? Maybe kick you out of school? Certainly tell your family."

Tears prick the backs of my eyes as everything he says churns inside me.

When I remain silent, his voice turns harsh. "All of you girls are the same. You think you can bat your eyelashes and wear lowcut tops that show off your tits and you'll get a higher grade. Well, it's not going to work this time. You picked the wrong guy to play games with."

His fingers loosen before they slide from my shoulders to my breasts. The moment he squeezes them, I come alive, twisting in his arms until we're facing each other. His eyes flare as I bring my knee up and slam it into his crotch. I do it exactly the way Brayden taught me when I was in middle school and attended my first dance.

With a grunt, Dr. Holloway doubles over and staggers back a few steps. "You fucking little—"

"Don't you dare say it," I snap. Even though I'm pissed off, my hands tremble as I grab both my jacket and scarf. Instead of pulling them on, I rush toward the closed door.

"Where do you think you're going?" he wheezes, still stooped over. It's tempting to kick him again for being a lecherous asshole in sheep's clothing. "We're not done discussing this."

"Oh, trust me, we're finished." As I reach out, wrapping my fingers around the handle and yanking it open, I pause, turning back to meet his gaze. "And I'll be the one talking to the head of your department about you attempting to sexually assault me. I don't care if it means I have to retake statistics next year, I'm not going to allow you to take advantage of any other students."

His eyes widen as he blanches. "Wait—I think there's been a misunderstanding. Sit down so we can discuss this."

I shake my head as adrenalin continues to pump wildly through my veins. "No. There haven't been any misunderstandings. You were perfectly clear about your position."

"Elle—"

As I step over the threshold, I slam the door closed behind me. For just a moment, I lean against the thick wood before sucking in a deep breath. My head swims, unable to believe this actually happened and that Dr. Holloway turned out to be such a creep. My legs quiver as I push away from the door and walk down the long stretch of hallway to where the secretary of the department is parked behind her desk.

I have to remind myself to breathe the entire time. My hand flutters to my lower abdomen as if that will stifle the queasiness roiling inside. I don't think I've ever felt this nervous in my life. Not even when I've performed on stage in front of a packed theater.

"Hi." I glance at the name on the office door behind her. "Is Dr. Redham available?"

Her gaze drops to the schedule on her desk. "He's on the phone right now, but if you'd like to take a seat, it shouldn't be long."

I nod before forcing myself to one of the plush chairs and settling in to wait.

It turns out to be the longest five minutes of my life, but not once do I waver on what needs to be done.

Chapter Forty-Three

CARSON

I hitch my backpack onto my shoulder and wind my way through the crowded union. It might only be eleven in the morning, but there's already a ton of people grabbing lunch or a quick snack before their next class.

When my phone chimes with an incoming text, I slide it from my back pocket. Even though I know it isn't Elle, I can't help but hope I'm wrong. Keeping all this distance between us is killing me. Once my cell is in hand, I glance down at it. Disappointment bubbles up inside me as I scan the message from Mom.

Looking forward to the game this weekend. Can't wait to see you.

I should be happy they're carving time out of their busy schedules to make it to the game. They've missed most of them. And with the season ending, there won't be—

A soft grunt escapes from me as I truck into someone. Or maybe it's the other way around. At this point, I can't be too sure. My hands automatically shoot out, catching the person before they can tumble backward. It's only when my fingers wrap around slender arms that I realize who I've caught hold of.

"Hey." It takes every ounce of self-restraint not to drag her to me and bury my face in the delicate hollow of her neck in order to inhale her sweet scent.

Elle blinks. "Carson...hi."

My brow furrows as I carefully search her face. There's a tightness to her features that usually isn't there. A strain that brackets her mouth. A distressed look filling her eyes.

Whatever is bothering her, it's more than our relationship.

"What's going on?"

When her teeth sink into the plump flesh of her lower lip, I know my intuition is correct.

With my fingers locked around her upper arm, I glance around the congested space, looking for a place where we can talk in private without being interrupted. No longer do I care if I'm late to class. Or miss the damn thing altogether. I have no idea what happened to put that expression on her face, but I'm going to damn well find out.

People scurry out of my way when they see me barreling through. I scan the area, looking for an empty table. There's nothing. Instead of staying inside, I push through the glass doors into the fresh autumn air. There's an unoccupied picnic table on a grassy knoll about twenty yards away. It's fairly chilly out, so it isn't a total shocker to find it abandoned. I should probably release her, but I can't bring myself to let go. The connection feels much too good, and I've missed laying my hands on her. I have no idea how long this conversation will take, but I'm going to keep her as close as I can for as long as I can. Once we reach the table, I drop onto one side and pull her down next to me so that she's practically sitting on my lap.

"Now tell me what happened."

Only when we're settled do I realize that she's trembling.

I drag her closer and wrap my arm around her. "Are you cold?"

Her silence is disconcerting. All it does is jack me up.

"You need to tell me what's going on." Before I burst out of my skin.

Her gaze flickers to mine before dropping to her fingers, which twist together in her lap as she shakes her head. "You were right."

My face scrunches, not following the conversation. "What are you talking about?"

When she continues to avoid eye contact, my hand settles under her chin before lifting it until she has no other choice but to meet my steady gaze.

"You need to tell me what's going on, Elle," I say patiently. "What am I right about?"

Her tongue darts out to moisten her lips.

Distracted by the movement, my attention drops as she whispers, "About Dr. Holloway."

Motherfucker!

My gaze snaps back to hers as a punch of anger hits me in the gut. "What did he do?" The growl that leaves my lips sounds nothing like me.

Her eyes widen as her muscles tense. When she attempts to glance away for a second time, my grip tightens on her chin until her gaze returns to mine.

"I stopped by his office to start on the filing he offered for extra credit. While I was working, he came up behind me and put his hands on my shoulders." There's a pause and I have to strain to hear her words. "He started to rub me, and it was really uncomfortable."

A red haze of anger descends, clouding my vision, making it impossible to think clearly. "Are you all right?"

Not only will I kill him if he hurt her, but I won't be able to forgive myself for not doing more to stop him. Instead of paying a visit to his office, maybe I should have gone straight to the chancellor. Maybe then Elle wouldn't have been put in such a position.

"I'm fine," she says quickly as her palms settle on my chest before her fingers curl into my sweatshirt. It's as if she's holding on for dear life. "Really."

My grip on her chin loosens until I can cup the side of her face. A soft sigh escapes from her as she closes her eyes and presses her cheek into the tender touch.

"Tell me everything that happened. I want all the details."

It takes a handful of minutes for her to get the full story out.

The only thing capable of making me smile is when she tells me about nailing the bastard in the nuts. "Your brother would be proud. You know that?"

Just a hint of a smile plays around the edges of her lips. "Yeah, although I dread telling him about this. He's going to totally lose it."

She's right about that. Brayden will fly off the handle when he finds out about this incident. Thankfully, the dean of the department took Elle seriously and had her fill out an incident report before speaking with someone from the chancellor's office along with campus police. He told her that Dr. Holloway would be put on immediate administrative leave and, pending the outcome of an investigation, would be fired if any misconduct on his behalf was found. Since another professor will be taking over for the remainder of the semester, she won't need to transfer out of the section.

"I'm really proud of you," I say, gently stroking her face.

"For what?" Confusion fills her eyes as she frowns. "Not listening to you when you tried to warn me that the guy had ulterior motives?" She shakes her head. "I feel stupid for believing he was nothing more than a nice guy concerned about my grade."

"Nope," I murmur. "I'm proud that you stood up for yourself and didn't allow that asshole to intimidate you. Instead, you went straight to the dean and told him what was going on."

Some of the regret and embarrassment swirling in her eyes fades as her expression lightens. "I didn't want him to take advantage of anyone else."

I nod. "You're smarter and braver than you're giving yourself credit for. Not everyone could have handled the situation the way you did."

She releases a puff of air before holding up one hand. "It's been more than two hours and I'm still shaking. It's all churning in the pit of my belly."

I tug her closer until she can rest the side of her head against my chest before wrapping my arms around her body. "I'm sorry this happened to you. I wish there were something I could have done to stop it."

"You did try," she murmurs, "but I wouldn't listen."

I press a kiss against the crown of her head. "You're not to blame for taking him at face value and wanting to believe his intentions were pure."

"I feel like an idiot."

When I pull away, she lifts her head to meet my gaze. "You're the furthest thing from that. Do you hear me? He's the one in the wrong, not you. That asshole was given a position of power, and he abused it. That's unforgivable. My guess is that if the university digs back far enough, they'll discover this isn't the first time he's pulled this crap with a student."

A mixture of guilt and remorse continue to swirl through her dark depths. I have no idea how long we sit in the cold with her encased in my arms. For the first time since the cabin, I feel whole again. And that has everything to do with this girl.

"I wish it could be different between us," she whispers against my chest.

"I know." My grip tightens when I realize that I'll have to let her go.

She's no longer mine to hold.

Chapter Forty-Four

ELLE

A s soon as I step foot over the threshold, Mom tugs me into her arms and holds me close. "I've been thinking about you so much, sweetie. I'm glad you decided to come home for dinner. Although, you didn't have to borrow Madison's car, I would have been more than happy to pick you up."

"It's fine," I say with a shrug. "Maddie doesn't mind."

Honestly, it's a relief to escape from campus. I need the break, even if it's just for a few precious hours. The weight of what happened has settled heavily on my shoulders and now feels as if it's pressing me into the ground. Walking through the front door of my childhood home has the most crushing part of it falling away, giving me the smallest of reprieves.

It's only been a handful of days since the incident with Dr. Holloway and rumors continue to sweep through campus as to why one of Western's most beloved professors has disappeared without a word. I've heard a bunch of crazy stories but none of them come close to touching the truth. Other than Carson, my brother, Sydney, and Mike, I haven't told anyone else at school what transpired in his office.

Mike has stopped by my suite several times to make sure I was all right. Honestly, I don't know what I would do without him. To say he was shocked about what happened with our professor is an understatement. Even though I'm not ready to open up about the situation, he's been a strong shoulder to lean on. And right now, that's exactly what I need.

Mom nods before retreating a step to search my face. "Are you sure you're okay?" Her voice turns hesitant. "Do you want to talk about it? Every time I ask, you brush me off."

Guilt slices through me as I glance away. She's not wrong. Even though there's not much to what happened in his office, I'm still unclear if I perpetuated the situation and led him on. When it comes down to it, I agreed to dinner, drank wine with him, and allowed him to input his number into my phone. when he sat too close at the coffee shop, I didn't move away. When he texted during class, I didn't tell him it made me uncomfortable.

And I should have.

In hindsight, all of these incidents stick out like a brightly flashing neon sign. Just like I told Carson, I'm embarrassed by my own stupidity.

Pushing away the ugly memories, I release a steady breath. "I appreciate you asking, Mom. But I'm not ready to discuss it right now. I just need a little time to process what happened."

As soon as the words escape from my lips, she tugs me back into the warm circle of her arms and holds me close. "Oh, Elle. I hope you realize that you didn't do anything wrong."

That's what everyone keeps telling me. But if that's true, then why does it feel like I did?

"I know." It's so much easier to agree with the sentiment than argue.

"When you're up to it, I think it's important that you speak with a professional who can help you work through your feelings. If you don't want to talk with the counselor at the university, then we'll get a referral and find someone else."

"Yeah, maybe," I say vaguely, uncomfortable with the idea of sitting down with a total stranger to discuss something so personal. Then again, maybe it would be easier to talk with someone who doesn't know me. It's a lot to think about. And right now, I'm not ready.

Looking as if she wants to argue, Mom presses her lips together as concern brims in her eyes. I really wish there were something I could do to wipe it away. I'm tired of her, Brayden, Carson, Sydney, and Mike staring at me like that.

"It's really not that big of a deal, okay?"

"But it is," she says softly. "One of your professors tried to coerce you into a sexual relationship, and that's not okay."

"You're right. He tried, but he didn't succeed."

She squeezes my hand. "Your father would be proud of you for handling the situation the way you did."

My lips lift a fraction. "You can thank Brayden for teaching me how to knee a guy."

"Already have," she says, pressing a kiss against my forehead. "What Dad would be proud about is that you went straight to the administration instead of sweeping the incident under the rug and pretending it never occurred."

As difficult as it had been, there's no way I could slink off and do that. How could I live with myself if he tried to take advantage of another student and I could have stopped him?

"I love you, Elle."

Her softly spoken voice knocks me out of my tangled thoughts and does the impossible—lightens my heart. No matter what happens in life, I'll always have my family. And that means everything.

"I love you, too."

She slips an arm around my waist. "Just promise that if you need to talk, you'll reach out." Before I can respond, she tacks on, "And if you're not comfortable doing that with me, then you'll speak to a counselor."

My shoulders fall. "I promise."

"All right."

With her arm wrapped tightly around me, we walk into the kitchen. The rich scent of beef stroganoff permeates the air. It's normally one of my favorite dishes, but I haven't had much of an appetite lately.

"It smells delicious," I say, sliding onto one of the stools tucked under the long stretch of island.

She glances at me before moving to the stove and pulling off the cover, stirring the meat sauce. "I made it especially for you."

"Thanks."

"After everything..." Her voice trails off and she clears her throat. "I thought it might make you feel better."

"It does."

She nods, hustling to the marble counter and grabbing a bag of egg noodles before dumping them into an oversized pot of boiling water.

"I'm glad you and Brayden are finally on speaking terms again. I don't want there to be a rift between the two of you."

I stare at my fingers as they twist on the counter. "I know."

It wouldn't have happened without Carson. He's the one who called Brayden while I clung to him and retold the story. Within ten minutes, he was at the union with Sydney in tow. She wrapped me up in her arms and held on tight, all the while whispering that it wasn't my fault. She might be my brother's girlfriend, but I really hope that one day, she'll be part of our family. They've only been dating a month or so and already, I love her fiercely.

In true form, Brayden wanted to stomp over to the math building in order to get his hands on Dr. Holloway. Carson talked him down from the ledge and kept him from doing that. The last thing I'd want is to see Brayden ending up in trouble or even suspended because of me.

It's unfortunate that it took a situation like this to let go of my anger and forgive him. No matter how irritated or frustrated I get with my brother, I'll always love him. And nothing will ever change that. At some point in the not-so-distant future, I'll have to sit down with Carson and resolve our relationship, but there's been too much going on to do that.

Ten minutes later, Mom sets a steaming plate of stroganoff with broiled asparagus in front of me. Even though it smells delicious, my appetite remains elusive.

"Dig in before it gets cold," she encourages, settling next to me at the island.

I pick up my fork and push around the noodles and beef on my plate, trying to give the illusion that I've at least eaten some of it. I don't have the heart to confess that I'm not hungry after she went through all this trouble.

"Sweetie," she sighs, "you need to eat. It'll make you feel better."

"I know." I spear a noodle and pop it into my mouth before chewing it methodically and swallowing it down.

"At the rate you're going, you'll be here until tomorrow morning."

"Sorry, Mom. I really appreciate you taking the time to make this."

She slips a comforting arm around my waist. "It'll get better, I promise."

I nod, hoping she's right.

Before we can steer our conversation to a more pleasant topic, the front door opens before being slammed shut. Mom straightens on her chair as we both stare at the hallway that leads to the foyer.

"Were you expecting someone?"

She shakes her head. "Nope. I had extended an invitation to your brother, but he'd said he wouldn't be able to make it."

The only other person who would walk into the house without knocking would be Theo. I'll admit that seeing them together the first time was a bit of a shock to my system, but now that I've gotten used to it and become better acquainted with him, I've discovered he's a really nice guy and Mom seems genuinely happy.

Happier than I've seen her in a long time. Once I realized he wasn't trying to come in and take Dad's place, it was easier to let go of my concerns and accept their relationship for what it was.

Instead of the older man walking into the kitchen, Brayden strolls in.

"Hi, hun." Mom rises from her seat and quickly crosses the large space. "I didn't think you'd be able to make dinner."

Just as I lift my hand in greeting, Carson appears behind him and the movement stalls midair. When my surprised gaze bounces to my brother, he shrugs, a sheepish expression settling on his face.

As the silence stretches, Brayden clears his throat. "Can we talk for a minute?"

Surprised, I automatically rise from my stool. "Yeah, of course."

"Want to go to Dad's study?" he asks, already swinging around and heading toward the entryway where our father's office is located.

"Sure." My gaze flickers to Carson's as I walk past. Even though we've been in touch over the last few days, it's mostly been him texting or calling to check in and see how I'm doing. No matter what has happened in my life, he's always been a steady presence I can count on.

Once inside the room, Brayden closes the door, sealing us inside the space where all of Dad's trophies and football memorabilia is still proudly on display. There are photographs of him at different stages in his career, from high school through to the professional teams he played for. Everywhere you look, there are pictures, framed news clippings, and awards. Being here always makes the ache in my heart throb a bit harder for all that was lost.

Just like I always do when I step over the threshold, I gravitate to the last photograph that was taken of our family before the accident and pick up the silver frame. I don't realize I'm running my finger over the glass that covers his face until Brayden murmurs from beside me, "Sometimes it doesn't feel like the loss will ever fade, does it?"

I glance at him, surprised by the question. "No." Lifting my lips into a slight smile feels impossible. "There isn't a day that goes by I don't think about him."

"Same." His shoulders deflate as he hefts out a heavy sigh and gets straight to the point. "I'm sorry, Elle. I hope you realize that it was never my intention to hurt you."

Thick emotion gathers in my throat as I nod. "I know."

His gaze shifts to the photograph still clutched in my fingers. "All I've tried to do is protect you the way Dad would have wanted."

That statement is enough to have hot tears pricking the backs of my eyes. "I know that too, Bray." Carefully, I return the silver frame to its home on the bookshelf. "And I realize that everything you've done comes from a place of love, but sometimes it feels like you're smothering me."

Guilt flashes across his face.

"It would have been nice to have a boyfriend in high school. No one would even look twice at me because they were so afraid of you.

And it's been the same at Western. You need to back off and let me live my life. I'm more than capable of taking care of myself, Bray." There's a pause before I force out the rest. "Haven't I just proven that?"

He stiffens, fury igniting in his eyes as his hands tighten at his sides. "I swear to god that if—"

I shake my head. "I don't want to talk about how the situation with Dr. Holloway will play out. My point is that he tried to do something I didn't want, and I handled him on my own." I press a hand to my chest. "I know who I am and what I want. I didn't let him take advantage of me. You need to trust that I can protect myself and make good decisions."

The anger that had flared to life so easily moments ago drains away, and his voice softens. "I do trust you, it's everyone else I have a problem with."

"Dad wouldn't have wanted you to keep me safely protected in a bubble. He would have wanted me to experience all that life has to offer and be confident in my own abilities to handle whatever situation comes my way. You don't have to worry so much."

He releases a steady puff of air. "That's kind of difficult to do. You're my kid sister, and I've spent my entire life looking out for you."

"I know, but you're going to have to back off eventually. Next year, you won't be around to take care of me. Take a few steps back and give me a chance to prove that I can handle myself."

He drags a hand through his dark hair before gazing out the large picture window that overlooks the front lawn. "It's not that I think you're helpless or incompetent. I just..." His voice trails off, and for a long stretch of moments, silence fills the air before his gaze returns to mine. "I don't want to let Dad down."

That's all it takes for me to close the distance between us and slip my arms around his ribcage. "You could never do that. You've taken care of this family the best you could. Don't forget that you were only seventeen when he died. Way too young for that kind of responsibility."

His arms band around me, squeezing me tight. "I'll try to do better in the future, okay, squirt?"

"That's all I can ask for."

"So, about you and Carson..."

When his voice trails off, I pull back until I can search his face.

He shrugs. "I'm cool with it."

My brows rise. "Really?" That's the last thing I was expecting him to say.

He glances away before murmuring, "Yeah. I'm good if you two want to, you know, *date*."

Another wave of shock crashes over me. I can't believe I'm actually hearing these words fall from his lips. Especially when he was so vehemently opposed to it. Until that terrible morning at the cabin, I'd never seen the two of them have so much as a disagreement. I didn't think there was anything that could drive a wedge in their friendship.

"What changed your mind?"

"He's a good guy." There's a pause before he tacks on, "And he really cares about you."

My heart swells with love as I pull him in for another embrace. "Thank you."

"All I want is for you to be happy, and if Carson does that, then I don't want to stand in the way of your relationship."

For the first time since the morning he barged into the cabin, a genuine smile spreads across my lips before I stretch onto the tips of my toes and press a kiss against my brother's cheek. "I love you, Bray."

"Right back at you, squirt," he says with a smirk. "Now, I'm not saying it won't take time to get used to seeing you two together."

I nod. Totally understandable. "We'll try our best not to make out in front of you."

He scrunches his nose. "Don't even joke about that."

A chuckle escapes from me before I grab his hand and tow him from the room. It feels so good to finally hash everything out. We've always been close, and not talking to him on a daily basis was difficult. Once we return to the kitchen, my gaze settles on Carson, who sits at the island with a plate of stroganoff in front of him.

As soon as he sees me, he pops to his feet. "Do you want to—"

"Talk?" I fill in with a smile. "Yeah, I do."

The edges of his lips tilt upward as he jerks his head into a nod. "Maybe we could take a drive?"

"I'd like that."

Mom smiles as I hold out my hand for him to take. He eats up the space between us before slipping my fingers into his and squeezing them tight.

Chapter Forty-Five

CARSON

I hold open the passenger side door as Elle slides onto the leather seat. Our gazes catch before I slam the door closed, locking her inside the vehicle and jogging around the hood. Once settled next to her, I shove the key into the ignition and start up the engine, pulling out of the circular drive and onto the subdivision road.

With my attention focused straight ahead, I slip my fingers around hers. After being apart for this long, I need the physical contact. We're both silent, simply content to be together, as I pull into the main driveway for our old high school. There's only one in town, so it resembles more of a college campus with its main building, separate auditorium, and athletic center. The school's booster club made sure that the football stadium could rival any Division I arena. Playing under the bright lights on a Friday night was always a blast, and I enjoyed all four years spent here. Especially with Brayden by my side. And knowing Elle was in the stands, cheering us on, always forced me to take my game to the next level. I never wanted her to see me doing anything less than my best.

Once in front of the football stadium, I ease into a parking space and kill the engine before squeezing her fingers. "Come on."

With a furrowed brow, her gaze bounces from me to the stadium before sliding back again. "What are we doing here?"

"You'll see." I exit the truck before she can ask any more questions.

By the time I make it around the vehicle, she's slamming the door shut. I slip her hand back into mine and pull her through the entrance that leads to the bright green turf. Now that it's November, the high school season is over, and the teams are no longer holding practice.

We walk through the dark concourse before reaching the field. The only light that filters down is from the sky, illuminating the arena. My feet slow before grinding to a halt as I glance around, remembering all the times we ran through the tunnel to the sounds of cheering fans. Some of those memories are as fresh as if they'd happened yesterday. Especially the ones where I'd look up and find Elle sitting with her parents.

Those were good times, but it's nothing compared to now— because back then, Elle didn't belong to me, and I didn't think there would ever come a time when she'd be mine. And that's the difference.

I tug her into my arms and hold her close. There's something about her slim body pressed against mine that feels so right. Better than anything or anyone else ever has.

"One of the things I loved most about playing at this stadium is that I always knew where you were sitting. I could glance over at the fifty-yard line and look ten rows up and there you'd be. It was easy to make myself believe that you were there for me, watching me the entire time. That was all the incentive I needed to push myself harder."

She presses into me, molding to my body. "I always watched Brayden, but I was there for you, too. My attention was always locked on you, cheering you on."

I drop my forehead to hers, continuing to hold her gaze. "For as long as I can remember it's been you, Elle. No one else. Even when I didn't think there was a chance in hell you would ever belong to me, it was you. In my thoughts and dreams, it was you."

"You have to know I felt the same way. There was never anyone else in my heart."

My heart swells with thick emotion.

"The only reason I kept you at a distance is because I didn't want to do anything to hurt Brayden. I still don't." I reach up to stroke my fingers over the curve of her cheek. "But I can't stay away any longer. I need you in my life and by my side."

When she tilts her face, I brush my lips across hers. "There's no one who matters more than you."

"I'm yours, Carson. I always have been."

My hand slides around the side of her head until I can cup the back of her skull in my palm. "I hope you mean that, baby. Because you're mine now, and I don't plan on ever letting you go. I've spent enough time without you. I refuse to give up any more."

When her breath catches, my mouth crashes onto hers. One sweep of my tongue against the seam of her lips is all it takes for her to open and then I'm plunging inside, licking and sucking at her sweetness. There's something so right about the feel of her in my arms. It's as if she was always meant to be there. I tried for so long to put her out of both my head and heart, and I couldn't do it.

I refuse to try any longer.

When I finally break away, we're both breathing hard. Her heavy-lidded gaze is filled with arousal. Have I ever seen anything as sexy in my life?

This girl, she's the one for me.

And I'm the one for her.

The only one she'll ever need.

EPILOGUE

Elle

T *wo years later...*

With the strap of my carry-on bag resting against my shoulder, I navigate the thick crowd at the airport before heading outside to grab a cab. Pushing through the heavy glass doors into the cool air, I'm inundated with the scent of exhaust fumes. I pause at the curb and search the surrounding area before lifting my hand and hastening my pace toward an empty yellow taxi. A few moments later, I slide into the backseat before rattling off the address. A breath of relief escapes from me as the cab takes off, merging into traffic. Only now does my head fall back onto the cushion and my eyelids flutter shut.

It's been four weeks since Carson and I have been in the same city, and I can't believe how much I've missed him. FaceTime, calls, and texting is in no way the same as being in the same room together. Or being able to reach out and touch each other. And late-night calls with lots of sexy talk and self-love sessions are in no way the same as having the person you love stroke their hands or lips over you.

Even the thought is enough to have me clenching my thighs together in anticipation.

We've been living in separate cities since Carson graduated and moved to New York where he was drafted. He's renting an amazing apartment in the heart of the city. I love spending my breaks with him. Hand in hand, we walk around the crowded streets and take in Broadway shows, eat at amazing restaurants, and attend concerts.

I'll admit that it was tempting to transfer colleges after he moved. For me, New York has always been the end goal. I want to act on Broadway, and there's no better place to be than here. Even though I'm sure about us and the direction we're headed in, I didn't want to rush our relationship. I wanted to give us time to grow as a couple. Plus, I love my professors and roommates. So, I'm enjoying my last year at Western before graduating in the spring and moving in with him.

With traffic, it takes about an hour to reach his high-rise. As we pull to the curb, I pay the driver and grab my bag from the seat beside me before exiting the vehicle. As soon as I get out of the taxi, a couple outfitted in a gorgeous dress and tuxedo emerges from the building and climbs into the yellow vehicle. For just a second, I stand on the sidewalk before inhaling a big breath of air. I love everything about this city. The energy is like nothing else I've ever experienced. It's infectious.

The doorman tips his hat before opening the door with a flourish. "Nice to see you again, Ms. Kendricks."

"Thanks, Frank. It's good to be back," I say with a smile.

"Pretty soon it'll be permanent."

"Yup, can't wait!"

With a wave, I step inside the elaborate lobby with its high vaulted ceiling, crown molding, and crystal chandelier. My shoes click against the ocean of white marble as I move through the space. I greet the manager loitering behind the wide expanse of counter before heading to the bank of elevators. The place is over-the-top swanky and comes with every conceivable bell and whistle. Underground parking, a private gym, a rooftop pool, dry cleaning, and concierge service, just to name a few.

Once inside the mirrored car, I hit the button for the twentieth floor. Most of the walls in his apartment are floor-to-ceiling windows with breathtaking views of the city. Especially at night, when all of the lights are illuminated and stretch as far as the eye can see in every direction.

Has he pressed me against them a time or two and fucked me so hard that I've screamed my head off before nearly slumping to the floor?

I'm going to plead the fifth on that one. I'm not really a girl who likes to kiss and tell.

When the doors slide open, I step into the carpeted hallway and walk down the long stretch. Beautiful artwork hangs on the walls along with well-lit sconces that are strategically placed at set intervals. There are always vasefuls of fresh flowers set on narrow antique tables. I have no idea how much Carson pays each month for the place. When I asked, he refused to tell me, but it must be a pretty penny. I know he wanted to make sure that we were in a central location near all of the amenities. And that includes Broadway.

I slip the apartment key from my purse before inserting the thin metal into the lock and twisting the handle. I wince when the door creaks and carefully step into the foyer, closing it behind me just as quietly. With my head cocked, I pause and listen for the telltale signs of movement from within, but everything remains silent.

Perfect.

I texted Carson before I left for the airport to see what his plans were for the day. He mentioned going to practice and then heading back home again. So, we made plans to FaceTime later in the afternoon. This trip is a surprise, and I can't wait to see the look on his face when I walk in. We weren't supposed to get together for another two weeks, but I was able to talk one of my professors into allowing me to take my exam early.

I peek into the living room but don't catch sight of him. The apartment is almost three thousand square feet with three bedrooms, a spacious kitchen that's all black marble, high-end fixtures, and shiny stainless-steel appliances. There's a massive island with tons of room for prep. When I'm in town, we'll stop at Wholefoods and pick up groceries before preparing our meals together. I never thought I'd enjoy cooking, but with Carson, it's been fun. When the weather is nice, we take our plates to the balcony and enjoy the view along with our dinner. I can't wait until I'm here full time.

I tiptoe past the wood panel study with its fireplace, endless rows of bookshelves, and fancy antique desk before looking inside, but he continues to remain elusive.

With a turn to the left, I head down the hallway, passing by the two generously sized guest bedrooms and a bathroom before arriving at the master suite. As I step over the threshold, the sound of running water hits my ears. Quietly I set my bag on an overstuffed armchair before peeling off my sweatshirt, bra, leggings, and panties. Once I'm naked, I walk into the spacious bathroom. It's all blue-gray marble tile and ivory cabinetry. Standing inside a clear enclosure that is spacious enough for five people is where I find Carson.

Even though the glass is steamy, I'm able to make out his shape as water cascades down his body. I can't help but pause and drink in the sight of him. It's one I could never grow tired of.

Carson has always been muscular, but now that he's playing in the NFL, he's bigger, stronger. More well-defined.

It's only made him hotter.

He has everything going for him. He's sexy, young, and talented. With his good looks, he's exploded on a national stage. He's already got a few endorsement deals under his belt—a Calvin Klein underwear advertising campaign included. Girls have always gone wild for him, but now that he's been splashed across billboards, women crawl out of the woodwork to throw themselves at his feet. Even when I'm standing right next to him and his arm is draped around my shoulders, it still happens.

If I wasn't so secure in our relationship, it would bother the hell out of me and probably cause problems. But it doesn't. At the end of the day, I know whose bed he wants to be in. He could have moved on in college, and he didn't. It's not going to happen now just because there are more females vying for his attention than ever before.

Unable to hold off any longer, I pull open the glass door and step inside. With his hand gripping his thick erection, he swings around, and his eyes widen. "Elle?"

I grin. "Were you expecting someone else?"

As the shock fades, an answering smile curves his lips before he reaches out and tugs me against his hard body. "I thought we weren't going to see each other for two more weeks."

I rise onto my tiptoes and press a kiss to his mouth. I've missed him more than I thought possible. "I was much too frustrated to wait that long."

My hand slips down his rock-solid body before arriving at his cock. "Seems like you were, too."

He shrugs, not looking embarrassed in the least to be caught red handed. "Gotta do what I gotta do to make it through, right?"

My fingers tighten around his girth as I slowly slide along the steely length. God but I love the feel of him beneath my fingertips. "As long as what you gotta do involves your own hand, I'm good with it."

Water rains down on us as he presses a kiss against me. "You know it does. There's never been anyone but you." He lifts his head until he's able to search my eyes. "How could there be when you're the only girl who has ever filled my dreams?"

A little piece of me melts as I reach up and nip at his lower lip. "I love you."

"I love you, too."

"Now that we've gotten that out of the way, why don't you screw me nice and hard before I self-combust?"

A wicked grin curves his lips. "If you insist."

"I do."

There are no more words as he does precisely that.

A few times, actually.

And each one is somehow better than the last.

But that's the way it is with Carson. It just keeps getting better and better.

The End.

Subscribe to my newsletter to receive a free bonus epilogue that
includes all of the couples from the Campus series!
Get it here -) https://dl.bookfunnel.com/et1elg7ht6

Want to read the next story in the Campus Series? Pre-order it here -)
https://books2read.com/campusgod

Have you read the other books in the Campus Series?
Campus Player (Demi & Rowan)
https://books2read.com/u/mYAxqV

Campus Heartthrob (Sydney & Brayden)
https://books2read.com/campusheartthrob

KING OF CAMPUS

Ivy

Ladies, and a few guys as well, ;) keep those Roan King sightings pouring in. Especially the ones of him at football practice. Hot, sweaty, with an extra shot of gorgeous is exactly how I take my Roan King. Don't mind me while I type away with one hand... KingOfCampus.com

"*H*oney," I holler at the top of my lungs before kicking the door shut, "*I'mmmm home!*"

Those words are met with a loud shriek as Lexie flies around the corner before hurtling her small curvy body at me. I'm given roughly two seconds to drop my bags in anticipation of impact. She's lucky I have fairly decent—

The breath gets knocked out of me as we both go crashing to the floor.

Apparently, reflexes are no match when that much force and weight are careening toward you at the speed of light. Physics, I'm guessing, is exactly how I end up sprawled on my back with my best friend and roommate spread out on top of me in our brand-spanking-new apartment. There's a completely manic light filling her big brown eyes. Matching the look, I can't help but beam up at her because it is so freaking good to see her gorgeous face.

It's been precisely fifteen months since we've been in the same room together. Actually, it's been fifteen months since we've been on the same continent. I spent my sophomore year of college studying abroad in Paris.

Needless to say, it was as amazing and spectacular as you'd imagine it would be. Even thinking about it leaves me with a tiny pang of nostalgia for the life I'd left behind.

"Damn, now that's hot! Can I snap a shot for my wallpaper?"

We turn to stare at the tall, good looking male grinning...or maybe the correct term would be—*leering* down at us. His eyes slide oh-so-slowly over our entwined bodies as if he's trying to singe this moment into his memory for all eternity. But it's not in a pervy way...what the heck am I saying? Of course, it's in a pervy way. Which is precisely when I realize that my dear friend, Lexie, seems to be missing the lower half of her outfit.

Yep...she's only wearing panties.

She smothers a giggle before clearing her throat. Rather impressively, her voice whips out in a perfect imitation of a mother scolding her three-year-old toddler. "You damn well better not snap a picture or you won't be seeing this ass for a very long time." To emphasize this point, she gives it a little shake and her boyfriend groans in response.

"Please?" There's a whole lot of whine filling his deep masculine voice. Which is kind of hilarious because he's well over six feet tall and is seriously broad in the chest and shoulders. This one is definitely all man. Lexie, of course, filled me in via Facetime on the football playing boyfriend she acquired about seven months ago. Needless to say, she wasn't exaggerating.

He's pretty damn hot.

If you're into big and muscly.

Which I'm not going to lie... I am.

"The mental snapshot you're burning into your brain will have to suffice."

Folding his muscular arms in front of an equally solid looking chest, he grumbles under his breath, "You always have to be such a hard ass."

Lexie gives me a little wink. "You wouldn't have it any other way, babe."

"True," he sighs in agreement, "very true."

Since Lexie isn't showing any indication of removing herself from my person anytime soon, I'm forced to point out the obvious. "You might want to get off me before your boyfriend has an embarrassing moment in his shorts."

I'm joking, of course.

Sort of.

"You don't have to get off on my account," he quickly chimes in as he continues to ogle us.

Lexie rolls her eyes at me.

"Have I mentioned just how hot you look in that thong?" His voice sounds all heated up and I'm seriously considering shoving Lexie off me before something unfortunate, not to mention awkward, happens and I'm no longer able to look this dude in the eyes again.

"Jeez, Lex, did you have to molest me while only wearing a thong?" No wonder her boyfriend is all but sporting a woody over there.

"Be happy you didn't arrive ten minutes later, I wouldn't be wearing anything at all."

I shake my head to loosen that mental image from my brain. "That wasn't something I needed to know."

Continuing to grin, Lexie smacks my lips with a big wet sloppy kiss. "Goddamn but I missed you, Ivy." Then she does her damnedest to squeeze the very life out of me before rolling gracefully to her side.

"I'm glad to be back, too." As the words automatically spill from my mouth, I realize that I don't necessarily mean them. There's a large part of me that wishes I were still living my life in Paris. With an ocean between me and my dad, I didn't have to dwell on him and the new family he created for himself so quickly after Mom died.

Dad's life carried on while mine fell apart. Even though it's been five years since she died, the ache still feels painfully tender. Returning to Barnett means that I no longer have an excuse not to visit them.

Shaking those thoughts away, I realize I'm still sprawled on the carpeted floor. I blink my eyes a few times as a handsome face peers down at me before crinkling into a large friendly smile. I don't bother hoisting myself up just yet. Instead, I say in my most formal tone, "Mr. Sullivan, I presume."

His grin intensifies, making him appear even more striking than I'd originally thought. Lexie had gushed about how gorgeous her new guy was. And it's not like I didn't believe her, but it's obvious she wasn't exaggerating.

Like at all.

Because Dylan Sullivan is seriously hot.

Golden blond hair, deep brown eyes, sculpted jaw, and athletic body.

According to Lexie, he treats her like a total princess. Which is exactly how it should be. Lexie deserves someone who appreciates how smart, loyal, and gorgeous she is. She's a damn good friend and I'm lucky to have her in my life.

"The one and only," he beams in response, throwing a flirty wink in for good measure.

Oh, this guy is totally dangerous.

Could they be more perfectly suited to one another?

I absolutely love it.

"Umm, isn't your father Dylan Sullivan the first?"

He shrugs his broad shoulders. Self admittedly, I'm kind of a shoulder and arm girl myself. And Dylan Sullivan certainly has nicely chiseled ones.

"Shhh, you're ruining the moment, babe."

That being said, Dylan offers me a hand, which I grab hold of, before being hauled off the floor and set back onto my sandaled feet. I dust my backside off before my gaze slides to Lexie. The unexpected glassy sheen of tears shining in her big brown eyes has my own widening in confusion.

"Lex, why are you—"

I don't get a chance to wrap my lips around the last word before she's hurtling herself in my direction. Her arms slip around my body before tugging me close.

"I missed you, Ivy-girl," she whispers fiercely against my ear, "so damn much! Fifteen months is a long time to stay away. Don't ever leave me like that again."

I'm not normally an emotional person, but her heartfelt words have me choking up and I squeeze her to me.

She pulls back to search my eyes before admitting quietly, "I was afraid you might decide to stay over there."

That just goes to show you how well Lexie knows me. What I don't mention is that I tried my damnedest to make that happen. To finish out college, find a permanent place to live, a dance gig, all so I could postpone coming home indefinitely. Being back here, even though this is a new apartment, still reminds me that my mom is dead, and my dad has moved on and I no longer have a home to return to.

Not one that feels like home used to feel.

"I'm just so glad you're finally back."

"Me, too," I whisper as hot licks of emotion prick the back of my eyes. I hug her tightly one last time before releasing her.

Lexie and I have been best friends since fourth grade when her family moved in down the block from mine. We made it through middle and high school with our friendship intact and decided to apply at some of the same colleges so we could room together. Luckily, Barnett was on both of our short lists. It has a highly regarded fashion design program for Lexie and a kickass dance program for me.

There's absolutely no one in this world I can count on like Lexie Abbott. I'm actually a little ashamed of myself for failing to remember that. In trying to escape all the painful memories, I forgot about the good stuff, too.

Lexie backs up until she's standing directly in front of Dylan. As soon as she's close enough, he wraps those huge arms around her before pulling her flush against the front of his body. Looking ridiculously contented, he settles his chin on top of her head like he's done it a hundred times before.

Like it's the most natural thing in the world.

I can't help but feel thrilled that Lexie has found someone who appreciates the amazing woman she's grown into.

Unwilling to get anymore sappy than I already have, I shake my head. "Do you two come with barf bags? I've only been here for ten minutes and you're already making me sick to my stomach."

They both flash big cheesy grins at me. I want to roll my eyes before sticking my finger down my throat like I'm going to puke. "I suppose you're going to be practically living here with us?" Yep, I can already see how this will go. Dylan will be our unofficial apartment mascot.

With big innocent eyes, she says, "Didn't I mention that Dylan lives in the apartment next to us with two guys from the football team?"

"Nope," I shake my head, "you definitely did not mention that. I guess that makes things convenient."

"Totally convenient," Dylan adds with a sly grin aimed in my direction.

This time, I actually roll my eyes. "So which room is mine?"

In her exuberance, Lexie all but jumps out of Dylan's arms before leading me down a short hallway. As I trail after her, I'm reminded that she's only wearing a thong.

I mean, sure, she has a great ass but still...

"Er, maybe you should put your shorts back on before you give me the grand tour." Out of the corner of my eye, I see Dylan open his mouth. My narrowed gaze slices to his. "Don't even say it," I warn.

Biting her lip, Lexie stifles another laugh before dashing into her bedroom. In twenty seconds flat she rejoins us sporting tiny white shorts. Then she leads the way into a sunny little room before doing her best auto show model imitation as she gestures with wide sweeping movements to all the wonderful amenities my room has to offer.

She points toward the two large windows lining the wall. "Look at all the gorgeous sunlight that pours in!" Then she throws open the bi-fold closet doors. "And a humongous closet for all the clothes you brought back from Paris." Her arms drop to her sides as she swivels toward me. Her auto show model imitation is forgotten in lieu of possible new stylish European clothing. "You *did* bring me back some clothes, right?"

For a moment, my eyes travel around the room, taking everything in. It's not huge by any means but after living in Paris, it sure feels like it is. I'm used to about a third of the space. So this feels pretty damn luxurious. I can't imagine what I'm going to do with all this space to myself. Then my eyes fall to the double sized mattress shoved up against the far wall and my heart actually swells with unfettered joy.

Oh my god, it's so big! I've been sleeping on a twin bed for the last fifteen months. I literally can't wait to spread out on that huge mattress. Maybe roll around a bit. Make some snow angels…minus the snow. Already I'm looking forward to hitting the sheets tonight.

I spent a little more than eight hours on a plane with a two-hour layover in Amsterdam. And France is six hours ahead of us. So, I'd like nothing more than to fall into bed for a nice long nap.

When I don't respond, a thread of worry weaves its way through her voice. "Ivy?" Her concerned tone snaps me right out of my thoughts.

"Of course I did," I say. "There's a short, thigh length pleated skirt, two hand woven scarves, one cashmere sweater, a gorgeous black knit top and these creamy trouser pants that your ass will thank me for."

If watching Lexie sprawled out on top of me, wearing nothing more than a lacy little thong and a tank top is Dylan's idea of a wet dream, hearing about all the beautiful clothes I brought back from Paris is hers. We're talking flushed cheeks and dilated eyes.

And yes, it's entirely possible Lexie could have an embarrassing moment in her shorts. Although I hope not.

"Oh, I can't wait to see them," she squeals in delight, practically jumping up and down with unbridled enthusiasm.

Fashion design is Lexie's life. She was a budding fashionista way back in middle school before I ever cared about what top went with what bottoms. Thank goodness for Lexie or I probably would have been much more of a walking fashion disaster than I was.

I scraped together enough money and perused a few vintage boutiques to find unique pieces I knew she wouldn't be able to get here in the States. I hope she loves them half as much as I think she will.

"What about some hot French lingerie?" her boyfriend asks.

Since Dylan is standing directly behind Lexie, she doesn't bother turning around to admonish him. Instead, she rams her elbow into his gut. He grunts in response. If she hadn't done it, I probably would have.

"Just stand there and look pretty," she mutters under her breath.

My lips twitch because he is definitely pretty.

Lexie gives me a little wink as if she can read my mind. "Don't let his good looks fool you, he's smart, too."

Of course he is.

Because gorgeous and smart are exactly the kind of guys Lexie attracts. While I, on the other hand, had the sad misfortune to fall for a hot athletic jerk who assured me he was going to remain faithful to his study-abroad-girlfriend when in actuality, he started hooking up with other girls as soon as above-mentioned-girlfriend was out of the country.

I've had the last fourteen and a half months to get over Finn McKenzie. And I have. I am totally over him. Unfortunately, he's been calling and texting almost relentlessly for the last week, which means he's been occupying my thoughts way more than I'd like.

Perhaps I should say he's been *trying* to call and text. I haven't bothered to pick up his calls or respond to his rather lengthy and apologetic text messages. I mean, can you seriously believe that? The guy has some nerve reaching out to me after what he did. Is he so delusional as to think we're going to pick up where we left off now that I'm back at Barnett?

Apparently, he is.

We'd been together for about six months before I left for Europe. And yes, I knew having a long-distance relationship would be difficult, but I was willing to give it a shot. I'd grown to like Finn. I hadn't been gone more than two weeks when Lexie FaceTimed me about what Finn had been busy doing...which had been, in case you're wondering, other girls.

And that, my friends, had been the end of that.

Lexie's advice was to forget about my cheating asshole of an ex by hooking up with a bunch of hot French guys.

I hooked up with two semi-hot French dudes and buried myself in dance which was the reason I'd been accepted to study at the Conservatoire de Paris in the first place. After a few months, my heartache lessened. I stopped thinking about Finn, my dad, his new wife, their kids, and I concentrated on soaking up everything I possibly could.

It took some time to adjust but after two months, I found myself with an amazing new life in a city renowned for its art and culture. There was no way I was going to allow anything to ruin this once in a lifetime opportunity. Right around the year mark, I stopped thinking about Lexie and returning to Barnett University and started wondering if maybe I could live here for the rest of my life.

Or, at the very least, the next few years.

When I mentioned this possibility to my dad, he made it perfectly clear that he would not be footing the bill for a life in Paris and said, in no uncertain terms, he wanted me back at Barnett come August. Undeterred by his directive, or perhaps because of it, I'd searched for enough scholarship and grant money to pay for me to continue studying in Paris. Needless to say, I hadn't been able to pull it off which is exactly why I was back at Barnett for my junior year.

"So, do you like it?"

My eyes swing back to Lexie who is standing there with all this hopeful expectation lighting up her face. A tiny smile tugs at the corners of my lips because it really is good to see her after all this time apart. "It's absolutely perfect."

Looking very much like the best friend I left behind fifteen months ago, a huge grin spills across her beautiful face before she hurtles herself at me for a third time.

Want to read more? You can buy King of Campus here -)
https://books2read.com/u/bPX7WY

THE GIRL NEXT DOOR

Mia

*S*ummer *before freshman year of college...*

"*G*et your butt over here," my best friend squeals from the window where she's taken up sentinel, "you *need* to see this!"

That's a negative, Ghost Rider. I'll take a hard pass. I have zero interest in spying on a yard full of drunken classmates who are partying it up at my neighbor's house. Reluctantly, I glance up from the toes I'm painting with a pale pink polish. Coney Island Cotton Candy, to be precise.

When our gazes lock, Alyssa waves me over. She's practically vibrating with excitement. Kind of like a schnauzer.

"Everyone is over there!"

"Not true," I mutter, lacquering my baby toe with an impressively steady hand. "*We're* right here." And that's exactly where I plan to stay.

"Yeah, that's kind of the problem." She steeples her hands together before shaking them at me. "Please?" she begs. "Can't we go over there for a little bit? *Just a little*? That's all I'm asking."

That's all she's asking...ha!

I'm calling bullshit.

Alyssa knows I'd rather chew my arm off than crash one of Beck Hollingsworth's parties. I didn't mention it to her, but Beck shot me a text earlier this afternoon with all the details. If she even suspected an invitation had been issued, she would have dragged my ass across the lawn that separates our properties as soon as the first guest pulled into the drive.

No, thank you.

It's obvious from all the commotion coming from next door that the entire senior class has shown up to celebrate our newly graduated status. If we didn't live on a quiet cul-de-sac tucked away in a gated subdivision, I'd expect the police to make an unannounced visit and shut down the festivities.

Then again, no one wants to mess with Beck's father, Archibald Hollingsworth. He's a high-priced attorney with a fleet of underlings working for him. He's one of those overly tan guys with blindingly white veneers you see on television yapping about if you've been injured, you need to call them—they fight for the little guy! The dude is everywhere. Billboards. Commercials. Newspaper and magazine advertisements.

The local police have tangled with Archibald several times over the years because his son is a magnet for trouble. Let's see, there was the time (or five) when he was picked up for underage drinking. When Beck was fifteen years old, he *borrowed* his parent's brand spanking new Range Rover and did a little off-roading. And the police were involved when he super glued the locks on the high school building doors for senior prank day.

Instead of hauling Beck to the station every time he's picked up, they drop him at his front door and don't bother talking to Archibald about it. Beck is on a first name basis with a number of guys on the force. A few showed up to his graduation party in June.

It shouldn't come as a surprise that Beck always figures out a way to circumvent the obstacles standing in his path. His parents. School. The law. It's as irritating as it is impressive. Maybe one of these days, he'll use his powers for good instead of evil.

"Come on, Mia!" Alyssa whines, all the while flashing sad puppy dog eyes at me.

Double whammy.

My bestie knows I have a difficult time resisting puppy dog eyes.

I wiggle my toes from the bed and grumble, "I can't go anywhere until my nails dry." I'm doing my best to prolong subjecting myself to the aggravation of being anywhere near Beckett Hollingsworth. The guy drives me bat shit crazy.

And that's putting it mildly.

"Great! So...five minutes?" She swings away before pressing her face against the screen as her voice turns dreamy. "I bet Colton is already there."

Ugh.

Colton Montgomery is Beck's righthand man, so it's not a wager I'm likely to win.

Against my better advice, Alyssa has been crushing hard on Colton for more than a year. Not only is he popular, but he's a football player. Heavy emphasis on the *player* part. If Alyssa were smart, she'd find a nice guy to fall in lust with, but she has tunnel vision when it comes to the blond-haired, blue-eyed heartbreaker.

Colton has it all going on. Brains, brawn, and more than likely, a one-way ticket to the NFL after college.

The only problem is that he's aware of his own appeal.

His ego is as massive as other parts of him.

Or so I hear.

And not from Alyssa since he refuses to sleep with her. I can't decide if the situation is amusing or sad. The more Colton keeps Alyssa at a firm distance, the more determined she is to have him.

Last football season, Alyssa dragged me to every game. Even the away ones. My greatest fear was that Beck would assume my ass was in the stands in support of him. His fan club is already legendary without adding me to the ranks.

When it comes to the ladies, Beckett makes Colton look like an innocent babe. He goes through girls like most people go through underwear. Speaking of panties, the girls at our high school are always happy—hell, I'd go so far as to say thrilled—to drop theirs for him.

It's ridiculous.

He's a chronic user and abuser.

There should be a warning label slapped across his forehead.

Beware. Toxic to the female species.

But you know what?

That wouldn't stop these bubble-headed chicks from spreading their legs wide for him. I've stopped trying to figure out the appeal. All right, I'm well aware of what the attraction is. As much as I've tried to pretend I'm immune to his charms, I'm not. I just do a damn good job of burying them deep down where they never see the light of day. If I didn't, Beck would annihilate me in a heartbeat, and I have zero desire to end up a casualty on his hit list.

Given the choice, I'd rather flip through Netflix and find a movie to watch rather than be dragged over to Beck's bash.

Doesn't sitting around in pajamas and stuffing our faces with pizza sound way better than watching a bunch of our classmates get sloppy drunk, engage in way too much PDA, puke all over the place before alcohol poisoning sets in?

I won't bother posing the question to Alyssa. There is no way she'll willingly opt for sitting home instead of stalking her crush.

Would you like to guess what Colton will be doing while I wipe drool from Alyssa's chin?

You guessed it. He'll be flirting with every vagina he thinks he has a chance of penetrating.

Honestly, it's one of the most masochistic things Alyssa could do. I have no idea why she insists on putting herself through this kind of agony. Apparently, my job as her best friend is to support her decision to inflict untold amounts of mental anguish onto herself. I'd slap her upside the head if I thought it would knock sense into her.

My prediction for the evening goes a little something like this— Alyssa will have a few drinks, moon over Colton, before dissolving into a puddle of tears while that manwhore makes out with other girls in front of her face. Then I'll drag her home and she'll end up knuckle-deep in a gallon of triple chocolate ice cream.

But that's what friends are for, right?

Don't worry, I've already made my peace with it.

"Fine," I grumble with a scowl, hoping she understands the depth of my reluctance. "But let it be known that I won't be staying for more than an hour. So you better make good use of your time, girl."

She swings around to face me, bouncing on the tips of her toes as she claps her hands together with excitement. "Yay!" As soon as she gets the affirmative, she beelines for my closet, which is half the size of my room.

I have the kind of closet most girls my age can only dream about. Shoes, purses, clothes, jewelry. It's all there and organized.

"Cue the montage music while I find something schmexy to wear!" she squeals.

"What you have on is fine." I roll my eyes and yell, "It was good enough for me, wasn't it?"

From within the depths of my closet comes a snort.

For the next ten minutes, I'm treated to an impromptu fashion show. At the rate Alyssa is going, we won't make it to the party any time soon.

Take your time, girlfriend. I'm totally good with that.

A dozen outfit changes later, Alyssa settles on a black knit tank and white skirt that showcases her sun-kissed legs to their best advantage. Alyssa has been taking dance classes since she was three years old. She's toned with long, lean muscles.

"Damn girl, you look hot." Not that her crush will appreciate the effort. Alyssa needs to move on. I'm thinking a twelve-step program would help kick the Chase Montgomery habit.

"I would gladly live in your closet if you'd let me." She grins before doing a little twirl. "It's my happy place."

A reluctant smile quirks my lips.

My mother is a card-carrying shopaholic and has the Amex Black Card bills to prove it. She buys clothes like our house burned to the ground and nothing could be salvaged. Even with racks and racks of space, my wardrobe is bursting at the seams. Three quarters of the stuff has never seen the light of day. Alyssa is lucky we're roughly the same size so she can borrow whatever she wants.

Now that she's dressed and ready to mingle, her eyes narrow as she takes a hard look at me. Wordlessly, she spins around and races back inside the closet only to resurface a handful of minutes later.

"Here you go," she says, tossing two garments at the foot of my bed.

I glance at the shimmery gold tank and dark wash jean skirt that resembles a folded-up napkin. The skirt is cute as hell, but I would strongly advise against going commando while wearing it unless you're looking to flash everyone your goodies.

Since that's not my usual style, the price tag is still dangling from the pocket. I have no idea what my mother was thinking when she picked it up.

Unsure why she's throwing clothes at me, I point to the small pile. "What's that about?"

"You need to change." She gives me a look that says—*duh* before clapping her hands together. "Chop-chop."

Changing my clothes was not part of the plan. I'm fine with going in my pajamas. It's not like I'm looking for a hookup. Or anything else, for that matter.

I shake my head and fold my arms across my chest. "No, thank you."

Her gaze rakes over me as she points at my T-shirt. "Is that a coffee stain on your boob?"

With a frown, I glance at my chest and inspect the dark spot marring the fabric of my right breast. My guess is that she's right. Caramel Macchiato, to be specific. "Possibly."

Her lips flatten. "I refuse to go anywhere with you looking like *that*."

"Great!" I stretch out before stacking my hands behind my head. "What kind of movie night does it feel like to you? Romcom? Horror? Psychological thriller? Angsty tearjerker?" A benevolent smile curves my lips. "You can choose."

Alyssa stomps her foot on the carpeted floor. "Mia!" she wails at a decibel that could shatter eardrums. A few neighborhood dogs howl in response. *"You promised!"*

Promised?

No, I don't think so.

I scrunch my nose and tap a finger against my lips. "I don't believe I ever *promised* to do anything. *Reluctantly agreed?* Yes. *Was browbeaten into capitulating?* Definitely. But *promised?* Not in this lifetime."

When she straightens to her full height, I groan, knowing exactly what's about to happen. "*Mia Evelyn Stanbury!* Do I need to remind you who was there when—"

Argh.

This is the portion of the evening where Alyssa trots out every damn thing she's ever done for me until I relent. And she'll start with Harper Hastings. The girl who bullied me relentlessly in seventh grade because Xander Rossi asked me to the movies instead of her. After months of Harper's meanspirited attacks, Alyssa waited for the girl after school. My bestie let it be known that if Harper didn't cease and desist, she'd spread the good word that the other girl was a known bra stuffer. It must have been true, since Harper immediately backed off and I never heard a peep from her again.

"*Yes, yes, Harper Hastings,*" I mutter, not appreciating the direction this conversation has swerved in.

Alyssa folds her arms across her chest as a smug smile twists her lips upward. "Harper Hastings is only the beginning, my friend." She arches a brow. "Need I continue?"

Silently we glare before I fold like a cheap house of cards. "Fine, I'll change." I straighten before scooping up the skirt and top and shaking them at her. "It's only because I love you and you're my best friend that I'm even willing to step foot next door."

An angelic smile spreads across her pretty face before she blows me a kiss. "Love you, too. Now kindly move your assets."

"An hour," I remind. "That's all you get."

Looking unconcerned, she waves a hand. "No worries, that's more than enough time to work my magic."

What she means to say is that it's more than enough time for Colton to ignore her, all the while hooking up with another girl. Part of me almost wishes he would sleep with Alyssa. Maybe then the rose-colored glasses would come off and she would realize what a douche the guy is.

In one fluid motion, the stained T-shirt is stripped from my body and replaced with the shimmery gold tank. Then I slide off the comfy shorts I've been lounging in and yank on the tiny rectangle of material that doubles as a skirt.

I step in front of my floor-to-ceiling mirror that's propped against the wall and stare at my reflection before attempting to tug the skirt further down my thighs, but it's useless. There's not a spare inch of material to be found.

What the hell was my mother thinking when she picked this up? Was she mistakenly shopping in the toddler section? That's the only reasonable explanation.

I turn around and bend over, touching my toes before peering over my shoulder to the mirror. It's as I suspected. My thong is on full display. Actually, it doesn't even look like I'm wearing underwear since the material is wedged between the crack of my ass like dental floss.

Lovely.

Not to mention uncomfortable.

"Is there a second option to consider?" My gaze slides to Alyssa's in the mirror. "One where my ass isn't hanging out?"

"'Fraid not. I'm seriously loving the whole—is she or isn't she wearing panties guessing game you've got going on." She winks. "Play your cards right and maybe you'll get lucky tonight."

I narrow my eyes as my lips thin. "Believe it or not, I'm perfectly content being unlucky."

"That, my dear, is only because you don't realize what you've been missing."

"Heartache, STI's, and the possibility of an unplanned pregnancy?" I flutter my lashes and smile. "You are so right."

Ignoring my comment, she tosses a pair of gold sandals at me before sliding her feet into black leather ones that strap up her legs, giving her that whole Grecian goddess vibe. She looks amazing. But then again, when doesn't she? Alyssa has long blond hair and dark blue eyes. Her skin has a natural sun-kissed glow that darkens under the summer sun.

It almost offends me that Colton refuses to fuck my friend.

What the hell is wrong with him?

"Ready to go?" she asks, checking her reflection in the mirror one last time.

I slip the sandals on before rising to my full height. "As I'll ever be."

Five minutes later, we've traversed the lawn and are walking around the side of the Hollingsworth mansion. All sixteen thousand square feet of it. Needless to say, Archibald has turned ambulance chasing into a lucrative art form.

With every step we take, the sound of drunken laughter and the pulsing beat of music grows louder, assaulting our ears. As soon as the party comes into view, I wonder why I let Alyssa talk me into this.

It's complete chaos.

As much as Alyssa would like to convince you otherwise, I'm not a complete dud. I like to party as much as the next girl. But Beck enjoys taking his antics to the next level. He's not content to have a low-key get together where people sit around and chill.

This party is moments away from becoming one of those teen movies where all hell breaks loose and the host wakes up naked the next morning in a dumpster five states away next to a goat.

Over to the left, a few people are holding a guy upside down while he performs a keg stand.

Chants of—*chug, chug, chug* permeate the air.

It wouldn't surprise me if one of these drunken idiots is found floating face down in the pool come morning.

It begs the question of why Beck's parents would leave him alone without supervision. He might be eighteen years old and technically an adult, but he needs an adultier adult to keep him in check. Someone who can put the kibosh on his hijinks.

Good luck with that. His older brother, Ari, is out of the country for the summer.

Archibald and Caroline, his parents, must have realized this was inevitable. Every time they go out of town, Beck throws a huge bash. Depending on the amount of damage, he gets grounded anywhere from a couple of days to a couple of weeks. The threat of conse-quences—hell, actual consequences being enforced—are in no way a deterrent.

Believe it or not, before our parents left town for a long weekend in New York, Archie asked me to keep an eye on their son. His actual words were—*make sure no one dies.*

As if I exert that much control over Beck?

Yeah, right. Beck doesn't listen to anyone, let alone me.

Exactly what am I supposed to do?

Tattletale?

Facetime his parents so they can get a first-hand glimpse of the ensuing pandemonium?

As much pleasure as that would give me, it's not going to happen. I might be a lot of things (a rule follower and a goody-goody, if you listen to Beck) but there are lines that can't be crossed and snitching is one of them.

This will be one more antic Beck gets away with. I suppose that's the beauty of being Beckett Hollingsworth. He doesn't give a shit about anything other than football.

The Neanderthal sport is his life.

By the time Beck was a freshman in high school, he'd already drawn the attention of Big Ten college coaches. They couldn't wait to get him on their roster. If he could have gone straight to the NFL after gradua-tion, he would have. But that's not a possibility. Players aren't eligible to enter the draft until after their sophomore year of college. Beck's father has taken it one step further by insisting he wait until senior year because—and I quote—*no damn son of mine is going to be a college dropout.*

Beck will be proof positive that C's really do earn degrees.

As my gaze drifts over the thick crowd of glassy-eyed stares, it collides with bright green ones. A little zip of electricity sizzles its way through my veins as our gazes fasten. The muscles in my belly tense with awareness. Once I realize what's happening, I tamp down the reaction. My life has been filled with a thousand little moments like this one. Moments I like to pretend never transpired.

For all I know, it's gastritis from the sushi I picked up at the gas station last night.

Anything's possible, right?

Instead of glancing away, I hold his stare and scowl. What I've learned is that it's better to brazen out these situations than turn tail and run. Beck's perfect cupid's bow of a mouth lifts into a knowing grin before he crooks his finger.

A gurgle of laughter bubbles up in my throat.

I don't think so, buddy.

I'm not like the bubbleheads he usually toys with. I have a working brain and I enjoy using it to make good decisions that won't come back to bite me in the ass. Unlike Beck, I have a healthy amount of self-preservation.

I press my lips into a tight line before emphatically shaking my head.

A wolfish grin spills across his face, giving him a boyishly handsome appearance. With dark tousled hair, sharp cheekbones that scream his Russian heritage, and thick eyebrows, he's a danger to females everywhere. I won't mention the chiseled body that looks like it was carved from stone. Broad shoulders and a tapered waist complete the package.

It's almost a relief when a bikini-clad girl steps between us, severing the connection. Now that his sharp gaze is no longer pinning me in place, I'm able to exhale all the air from my lungs.

Alyssa grabs my hand. "There he is," she whisper-yells excitedly over the babble of voices and music. "Oh my God, he's so freaking dreamy."

I regard the crowd of newly minted high school graduates before finding Colton.

Sure, I'll admit it. He's as hot as Beck. Instead of short dark hair, he's golden blond. It's buzzed on the sides and left long on top, so he's constantly pushing it away from bright blue eyes. He's tall and brawny. If I hadn't gone to school with him since elementary, I'd suspect he flunked a few grades. Even his muscles have muscles.

Girls are already circling around him, vying for his attention. The guy is like a rock star picking out groupies to sleep with at the end of the night.

"He's okay," I mutter, wanting to downplay his attractiveness.

"You're so full of shit, your eyes are turning brown. He's way better than *okay* and you know it."

"Ewww." I scrunch my nose. "That's gross."

"Focus!" She snaps her fingers in front of my face.

I make one last-ditch effort to sway her. "You can do better than Colton. He knows exactly how hot he is and takes full advantage of it every chance he gets. Find someone like," I stand on my tiptoes and pick through the mass of bodies before zeroing in on the perfect guy for Alyssa, "Landon Mathews. Not only is he good looking, he's a sweetheart."

Alyssa's expression turns thoughtful as she assesses the tall guy with inky-black hair and unusual blue-green eyes. He's standing around with a bunch of football players, laughing at something one of them said.

"He's definitely yummy," she admits.

For one glorious moment, my spirits soar. Maybe she'll drop this whole Colton Montgomery nonsense and go after someone more attainable. Landon is a great guy. He's as hot as his friends, but he's not a total asshat. Unfortunately, he doesn't get nearly the same amount of hype that Colton or Beck do since he's been labeled a good guy.

I mean, who wants to date a nice guy when you can have one who treats you like total crap?

Said no one ever.

Except...there seems to be way more truth to that statement than most females are comfortable acknowledging. Whether they realize it or not, these girls have been conditioned to crave unattainable jerks.

It's disturbing on so many levels.

"Added bonus," I continue, "he knows you're alive!"

"Um, excuse me, Colton knows I'm alive," she grumbles.

"Are you certain about that?"

She bites her lip as we glance at the guy in question who is—surprise-surprise—surrounded by a bevy of scantily clad girls competing for his interest.

Uh-oh.

Alyssa's got that look in her eye. The one that tells me not to bother trying to talk her out of her plans.

She confirms it by saying, "Wish me luck, I'm going in."

It was worth a try.

"Good luck."

One of Alyssa's best qualities is that she's not a quitter. That girl can be as tenacious and persistent as a terrier. And sometimes, just as yappy.

In this instance, it's a negative.

When she's a few steps away, I cup my fingers around my mouth and yell, "Maybe you should take off the panties so you can flash him your puss. That way he'll know you're a sure thing."

She whips around with a grin. "Excellent idea!"

My jaw drops when she shimmies out of her panties and tosses them in my direction.

"Christ, girl! I was joking! That was sarcasm!" I glance at the wadded-up material I now clench in my hand. "What am I supposed to do with these?"

She shrugs. "Keep them as a souvenir?"

Gross.

"I don't think so." I stalk to a garbage can and pitch them. When I turn around, Alyssa is pushing her way through the crowd, moving steadily closer to Colton and his harem.

If nothing else, this should be entertaining. It takes a moment to realize I'm alone at a party I didn't want to attend in the first place. I slip my phone from my back pocket and glance at it.

Fifty minutes and counting.

This is shaping up to be the longest hour of my life. Maybe I should head inside and grab a drink. By the number of drunken idiots I'm surrounded by, my guess is that the booze is flowing freely. I maneuver my way through the crowd and into the kitchen before taking in the scene.

If Beck's mom saw all these people sitting their asses on her polished-to-a-high-shine marble countertop, she would probably have a conniption. She's kind of a germ-o-phobe. There's a half-naked girl stretched out on the island with a lime clenched in her teeth as one of the football players slurps tequila from her belly button.

I'm no aficionado on hygiene, but that definitely doesn't seem sanitary.

A few people greet me as I make my way to the keg and take my place in line. I'm in the middle of chatting with a girl from my French class when she turns an unflattering shade of green and bolts to the nearest bathroom with her hands slapped over her mouth. All thoughts of a refill are abandoned as she pushes her way to the back hall. I really hope she makes it in time. Caroline will be furious if she finds out someone has thrown up on her marble floors.

Once I have a frothy cup of beer in hand, I head to the patio to check on Alyssa's progress.

Am I a terrible friend for hoping she's already been shot down and has thrown in the towel for the night?

Probably, but I can deal with that.

Instead of finding a dejected Alyssa crying in the corner, I'm amazed to discover that she's clawed her way to the front of the pack. Who knows, she may actually have a shot of getting picked from the crowd.

This could be a real game changer for her.

Guess that means I'm stuck here. I look around the patio, searching for a place to park my ass. The Hollingsworth property is about an acre in size, which is the same as ours. The space around the pool is gated with a black iron fence and tall arborvitae that spear into the dark night sky. Toward the back of the gate is an unoccupied lounge chair with my name on it. I'll hang out there for forty minutes before dragging Alyssa's panty-less ass back to my house.

Before I can take three steps, a deep voice cuts through the raucous noise of the party.

"Well, well, well. Look who decided to make a cameo appearance tonight."

I swing around, knowing exactly who I'll find.

Beck.

As difficult as it is, I try not to notice how delicious he looks in plaid board shorts that hang low on his hips, showing off the cut lines of his abdomen before disappearing beneath the waistband. The chis-

eled strength of his arms and chest are enough to bring most girls to
their proverbial knees.

The operative word in that sentence being *most*.

I, however, am not one of those idiotic girls.

"Coming here tonight wasn't my idea. I was dragged under duress."

"Yeah, I figured you would have better things to do than hang
around with a bunch of wasted assholes."

He's got me there.

"You know me too well." When my throat grows dry, I lift the red
Solo cup to my lips. Before I can take a sip, he snatches the drink from
my fingers and brings it to his mouth. I watch his throat constrict as
he drains the contents.

"Rude much?" My fists go to my hips. "What did you do that
for?"

He shrugs. Even though it's a slight movement, his muscles ripple
and attraction bursts to life in my core. "You shouldn't be drinking."

"Excuse me?" My eyes pop wide as laughter tumbles from my
mouth. "Are you being serious right now?" I wave a hand toward the
drunken mass that surrounds us. It's not even eleven, and already
people are passed out on loungers. "Look around, dude, everyone is
shitfaced." Hopefully, there are a few designated drivers among this
group or Uber will make a hell of a lot of money tonight.

As soon as Beck smirks, I know his answer is specifically designed
to piss me off.

"That might be so, but everyone knows you're a good girl. And
good girls don't drink. I wouldn't want the society to revoke your
membership. You've worked so damn hard for it."

My eyes narrow to slits. The attraction that had flared to life so
quickly is extinguished by his teasing.

I hate when he calls me that. And he knows it, which is precisely
why he continues to do it. Beck loves nothing better than to crawl
under my skin. He's like a rash I can never quite get rid of, no matter
how many steroids I use.

It's irritating.

"I'm not a good girl," I growl before stabbing a finger at his ridiculously hard chest. "And *you* are not my keeper. I can drink if I want to."

In a haughty voice, I remind, "I'm the one who was requested to babysit *your* ass. Not the other way around."

He crowds into my personal space. Instead of retreating, I stand my ground. I refuse to let him intimidate me.

"Babysitter, you say? Hmmm...I could definitely use one of those tonight." His fingers trace a path down the center of my chest, lingering in the valley between my breasts. "Should we take this elsewhere and you can demonstrate everything your service entails?"

His nearness does funny things to me and clouds my better judgment. Instead of pushing him away, I'm tempted to pull him closer.

My body wavers before sanity crashes down on me and I bat his hand away. "Go to hell."

"See?" He laughs as if I've proven his point for him. "A good girl through and through."

"I'm not as good as you think." The words shoot out of my mouth before I can rein them back in. To be clear, they are a total lie. I *am* as good as he thinks. Probably better. I have to be.

"Is that so?" He steps closer until the tips of my breasts brush against his bare chest. "Sweetheart, I'd love nothing better than to test that theory but we both know you'll always be Mia Stanbury, little miss perfect."

And he'll always be Beckett Hollingsworth. The guy with little-to-no impulse control who can't walk down the school hallway without finding trouble. The same one who can't be left alone in his own house for a night without inviting a hundred of his closest friends over for an impromptu party.

We are opposites in every sense of the word.

"Shut up, Beck." I've never met anyone who has the power to turn me on and piss me off at the same time. If he ever cranked up the charm, I'd be toast. He's capable of melting the panties right off a girl with one well-aimed look. I've seen it happen with my own eyes. I refuse to be one of those ridiculous females. I won't be used and tossed aside like dirty Kleenex.

I don't realize that I've become trapped in my own thoughts until his fingers settle under my chin, lifting it so I'm forced to meet his bright gaze. "What's the matter? Truth hurt?"

"There's nothing you can say that will hurt me." If only that were true.

His face looms closer until it fills my vision, blotting out the party. My world shrinks around us until it only encompasses Beck. My breath gets clogged in my lungs and burns like a fire before spreading to the rest of my body. Any moment I'm going to self-combust.

What am I doing?

I should pull away, but I'm powerless to do anything other than stare into his eyes and fall under his spell.

"Beck, baby!" a loud female voice booms over the rowdiness of the party, "over here!"

Even when she continues to bleat like a sheep, our gazes remain locked for several long heartbeats and I almost wonder if he'll ignore her. But she's persistent and continues to repeat his name until he severs the connection between us and swings around.

As soon as I'm released, the air rushes from my lungs and my body sags with relief. Or maybe it's disappointment. I tamp down the emotions so I can't inspect them too closely.

What would have happened if we hadn't been interrupted?

Nothing good.

This is *exactly* why I avoid Beck at all costs. Even though we're constantly sniping at each other, there's an undercurrent of attraction that hums beneath the surface. No other guy has ever provoked these kinds of emotions in me. I want to slap him almost as much as I want to kiss him.

Sanity returns with a rush as I focus on the statuesque blond twenty feet away. Ava Simmons is wearing a teeny tiny bikini that leaves very little to the imagination. Once she has Beck's full attention, she reaches around and unties the strings that hold the tiny triangles in place. The material floats to the cement at her feet. She lets him—and everyone else in the vicinity—ogle her perky breasts before running and jumping into the pool.

People cheer, and more girls ditch their tops, following Ava into the water.

A grin slides across Beck's face as he glances at me. A challenging light enters his eyes as he jerks his dark head toward the pool. Water sloshes over the edge of the azure-colored tile as more bodies dive in.

Oh, hell no.

My heart pounds as I throw my hands up in a *what can you do* gesture. "Sorry, didn't bring a suit."

His grin turns predatory. "Doesn't look like you need one."

Yeah...not going to happen.

"As fun as that seems, I'll pass," I wave an arm toward the pool, "but don't let that stop you from mingling with your guests. Ava's waiting." Topless. From the corner of my eye, I see her breasts bobbing like inflatable safety devices.

When his focus is drawn to the people splashing around, I follow suit. It's so much easier to stare elsewhere than hold the intensity of his gaze. Even when that option includes watching a bunch of topless girls I've known since elementary school. I don't check out the guys loitering in the area, but I'm sure most are sporting wood. Honestly, if it weren't for Alyssa, I would get the hell out of here before it turns into a raging orgy.

Beck steps closer and my gaze snaps to his. "Sure I can't persuade you to go for a swim?"

"Nope." I shake my head.

"That's too bad. This would have gone a long way to prove you're not the good girl I always pegged you to be."

Before I can summon up a pithy retort, he runs and dives headfirst into the water. I catch a glimpse of plaid as he disappears beneath the surface.

A mixture of relief and disappointment bubble up inside me until I'm nearly choking on them. It's the latter emotion I'm having a hard time accepting.

With a huffed-out breath, I stalk to one of the many loungers that surround the pool and settle on top of a plush cushion. I glance around for Alyssa, hoping she's given up on Colton so we can head home. It's not too late for the evening to be salvaged with pizza and a movie. Instead, I find her in the pool.

Topless.

Sucking face with Colton.

Great.

As much as I want to take off, I can't leave her here alone. God only knows what will happen if I do.

With a groan, I squeeze my eyes tight and prepare myself for a long night.

Want to read more of Mia and Beck's story? You can do it here -)
https://books2read.com/u/4EPQPg

ABOUT THE AUTHOR

Jennifer Sucevic is a USA Today bestselling author who has published twenty-one New Adult novels. Her work has been translated into German, Dutch, and Italian. Jen has a bachelor's degree in History and a master's degree in Educational Psychology. Both are from the University of Wisconsin-Milwaukee. She started out her career as a high school counselor, which she loved before moving to the Midwest with her husband, four kids, and a menagerie of animals. If you would like to receive regular updates regarding new releases, please subscribe to her newsletter here-
Jennifer Sucevic Newsletter (subscribepage.com)
Or contact Jen through email, at her website, or on Facebook.
sucevicjennifer@gmail.com
Want to join her reader group? Do it here -)
J Sucevic's Book Boyfriends | Facebook
Social media links-
https://www.tiktok.com/@jennifersucevicauthor
www.jennifersucevic.com
https://www.instagram.com/jennifersucevicauthor
https://www.facebook.com/jennifer.sucevic
Amazon.com: Jennifer Sucevic: Books, Biography, Blog, Audiobooks, Kindle
Jennifer Sucevic Books - BookBub